I0635510

Blind Fate

a Romance Novel

Blind Fate

a Romance Novel

Robin M. Manley

Rivers of Water Publishing
Rocky Mount, NC 27804

Copyright ©2015 by Robin M. Manley

All rights reserved. No part of this publication may be reproduced or transmitted in any form or by any means, electronic or mechanical, including photocopy, recording, or any information storage and retrieval system now known or to be invented, without written permission from the publisher, except in the case of brief quotations in critical articles and reviews.
Published in the United States of America by

Rivers of Water Publishing
Robin M. Manley, Owner
Rocky Mount, NC 27804

This book is a work of fiction. Except for brief mentioning of world-renowned preacher(s) and their specific sermons, all other characters are a product of the author's imagination. Any resemblance to real persons or events is purely coincidental. All songs associated with this work and used in conjunction with this book series are the original work of Jasmyne Williams (a.k.a jDenea') and are subject to the same copyright laws as ascribe above. The songs, *Why Can't You Do Better? Love is Patient, Let's Make Things Work,* Petty Girl Talk, *and Divvy That* are all original song written by Jasmyne Williams, marketed under the stage-name jDenea' and are copyrighted under Jasmyne D. Williams' name in the Library of Congress in 2017. These songs are not to be used without written permission of Jasmyne D. Williams a.k.a jDenea'.

Visit us at: www.rowpublishing.webs.com
Designs by Robin M. Manley
Library of Congress Control Number: 2017947212
ISBN- 978-1-947513-00-6
First Edition

All scriptures are from the New King James Version (NKJV) or the New International Version (NIV) unless otherwise noted in the reading. The sermons presented and mentioned in this book are the workmanship of the world-renowned Dr. Bernard Grant of Showers of Blessing Christian Center in Rocky Mount, NC.

Acknowledgments

I would first like to give honor to God and thank Him for providing such wonderful earthy support as I completed this, my third book.

I would like to acknowledge a few of the many people who provided multiple types of help. I began by giving many thanks to Geneva Reynolds, my mother, for years of encouragement, for always seeing more in me then I saw or see in myself, and for helping me with suggestions and edits of this book. I also thank her helping me with *To Hungry Souls Every Bitter Thang Taste Sweet* and *Entangled Again in the Yoke of Bondage.*

Thanks to children, Jasmyne and Jerika Williams, Denzel Davis, and my godson Marquise Hines for unconditional love, support, and believing in me. I will forever be thankful to you for always inspiring me.

Thanks to my pastor, Dr. Bernard Grant and first lady, Phyllis Grant (Lady P) for always encouraging me to allow God to use me, for believing in me, and installing wonderful and profound Biblical insight, wisdom, knowledge, and understanding. Finally, thanks to the Grants and the Showers of Blessing Christian Center family for entrusting me as the head of the Drama Department which allowed me to see possibilities with my writing creativity and imagination with wonderful biblical messages.

Thanks to my brother, William Manley, a.k.a Steve for always providing excellence pictures for my projects, portfolio, and/or flyers. Manley's Photography will forever be my favorite photography business.

Thanks also goes out to my special friends, often referred as my spiritual mother, Betty Barnes and her husband Eugene Barnes. This couple has also seen the best in me, no matter what. Brother Barnes often refer to me as Doc or Dr. Robin which encourages me to continue my educational journey towards my PhD. I would also like to thank another special friend, Verlyn Tarlton who refers to me as Coach Robin. Thank you for all your encouragement and insights.

Thanks to everyone mentioned and even those not mentioned (you know who you are). Your love, support, inspiration, and encouragement will always be remembered.

To God be the Glory!

Dedication

This book is dedicated to anyone who feels that true romance will never exist because of how you look or feel about you and your appearance. Be the 'you' that God created you to be and believe that real love and romance can and will happen, if you believe in you and that it can and will happen. Your faith sets the possibilities and/or limitations. Don't allow a lack of faith to set you up to believe that your body size or shape has control over your destiny to have real romance and your true soul mate. Don't allow someone else's life experiences and beliefs to cause you to be afraid to set high expectation for love and romance all it has to offer. Believe with your heart that God has created us all to be loveable and loved. Learn to love yourself and be open to receive love. Learn to love past the pain of your last broken relationship and you can become the ideal woman or man for someone who has God's spirit of love living inside him or herself. To God be the Glory!

Love Robin

Fate: the development of events beyond a person's control, regarded as determined by a supernatural power.

Chapter 1

"I'm serious man. Y'all know me, so I don't even know why you're acting so surprised," Jeremy said, pulling his 6 feet 5-inch, medium size, well-built body off the bench. "Look," he continued, palming the basketball. "I don't want a big, thick, fat, or chubby..." Jeremy began. He held up his hand to stop his friends, who all looked as if they were about to object. "Wait! I'm not finished. I don't want a P-H-A-T," he said, spelling out the word phat, which to him was the same thing as fat. "Oh, what else do ladies call themselves to avoid the word fat or any words that are synonymous with it?" Jeremy asked, snapping his figures trying to think of something else. "Oh yeah! I know, 'stacked-in-all-the-right-places." He remembered seeing that one on some ladies' dating site profile page and other social media websites.

"So, you are telling me that if you found a beautiful, loving and caring, plus-size woman..." Chris began, but was instantly interrupted by Jeremy.

"Oh yeah, that's the other word, *plus-size*, and to answer your question, No! I wouldn't date her. She and I might could be friends," Jeremy said, studying the disapproving looks on his friends' faces. "Besides, all of you guys would have agreed with me a few years ago."

The guys stared at Jeremy waiting for him to say whatever else he had to say about the matter.

"Guys, I have a right to like who and what I like, just like you. No one says a thing when a woman rejects an unemployed, beer belly, four kids and three babies' mama having dude."

"Man, now you know that is not a good comparison at all. I don't blame a woman who doesn't want a broke man, with kids he can't feed, but got money for beer," Johnathan said, as he pretended to be shooting an invisible ball from his seated position on the gym floor.

Jeremy repositioned the ball and released it for a nothing-but-net shot.

1

"Easy to do with no one blocking you," Johnathan said as he pulled his 5 feet 1 inch, 235-pound, and desperately-in-need-of-some-exercise-body off the gym floor. "You should be more like God," Johnathan continued. "He has no respect of person. He loves us all the same."

"I didn't say that I don't respect big gals. I just don't want to date one," Jeremy replied. "Besides, is God dating any of them?"

Johnathan stared at Jeremy with disbelief.

"What?" Jeremy questioned. "You mean to tell me that y'all don't have preferences too?" He scanned the faces of his friends. He was sure that they all had preferences, even if they were different from his own. He even knew some of their preferences.

Jeremy, Chris, Malcolm, Myles, and Johnathan had known each other for over 25 years. They all grew up in the same neighborhood and went to the same elementary, middle, and high school. They played together as children, but they were not best friends. Their parents knew each other; therefore, they spent time around each other throughout their entire childhood. College, relocations, and other life events had separated them throughout the years, but they would all end up back together for wedding, special events, and funerals. Their love for basketball created many opportunities for them to plan to come together for one-on-one, two-on-two, and later three-on-three games at the park. During cold months, they would meet at the local gym. Broken relationships, job transfers, and deaths of their love ones, eventually caused them all to move back to the same old hometown city. They began to meet at the gym or park more regularly. Even though they did not always see eye-to-eye and sometimes fussed as if they were enemies, they always had each other's back which lead to a very close friendship. Eric was the last one to later join the group.

"Jeremy is right. We all have preferences, at least I do, but I don't allow my preferences to limit me," Myles said and then paused to think of some of his likes and dislikes. "I don't like women who are taller than me or those who are as tall as I am. I love my little shawties, but I have dated some who were taller than me. Even had a good time," Myles said.

"But," Jeremy questioned, knowing that Myles would never completely agree with him on anything.

2

"But, well she was too loud and too controlling. I didn't know which one of us wore the pants," Myles responded. "If not for that..." Myles said, but was cut off by Johnathan before he could finish what he was saying.

"I'm telling you Jeremy," Johnathan chimed in. "I have seen it. You are going to be like Job in 3:25, the thing you fear will surely come upon you," Johnathan said and then paused and waited for a response from Jeremy.

"I don't fear them. As a matter of fact, I love them," Jeremy replied. "I just don't want to..."

"We know," Chris interrupted. "You fear being in love with one. You fear that you will end up an old man, with a well-built body, muscles everywhere, and married to a loving and caring big woman, because judging by the success rate of your relationships, you will be an old man by the time you finally settle down."

"They're not plaques. They are human beings, just like your plus-size mama and sister," Johnathan interjected.

"Look, let's leave Jeremy alone," Malcolm said as he grabbed the ball, indicating that the break was over. "I'm ready to get this game over with, so I can go home to my plus-sized, beautiful, got-it-all-in-the-right-places, P-H-A-T wife," Malcolm said, spelling phat out just as Jeremy had done earlier. Malcolm aimed the ball in the air and pretended to fake someone out as the group walked back onto the gym floor. "There is nothing like a woman who's as soft as a pillow to run home to. Personally, I don't want to see or feel a woman's bones poking through her skin. I definitely don't want to feel her bones digging in me. So, let's get this game over with so Jeremy can jump in his skinny little sports car," Malcolm said, then paused. "Oh, that's right, you drive a huge suburban now. Is that so you can drive your plus-size mommy and sister down here to the gym to work off a few Twinkies?" Malcolm jokingly said, releasing the ball with confidence that he was going to make the shot.

Jeremy laughed as he jumped and blocked Malcolm's shot. "I don't date my mommy or my sister, so they can look any way they want to, but now, I bet you won't let my mommy hear you talking like that. She would shove her big fat fist, down your fat throat, and give you a plus-sized lip," Jeremy replied, knowing that Malcolm was only using his mother and sister to make his point.

"Man, I ain't crazy. Ma Phillips would never hear me say that and if you tell her I said it, I will deny it all the way to my grave."

3

The guys all laughed as they divided up into their usual teams. As they began the three-on-three game, they continued to try to convince Jeremy that he was too opinionated. They all stopped the conversation when the gym doors swung open and three women swung in. The ladies sat down on the bleachers and watched as the guys played ball. Jeremy eyed the women every chance he got.

"Foul!" Chris yelled, feeling the sting from a smack on his wrist delivered by Johnathan.

"Foul! Are you serious? Since when we have been calling fouls?" Johnathan questioned as if it was acceptable to smack an opponent on the wrist so hard that it could be heard on the outside of the gym.

"Since now," Chris replied. "That wasn't a baby tap. That seems personal. Did I do something to you?"

Jeremy was glad for the break. He wanted to get a good look at the three women who were huddled up on the bleachers.

"That's it for me guys. I have to go," Eric said, taking a jump shot.

"Man, in the middle of a game, you just gonna walk?" Myles asked.

"Yeah, y'all suddenly got distracted and I'm tired of being a one-man show," Eric said, glancing at the three women sitting on the bleachers. "Why don't you request a sub? The way you're playing, one of those ladies over there can take you all on," he said as he walked past the ladies and winked. "Ain't that right ladies?" Eric questioned as he grabbed his gym bag and waved goodbye to his friends.

The tall, slender woman left the bleachers and walked towards the guys. "Need a sub, I hear," she said and looked at each of the guys waiting for a response.

The guys looked at the tall, brown-skin woman who stood staring at them with her hands on her hips. Chris scanned her entire body up and down and then returned his attention back to her face.

"Fine with me," Chris replied as if he was the spokesperson for the group. He threw her the ball. He wanted to check her reflexes. She caught the ball and threw him a chest pass.

4

"What's your name sweetheart?" Chris asked.

"Danielle, but everybody calls me Dani," she replied with a smile on her face.

"I'm Chris. Short man over there," he said, pointing in Johnathan's direction, "that's Johnathan. This is Malcolm. Mr. Opinionated over there is Jeremy. Oh, and the guy with the hat, that Myles-a.k.a. Snake."

Danielle waved to all the guys.

"You on my team-the Blacks," Chris said.

"Okay," Dani said, immediately noticing that Chris and Jeremy had on black t-shirts and Malcolm, Johnathan, and Myles had on blue t-shirts.

"Come on y'all, let's beat these girls so we can go home," Chris said.

He threw the ball to Jeremy, not ready to test Dani's skills, although he was impressed with her quick reflexes and chest pass. Jeremy moved the ball in closer to the hoop, faked a jump shot, and threw the ball to Danielle. She immediately took a shot from the three-point area. Malcolm tried to block the shot, but he didn't jump high enough.

"Nice shot!" Jeremy yelled to his new teammate.

"Thanks," she replied as she ran to catch up to Johnathan, who dribbled the ball down the court.

"Yeah, nice shot," Johnathan said with a hint of sarcasm.

"What? Nice for a girl?" Danielle questioned.

"You said it, not me. Now watch this," Johnathan said. He tried to pass the ball to Myles, but Danielle stole the ball and quickly pass it to Jeremy.

"That's what I'm talking about, a woman that ain't afraid to take what she wants," Myles jokingly said.

"Whose team are you on?" Johnathan questioned.

"Man, shawty got game. I'm just giving the girl her props," Myles replied and winked at Danielle.

Danielle winked back at Myles and then glanced at her friends sitting on the top row of the bleacher, watching her. Once the game ended, Danielle retreated to the bleachers.

"Good game," her friends said.

"Thanks. It's been a while, but I still got it," Danielle replied.

"Yeah girl, you still got it," her friends said, agreeing with her.

"Hey Danielle, same time next week. Maybe ya' girls can join next time, if you all are interested," Chris said.

"Sure," Danielle responded.

Chris walked over to the three women and introduced himself to the other two ladies.

"I'm Christopher Jacobs," Chris said, extending his hand to the slender, brown-skinned woman with a short bob haircut.

"I'm Jasmyne," she said. She shook Chris's hand. "And this is Stacy," Jasmyne said.

Chris looked around for his friends. As they approached the bleachers, Chris introduced the guys to Stacy and Jasmyne.

"We try to do this weekly," Jeremy explained. "Join us sometimes."

"Thanks, maybe I will," Danielle replied as if the invitation was only for her. "Stacy and Jasmyne are usually only spectators," she quickly explained.

"That's not true," Jasmyne interjected. "I play. I just haven't played with you," she said as she looked at Danielle with a hint *you don't know me*.

Danielle had been her high school's MVP for three years and often made her friends feel as if their skills were inferior to hers; therefore, they would often decline the opportunity to play with her. Stacy was also on her high school's team and was noted to have skills, but her humble attitude and well-kept secret led Danielle to feel that Stacy's skills were limited to a few lucky shots from time-to-time. Jasmyne's skills were limited, but she refused to be outdone by her best friend of 15-years. Jasmyne's skills included knowing what to do with the ball, even if she could rarely even touch the rim.

"Anyway," Danielle said, playfully rolling her eyes at Jasmyne. "We'll be here."

~

"Stacy is kind of cute," Jeremy said as the guys headed to the parking lot.

"Yeah, but Jasmyne is gorgeous," Malcolm said. "If I was single..."

"She is cute, but..." Jeremy said, interrupting Malcolm.

"But what?" Johnathan questioned, interrupting Jeremy even though he already knew what Jeremy was going to say.

"You know. I don't have to say it," Jeremy replied.

"Yeah, I do and that's exactly why you are alone right now, because you are too judgmental," Johnathan responded.

"No, it's called having preferences," Jeremy corrected him.

"Oh no. Not this again," Chris said, putting his hand over his ears. "Just drop it."

"Well, it doesn't matter what I think anyway. I am not interested in dating either of them. I am not looking for anyone right now. I like being single. I like coming home and finding my house the way I left it. I like not having to beg to watch what I want to watch on my own new smart TV. I like sleeping on whatever side of the bed I want to sleep on," Jeremy said as he tossed his gym bag in his truck.

"You mean you like being lonely," Johnathan replied as he slapped Chris a high-five. "Sounds like you have no choice to me."

"Oh, I got choices. Got plenty of choices. Do you know how many women are just waiting for a fine man like me to step in and help them to subsidize what their paycheck and what child-support won't do. Man, I can have a woman anytime I want one, but I just don't want to settle for being someone's sugar daddy," Jeremy said as he leaned against his truck.

"I feel you there, man. That's all I had with Janet. She didn't care about me at all. All she wanted was a man to help her raise the kids and pay some bills. After being alone for five years, she didn't care what I did, where I went, or who I went with, as long as the rent was paid, and the kids were fed," Malcolm rattled off as if he was having a flashback. "Yeah, that was good at first, but after a while I just..." Malcolm hesitated to finish.

"You just what?" Jeremy questioned.

"Well, I guess there comes a time when a man wants to feel loved and wanted and not just needed and used. I wanted more, and she didn't," Malcolm explained.

"Oh, so what? You wanted a house, your own kids, and a mini-van?" Chris jokingly asked.

"If that's what you want to call it," Malcolm said. "I wanted something real, like what I have now."

"You, Mr. Malcolm Mac Daddy?" Jeremy replied.

"Yeah, Mr. Malcolm Mac got macked. I finally wanted to hang up my jersey. I hooked up with Ms. Female Mac. I mean that girl was smooth. I'm telling you, women are the true masters of macking. They talk sweet, cook for you, tell you what you want to hear, and then BAM they got you leaving your wife and disowning or neglecting your kids. They have you burning bridges you don't even know exist. Then when they drain you dry, they say they found the Lord and suddenly feel guilty and think you should go back home to your wife," Malcolm said.

"So that's what happened?" Chris questioned.

"No, I'm just saying," Malcolm replied, hoping to drop the subject.

"I know. You just saying that you got macked, played, used, all that, and now you have burnt your bridges with your wife and your girlfriend. Oh," Jeremy paused. "That's right, you and Lesia are back together now. Right?" Jeremy questioned, glad that the attention was finally off him.

"But remember," Johnathan interrupted. "God can restore your marriage. I know Lesia still loves you."

"I know she does, but I'm telling you, she so hurt she ain't never going to forgive me. I have tried everything," Malcolm said with a hint of disappointment in his voice.

"You have to keep trying," Johnathan said. "You cannot expect her to forget everything instantly. It's not going to change overnight."

"I know, but look y'all, I don't feel like talking about this right now," Malcolm said and then he paused as if he was trying to come up with something else to say. "Anyway, I will see you later Johnathan, at Bible study. Oh, Chris when is the party?"

"Oh, yeah man," Chris said, suddenly remembering that he had not told all the guys. "My brother-in-law is having a special party for my sister and y'all have to come. Please, I don't want to be trapped around a bunch of twenty-one-year-olds, walking around with a beer in their hand, trying to act mature."

"Pass," Malcolm said.

"Me too," Johnathan echoed.

"Come on man. Why y'all going to be like that. Myles, you know nothing would make Kimberly happier than for you to be there. You know how much she loves you."

"Okay, maybe for an hour. It is her 21st birthday, but only an hour," Myles reiterated.

"I got it," Jeremy responded.

"Is that yes or no," Chris asked, knowing Jeremy's cunning ways.

"Okay," Jeremy said. "I got nothing to do next weekend, besides Kimberly is like a little sister to us all," Jeremy hesitantly replied.

"So, we all have to be there just because we are," Malcolm began, but was cut off by Chris.

"Y'all have been all the family that we have, but you don't have to come if you don't want to. Just let me know if you change your mind," Chris said as he pulled his truck door open and got in. "I will see y'all later. I got to go."

The guys slowly walked to their cars and waved goodbye.

Chapter 2

"Hey little Sis," Chris said and gave Kimberly a big hug. "Guess who I found lurking around?"

"Hey birthday girl," Jeremy said as he peeped from behind the door.

"Uncle Jay! Man get in here," Kimberly said.

"Where's your husband?" Jeremy playfully questioned as he looked around. "Got to be careful, women like you are worth fighting for."

"Hey kiddo," Johnathan greeted Kimberly as he stepped from behind Jeremy and handed her a birthday present.

"Hey kiddo. The whole gang is here. Let's move a little, groove a little," Eric said as he entered the house and quickly pulled his wife past the crowd standing around in the kitchen. "We got a babysitter for the next five hours and we going to enjoy every single minute. That's right," Eric said as he kissed Kimberly on the cheek and then grabbed his wife around the waist and began rocking her back and forth. They headed towards the family room. Eric scanned the scarcely filled room and noticed that most of the guest were friends of Chris. He also noticed that he was the only one that seem to be enjoying himself.

"Party's outside man. What are you doing in here?" Jeremy said as he glanced at Eric dancing.

"Don't want to share this fox with the guest," Eric replied.

"So, what's up? Why are you two so happy?" Jeremy asked as he looked out the patio door to see how many people where at the party.

"Love!" Eric said as he glanced into his wife's hazel eyes.

Jeremy stared at another couple sitting on the green leather sofa. The couple looked as if they had just had a serious discussion and were not happy with each other's company at that moment. "Wow you two make me want to give up the single life and hang up my player's jersey," Jeremy said, turning from the sad looking couple and back to Eric and Tesha.

"Yeah right," Eric said. "You won't even commit to a lunch date. I know you ain't going to commit to having just one woman."

"I didn't say I was going to commit to just one," Jeremy said and then laughed.

Eric looked at his wife and they both shook their heads in disbelief at Jeremy response. Jeremy turned and walked into the kitchen and grabbed the birthday cake off the table. "Come on! Time to go sing happy birthday to Kimberly."

"People still do that?" Eric questioned while opening the sliding glass door that led to the patio. Eric waited until Jeremy walked out with the cake, followed by his wife, and then he slid the door closed behind them. As soon as they were outside, they heard the doorbell. Eric ran down the back steps and peeked around the side of the house to see who was standing at the door, as if it were his house and not Kimberly and her husband's house. He knew that most of the usual crowd were already there. Eric glanced at the crowd gathered around the table on the patio singing happy birthdays. "Hey!" He yelled to the ladies who were standing at the front door. "Over here!" He said, but they didn't seem to hear him. "We are around back. Hurry up, we are singing happy birthday." As Eric waited for the ladies to join him in the back yard, he noticed that one of them looked familiar, but he couldn't figure out where he had seen her before. "Come on!" He said and waved his hand in the direction of the backyard. "Hurry, hurry!"

"Happy birthday to you," the crowd sang.

As the crowd sang and swayed from side-to-side, Eric noticed that one of the newcomers was staring at Jason, Kimberly's husband. Kimberly also seemed to notice the lady making facial gesture at Jason.

"Make-a-wish," Jason said, turning to face his wife and locking eyes with the tall slender woman flashing a huge smile.

The woman winked at Jason and then quickly turned to Kimberly and smiled. Kimberly could tell by the blank look on her husband's face that something was seriously wrong.

"Go ahead honey. Make a wish," Jason said, forcing a smile on his face.

Kimberly closed her eyes and made a wish. She blew out the 21 candles on the cake and handed Jason the knife.

"Why are you giving me the knife," he asked.
"Because my wish was for you to serve me," Kimberly responded.

11

"Oh, I see. Your wish, my lady, is my command," Jason said, cutting his wife a slice of cake. He put it on her plate. "Wait!" He said as she picked up a fork. "Let me."

"Let you what?" Kimberly questioned.

Jason took the plastic fork out of Kimberly's hand. He then cut a small piece of the cake with the folk and fed it to her.

"You been watching too much lyfetime," Kimberly joked. Everyone laughed.

"Lyfetime! Man are you serious?" Jeremy said as he moved from his seated spot at the patio table.

"Yeah man. I actually watch Lyfetime with my baby," Jason said as he kissed his wife on the cheek.

"I bet you really get a kick out of a whole network dedicated to making men look like wimpy men who can't protect their families, men who works 60, 70, 80 hours a week, then come home to an unappreciative woman, complaining that he never spends any time with her or the kids, or that he never does anything for her. All the while she pranced around in her 4000-square foot, five bedrooms, three hundred and eighty-thousand-dollar house. He's too busy working so that he can afford to buy the house she wants, only to hear complaints," Jeremy said.

"I know that's right," the tall slender woman said. "Some women complain about every little thing. Just ain't never satisfied with any of the man's efforts."

Chris turned around to see who was talking.

"Danielle, what are you doing here?" He questioned.

"Oh, I'm an old friend of Jake."

"Jake," Chris said, looking around for someone name Jack.

"Jake from State Farm?" Myles joked.

"Oh, forgive me. I must have the wrong house," Danielle said as she stared at Jason.

Chris could tell that something was wrong and that somehow Jason was involved. Chris walk over to the radio sitting on the small accent table and turn the music back up. A few people retreated to the lawn chairs

12

scattered around the backyard. Malcolm, Johnathan, Eric, and one of Kimberly's coworkers headed to the round-table for a game of spades.

"Excuse me," Chris said to Danielle as she turned to walk down the patio steps. "I got a feeling that you found the right house. I'm just not sure who you're looking for. What's going on?" He questioned.

"Oh, don't worry. I'm not stalking you," she sarcastically said.

"Oh, I'm not worried," Chris quickly responded.

"Look, I have to go," Danielle said and quickly walked towards the front of the house.

"Brandi," a voice yelled. Danielle turned around.

"What?" She responded.

"What are you up to?" Jason questioned.

"My name is not Brandi. It's Danielle."

"Yeah, I got that now. Why are you here? What are you doing?" Jason questioned.

"What are you doing, Jake? I mean Jason? Other than playing the loving and faithful husband."

"What are you talking about? You knew I was married, and you knew that I was not going to leave my wife for you. You knew that," Jason said. He spoke so low Danielle could barely hear him.

"I knew what you told me," Danielle said with hurt and anger in her voice.

"Stop it! You got what you wanted. Women like you always have to prove that you can get a man to jeopardize his family, just to be with you. Okay, you almost had me. I made one mistake, but the one thing you didn't count on was that I would refuse to do it again. You want to tell her, okay go ahead, tell," Jason said, stepping aside, letting her go back to talk to his wife.

"Maybe I will. I'm sure your wife would love to know about her husband's dirty secrets and that he's a..."

"He's a what? Say what you have to say, so you can leave," he commanded.

Danielle smiled as she turned and walked to the car where her friends had already returned to and were waiting with the engine running. Jason watched them drive off.

"Jason!" Chris yelled as he approached.

13

"What's up?" Jason replied hoping that Chris had not heard the conversation between him and Danielle.

"You know her?" Chris questioned as he stared at the ladies slowly driving off in the tan 86 Lexis.

"Yeah, our paths crossed once," Jason nonchalantly replied.

"What was she doing here?" Chris asked, knowing that something was going on.

"I don't know. You would have to ask her," Jason said as he walked off to return to the party.

~

Jason scanned the backyard for Kimberly. He spotted her dancing with Myles and headed over to them. "Mind if I steal my beautiful woman from you?" Jason questioned as he grabbed Kimberly by the hand.

"Sure!" Myles said as he watched Jason practically pulling Kimberly from his arms, across the yard, and up the patio steps. Myles watched Kimberly and Jason as they took a seat. He watched Kimberly's facial expression change from happy, to a concerned look, and then to sadness. He also noticed that she no longer looked like the sweet little girl that use to ask a million questions. She no longer seemed like just his best friend's sister. She was a grown woman.

"What's up man?" Johnathan questioned as he walked up, stopped, and stood beside Myles, and glanced in the same direction as Myles.

"Something is wrong. I can see it on her face," Myles said without taking his eyes off Kimberly.

"Who?" Johnathan asked.

"Kimberly," Myles replied. "I watched her eyes dancing with happiness less than three minutes ago. Now look at how sad she looks."

They both stared at Kimberly and watched her eyes fill with tears.

"Told you man. I could tell when Jason dragged her away from me that something was wrong," Myles said.

"He has been acting a little strange since Brandi, a.k.a Danielle, a.k.a Dani from the gym showed up," Johnathan said with more than a hint of suspicion in his voice.

14

"I knew she look familiar," Myles replied. "Claimed she was looking for someone else." Myles paused and looked at Kimberly again. "Yeah, right."

"I heard that too," Johnathan said. "Hey, I love Kimberly like a sister, but this is between her and her husband. Let's just try to enjoy the party and make it special for her."

"I hear you man," Myles said with his eyes fixed on Kimberly as he quickly headed towards the patio.

"Where are you going?" Johnathan asked, tracking behind Myles 230-pound, well-built body that seemed to float through the air as if he was as light as a feather.

Myles climbed the twelve steps leading up to the patio deck where Kimberly and Jason sat hand-in-hand. Myles smiled as he scanned Kimberly's face and body language. Jason looked up at Myles as he walked past the couple and grab an empty chair at the opposite end of the table.

"I'm not interrupting anything, am I?" Myles questioned as if he had not noticed Kimberly's teary-eyes.

"Look Myles!" Kimberly said as she turned to face him. "Jason gave me this beautiful ring for my birthday. Isn't it nice?"

"Yeah! Nice," Myles said as if he was disappointed. "So, what, you getting engaged again?"

"Just doing what I should have done years ago," Jason replied.

Myles took a sip of the soda that he had been nursing for almost ten minutes. He stared at the party goers standing around, enjoying the food, relaxing in the pleasant atmosphere, and the calm North Carolina weather.

"Here! Got you another drink. I know that's hot by now," Johnathan said as he mustered up enough courage to join Myles at the patio table with Jason and Kimberly. "And why did you leave me just standing there."

"You a big boy," Myles said and then paused and waited for a response. "Oh, don't tell me all those fine single women scare you? You scared that the lust of the flesh gonna take control?"

"I got my flesh under control," Johnathan said.

"So why do you need me to babysit you?"

"So, Kimberly," Johnathan said as he pulled a chair out from the table and sat down. "What's good with you? When you and Jason going to start a family?"

Jason and Kimberly stared at Johnathan as if he had cursed at them.

"We have a family," Jason replied.

"Oh yeah, Jason, I forgot you have kids."

"No! I have a god-child. One."

"I'm sorry man. Did I strike a nerve?" Johnathan teased.

"No, Holy Ghost Junior," Jason replied.

Johnathan chuckled. He was accustomed to being called Holy Ghost Junior. Myles studied Kimberly's body language as Johnathan and Jason exchanged gestures. Myles knew that the ring was not the object of Kimberly's teary-eyes. Kimberly seemed to be withdrawn and defensive.

"What's up Kim?" Myles said as he reached out and grabbed her hand. He did not seem to have any regards for Kimberly's husband sitting right in front of him. "That smile I saw on your face as we danced a few minutes ago has faded. I need to see that again. It is your day lady," he said as he smiled at her.

Kimberly smiled at Myles as he stared into her eyes. She had been around Chris's friends almost her entire life. When their parents were killed in a car accident, Myles, Malcolm, Johnathan, and Jeremy had become her substitute big brothers, dads, and uncles. Kimberly was referred to as Kiddo, Kimberly, Little Mama, and Kim, but she had never heard any of them at any time indicate that she was a *woman* or even a *lady* for that matter.

"I'm fine, nothing for you to worry about," Kimberly replied.

Jason looked at Kimberly as if she had violated some unspoken vow of silence.

"Okay, but if you need to talk about anything, you got my number," Myles said as he softly patted Kimberly on the hand. He pushed his chair from the table and looked at her one last time. "I'm out of here. I got to work a few hours today, so I'll check y'all out later." Myles eyes connected with

Jason as they looked at each other as if they were challenging each other to a duel. "You all be good and enjoy the rest of your day." Myles and Kimberly embraced in a warm hug for a few seconds, then he released her suddenly. He walked through the sliding door that led into the small family room. As he glanced at the scarcely furnished, two-bedroom house, he grabbed Kimberly and Jason's wedding picture. "She's done a lot of growing up in such a short time," he said as he placed the picture back on the coffee table. He held his soda can up towards the ceiling as if he was making a toast. "Here's to you Mom and Pa Jacobs. She turned out to be a beautiful young lady. You would be so proud of her." Myles gulped down his last drop of soda and placed the can in the recycling bin beside the refrigerator.

~

"Where did Myles go?" Jennifer asked as she approached Kimberly and Jason.

Kimberly and Jennifer had formed an instant friendship. Jennifer was more commonly known by others as, Miss Home Wrecker.

"Oh, I don't know. All I know is, he left," Kimberly replied. "Why?"
"Just asking," Jennifer said. "By the way, who were those three ladies that showed up for ten minutes, empty-handed, and then left without a proper introduction?"
"I'm not sure who they are-were," Kimberly quickly replied. "I think someone said they had the wrong address."
"Oh really, they looked too comfortable to me to be at the wrong house. Sounds like a deliberate mistake to me," Jennifer said as if she was trying to give Kimberly some hint.

Kimberly stared at Jennifer.

"Are you trying to tell me something?" Kimberly asked after a fifteen second stare down.
"No," Jennifer hesitantly said, looking around. "Look Kimberly, I can tell a woman on a mission and that woman was on the prowl. Trust me, I know."

"Yeah, where have I seen that look before," Kimberly said as she stared at Jennifer. "Oh yea, that's the look I saw on your face when you first arrived. You know, when you first got here."

"I am not on the prowl," Jennifer quickly said, defending her-self.

"Yeah right, so you weren't just on the prowl for Myles?" Kimberly questioned.

"I was just asking a question. Honey, that man got too many issues for me," Jennifer said in a matter-of-fact tone. "Really! He's 33, no kids, a good job, nice house, so I heard, ride on fleek, yet I have never seen him with a girl on his arms."

"From what I can tell, he only deals with women," Kimberly replied.

"So, what are you trying to say?" Jennifer questioned. "And does he have a woman or not?"

Jennifer's sudden interest in Myles caused feelings to evolve in Kimberly that she had never felt before.

"Why is that any of your business?" Kimberly questioned. "Besides didn't you just say that he has too many issues for you?"

"I know what I said. Actually, I'm wondering if he's gay or bi, and on the down low or low down," Jennifer sarcastically said. "It's his business if he is, but I just want to know."

"You just saying that because he is not and has never tried to holla at you," Kimberly said as if she was defending Myles' reputation.

"Please," Jennifer said, rolling her eyes. "If I want that man. I can get him just like I can have any other man I want."

"Yeah, you and all the other girls that profess how irresistible y'all are, you can get a man, but the question is, can you keep him?"

Jennifer smiled as if she had been given an ultimate compliment.

"Sweetie," Jennifer said, leaning towards Kimberly and whispering in her ear. "You'll be surprised at how many men wanted to be mine, but I didn't want to keep them." Jennifer turned and looked at Jason who was returning from watching his friends play spades at a nearby table. "Isn't that right Jason?" Jennifer asked as Jason sat down at the table beside his wife.

18

Jason looked at Jennifer and then at his wife. "Since I wasn't a party to the conversation, I think it is best that I remain silent."

"Good answer Bae," Kimberly said as she pulled her chair from under the table to leave. "Now, I think I am going to mingle a little with those that came to celebrate with me."

As Kimberly walked down the step, she quickly looked back rethinking her decision to leave her husband sitting at the table with a woman who was known as a home wrecker. Kimberly cared about Jennifer and tried not to judge her like everyone else had, but she didn't trust her.

Chapter 3

"Hey, did anyone find it strange that Brandi looked like Danielle's body double?" Myles asked as he did his normal stretching exercises before the game.

"You know what?" Chris said as he sat his gym bag down on the floor. "I knew she looked familiar, but I wasn't sure where I recognized her from."

"Hey-hey-hey-hey," Eric said as he entered the gym sounding like DeWayne from *What's Happening.* "What's good?" He said as he dropped his gym bag beside the bleachers.

"Just discussing Brandi slash Danielle," Myles replied.

"What about her?" Eric asked.

"Why do you think she said her name is Danielle if it is Brandi?" Myles questioned.

"Maybe she goes by her middle name, but others know her by her first name," Eric replied as he tied his shoes.

"True, but for some reason, I don't think her name is Brandi and I don't think she had the wrong address," Myles said as he took a practice shot.

"Well, I don't know what's going on, but I bet Jason does. I got a feeling that he is involved somehow," Chris said. "Dude looked as if he had seen a ghost when he saw her."

"Yeah, I noticed that," Myles replied as he lowered his voice as if he was about to solve a mystery.

"Well," Eric said, interrupting Myles. "Let's get this game over with. I am ready to burn off some unused energy."

"Ain't getting none," Myles joked. "Oh, church girl to holy."

"Man, that's really one thing I don't have to worry about. You have forgotten this, huh? The Bible says the bed is undefiled."

"That don't mean you getting any," Myles rebutted.

"Man, the best thing my wife ever did for our sex life was to take me to church," Eric said.

"What?" Myles asked with a questionable look on his face.

"Look, I started going to church and found out that God orders the wife to submit to me, her husband. I memorized the verse and when oh girl starts with that 'I don't feel like it. I got a headache," Eric said in his best wife's voice impersonation. "I stop her mid-sentence. I say, 'Hey honey,

Ephesians 5:22 says, 'wives submit to her own husband as to the Lord," Eric laughed as he continued. "Man, while I'm on a roll, I take it one step further. See, if she really had a headache, I could understand and wouldn't persist, but she be faking sometimes. So, I quoted the next verse; Verse 23 says, 'For the husband is head of the wife as also Christ is head of the church and He is savior of the body. Then I'll go ghetto on a sistah, and I look her right smack dead in those beautiful big hazel eyes and I say to her, 'Girl, God orders you and commands you to give it up to me, for I am the head and the owner of that body," Eric said and then gave Chris a high-five. "Man, you want to turn a real woman on, throw the Word on her," he said as the guys took their positions on the court.

"That's it," Johnathan said as he tried to high-five Eric.

"Man, you ain't getting none," Eric said as he pretended he was going to high-five Johnathan but missed his hand on purpose.

"I know, but I see how them women be looking at a brother at church. I have seen the ladies looking at me when I'm praying and crying out to God. They even be stalking me after church. Talking about, 'You know pastor said we should fellowship with each other. Treat someone out to lunch," Johnathan said with his best female voice.

"Man, they just want a free lunch. If not, why don't you have a wife yet, Boaz? The Bible does say, it's better to marry then to burn. I think that's in 1st Corinthians 7," Myles said and then paused as he tried to remember what verse. "I think verse 8 or 9."

"I know, but I can contain myself," Johnathan said. "Besides it is better to stay single than to get burnt. If you know what I mean."

"Man," Chris chimed in as he bounced the ball down the court. "Do you know it's so important to God that he called it fraud for a woman to withhold the goodies from her husband?"

"Yeah, like God really cares if you are getting any," Malcolm said.

"He does, 1st Corinthians 7:5 says, 'Defraud ye not one from the other," Eric said sounding like a preacher. "Interpretation- don't withhold one's body from the other. Watch this," he said sounding even more like a Baptist preacher. "Except it be with consent for a time that you give yourself to fasting and praying and only if you agree. Not because you are fighting, and you claim to have a migraine. So, I say to you brothers, fast early and go to bed after she prays so she can deliver up the goodies. But even after fasting and praying, ye shall come together again, so that Satan will not tempt you in someone else's bakery shop."

21

"Okay, can someone give the benediction, dismiss the services, and shake the pastor's hand so we can get on with this game? We can all contain ourselves through this game, right? Then you all can give yourself to whoever or to fasting and praying or defrauding whomever. Man, you can even render unto each other due benevolence if you feel like fornicating," Myles said as Eric and Johnathan both stopped and stared at Myles, who almost never mention God, church, or any other word that related to religion or religious practices. "Surprised, are we?" Myles said as he stole the ball from Johnathan who was standing still, bouncing the ball.

"Well! Yeah, I am," Johnathan replied as he watched Myles shoot the ball.

"Romans 13:7," Myles stated "says let the husband render unto the wife due benevolence; and likewise, also the wife unto the husband. Not everybody is walking around quoting scriptures, but that does not mean that they don't know them," Myles said as he walked towards the bleachers and grabbed his water bottle.

"Hey guys," a familiar voice said as the gym door flew open.

"What's up?" Another voice chimed in.

Eric stopped bouncing the ball and turned to meet Danielle's big smile.

"Hey! It's Brandi," Myles said as he stared at her.

"I prefer Dani," she replied as she walked in the gym with a ball popped under her arm. "Mind if we play," she asked as she stopped at the bleachers followed by Jasmyne, Stacy, and one of the ladies who had been with her at Kimberly's party.

"Sorry, didn't mean to interrupt. I see you are in the middle of a game; we'll just take the other court," Dani said.

As the ladies walk onto the court, Myles stared at Chris to see if he expected him to say something. After all, it seemed that after Dani/Brandi showed up at his sister party, Kimberly no longer seemed happy.

"Hey," Stacy yelled as she placed her arm over her head and stretch from right to left. "Maybe we can have a three-on-three game. Women versus men, if you aren't too tired after you finish your game," Stacy said while staring straight at Myles. She stretched from left to right, back and forth, and then she began rotating her upper body in a circular motion.

"We'll see," Chris said as if he was seriously considering it. "About time," he said as he turned his attention to Malcolm who had just arrived. "Where's Jeremy?"

Malcolm look around as if he was looking for someone and was confused. He walked to the bleachers and sat his bag down. "Not there," he said as he pretended to look in his front pocket. He then pretended to look in his gym bag. "Not there either but wait. I did pack in a hurry; I might have overlooked him."

"Funny," Eric said then pointed towards the women taking turns practicing lay-ups.

"Might as well," Chris said knowing what Eric was thinking about.

"What?" Malcolm questioned.

"Five of us and four of them," Eric said as he quickly glanced in the ladies' direction.

"You all go ahead," Malcolm said as he grabbed his cell phone. "I have a few calls to make anyway."

"But seriously guys, I have not heard from Jeremy at all today," Malcolm said as he checked to see if he had any missed calls.

"Me either," Johnathan said, "but then again, he never calls me."

"Try his home number," Chris suggested.

"I did, it went straight to voicemail," Malcolm replied.

"That's strange," Chris said as he palmed the ball and walked over to the bleachers. I called him four times this morning and each time someone picked up the phone and then hung up."

"Maybe he's busy rendering due benevolence," Johnathan smiled.

"You probably right," Myles replied. "So, let's get this game on."

"I'm going to chill," Malcolm said, "but you all continue your game."

The guys went back to their two-on-two game as the ladies seem to just toss the ball around. From time-to-time when it appeared that one of the guys was looking in the ladies' direction, Dani would do a lay-up or attempt a three-point shot.

Malcolm had made all the calls he needed to make while watching his friends play ball. He watched for almost thirty minutes. He thought about joining his friends but didn't want to bully Johnathan off the court as he had done in the past whenever someone was not there, late, or left early. From time-to-time, Malcolm glanced at Danielle and her friends.

"Hey," Danielle yelled to Malcolm. "Why don't you join us?"

Malcolm glanced at his friends as if he needed permission, but he didn't wait to see if they would give it to him. He hesitantly strolled over to the court occupied by Danielle, Stacy, Jasmyne, and the newcomer.

"Malcolm, right?" Danielle questioned.

"Yeah," he responded as he stared at the brown-skin woman wearing gray sweatpants that looked a little well worn.

"This is Melody," Danielle continued with the introductions.

"Call me Mel," Melody replied as she extended her hand towards Malcolm. "Nice to meet you."

"Like-wise," Malcolm said.

"I'm sure you remember Stacy and Jasmyne, don't you?" Danielle continued.

Malcolm motioned his head yes, indicating that he did remember Jasmyne and Stacy.

"Jasmyne is having some issues with her ankle, so she's sitting this one out."

"Cool," Malcolm said not knowing what else to say. "I mean.... I don't mean it's cool that you hurt your ankle. I just..."

"I understand," Jasmyne replied as she hobbled to the bleachers trying not to put too much weight on her right ankle.

"Maybe you need an ice pack or do people put heat on it," Malcolm said, not really knowing which was best, heat or ice.

"I'm good," Jasmyne replied.

From time-to-time Malcolm got the impression that Danielle and Stacy might have been a couple. They seemed to whisper to each other a lot and they hung onto each other real tight. Malcolm was sure that the other guys had noticed too, but before he had a chance to say anything to the guys, he spotted the women eyeing the men every chance they got, when it appeared the guys were not looking. "Nah," he said to himself, "These ladies checking us out on the sly. They are straighter than arrows."

Malcolm and Stacy made a good team. They played as if they had been playing ball together for years. They seemed to know each other's every move and thought.

"We make a good team," Stacy said as Malcolm grabbed his water bottle after the game ended.

"Yeah, I must admit you got skills. I thought Danielle was the MVP of the group.

"She think she is," Stacy said as she lowered her voice.

"Why is that?" Malcolm questioned.

"Because I let her think that."

"Why?"

"Some people need to feel as if others think that they are the best. So, I let her have her moment in the spotlight."

"Well, I think you took that away from her today," Malcolm said as he gave her a high-five. "Great game!"

"I'll just call it luck to keep the peace."

"That's mighty humble of you."

"Not really. I had my time in the spotlight before and regardless of what people think of me, I know who I am. Some people continue to need validation from others. I don't. So why take the little bit of happiness from her. Sometimes it's all some people have."

"Good point."

"When I use to seek that type of attention, my dad used to tell me that showboating is for insecure people. Dani and I have always been on the same team, so I've never really had the opportunity or need to bring my 'A' game. Except six years ago in high school."

"Well, you were on it today."

"Thanks, so were you."

Mel and Dani walked over to Malcolm and Stacy and sat down on the gym floor.

"Good game you guys," Melody said, grabbing her water bottle.

"Thanks, same to you," Malcolm said.

"Yeah," Danielle said. "Great game. Stacy, you've been sneaking in some extra practice, haven't you?"

"Been keeping that a secret but looks like the cat is out of the bag now. MJ has been giving me private lessons," Stacy said and then laughed as she winked at Malcolm. "No seriously, I guess I just got lucky today."

"That or you're showing off for Malcolm here," Jasmyne said.

"Another game?" Malcolm asked.

"Fine with me," Stacy said as she stared at Malcolm's friends. "Look like they are about to leave or something."

Malcolm turned and saw Eric on his cell phone and the other guys were quickly approaching Eric. Malcolm studied Eric's face and could tell that something was wrong, seriously wrong.

"What?" Eric yelled in the phone.

"What's wrong?" Malcolm asked as he ran up to Eric. Everyone stood around anxiously waiting for Eric to get off the phone.

"Calm down, Kimberly. We'll be there," Eric said as he looked at his friends and made a quick circular motion with his finger to indicate to his friends to hurry up and pack up. He began to quickly shove his things in his gym bag. "I know, I know baby, we are on the way." Eric stared at his friends with disbelief as he hung up with Kimberly. "This can't be happening," he said in disbelief.

"What?" Chris questioned.

"What is it?" Malcolm asked before Eric had time to reply.

"What? Is something wrong with Jason?" Chris questioned.

"He better not had done something to Kimberly," Myles replied.

"No, he didn't. It's Jeremy; he has been shot," Eric said as he zipped up his bag. "We have to get to the hospital. Kimberly said it's not looking good."

"What? What happen? When?" Johnathan began to ask. "Lord we need to pray."

"Let's just get to the hospital, we can pray on the way there. I'll tell you all about it in the car," Eric said.

Everyone grabbed their things and rushed out of the building. Eric, Myles, and Johnathan all piled into Chris' truck. Danielle, Stacy, Melody, and Jasmyne walked out behind the guys as if they had been invited to dinner.

"Malcolm," Danielle yelled as he headed to his car instead of getting on the truck with the rest of the guys. "Are you going be okay? You seemed a little too emotional. I'll be glad to do the driving."

"I'm okay. I just have to find Jeremy's mom and sister," Malcolm said and then paused. "Okay, on second thought, if you don't mind, you can drive for me. I need to make a few calls."

"Your car or mine?"

"Doesn't matter," Malcolm replied.

"My car," Danielle volunteered.

Malcolm tossed his gym bag in his car, locked the doors, and headed towards Danielle's car. Danielle waved goodbye to her friends.

"I'll call you," Danielle said as she slapped Stacy and Jasmyne a high-five and then returned her attention back to Malcolm. "Ready," she asked Malcolm as he opened Danielle's passenger door and got in the car.

"Yes, I think so," Malcolm said as he immediately pulled out his phone and began dialing and quickly placed the phone to his ear.

"Hello," Malcolm yelled as if he was talking to an elderly person or someone with a hearing problem. "No, this is not Eric; this is Malcolm."

"Okay baby, I'm sorry. I always get you two mixed up," Jeremy's mother said.

"It's okay Ma Phillips,' he said. How are you doing today?" Malcolm asked.

"I'm fine. Just worried about that gigolo son of mines."

"Why would you be worried about him?" Malcolm asked trying to figure out if she had already heard the news about Jeremy.

"They say one of them Jezebel women he be messing with, shot him," she said then paused for a second. "Well, that's what someone told Poochie. Wait, that's not right, I think she said he got shot over one of them Jezebel women, so I guess Jezebel wasn't the one that shot him. You know, in the Bible Jezebel died. Think she fell out of a window. Dogs ate her body or maybe it was crows," Ma Phillips said, as if she really wasn't concerned about what happened to Jeremy.

"Where's Poochie now?" Malcolm interrupted.

"She might be looking for Jezebel, so she can push her out of the window," Ma Phillips laughed. "I'm just joking son. I think she's on her way to get me, so we can go to the hospital, but I told her I don't need to go. It's in Gods hand, been telling him that them pretty girls always got 'em a man on the side. I love him Eric, but I can't kill myself worrying about him. Done gave it over to the Lord, but I'm going down there when Poochie get here."

"Ma Phillips does Poochie have license?"

"No Jeremy. You know Poochie ain't going to get no license. 'Fraid she's gonna be like me and always be dependent on somebody to drive her around. I told that girl that she needs to do better than I did."

"This is Malcolm, Ma Phillips," Malcolm said, correcting her again.

"Malcolm, sweetheart, I know who you are, and you know who you are. Sometimes I just say the first name that comes to my mind. Take too much out of me to keep correcting myself, but I know you are Malcolm. I know all of Jeremy's friends, the male friends anyway. I don't know all thems' women. Don't none of them hang around long enough for me to remember their name. Be a new one all the time, but none of them make my boy happy. I try to tell him to stop looking at the body and face and look at the heart, but he doesn't listen."

"I know Ma Phillips. Well, I'm glad you got a ride because I was going to come get you and Poochie," Malcolm said.

"I know you will baby. How's that wife of yours," Ma Phillips asked and then paused as if she was thinking of what to say next. "She a nice girl and she loves you. Don't you ever trade that for someone who just want to be with you, okay?"

"Yes, ma'am. I won't," Malcolm said as he suddenly looked at Danielle. *What was I thinking?* He said to himself. "Ma Phillips, um I will see you at the hospital," Malcolm said and then hung up the phone. "Look, Danielle, this was a bad idea. I was not thinking. If my Lesia see us together, she's going to kill me and then she's going to kill you."

"Who is Lesia," Danielle questioned, hoping she was a girlfriend and not Malcolm's wife.

"My wife," Malcolm quickly replied.

"Look, I was just offering to help. I'm not trying to mess up your happy home. You just seem so pre-occupied. I could tell that you are the thinker in the group. You could have gone with your friends, but you were thinking about Ma Phillips and Poochie, whoever they are. I'm assuming they are relatives of Jeremy, who don't have a car or license," Danielle replied as if she was trying to stroke his ego.

"His mother and sister," Malcolm confirmed.

"Look, I could drop you off and leave. I'm sure that one of your boys could take you to get your car," Danielle said and then stared at Malcolm and waited for a reply. "Better yet, I can turn around now and take you back to get your car."

"No, we are more than halfway there, no point in turning around now," Malcolm said. "Look Dani, I really appreciate this. And believe me, I didn't mean..."

"You don't have to apologize," Danielle interrupted.

"Apologizing for what? I wasn't apologizing. I was going to say that I didn't mean to inconvenience you, but I thought I was going to have to run through my entire phone book to get a hold of Poochie. She's a grown woman, living with her mom and don't seem to think that she should have to tell anyone where she is going. She changes her number every other month."

"How do you know so much about her? Did you ever date her?" Dani asked.

"No, but I did live with them for a few months when my wife and I were separated," Malcolm hesitantly replied.

Danielle looked at Malcolm to see if he looked as if he might be willing to share more.

"How long ago was that?" Dani questioned.

"About two years ago," Malcolm said and then paused. "No wait. Yeah-yeah, that's right, about two years ago."

"What happened? Why did y'all separate?" Danielle asked.

"Well," Malcolm hesitatingly began. He wasn't sure he wanted to discuss his business with someone he barely knew. "Well, I guess we were both just too stubborn to compromise on certain things."

"Like what?" Danielle persisted.

"Like stuff, little stuff that led to constant nick-picking."

"Don't tell me it about the toilet seat up, cap left off the toothpaste, or squeezing it from the middle. No, wait. I know. The toilet paper over and not under."

Malcolm laughed, indicating that Danielle had at least named some of the usual arguments.

"Are you serious?" She chuckled. "People really separate over stuff like that?"

"Well, of course there were other major issues," Malcolm replied, not wanting to sound as if petty arguments cause him to separate from his wife. "Things like me coming home and the kitchen would be spotless," Malcolm said. He did not want anyone to think that a cap off the toothpaste could ever cause him to leave his wife.

"And that's a problem, a spotless kitchen?" Danielle questioned.

"Nah, really its normally not or it wouldn't have been if she had cooked first, then cleaned."

"So, she didn't cook?"

"Nope, didn't know how and didn't even want to learn."

"Oh, I see. You are one of those male chauvinists, aren't you?"

"No, but if a woman doesn't have to work, she can at least cook for her man," Malcolm said and then paused. He didn't want to paint a bad picture of his wife. He had learned never to give another woman any ammunition that she could use against him later. "But that's all changing. My baby takes good care of me now, so it's all good."

"And you?" Danielle questioned, not willing to drop the subject.

"What about me?" Malcolm asked.

"I'm sure you did stuff too."

"I did a little dirt, and I'm not proud of that. Hate I ever hurt her."

"Cheated?"

"Why is that the first thing that comes to y'all minds?" Malcolm questioned as if he was insulted.

"So, you didn't cheat?" Danielle asked.

"Well, not at first," Malcolm responded.

Danielle waited for him to finish. She knew there was more to the story. Malcolm didn't want to share anymore of his personal business, but for some reason he felt compelled to do so. It was the first time that he had been asked about the things that he had done to cause the separation. Normally, he would pretend that he started hanging out to avoid her nagging, when really, he just wanted to hang out with his friends and drink.

He felt as if hanging out with his friends was the only thing that signified independence and freedom.

"We began arguing over the little stuff. I began hanging out more and more and stayed out later and later and coming home drunk and broke. Yep, I was blowing too much money. Money that she thought should be going toward a house. A house she wanted," Malcolm stated. "Me, well I guess all I saw was responsibilities. Fix this, cut the grass, buy that, or you need to do this and do that. I just wasn't ready for all that responsibility plus a mortgage. She felt cheated. Just kept complaining about our life and what we had to have, in order to compete or compare to someone else."

"It made you feel like less than a man, didn't it?"

"Sure did. I wanted her to have it all. I just felt that if we were going to go into all that debt, she should help me more. Eventually, I did try to give it to her, but by then, it was too late. I had messed up my credit and blew all of my savings." Malcolm laid his head back on the head rest. "Now, I want it all with her and can't give it to her. Sometimes it was really hard to see all the disappointment in her eyes as she looks at other people's beautiful homes."

"So that's gone now, the disappointment?" Danielle questioned.

"Well, she knows that I'm working on giving her everything, but I think she knows that it is going to take some time."

"You sure that she is not going to get tired of waiting?"

"I am making progress and the funny thing is, I thought she was getting tired of waiting too, but what she really needed to see was that I was making constant effort and gradually progressing towards building up our credit and saving for a down payment."

"She should have been showing gradual improvement also."

"That's true," Malcolm said. He began to realize that Danielle would gradual make him resent his own wife if he kept listening to her. "But when people start blaming each other, they sometimes don't see the roles that they play in the destruction. I was blaming her and didn't see what I was doing, nor did I see the things that she was doing right. Nor did she see the things that I was doing right. We were both just too busy looking at each other's faults and blaming each other for everything that we were unhappy about. Now that I think about it, she was really doing the best that she knew how to do."

"What about you? Were you doing the best that you knew how to do?"

"In some areas, I was doing my best, but to be perfectly honest, in other areas, I wasn't. I did what was comfortable for me to do. I did what was easy and convenient; sometimes I just did what was fun."

"Wow, most men I know would never admit their part. They always blame the woman. I can't tell you how many times I have heard men pretend that they cheated because the woman was too fat, or they argue all the time because she's just too sensitive or moody," Danielle said. "If memory serves me correctly, didn't you start off that way, blaming her, saying she never cooked?"

Malcolm ignored Danielle's statement and turned the radio up. He sang silently along with the song on the radio.

"My strength is weak, can't take your mess. I'm packing my bags and I'm out. And don't try to stop. Why work this out, if you in and out of her house, can't pay the rent, the lights out. Don't want a job, can't keep a job. Keep smoking crack at Jack house. Don't want no more, can't take no more. I'll let myself out."

"Who is that?" Danielle asked. "I've never heard that song before, but it's on point with what a lot of us have experienced and are feeling.

"Oh, that this hot new R&B, slash Hip Hop, slash Gospel singer, slash rapper, slash writer, name jDenea'," Malcolm said. "I think the name of that song is, *Why Can't You Do Better.*"

"Is she also the same lady who wrote that song, *Stay on Ya Grind?*" Danielle asked and then started humming the words to the song.

Chapter 4

"You can drop me off at the door," Malcolm stated.

"I'm coming in too. If that's okay," Danielle said as she pulled into the first empty parking spot that she saw.

"Suit yourself," Malcolm said with a hint of coldness in his voice.

The reality of his journey had hit him. The conversation about his marital issues kept his mind occupied. He had almost forgotten the fact that he was going to the hospital to see about his best friend who had been shot and was on an operating table, fighting for his life. Malcolm opened the door and jumped out of the car before the car even came to a complete stop. He ran up to the emergency entrance so fast, he had to wait for the automatic doors to open. As soon as Malcolm walked through the double doors, he immediately spotted his friends.

"How is he?" Malcolm asked as he approached his friends.

"Don't know. We just got here too, but Kimberly is with him. Ma Phillips and Poochie are on the way," Eric said as he glanced at Danielle walking through the double doors of the emergency room.

"Yeah, I know. I talked to Ma Phillips on my way here," Malcolm replied. "Does anyone know what really happened? Ma Phillips said something about a woman shot him or he got shot over a woman."

"Kimberly said that Jennifer..." Chris started, but was interrupted.

"Jennifer?" Malcolm questioned.

"Yes, Jennifer. Well, from what we gathered, Jennifer ran into Jeremy and they got into a little argument about Jason."

"Jason," Malcolm said with an 'I-should-have-known tone."

"Apparently, Jennifer made some inappropriate comment about Kimberly pleasing her man or keeping a man," Chris said.

"When was this?" Malcolm asked, trying to figure out if any of this had anything to do with Danielle and the other women who had showed up at the party uninvited. Malcolm began to feel a little uncomfortable with Danielle listening.

"Anyway, Jeremy told her in no uncertain terms to stay away or else," Chris continued. "Jeremy and Jennifer got into a little argument. I guess Jennifer wanted to prove that he didn't scare her. She made a big deal out of it and had one of her boyfriends to put a little scare in Jeremy, or at least that was the plan."

"Are you serious?" Malcolm questioned as he looked from Chris', to Eric, to Johnathan, to see if anybody displayed any signs that would indicate that this had to be some horrible misunderstanding or a joke. "A man is about to lose his life over a juvenile argument."

"Well," Eric continued the story where Chris left off. "It appears that when the guy saw who Jeremy was, he claimed that Jeremy had dated his wife. It turned into a big mess. Jennifer got upset because she didn't even know the man had a wife. She reached for the gun. They got into a little scuffle, the gun went off, and you know the rest. Jeremy got shot."

"The guy claimed he thought the gun was empty. He claimed that he was only trying to scare Jeremy." Chris paused and shook his head as if there was more to the story. "Man get this. The guy told the police that Jennifer told him that Jeremy tried to rape her."

Malcolm sat down in the nearest chair and placed his hands over his eyes. "This has got to be a nightmare."

Eric, Johnathan, Chris, and Myles all set down beside Malcolm. Danielle could tell that Jeremy was well loved by his friends.

"Where's Jason?" Malcolm asked.

"Nobody knows," Johnathan replied. "Well, Kimberly might know. Nobody thought to ask about him."

"He could be back there with Kimberly for all we know," Myles said.

Myles had been silent the entire time as the group discussed what had happened. He had been praying and asking God to spare his friend's life. "You know, I knew that trick was trouble from the moment I set eyes on her. I knew I should have warned Kimberly about her." Myles chuckled a little. "Not that she would listen to me. That girl is too accepting of everybody. She's gonna have to learn to be careful of the company she keeps."

"Sounds like Kimberly is a loving person," Danielle said.

It was almost as if Kimberly was the one laying on the hospital operating table, fighting for her life.

"She is very loving. That girl used to take in every stray cat in the neighborhood," Myles said then paused, looking up in time to see Poochie and Ma Phillips making their grand entrance.

"I knew the day that Jennifer moved next door to Kimberly and Jason that she was going to be trouble." Malcolm began, but stopped almost as abruptly as Myles had stopped talking when he looked up and saw Ma Phillips and Poochie. Malcolm practically had to bite his lip to keep from laughing.

The sight of a 350 pound, 5' feet 1" inch woman, walking through the emergency room doors, gave a momentary relief from the sadness and anger that the group was feeling as they anguished over the condition of their beloved friend. Ma Phillips had on a big red hat with a veil all around it, matching gloves, a black and white striped skirt that looked hi-jacked in the back and dipped low in the front, a yellow blouse with a large blue button across the bust area. She looked as if she had gotten dressed for church and the circus at the same time. She had on pink bedroom shoes with bunny ears and thick black socks. Malcolm had been around her long enough to know that her dress attire was deliberate. He knew she had no sense of fashion and her style was anything that was comfortable. Malcolm could tell that Ma Phillips' fashion ensemble had amused everyone in the emergency room.

"I need to see my boy," Ma Phillips said as she approached the front registration desk.

"Okay ma'am, what's his name?" The receptionist asked.

"Jeremy Phillips Junior," Ma Phillips said with all the pride that she could muster up.

"I'm sorry Ma Phillips," the receptionist began, but before she could finish her sentence, Ma Phillips threw her hands back and let out on a loud yell.

"Oh Lord, Jesus," Ma Phillips began to cry out. "Don't fail me, Lord."

Malcolm and Eric ran to grab Ma Phillips as she threw her hands in the air again and leaned back so far, she looked as if she was about to do a back flip. Realizing that Malcolm and Eric might not be able to hold her weight if she began to go down, Myles and Chris jumped up and ran to help keep her from falling. Myles figured it would be easier to keep her from falling than to help try to pick her up, if she fell.

"What's wrong Ma Phillips?" Malcolm asked, while the four guys braced her body.

"My boy, he gone. Lord done took him."

"What is she talking about?" Myles asked the receptionist. "When?"

"Sir, I'm sorry for the confusion. She got irate before I finished my sentence. She asked to see her boy and before I could finish saying, 'I'm sorry, but he's still in surgery right now.' I guess she just assumed that I was about to say something else."

"Oh," Ma Phillips said. She was breathing so hard and heavy that she could barely hear the receptionist as she continued to talk with Myles. Ma Phillips was breathing as if she had run a 10-mile marathon nonstop.

"Is he going to be okay?" Poochie asked. "I'm Penny, his sister," Poochie said to the receptionist as if she was annoyed that the receptionist seen overly friendly with Myles.

"The doctor will be out to talk with you as soon as the surgery is over," the receptionist replied. She then looked at Myles as if he was the one who had asked the question and not Poochie. "We have a waiting room upstairs. You will probably be more comfortable there," the receptionist said and pointed to the double doors to the right side of the receptionist desk. "Once you go through those double doors, just ask someone at the nurses' station to point you to the elevators. Go up to the third floor and someone will be there to show you where the waiting room is."

"Thank you, baby. You are so sweet. Gods gonna bless you really good," Ma Phillips said as she headed through the double doors.

"Thank you," the receptionist said and smiled at Myles as he winked at her.

"Y'all coming?" Ma Phillips asked as she turned to face Chris and Eric who were still standing by her side.

Everyone followed behind Ma Phillips. As soon as the double doors closed behind them, Ma Phillips turned to face the group as if she were going to make some profound announcement.

"Now, I might be an old lady and I'm sure I act senile from time-to-time. I know I even look a little crazy with what I am wearing, right?" Ma

Phillips waited for a brave soul in the group to confirm that her ensemble was crazy, but no one dared to answer, so she continued. "But I do have enough sense not to start a sentence with 'I'm sorry, when someone asks to see a gunshot patient. Am I right about that?"

Everyone let out a sigh of relief and a few chuckles.

"Yep, you right about that, Ma Phillips," Johnathan said.
"Then she got the nerves to say I began acting irate. Child didn't know I was calling on the Lord for strength. Thought I was about to come crashing down to that floor. How she expects me to act? With her fast tail self; over there flirting with Eric. I mean Johnathan."
"Myles," Johnathan corrected her. "She was flirting with Myles."
"Johnathan, did you see her flirting with Myles," Ma Phillips asked.

Malcolm snickered a little because he knew Ma Phillips was about to get Johnathan straight; the same way she corrected him on the phone earlier.

"Yes ma'am. I saw it," Johnathan said like a proud schoolboy who knew he had just answered the question correctly.
"If you saw that it was Myles that the Jezebel was flirting with and not you, no need to tell me who it was, long as you know it wasn't you; it doesn't matter what I think or what name I call out. Boy, I told you earlier, I just call the first name that comes to my head. It is many of y'all. Now where's that elevator that girl was talking about. As long as I've been standing here talking, I know one of y'all done had enough time to ask someone."
"It's over there," Malcolm said and quickly turned and walked away so he could laugh without Ma Phillips hearing him. He didn't want to seem insensitive considering the serious situation they were facing, but he was grateful for the opportunity to not think about it for at least a minute. He had a feeling that a comedy show was about to go down with Ma Phillips, Poochie, and Myles all in the same room.

Chris and Johnathan hesitated as they headed to the elevator. They were unsure if they wanted to be trapped in a room with Ma Phillips and Poochie.

"Come on," Malcolm said as if he knew what Chris and Johnathan were thinking. "I am sure Ma Phillips want to be there when Jeremy gets out of surgery. Besides, I am sure that Kimberly could stand some company in the waiting room upstairs." Malcolm didn't bother offering an invitation to Danielle to join them; nor did he say goodbye to her. He glanced back to see if his friends were following him. Everyone piled in the elevator in complete silence. When the elevator doors opened again, Kimberly was standing at the nurses' station. Everyone rushed out of the elevator towards her.

"What's his status?" Malcolm asked as he jetted out of the elevator first and rushed up to her.

"He's out of surgery," Kimberly said looking from Malcolm to Ma Phillips not sure who she needed to be giving the update to. "The doctor said he's in good shape, but he is still asleep. He was heavily sedated doing surgery."

"Can we see him?" Chris asked.

"No, they won't allow anyone to see him just yet, but we can wait over there in the waiting room."

Kimberly led the group to the waiting room. She noticed that Ma Phillips seem to allow everyone else to be in charge. She did not ask any questions, nor did she respond to the status update.

As they walked into the waiting room, everyone quickly took a seat. Ma Phillips struggled to sit down in the low sitting chair. Malcolm and Johnathan rushed to her side to help lower her plus-size body to the chair. Myles quickly grab a seat beside Kimberly on the sofa.

"You look exhausted. Have you been here the entire time?" Myles asked Kimberly.

"Yep," Kimberly said. "Jennifer called me crying. She didn't know what else to do." Kimberly lowered her voice as she finished telling Myles what happened. "She gave my name and number to the paramedics as his next of kin."

"When did all of this happen?"

"Last night," Kimberly said and then paused. "Well, actually this morning sometime around 2:00 a.m. Jennifer didn't call me immediately after everything happened. The police are involved and after Jeremy was rushed to the hospital, she was taken to the police station for questioning. I think she is going to end up in jail." Kimberly eyes flooded with tears. "Why would she go this far to try to prove a pointless-point?"

"Kimberly, women like that use any means to feel important. They like married men because they like the idea that a man would jeopardize his family just to have them, just to be with them, even if it's just for one night. They like men fighting over them for the same reason. It makes them feel important. They act bold and confident, but really, they have low self-esteem and very little confidence. Most of the time, men don't have an ounce of respect for those types of women. They are nothing more than tricks or one-night stands. Most men do very little for them and those that generally do anything at all, do so under the threat of *if he doesn't, she's going to tell his wife*. Jennifer knew he was a married man, and I suspect she got mad when he was willing to fight Jeremy over his wife, but not fight over her. That's why she yelled that Jeremy raped her."

"Kimberly," Ma Phillips began. "Where's that friend of yours? The one that my boy was fighting over."

"Ma Phillips," Kimberly said, barely above a whisper.

"Call me, Ma Phillips same as everybody else does. Now, I don't know much about you. You don't come around much since you got yourself all grown-up and married. But, I remember when Chris used to bring you around for Poochie to babysit after your parents passed on to Glory. You always have been in my prayers. I've seen all of you grow-up, go off to college, or get married. Well, some of y'all. And some don't act like you want no woman-like my boy. Anyway, you love my son just like he was your blood brother. I see that in your eyes. You listen to Myles. He's a smart man. And don't you be blaming yourself either because of that friend of yours. Sometimes we just put our trust in the wrong people when your heart's big enough to want to trust everybody. You hear me."

"Yes, Ma'am. I mean Ma Phillips," Kimberly tried to resist the urge to say what she had been feeling, but the words quickly formed in her head as they had been doing since she got to the hospital and before she could stop herself, she blurted them out. "But he got shot protecting my honor."

"Baby, this is not about your honor," Ma Phillips quickly interjected. "That girl is upset because of what Jeremy did for you, what she wants a man to do for her. He loves you enough to protect you without you asking, begging, or scheming to get him to do so. See, you don't have to sleep with any man to get his attention or affection. She's craving that, that attention, affection and no matter whether it was you or some other girl, she was going to try to get that attention by any means necessary. That's why she lied and cried rape. Most men, whether they love you or not, is going to get upset to hear that any man has tried to take advantage of a woman. That man thought Jeremy was a bully and rapists. He probably just meant to flex his muscles and use his gun as just a means to scare him. Now, he must go home and explain to his wife that he shot a man over another woman. No, I don't believe he intended to hurt anyone; I just believe he intended to scare him. See, Jennifer and women like her, they don't even realize or even care, that they make it hard for women all over. When you cry rape and you haven't even been touched, it's hard to trust any woman. Jeremy's going to learn too; he's going to learn to stay out of married women's bed," Ma Phillips said, taking advantage of her captive audience. "Yep, I've been a player and even been played. Don't let this old woman fool ya. I know the game. Probably created some of the rules." Ma Phillips continued to talk on and on.

~

"Malcolm, honey, are you okay?" Lesia asked, as she rushed into the waiting room.

Malcolm quickly stood and rushed to his wife and greeted her. "Yes, sweetie. I'm okay," he said as he walked her back to where he was sitting. Johnathan slowly moved down one seat so that Malcolm's wife could take a seat beside her husband.

Everyone spoke to Lesia, and quickly return their attention back to Ma Phillips.

"Hey, Lesia," Ma Phillips said in a soft tone. "Baby, you are picking up some weight. Looks good on you though. Your skin all shiny," Ma Phillips said then paused. "You know what? I almost forgot about it until just now, but I've been dreaming about fish for about two weeks now. Girl, you're pregnant, ain't ya?"

Lesia looked at Ma Phillips with a hint of *get-out-of-my-business* in her eyes; she turned to face Malcolm and smiled. "Ma Phillips is a trip ain't she. I don't know why all old people always think somebody got to be 'in the family way' just because they dream about fish. Maybe I was just craving a seafood meal. You know a two-piece fish dinner."

"Baby girl, there's something we need to talk about?" Malcolm questioned, but stopped mid-sentence when he saw a tall man wearing a white jacket, walking in the room.

"Mrs. Phillips," the man said as he stared at Kimberly.

"I'm Ma Phillips," Ma Phillips said as she stared at the doctor. "He's my son."

The doctor glanced at Ma Phillips and then back at Kimberly. Kimberly slowly knobbed her head at the thin white man indicating that it was okay to talk to Ma Phillips. As the doctor talked to Ma Phillips, Kimberly talked to Myles.

"I let them believe that I was his wife," Kimberly whispered to Myles. "It was the only way that they would talk to me. They said they could only talk to the next of kin. So, when the paramedics identified me as his wife, I didn't correct them."

Myles kissed Kimberly on her forehead. "Good! Ain't no telling how he would have been treated if they thought he was here alone. Might have left his black behind alone to die on a gurney in the waiting room or hallway."

Kimberly managed to smile. Myles had a way of making her feel good even when she messed up royally.

"Don't tell Jason that I got another husband," she joked.

"Your secret is safe with me," Myles replied as he turned his attention to Ma Phillips. He noticed that she was trying to get her body out of the chair, but before he could get up to help her, Johnathan and Malcolm were already at her side and Chris was standing two feet behind them waiting to see if his help was needed.

"These all your strong boys, Ma Phillips?" The doctor asked.

"Yup, these all my strong handsome young men," she replied. "Now, just tell me what you got to tell me. As long as you don't start your sentence with I'm sorry, I'm going to be okay. Done prayed and I know my son ain't dead."

"Well, Jeremy is awake, but he's a little groggy. He remembers being shot, but he doesn't remember everything," the doctor informed Ma Phillips.

"Well, I guess that's great news. Now can I talk to him?" Ma Phillips asked as she began walking out of the waiting room.

"Ma Phillips let me warn you," the doctor said as he followed Ma Phillips out of the waiting you. "He had a little brain damage and..."

"I don't need any warning. I just want to see my boy. Anything else you got to say, say it to one of my boys here or the other Mrs. Phillips over there," Ma Phillips said as she turned and looked at Kimberly and winked. "I ain't no slow leak," she said barely above a whisper as she walked out of the waiting room.

Ma Phillips followed the doctor down the hall. When they got to room 407, the doctor stopped and allowed Ma Phillips to enter the room alone. As soon as she entered the room, she noticed that Jeremy's eyes were bandaged up. She wanted to go find the doctor and ask him why, but she decided to ask Jeremy instead. She stared at her son, wondering if he was still asleep or just extremely silent. She wanted to say something, but she wasn't sure what to say. She was afraid that her words would not come out right, because she was both concerned about his condition, but angry at his actions. *How could he get involved with such reckless behavior that he would end up in a hospital fighting for his life?* She thought to herself.

"Jerry, son, are you awake?" She whispered.

Jeremy groaned a little and then tried to clear his throat. He tried to talk, but nothing beyond a whisper escaped his lips. He tried to adjust his body so that he could sit up but was unable to move. The more he squirmed in the bed, the more uneasy Ma Phillips felt. She was afraid that his hands would get tangled up in tubes and he would snatch something loose.

"Be still boy," she said as if he was a five-year child. "You're going to pull one or all of those tubes out. I don't know what they are doing for you, but I'm sure they are doing something to keep you alive."

Jeremy cleared his throat again and tried to talk. His voice was weak, but he managed to force words out of his mouth this time. "I can't see."

"Why don't you let your eyes focus for a few minutes? Maybe it's like when you first turn the lights on in the morning and your eyes need time to adjust to the light," Ma Phillips said in a very comforting and calm voice.

42

"You know it could have something to do with the fact that they have those bandages over your eyes."

"I can't see," Jeremy restated.

"I'll get the doctor," Ma Phillips said and quickly rushed out of the room.

As soon as Ma Phillips stepped into the hallway, she was bombarded with Jeremy's friends, who anxiously awaited an update about Jeremy's condition.

"How is he?" Malcolm asked as he studied Ma Phillips face and could tell that something was wrong. "Can we see him?"

Before Ma Phillips could answer, she spotted the doctor and briskly walked up to him. Malcolm scanned the faces of his friends then decided to follow Ma Phillips.

"He can't see." Malcolm heard Ma Phillips say as she approached the doctor.

"Whenever there is trauma to the head, there is a possibility that the sight can be temporarily affected," the doctor stated as if it was nothing to be concerned about.

"Will he get it back?" Malcolm asked.

"We don't know right now," the doctor said, hoping that the answer would suffice for now, but he could tell that it was not enough. "Normally, the condition is only temporary, but sometimes it can be permanent. We will monitor him for a few days and administer a test or two to see if we can give you a more definite answer."

"It's all my fault," Kimberly began to mutter as the doctor walk past her, headed to Jeremy's room.

Ma Phillips followed the doctor back to Jeremy's room. As she walked past the group with Malcolm following behind her, she touched Kimberly on her shoulder as a sign that everything was going to be okay. She wanted her to know that she did not blame her. However, she was too concerned about Jeremy to try to comfort her at that moment.

"You all go back in the waiting room and try to get some rest. I would tell you to go home, but I know that would be pointless because you ain't going nowhere. I'll come get you when he's up to visitors," Ma Phillips said and then disappeared into Jeremy's room without waiting for response from anyone."

"It's all my fault," Kimberly said again.

"Calm down, sweetheart," Myles said. "It is not your fault, so stop saying that. You can't keep beating yourself up for what happened. It's not going to change anything. We must remain positive about the outcome. Besides, Johnathan has been praying for him and you know how relentless he can be. Just like when Jacob said *he was not going to release the angel until he blessed him*, Johnathan ain't going to stop bugging God until all of Heaven open up and pour out the miracle that we need in this situation," Myles said as he turned to Johnathan and winked.

"That's right," Johnathan said, accepting the unspoken request to help cheer up Kimberly and encourage the others. "The Word of God says, 'by Jesus stripes he is healed.' Now that's what the Word of God says, and I don't know about nobody else, but I am just wise enough to believe that the Word is true. God is the truth because He cannot lie," Johnathan preached his sermon all the way to the waiting room. "God tells us to put Him in remembrance of His word and that's exactly what I'm going to do. I am going to remind Him day and night that according to His word, Jeremy is healed. What He said and what I believe in my heart is that Jeremy is healed. Now, I know it might not look like it now to the natural eye, but the spirit man receives it before the natural man sees it and we must believe and receive that for Jeremy. We have to intercede for him."

"Amen, brother Johnathan," Lesia said. "I really felt that."

"I know, right, me too," Eric said. He turned and looked at Lesia in agreement with her statement to Johnathan. "Amen." Eric took a seat in the chair directly across from the waiting room's entrance. He placed his hands behind his head and leaned back and closed his eyes. He immediately began to speculate about what was going on in Jeremy's room. He began to imagine the worse.

"The devil comes immediately to steal the word," Myles said. "The very worst-case scenario," Myles began as he touched Eric on the shoulder and sat down beside him. "He will be blind, but he will be alive. He will be here to see another day. Johnathan just preached victory and we are sitting around here as if we are mourning his passing. If we truly believed what

Johnathan just preached, we should be celebrating the victory. Just that quick, the devil tried to snatch that word from our hearts that was just preached. The Bible says the devil comes to steal the word that was sown in our hearts. Was it really sown?"

"What made you use the words 'worst case?" Eric questioned.

"Simple, it was all over your face man," Myles said to Eric. "You were thinking the worst, but your worst was worse than the worst that I was thinking."

"Celebrate?" Malcolm said as if he was considering the thought. "Yeah, man you are right. We have two reasons to celebrate. First of all, the devil is defeated, he lost again."

"Lost what?" Kimberly questioned as if she was confused.

"He couldn't take him out. He could not kill him. Even tried to make us doubt God's word," Eric said.

"But really, we have a reason to celebrate; we can celebrate his life. We can celebrate this victory," Malcolm said.

"But he is in there laying in that bed fighting for his life, can't see," Kimberly said as a flood of tears rolled down her face. "It feels selfish to want to be out here celebrating and he's in there hurting. I don't physically feel the pain that he feels, but I am hurting for him right now."

"But he is alive. He is winning the fight for his life. Faith requires us to act like what we believe, is our reality. It is so. If we believe he's gonna beat this, we have to act like he's going to beat it. He's not fighting for his life, God saved him already. He's fighting for sight. If he can't see, guess what? Well, he's alive. He has seen what he needs to see and even though he hadn't seen everything that God has ever created, what he has seen gives him the ability to imagine the things that he hasn't. He knows the color of the sky. He knows the beauty of the world and no one can ever take that from him. But he's here, still on this earth and like Johnathan, I'm wise enough to believe that God's word is true. If He healed one blind man, he can heal another." Myles got up and stood directly in front of Kimberly and then kneeled down in front of her. "You know I love you, right? I love you as if you were my very own biological sister, so just know when I tell you this. It's not to hurt you, but to snap you back to reality."

Everyone stopped and turned to face Myles.

"It seems to me that we are all more focused on our own discomfort of this situation than we are about Jay's," Myles said then paused. He slowly turned and looked around at his friends and then he turned back and locked eyes with Kimberly. "Kimberly, I don't think it is selfish to want to celebrate his life and the devil's loss. I think it is selfish to be more concerned about your own feelings, and not his feelings. If Jeremy wanted to play the hero for you, then let him be that hero, if he qualifies. When you go in there, you thank him for what he did for you. Let him feel like a hero. Maybe that's what he needs to feel. It's selfish of you to not be able to forgive yourself. The easiest way to release this self-guilt, is to forgive you, like God forgives you. If God can forgive you, you can forgive yourself. You're not better than God, are you?"

"Wow Myles." I have heard you speak more about God and wisdom today than I have heard you speak in 20 years," Johnathan said.

"Think of Jesus' discomfort, nails driven through his hands and head pierced, hanging on the cross. All of that and He even had to carry His own cross as He marched to His death." Tears began to flow rapidly as Myles envisioned Jesus hanging on the cross. 'He did all of that for us. He died for us. Yet, we act as if Jeremy is dead because he might have to live without sight. I bet Jesus would have loved to switch places with Jeremy at any given time. If all they wanted to do to Him was to take His sight that would've been a cakewalk for Jesus."

Chris entered the room. No one had even noticed that he had not returned with the rest of the crowd.

"Any word on how he's doing?" Poochie asked as she turned and looked at Chris.

"You mean other than being blind?" Chris question. "He's doing good." Chris answered without waiting for Poochie to respond.

Poochie glanced down at her ringing cell phone. "Well, that's good to hear. One thing is for sure, he's going to learn to stop judging things by the way they look, won't he?"

"You know what?" Malcolm began as he jumped up and walked towards Poochie.

Poochie didn't flinch or bat an eye. She had become accustomed to fighting with Malcolm. They were as close as sisters and brothers could be, without being biologically related.

"What?" She questioned as she looked up from the cell phone that was attached to the side of her ear. She shifted her plus-size body to the left so that she could pull her three sizes- too small, Rok-N-Wear tee-shirt down in the back. Despite her big body, she always wore the latest fashions, or the best knockoffs and look-a-like brands. "What, Mr. Righteous-when-it-suits-you?" Poochie responded as she stared at him eye-to-eye as if they were about to go to war.

"You are so self-centered," Malcolm replied.

"Oh! And you're not?" She asked. "And what about my brother? You want to tell me that he's not self-centered. Don't get me wrong, I love him and I'm glad to know that he's okay, but sometimes we have to live by the choices we make. We don't always get a chance to repent before the consequences of our actions manifest. And he has made some very bad decisions. I can pray for him and for his healing, but let's face it, we reap what we sow." Poochie looked at Malcolm as if she expected him to say something. "I bet that every one of us in this room would love a few crop failures because we have all sown some bad seeds. Now, I know y'all look at me and judge me because I act like nothing bothers me, but like you said earlier Myles, if we have faith, then we have to act like it is so. Doesn't that apply to how we talk about a person that is alive to live another day, who can clean up his act and get it together. So, I would have said the same thing to him that I just said about him. I ain't acting as if nothing has really changed other than he can't see. So, who's acting more in faith, those of you who wants to treat him like he's suddenly a saint because he's laid up in a hospital bed, or the ones who treat him like they would have always treated him, if this had not happened? Now, don't forget this. You know I was raised up in the church, just like to rest of y'all. I might not act like it sometimes; well, most of the time, but some of the Word is in me and what's in you, will come of out of you. Maybe my logic is a little twisted about how I demonstrate faith, but I do have faith to believe that he's going to make it."

Malcolm set down beside Poochie. "You know, for someone who acts as if you are only concerned with you..." Malcolm said, then stopped mid-sentence not knowing if he wanted to say what he was thinking or not. "Well, let's just say your heart-felt speech tells me everything that I need to know. You love your brother no matter how much you act like you can't stand him."

Poochie knew that regardless of what her brother's friends thought about her indiscretions and repeated mistakes, they knew she was right. She scanned the faces in the crowded waiting room. The blank stares and concern look indicated that everyone was pondering what she said or maybe even considering their own life and past mistakes. Poochie even thought about her life. She had a lot of men and many of which had about an ounce of respect for her. She knew that she was leading a destructive life, much like her brother whom she had just roasted. She knew that she used her multitude of men to disguise the fact that she was unhappy with her weight, her life, and her seemingly bleak future. She was tired of squeezing her size 28 body into size 22 clothes as if she was smaller than the story the scales revealed. Her insistence upon wearing anything that fit her because she thought she looked good in it, even if she revealed too much or even if she was about to bust it open, was her pretense at being confident. Squeezing into clothes that was two-sizes too small didn't make her any happier, but other people thought she was confident. She never tried to correct them. She walked into every room demanding that every man pay attention to her, as if she thought she was a brick house, no matter how she felt inside.

"Judge me not," Johnathan blurted out, then paused, breaking the uncomfortable silence that fell upon the crowded room.

Malcolm hugged Poochie as if he had been ordered to do so.

"I guess at a time like this, we all need to reflect on our own life values and not judge each other," Johnathan continued.
"You know what they say," Myles said as he strolled past Malcolm and Poochie. "There is a time and season for everything. Maybe we need to figure out what season this is for us all." As Myles headed out of the waiting room, he turned and looked at Kimberly. "Mrs. Phillips, I'm going to check on Jay." He winked at Kimberly.
Myles slowly walked out of the room. He looked back several times as if he thought someone might be following him. He walked down the hall and past the nurses' station. When Myles got to Jeremy's room, he paused

at the door. He was not really sure whether he should just walk in or knock on the door before entering. He didn't want to wake Jeremy, if he was sleeping. He slowly pushed the door open and peeped his head in.

~

"Hey man, it's me, Myles. Can I come in?" Myles asked.

When Jeremy didn't answer, Myles considered going back to the waiting room, but instead, he took one step further into the room and looked around for Ma Phillips. He discovered that Ma Phillips was not in there.

"Jay," Myles said as he entered the room. "Man, you good in here?" Myles questioned.

"Yeah man, I'm good, just..." Jeremy started, but his voice faded mid-sentence. Myles could tell that Jeremy was not okay.

"Jeremy man, everybody is out there waiting just to see you," Myles hesitantly said.

"I know, but I don't want to see anyone," Jeremy quickly responded, then paused and chucked. "See, now that's funny cause..." Jeremy paused again.

Jeremy slowly raised his hands to his head and massaged his temples. Then he slowly lowered his fingers to his eyes. Myles could tell that Jeremy was crying.

"I guess I should have said, I don't want them to see me," Jeremy corrected himself.

"Man, we are going to get through this together," Myles said. "Losing your sight doesn't mean you've lost anything to us. We have gone from boys to men together and we are going to get through this together as well. The same way you would be there for any of us, we are going to be there for you. And..."

"I know, it's just that..." Jeremy stopped talking as the tears rolled down his face. "Why me?" Jeremy began to question.

"Look, you lost your sight, you're lucky it's not your life, or an arm or a leg for that matter. I know it might be easy for me to stand here with

49

my sight and say this, but you have to be thankful that your sight is all you lost," Myles said then paused and looked at his friend and immediately felt thankful that he was not dead. "Man, it could have been your life. Besides, the doctors told your mother that it might be temporary."

"I know and lying here in this bed, all I can think about is that..." Jeremy paused for a few seconds then finished. "I have someone to bring me my meals, help me take four steps to the bathroom, and then help me back to my bed again. That's one thing. Man, I don't have a wife to help me around. Do you know how long I waited to move out of my mom's house?"

Jeremy tried to raise his right hand to wipe the tear that seem to refuse to roll down his cheek. His IV tube got hung up on his bed rail. Jeremy got frustrated trying to untangle it and snatched the IV out of his hand.

"Jay, I know you don't believe this, but something good will come out of this."

"What Myles? What good do you think is going to come out of this," Jeremy yelled.

They tried to ignore the beeping sound coming from the monitor. Jeremy covered his eyes again and blood ran down his hand. Myles walked closer to the bed, wondering whether to call the nurse, wash the blood that was running down Jeremy's hand, or try to comfort him.

"Jay, honestly, I really don't know what to say right now," Myles replied.

"Say anything. Say nothing. Do whatever you wanna do. You can't fix everybody's problem Myles. You can't give me my sight back," Jeremy yelled.

"What's going on in here?" An unfamiliar voice questioned as the door opened and a nurse entered the room. Myles stepped aside so that she could get to Jeremy.

"I'm DeAnna Wright and I'll be your nurse Mr. Phillips," the nurse said as she glanced at Myles and smiled.

"Hi, I am Myles," he said as he extended his hand trying to distract her attention from Jeremy. He knew that Jeremy wouldn't want anyone to see him crying. "And your name is?" He asked. "Oh, that's right, you just stated that your name is DeAnna Wright. Sorry! I just get so nervous around beautiful ladies."

Myles winked at DeAnna, hoping she understood that he was trying to cheer Jeremy up by indicating that he was about to be taken care of by a beautiful woman. DeAnna smiled at Myles as if she understood.

"Mr. Phillips, I see you decided to remove your IV," DeAnna jokingly stated.

"Must be nice," Jeremy snapped. "I see you're..." he stopped mid-sentence. "Oh, I forgot just that quickly. I can't see anything, now can I?"

DeAnna quickly began cleaning up the blood.

"Okay, that's much better. Don't you think?" She asked Jeremy. "I will check with the doctor and see if you need to be hooked back up. "

Myles watched DeAnna as she worked. She cleaned up the water that Jeremy knocked over and then checked the bathroom to see if anything needed restocking. She talked as she worked. DeAnna was very pleasant despite the fact that Jeremy complained the entire time she was in the room.

"Let me get you another pitcher of ice and some more water, Mr. Phillips," DeAnna said as she grabbed the small teal pitcher. "I'll be right back so don't you go anywhere, okay?" DeAnna said, but before she left the room, she noticed that Jeremy looked cold. "I'll get another blanket out of storage for you just in case you need it. Is that okay?"

"Sure," Jeremy said feeling a little bad that he had given DeAnna a hard time when all she was doing was her job.

DeAnna put the pitcher down and strolled across the room. She looked at the thermostat to check the temperature in the room. She opened the storage cabinet and grabbed a blanket.

"Look Jeremy," Myles began. "I'm going to let the guys know that you are okay. I am sure they are concerned about you," Myles said as he headed for the door.

"Okay, but I don't want to see anyone right now, only don't tell them that. I don't want to hurt anyone's feelings. Just tell them that I'm sleeping

51

or that the nurse is with me right now," Jeremy stated. "Tell them to go home and get some rest."

"Gotcha," Myles said as he quickly exited the room.

"Probably do you some good," DeAnna said to Jeremy as she placed the extra blanket across the foot of his bed. She gently patted his hand so that he would know that she was standing right by his side. "I'm really not supposed to do this, but I could probably find a few folding chairs if you would like me to."

"Would you please stop standing around feeling sorry for me as if I am some helpless victim or dying patient," Jeremy asked in a bit of a softer tone than he had used before. "I don't want no one's pity."

"True friends don't show pity; they show love and concern. They look for the silver lining. They encourage and pray for you," DeAnna said as if she knew exactly how it felt to be in Jeremy's position.

"I guess that's a silver lining; I can't see," Jeremy said and then laughed. His laughter turned into moans and groans.

DeAnna looked around the small hospital room as if she was looking for something to do. Despite his many complaints and grumpy demeanor, DeAnna could tell that Jeremy was probably a really nice guy. Jeremy could feel DeAnna presence almost as if he was touching her.

"That's Midnite that I smell," Jeremy said.

"Yes," DeAnna replied. "It's my favorite. I'm surprised you can smell it. When I have to work, I only dabbed a little behind my ears. I don't want to cause anyone to have any allergic reactions."

"Most people don't even think about that. Boy do I get so tired of women smelling like they bathed in the perfume bottle. They be 'bout to choke a brother to death," Jeremy said.

He felt a gentle push on his back, so he instantly lifted his head so that DeAnna could fluff his pillow.

"Wait now," DeAnna said. "Men do the same thing. They splash it on themselves, their clothes, and I even think some men wash their hair with it."

"You are probably right," Jeremy chuckled.

"I bet you've done that too," DeAnna replied. "That's probably why you chuckled."

"Who me?" Jeremy laughed. "Nah?"

"Yes, you," DeAnna replied. "I know you've been around here driving the women crazy and 'bout to choke 'em all at the same time."

Jeremy tried to resist, but he couldn't. He burst out laughing. "Okay, okay. I admitted it; I am guilty. I have tried that before. Sort of."

"Sort of! Huh?" DeAnna asked as if she was pondering something. "So, you have drove women crazy and then claimed innocent. Surprise you are not locked up."

Jeremy let out a slight laughter. "Looks like they didn't have to lock me up. All they had to do was pin me up in here and take my sight. That way, I can't find my next victim," Jeremy said and then let out another slight laugh.

DeAnna stared at Jeremy, wondering whether to laugh with him or to comfort him. She wasn't sure if he was trying to be funny or sarcastic. She didn't want him to slip back into feeling sorry for himself. He had turned around so quickly. She even thought he might be flirting with her. At least she hoped he was. It felt good to get some attention from a handsome man, even if he couldn't see.

"Relax," Jeremy said after a few seconds. "No pity parties here. After all, I don't have to see my victims. Now do I?" He asked as he reached out and grabbed her hand as if he could see it. "See, got you already."

"No, I guess you don't have to see your victims," DeAnna said as she chuckled.

She smiled at the fine, helpless man, lying before her. She began to visualize herself on Jeremy's arm. Her smile grew wider and wider. *Would he even give me a second look if he could see me, she* asked herself? Suddenly she began to feel a little sad. Doubts invaded her spirit. Her feelings turned from compassion for her sightless patient to self-pity. *Focus,* she told herself. *This handsome successful man, holding my hand is filled with thoughts of anger and can't even see the real reason he's still here. It's because of You God, she* muttered to herself. *I have to focus on him, not me.* DeAnna tried to block the romantic thoughts that kept manifesting in her head, but she couldn't. *Lord, I thought you finally sent me the man that I've been praying for, but this man doesn't even know you God and can't even see me. Probably wouldn't even be holding my hand if he could see me now,* she thought to herself.

"What's wrong?" Jeremy asked, sensing that DeAnna defenses were suddenly up. He could feel her tense up.

"Nothing, I was just thinking that I need to finish my rounds," she replied.

"Oh, Yeah. I understand. Hope you stop by later," Jeremy said.

"I will," DeAnna quickly replied.

"You promise?" Jeremy questioned.

"It's my job," DeAnna politely responded. "I get paid to come in here and check on you. So, I will be back in a few hours," DeAnna said as she walked out of the room before he could reply.

So, I guess all I am is just a job, Jeremy said to himself. His smile slowly disappeared from his face. He eventually leaned his head back and tried to think up pleasant thoughts. *Guess that's exactly what I should have expected,* he thought. *I am a patient. I am just her job. I guess I see how women feel when someone makes them feel special on the first date, then they expect ole dude to feel some kind of way about them from then on,* Jeremy said to himself. He closed his eyes and began to think about going home. The excitement about getting out of the hospital lasted a few minutes. *Who's going to help me then,* he thought. *I am sure the guys will help me from time-to-time, but none of them would want to live with me. Maybe Poochie, yeah. I can pay her to help me out for a few days.* As Jeremy tried to figure out how he would be taken care of, he became angry all over again. "God, why should I have to rely on someone to help me? I am a grown man. I should be able to take care of myself. This is not fair God. Why God?" Jeremy asked. "Why me? Who's going to help me? Who God?" Jeremy asked as he tilted his head up towards Heaven. "I'm waiting for an answer God. Tell me. Who?" Jeremy asked. He waited as if he expected God to answer him that very moment. "Who God?"

"Oh, now you're calling on God, huh?" Johnathan asked. He slowly pushed the door open to Jeremy's room and walked in. "I guess it's better late than never."

"Hey John," Jeremy said. "What's good man? I thought everyone had gone home by now."

"Nope. They all still out there, just hoping that you'd allow us to see you. We want to see for ourselves that you are okay. Myles told us to go home and give you some time to deal with… well."

"You can say it man. The fact that I can't see. I'm blind," Jeremy responded with bitterness in his voice.

"Yeah that, but remember, it's temporary. I know that this too shall pass. You're going to be back to your old self in no time."

"You really believe that?"

"Yes, I do." Johnathan said without hesitation. "You are healed."

"I don't have the faith you and Malcolm have," Jeremy said. As he talked, his word became a little more at ease, as he searched for the right words to say. "I don't go to church or pray every day. I don't even…"

"So, you think because you haven't gone to church or prayed in a while, that God won't hear your prayers? Is that it?"

"Well, I know He would hear them, but will He answer them?"

"Lots of people go to church every Sunday. Some even pray every day, but that's because they're following religious practices, but that doesn't mean they have any kind of relationship with God or faith in Him. Religion and relationship are not the same thing. If God answers their prayer, He surely can answer your prayers."

"But will He?" Jeremy questioned with more than a hint of doubt in his voice. "I might not know as much as you know about God, scriptures, and holiness, but I do know that the difference between me and the rest of the sanctified hypocrites is that, at least they have some faith. All they need is faith the size of a mustard seed. I know that much."

"Is that what you think? The truth is, most people pray about their problems or as religious folks say, they turn them over to God. Then a few minutes later they are telling their 'woe is me" story to whomever will listen. They got their fingers crossed, a rabbit foot in their pocket, and praying no black cat will cross their path. Operating in faith my foot. They are operating in that 'hope this story sound pitiful enough for listening hearts to help me.' They then end their story with the catch-all statement, 'I hope God lay it on someone's heart to help me.' Falling out in front of the congregation just to get attention. Then call it slayed in the spirit. Man, that ain't bit more faith. You got just as much, if not more than the holy sanctified church goers, more than the ones who are just praying, I mean playing church."

"You right about that. I have been the victim of one of those 'woe is me' stories before. The very next week, the dude and his family posting pictures on Facebook showing off their fabulous vacations. Guess, I helped pay for that. I said to myself, he and his family can be sitting in the dark next week and I bet I won't be giving him no money for another light bill." Jeremy let out a little chuckle. "He better stock-up on some Every-Ready batteries next time and some flashlights, because I am not giving him a dime. I can't stand hustlers like that," Jeremy said. "I know God can't."

"Think about it though. It might not sound right and it sho' ain't right, but they had faith for the money and it came. So, if they can have faith in their hustling ways, and it works for them, why you can't have faith in healing? Healing that God already gave you."

"I can," Jeremy said. He paused to think of how to explain the guilty feelings he was experiencing. "But, why should I?" He continued. "It's like friends that don't come around until they need you. Same thing with God. I do want to have a relationship with God someday, but it would feel like me only seeking Him now because I need Him."

"Do you think you are the only person who wants a relationship with God, but feel that they are only seeking Him when they need Him? It happens all the time. Its times like this that humbles us and makes us realize that we need God. Having a relationship, starts with accepting Him and having faith in Him. Faith for healing starts with you believing that healing is for you. You wouldn't have a reason to believe for healing, if you did not need healing. You have to believe that it is possible for your sight to be restored. If God has done it for one person, He will do it for you. God has healed the blind. By Jesus stripes you are healed, but you must believe that," Johnathan said. "But you should not have to wait to believe you are healed once you have built up the prefect relationship in God."

"So, you're saying that I should believe that I am already healed or are you saying that I should believe that I will be healed?" Jeremy asked as if he really wanted to understand how faith works.

"The Bible doesn't say that by Jesus stripes you will be healed. It says you are healed. You have to believe that you are healed already. I think that's why so many people are still suffering today; they're waiting on God to do what His word says that He has already done. We just have to believe, even though you don't see it or feel it. That's what faith is about, believing even when the situation is contrary to what you want and expect see," Johnathan explained.

"Okay, that's enough," Jeremy said as if he was ready to accept that he was healed. "I get it. I believe that I am healed. I just have to keep saying it until I believe it, right? And before you ask me again..."

"What?" Johnathan interrupted. "I was not going to ask if you've confessed Jesus as your Lord and savior, but since you brought it up, have you?" Johnathan replied as if he had read Jeremy's mind.

"Yeah, man I have. Do you know who my mother is? You can't live in her house if you are not saved. '*Satan ain't in my family and his children can't stay under my roof unless they get adopted into the Kingdom of God*,'" Jeremy said trying to sound like his mother. "Ask Malcolm. She told him the same thing when he stayed with us right before I bought my house."

"Man, I remember the first time I spent the night at your house. She got me saved. She thought she was John the Baptist; she tried to baptism me in y'all small plastic swimming pool," Johnathan said and laughed as he talked.

"I remember that," Jeremy said laughing so hard, he cried.

"You know that we have already sent up prayers to God on your behalf. We all prayed for you. Even that drama queen sister of your," Johnathan said and then waited for Jeremy to reply.

Jeremy turned in the direction of Johnathan's voice. He had a look of 'watch-it-now, that's my drama queen sister.' He had become accustomed to his friends talking about Poochie. It was a source of good-natured fun, but any one of them would defend her at any time. She was like a sister to them all.

"Yeah, I figured you had, and I really appreciate it," Jeremy said. "Oh, and I really do." Jeremy said in a low voice.

Johnathan could barely understand him. "You do what?" Johnathan asked.

"I accepted God as my Lord and savior, I believe that Jesus died on the cross for my sake," Jeremy spoke more clearly.

"I thought you said you already did?" Johnathan questioned with a puzzled look on his face.

"I did, but I can't say that I understood what I was doing when I was five," he said and then paused for a few seconds before he continued. "Or however old I was. I just want to be sure that I am saved. I just wanna make sure that if I die, I am not going to hell."

"Man, that's wonderful that you wanna make sure."

"Do you remember Jalania?" Jeremy asked.

"Who?" Johnathan playfully responded as if he was confused about who she was.

"Man, you know who I am talking about. Stop playing! It has not been that long."

"You right. It has not been that long. It's just been so many, I can't keep up with your ladies? I can't stand when you bring one around. I am always afraid that I will call one of them by the wrong name," Johnathan said staring at Jeremy for about ten seconds waiting for a response. Then he suddenly remembered that Jeremy had temporarily lost his sight.

"Don't look at me like that," Jeremy replied.

"You can see me?" Johnathan asked as he jumped up off the edge of the bed.

"No!" Jeremy answered and laughed. He could imagine the look on Johnathan's face. "I can just imagine you looking at me with doubt on your face."

"I guess in a way you can see, huh?"

"I guess so."

"Ok, so yeah," Johnathan replied. "I remember old Lana. I just didn't know her name was Jalania. What about her?"

"Well, while we were dating, she took me to church with her. I liked the flow; it was so pumped up. Man, that preacher had me wanting to shout. In fact, I think I did a few times."

"What did he preach about?" Johnathan questioned.

"I don't remember; it's been a long time ago."

"It must not have been that good. You were just emotionalized for the moment."

"It was good enough to make me want to be saved."

"Well, what happened?"

"Well, it seemed like all the sisters in the church were unhappily married, desperate, bitter, just plain fake, or trying to gather as many titles as they could; head of this, in charge of that, doing the announcements, singing every solo, but pick up a piece of trash-not in a million years."

"You had Jalania, so why did that matter to you?"

"Trust me, it matters. You get a lot of unhappy, desperate, bitter church women together, yapping in your woman's ear and man will she change on a brother."

"So, what did she do? Did she put it on lock? Which is where it should have been anyway," Johnathan said in a matter-of-fact tone.

"Nah, she won't that saved. She continued to bless a brother, but man she fussed about everything that I didn't do. 'You don't pray in the morning. You don't go to Bible study. You need to volunteer in the church.' Man, she made me think that serving God was worse than serving a prison sentence."

"Jay, man you should pray, serve the Lord, and go to Bible study," Johnathan replied as if he wasn't sure what point Jeremy was trying to make.

"I know, but she nagged about it every day. She would wake up complaining. If she were living as holy as she wanted me to live, she would not have let me in her bed. But yet, she was judging me. Those church women seem to size up every man that steps in the church. Judge them before he even makes it to the pew to sit down. Change comes gradually for some. I'm telling you, club women ain't got nothing on church woman when it comes to evaluating a man. I felt like a pig in the meat market and if you acted ungodly in public, you were like a hog in the slaughter house," Jeremy said as if he had some great point he was leading to. Sex in the dark, but no mistake in the public view."

"Well, what does that have to do with your relationship and God?" Johnathan questioned.

"Some of those women started brainwashing Jalania into believing that she should focus more on God or stop neglecting God for me. They were trying to get her to leave me."

"So, is that why she left you?"

"Yes. Well, I guess so. After I went out with one or two of the sisters at the church."

"I know you didn't. Really man, what did you expect?"

"Remember Anita?" Jeremy asked.

"The skinny one that had two kids?"

"She wasn't skinny. She was..."

"Man, she was skinny. Woman didn't have no meat on her bones, but she was fine." Johnathan paused. "Wait, you met her at Lana's church?"

"Yup and Tammy."

"Was that a church or a speed dating site?"

"I'm telling you, a brother can't stay on track in churches like that."

"So, you let them ruin your relationship with the one that was leading you back to God."

"She played her part too. I was in her bed, remember? That girl was so superior and controlling, she made me feel like I needed to check with her to make sure I actually had to go to the bathroom. I mean, she wanted me to be the head, but she refused to listen to anything I had to say. She acted like she was in charge of every decision, even what I ate. Didn't even want me to eat a piece of candy, unless it was peppermint," Jeremy said.

"So once again, what does this have to do with your salvation? God does not stop being God because of how others act. God is not the church. The church represents the building you go to and the people in it. They are not God," Johnathan replied.

"I know, but what example are they giving those that are seeking Him. Men typically turn to church because of a good woman."

"You know I hear women say that they got their man trained. Honestly man," Johnathan began and then looked around as if to make sure no one else was listening to what he had to say. "I don't see anything wrong with that."

"Man, I am not a dog and no woman is going to train me."

"No, wait. Listen," Johnathan interrupted. "The right one can train you in such a subtle way you're not even going to know that you are being trained. It is simply going to feel like love. A woman that has been trained by God will win you with her ways. Sounds to me, the ladies you have been messing with have not truly been trained themselves. They don't know God, no matter how much they fake in church. They don't know how to be a wife or a good girlfriend. They just know how to run after a title or position in the church."

"I think that's what Jalania was trying to do. I guess she had not been trained, but thought she was qualified to be a trainer."

"Yup and sounds like she was religious and publicly practicing religious customs. Perhaps she was just an untaught Christian."

"What's the difference?" Jeremy replied as if he was making more of a statement then asking a question.

"Religious people go to church, and..." Johnathan paused to think about the best way to address Jeremy's question. "Let me put it this way," he continued. "The religious people I'm talking about are playing in church. They are going through all the motions that are expected of church folks, but their hearts are still in the world, and are enjoying the pleasures of the world. Such as, having sex outside of marriage, cohabitating, and drinking alcohol. Some people who can't get corporate title to impress or compare to their friends, run after titles in the church or the pulpit. In charge of people and don't even know how to communicate with them. They act like they too good to even talk to anyone, unless they are holding a mic and being out front. Some are only impressed with trying to impress the headman. Ain't even about impressing God."

"I see, you mean like me?" Jeremy replied. "I mean corporate title and fornicating."

"Well, yes and no," Johnathan hesitantly said. "Title man, nah, but sex yes. But it's best that you be honest and admit that you are struggling with giving those things up than to pretend that you did give them up while in church on Sunday. God will work with people who are honest. Think about it. Some people act like they got it all together and don't need God's help. They got everyone thinking that they have it their way. Some are being led by leaders who do not know what to do, so they do it their way, and their way is wrong. Saying stuff like 'if God want me to do this or have that, He would give it to me.' Truth is, the Bible answers plenty of the questions for them, but they are resistant to God's way. They just don't know it. You can lead the sheep to the water, but if they don't want to drink, they are still going to perish. Some church folks are at the water, some playing in the field around the water, meddling with the flocks, but they are not drinking the water. They're going to perish. There are other sheep that will come to the water, drink it, and quench their thirst for the moment then go back in the wilderness until they need water again."

"I see," Jeremy said. "I guess there are some sheep who stay at the water constantly drinking and replenishing their supply. They know they can't live without the water. I guess those are the good old saints. Those with a real relationship with God."

"They never allow themselves to get too thirsty or stray too far from their water supply. If they do, that's when they get thirsty and began drinking from any and every water hole," Johnathan said.

Jeremy and Johnathan sat quietly for what seemed like forever. Jeremy wanted to be alone but didn't want to make Johnathan feel as if he was avoiding their conversation about God. He knew that all the talk about sheep and water was not over. He had known Johnathan long enough to know that Johnathan was allowing him time to digest what he had just heard.

"So, man, when are you going to stop pushing everyone away? Your mom and sister are out there praying for you and so is everyone else. They just want to know that you are okay. You know how we all are, even you. We like to see things for ourselves. They ain't interested in my second-hand information," Johnathan explained.

"I understand that, but I don't want them standing around feeling sorry for me and crying like I'm dead," Jeremy replied.

"You really don't know us at all, do you? After all these years, you haven't figured out that we don't feel sorry for you. To many praying people out there and too much faith running through our veins," Johnathan replied.

"Okay, I guess you're right," Jeremy said. "I guess I'm the one that's feeling sorry for myself."

"Now that's what I'm talking about, honesty. Healing cannot start until you are honest with yourself. Admit that you need, want, and receive healing."

"Okay, look, I know I'm being selfish by not allowing them in here."

"Well, they're being respectful of your wishes, but any one of them could walk in here at any time, just like I did and you gonna let them. You are not going to call security and you can't stop them. Well, the nurses might be able to and they know that but…"

"So, you don't respect me?" Jeremy questioned.

"It's not that I don't respect you. See, I don't think you want us to stay away. I think that you want to see us, but you think that we're going to judge you because of what got you here," Johnathan explained.

Jeremy grunted and closed his eyes.

"How are you doing in here," DeAnna, the nurse said as she tapped on the door and slowly opened it and walked in the room.

"Fine," Johnathan instantly responded as if she was addressing him and not the bandaged-up patient lying on his back in the bed.

"Glad to hear you are doing okay," she said and then turned to Jeremy. "Now, how's the patient?"

"Hey DeAnna," Jeremy responded. "Ask me that question after I eat lunch. Wait! Or is it dinnertime? I can't see my watch?"

"So, what are you trying to say?" DeAnna asked.

"Come on now, don't act like you don't know what they say about hospital food," Jeremy said.

"What?" DeAnna questioned. "That it's heathy or well balance."

"Johnathan, she's funny, ain't she man," Jeremy said and laughed. "But you better watch out for her. She's dangerous. She chokes men."

"I see why," Johnathan said, facing DeAnna. "A fine sister like you, I'm all choked up right now."

Johnathan watched DeAnna in silence while she worked.

"Mr. Phillips," DeAnna softly said. "If you don't mind, I need to check your blood pressure and your temperature."

Jeremy's mood instantly changed. It was as if for a moment, he had forgotten about his condition and where he was.

"I'm all yours; do your job," Jeremy replied, remembering DeAnna's words from the earlier conversation.

"Guess you are about ready to get out of here and head home, huh?" DeAnna asked as she worked.

'Yeah, I am," Jeremy said nonchalantly.

"Well, you are going to get your wish real soon. Maybe tomorrow, so I hear, but you didn't hear that from me, okay?"

"Okay, I guess I can do that. I will pretend I lost my sight and my hearing," Jeremy replied.

"Great!" Johnathan said. "I am gonna let everybody know, but on the hush-hush," he said as he rushed out of the room.

DeAnna looked around after she checked Jeremy's temperature. She wanted to clear the air about her comment regarding him being just her job.

"Jeremy, about that 'just a job comment,' if I upset you, I didn't mean it like that. I don't think of my patients as just a job. What I do to take care of your health is my job. But now, the interaction with the patient is my passion."

"Don't sweat that, you have a great bedside manner," Jeremy said feeling relieved that he wasn't just a job.

"I have to have it, in order to do this job," DeAnna replied. "People only come here when something is wrong. I don't want them to deal with an attitude from me on top of what they're already dealing with just to stay alive."

"I understand. I guess I was just feeling that when I go home, I'm gonna miss that personal attention," Jeremy paused and then continued. "To be honest, I don't know who is going to be there to help me make it through this transitional period."

"Tell you what, I'll give you my number and if you ever need help, I'll be there," DeAnna said.

"You do this for all your patient?" Jeremy jokingly asked.

"No, I don't and don't tell anyone either. Promise!"

"Okay, I promise to call you to come take my temperature and make sure my blood pressure is normal," Jeremy said and then extended his hand to DeAnna, so they could shake on it.

"Oh, your hands are so cold," DeAnna said, as she firmly grabbed Jeremy's right hand.

"Sorry!"

"Do you need another blanket?" DeAnna asked. "We keep it cold in here to keep the germs from spreading so quickly."

"Really!" Jeremy said.

"Really! Give me your hand," DeAnna ordered as she grabbed his right hand and gently began to rub his hand with both of her hands to warm his hand up. "That's better," she said as she released one hand and reach across his body and grabbed the other.

Jeremy could tell that DeAnna was a spirit-filled person. He could feel the heat from her body. "Well, I see why you didn't want to see us," Eric said as he walked into the room. "We'll come back later," he joked.

Kimberly rushed pass Eric and ran to Jeremy's side. "I am so sorry," she said as she placed her head on Jeremy's chest.

Jeremy felt her warm teardrops as they soaked through his thin hospital grown.

"It's all my fault," she said as Jeremy slowly stroked her hair.

"No baby, it's not your fault. You can't control what other people do. You were not the one who put the gun in his hand or hers or whoever had

64

it." Jeremy stopped for a second then continued. "Oh, that's right, the gun was pointed at my head," he laughed.

Kimberly stared at Jeremy for a few seconds with tears rolling down her cheek. Jeremy couldn't tell if she was laughing or crying. DeAnna quickly and quietly slipped out of the room.

Chapter 5

"You know what?" DeAnna said, returning to the nurse's station looking confused.

"What girl?" Kristie, a tall, thin Caucasian nurse said as DeAnna placed the clipboard on the desk.

"Mr. Phillips," she began.

"Who?" Kristie asked scanning the patient's list.

"The gunshot victim," DeAnna said and then instantly felt guilty. "I mean patient."

"Oh, okay. What about him, other than he's blind?" Kristie asked.

"I think he has a girlfriend," DeAnna said. "Or maybe a wife."

"What do you expect?" Kristie said, turning back to her computer. "I know you heard he got shot over a woman. Besides, you don't need a blind man."

"Well, you and I both know it's probably temporary. Besides most guys are so busy looking at wanna-a-be women like you," DeAnna said, playfully pointing to Kristie. "They miss out on good women like me."

"So are you saying that because I'm thin, that I cannot be a good woman too," Kristie replied, knowing that DeAnna was referring to weight.

"No, but you and I both know that women like you who think that they can get any man they want, but yet treat men any kind of way," DeAnna said as she looked at the other nurses. "Well, not all of them, but a lot of them do. They are those wanna-a-bee's that I am talking about," DeAnna said.

"But that's true for both thin and big gals," Karen, the head nurse said.

"Don't matter much now, does it?" DeAnna replied.

"So, did you think that he would never find out that you are, well, hum... a little extra fluffy?" Nancy chimed in.

Nancy was the closest that DeAnna had to a sister and very honest.

"No, but by the time that he did find out, he would be..." DeAnna stopped mid-sentence.

"Would what? Be in love with you?" Nancy questioned. "DeAnna, what makes you think that he wouldn't want you if he could see you?"

66

DeAnna stared at Nancy with her hands on her hips. "Girl you know what I'm saying."

"Dee, you know, you're judging him based on how other men act."

"Most of them are the same," DeAnna replied.

"Well, sounds like you are judging Ms. Christian, Ms. Speaking in Faith, Ms. Call Things That Be Not As if They Were."

"No, I'm not," DeAnna said. She did ponder what Nancy said.

"So, what do you call it?" Nancy asked, staring DeAnna eyeball-to-eyeball.

"Well, the way I look at it is," DeAnna began explaining and then stopped. "Look, it doesn't matter. He's got a woman and she's glued to his chest right now. He's going to be glued to her's too, once he gets out of here. I guess," DeAnna said thinking about the conversation she had with him earlier. It was a conversation that suddenly reminded her that he indicated that he lives alone and had no one to help him once he leaves the hospital. "

Blind Fate
Chapter 6

As Jeremy slowly walked from his kitchen and into the living room, he stumbled over the trash-can. He turned around in a rage and kicked at it, but he missed. "I can't do this," he yelled as he tried to find his way around his own house. "God, why me? What did I do to deserve this?"

Jeremy knew that at any time, he could call his mother, sister, or one of his friends and they would be willing to stay with him, but he wanted to maintain his independence. He didn't want anyone hovering over him all day treating him like he was totally helpless. He thought about calling one of his female friends, but he knew that none of them would be willing to actually cook or clean for him. Jeremy slowly made his way around the living room. He used his foot to find the oversized sofa which monopolized most of the room. He plopped down on the sofa. "Ouch," he yelled as he hit his knee on the coffee table. He placed both of his hands over his face as if he was trying to hide his face from someone. He began rocking back and forth. "Lord, I know I'm not one of your favorite people, but please help me. I can't do this. I just can't do this. Lord please help me," he cried out. *Ask once and thank him thereafter,* he could hear Johnathan saying. *Asking twice is like begging, as if you don't believe he already gave it to you.* Jeremy was about to lay down on the sofa, but the phone rang.

"Great," he yelled. "That's just great!"

Jeremy wanted to answer the phone but knew that the answering machine would probably pick up before he could even find his way to the phone. Most of his friends typically called his cell phone, so he had no clue who it could be. He decided to let it go to the answering machine. "I'll check to see who it was later," he said as if someone else was in the room with him.

'Call from Jalania,' Jeremy heard. "What in the world is going on?" He said as he looked around. He'd never been able to put his voicemail system on intercom, although he had tried several times. He would always have to wait to play the message back after the caller hung up. "This has Malcolm written all over it. The jack-of-all trades, master of none," he said. Jeremy sat back on the sofa and smiled. He knew that his friends were respectfully giving him the time he needed, but they had all showed their support in some small way.

Jeremy thrusted his 250-pound muscular body forward and pulled himself off the sofa and almost flipped over the coffee table. He slowly lowered his body to the floor and laid his head on the coffee table. "Okay, God. Jokes on me," he said aloud. "Ha-ha! Now what am I supposed to do?" He was trying to remain positive, but he was almost in tears. The words *'positive confession'* rung in his head. He looked toward Heaven and cried out. "I can do this," he slowly said. He began to repeat the words over and over and began saying them louder and louder, but his voice grew angrier and angrier. He was so loud that he didn't hear the doorbell ring until after the third time it rung. "Go away," he yelled. He didn't know who it was, and he didn't even care. He didn't feel like moving from his spot on the floor.

"Mr. Phillips," he heard someone yell through the closed door. "I am with UPS. I have a package for you."

"Just leave it at the door," Jeremy yelled back. "I will get it later."

"It requires your signature."

"Give me a minute please," he yelled. "Great, this is just great. First the phone, now the door. What next God?" Jeremy questioned as he began feeling around with his hand to find the sofa. He found the coffee table and pushed it back with his foot so that he would not hit his knee on it when he pulled himself up. He slowly pulled his body to the sofa and then he slowly stood to his feet. He stood still for a few minutes with the back of his feet pressed against the sofa. "The door is to the right," he said to himself. He slowly began to walk towards the door, feeling for furniture with his hands and feet. When he finally reached the door, he felt up and down as if he was trying to find the doorknob. Once he found it, he unlocked the door, but he had to find the deadbolt lock. He began feeling up the side of the door molding and then the door again. He unlocked the door and pulled the door open slowly, but he had forgotten to unlock the chain. He quickly closed the door back to unleash the chain. As soon as he opened the door again, the UPS man shoved the electronic pad towards him, but Jeremy couldn't see it.

"Sign here," the man said. "Anywhere in the box."

Jeremy felt a little intimidated. He didn't want to broadcast his condition, so he considered trying to reach out for the electronic pen. *This is crazy*, he thought to himself. "Sir, I have this little condition… so…I can't," Jeremy said and then paused. He didn't want to say he was blind. "Well,"

69

he continued. "The thing is, I am having problems with my vision. I can't see."

"Oh, I am sorry sir," the UPS man said. "We normally have things like that written in the note section."

"I probably ordered this, whatever this is, weeks ago; I had sight then," Jeremy joked.

"I understand sir," the UPS man replied. He placed the pen in Jeremy's hand. Jeremy wanted to repel his hand, but he instantly realized that he needed the help, whether he liked it or not.

The UPS man held the electronic pad in one hand and grabbed Jeremy's hand and guided his hand to the section of the pad that he needed to sign in. "You can sign anywhere in this box."

Jeremy felt around in the box with his left hand and began signing in the box with his right hand. He returned the pen to the UPS man, said thank you, and quickly closed the door. A sudden feeling of helplessness overwhelmed him. Jeremy pressed his back against the door and slowly lowered his body to the floor. He wanted to open the package, but he became overwhelmed with anger. He tossed the package to one side of him. "Lord, I can do this. It's not that bad. It's only temporary," he said as tears rolled down his face. "I can do this." Jeremy pulled himself off the floor. He slowly walked back to the sofa and plopped down. It had been over two weeks, and nothing had changed with his sight. He knew that he had to learn to deal with his current condition. He also knew that he needed help from his friends and family, whom he had pushed away.

Jeremy pulled himself off the sofa and slowly walked towards the dining room. He had a good sense of direction, but he'd had issues with knocking things over and stumbling over things. When he reached the dining room table, which doubled as his file cabinet where all his important papers were housed, he began feeling around for his cell phone.

"Rats," he yelled as he heard a glass hit the table. He quickly felt around to find the glass. "Good," he said when he found the glass and quickly patted around and determined that the table was not wet. "Still don't feel my cell phone, but glad I don't feel wet papers. I guess it will be easier to use the house phone," he said as he turned towards the kitchen, which was directly across from where he was standing. He walked straight into the kitchen. He knew he would have no problem finding the phone, since it was always in the phone cradle. It had been hanging there for almost four years without him ever using it.

"Okay," Jeremy said as he slowly walked towards the kitchen and then instantly turned around and began retracing his steps back into the dining room. He remembered that all the phone numbers that he needed were stored in his cell phone. "Where is that phone?" He questioned. He patted around the entire table still looking for his cell phone. "Oh, I know. I will call it." Jeremy turned around again and began retracing his steps to kitchen. "I'll call it," he said again. As Jeremy walked into the kitchen, he began reaching out from side-to-side with his hands to make sure that he wasn't about to bump into anything. When Jeremy touched the stove with his hand, he knew it was only about a foot before he reached the wall that the phone was attached to. He had no problems finding the phone once he found the wall. "Finally," he said as he grabbed the cordless phone out of the cradle. He began feeling for the dial pad. He dialed his cell phone number. When he heard his phone ring, he surmised that it had to be in the dining room somewhere. He couldn't get back into the dining room fast enough before the phone stopped ringing. He dialed the number again. He wanted to just call one of his friends, but none of their numbers were stored in his personal memory; they were all stored in his phone. Jeremy felt like crying like a baby. He was getting frustrated. "I just can't do this," he said. He had forgotten about his positive confession. "Lord, I need help."

Chapter 7

Jeremy wasn't sure how long he had been sitting at his dining room table when he heard someone at the door.

"Hey Jerry," Jeremy's mom yelled as she walked into his house without knocking. "I got a surprise for you," Ma Phillips said, slowly entering and looking around at the mess.

"What in the world have you been doing in here boy?" Ma Phillips asked.

"Tripping," Jeremy said with almost a hint of excitement in his voice. "Why, is it a mess?" He asked.

"Well, it's not as neat and tidy as it usually is," Ma Phillips said.

"Well, I've been feeling the place out a little," Jeremy jokingly said.

"What does that mean?" Ma Phillips asked, not catching Jeremy's attempt to be funny.

"That's cute," a familiar voice responded. "You've got a great sense of humor."

"I know that voice," Jeremy said. "That perfume. Is that you DeAnna," Jeremy asked with even more excitement in his voice.

"Wow, I see that you have a good sense of humor and an excellent memory," DeAnna said with a big smile plastered across her face. "So how have you been?" She asked.

"I'm fine," Jeremy said with a confused look on his face. "What are you doing here?"

"I ran into her at the hospital and she asked about you," Ma Phillips said as she made her way across the room and started picking up clothes, pictures, and odds and ends that Jeremy had knocked over as he felt his way around the room. "I thought it would be good for you to have some company, other than me and Myles and them. Have they even been over here?"

"Ma, you could have at least called," Jeremy said in a low voice. He wasn't sure where DeAnna was in the room or if she could hear him. He wasn't even sure if he should feel embarrassed about how his house looked, because he wasn't sure how it looked.

"Yeah, I did but," Ma Phillips began.

"It's okay Ma Phillips," DeAnna said. "I can leave." She could sense that Jeremy was probably a little uneasy or embarrassed. She wasn't sure if he was afraid that his girlfriend might walk in or if how his place looked, concerned him.

"No DeAnna," Jeremy responded in protest. "You don't have to leave. It's just that...well...I wished I would have, heck... could have at least cleaned up. I am sure that it's a mess. You know what they say about first impressions."

"Really, it's not that bad. I have seen far worse than this. Trust me," DeAnna said. As she walked towards Jeremy, she skillfully hooked her arm under his and guided him back to the dining room table. She placed his hand on the chair and watched him feel for the seat of the chair and then he sat down.

Ma Phillips continued picking up pictures and placing them back in their original location. She moved around in Jeremy's house as if she was deliberately looking for something to do. Ms. Phillip watched DeAnna as she sat down at the table with Jeremy.

"So, what have you been up to?" DeAnna asked. She reached over and instinctively began to feel Jeremy's forehead to see if he was warm. "Oh, sorry. Habit," she said and chuckled a little. "If I had a thermometer I would probably take your temperature and check your blood pressure too."

Jeremy chuckled. "You lucky my mom's over there," he said as he pointed to the right. He realized that he did not know if she was to the left of him or to the right of him. "Or there or wherever she is," he paused to see if she would speak up. "I guess she's still here," he said and paused again. "She is still here, isn't she?"

"Yes, she's cleaning up. I think she just folded your clothes and put them in your room," DeAnna said as she glanced at Jeremy's mother. "You're a lucky man."

"Lucky," Jeremy said. The smile slowly disappeared from his face. His mood instantly changed. "If I was lucky, I would be able to see and wouldn't need my mommy picking up behind me like I am a five-year-old child."

"Says the man that has his life after being shot," DeAnna said in a soft comforting voice.

"Okay, so I am lucky to have my life, but..."

"But nothing boy," Ma Phillips said as she walked out of the bathroom in time to hear the end of the conversation. "Stop complaining and man up, as you young folks say. I don't consider it luck either, but I do consider you blessed." She walked into the kitchen and grabbed the phone

73

off the hook and began dialing. "I'm about to go on home, but I want to call Malcolm and Myles to come over and re-arranged this furniture. Maybe it would help you to stop running into things and knocking over end tables. You had broken glass all over the coffee table, but I done cleaned it up."

"What? Ma, I am a grown man. How you just going to decide to re-arrange my house?" Jeremy protested. "And how you know everybody ain't busy?"

"Boy, you need to move things. It is too cluttered in here. Since you refused to stay with me until your sight returns, you can at least make it easier on yourself."

"Okay! Ma, whatever you say," Jeremy said. He did not want to argue with his mother in front of DeAnna.

"You got anything in there to eat?" Ma Phillips questioned.

"No, I have been ordering take-out. Is that okay with you?" Jeremy sarcastically asked.

"No, it ain't. I packed your freezer with dinners that I personally cooked just for you."

"Yeah, I remember you saying that, but I didn't want to burn my house down trying to warm them up."

Ma Phillips chuckled as she placed the phone back on the hook and quickly removed it again. As Ma Phillips continued to make phone calls, Jeremy enjoyed his conversation with DeAnna.

"Think God is trying to teach you a lesson," Ma Phillips said while waiting for the person she called, to answer.

"Oh yeah, what lesson would that be?" Jeremy asked. "A lesson before dying, huh? From what I have been told, God ain't the one behind bad incidents."

Ma Phillips ignored Jeremy and talked on the phone. Jeremy could not tell what she was saying. She appeared to be trying to whisper so that he couldn't hear her. As soon as Ma Phillips hung the phone up, she joined her son and DeAnna.

"Jeremy, I raised you..." Ma Phillips started, but Jeremy cut her off.

"I know mom, under the ammunition of the Lord. Look, let's just talk about something else because my relationship with God is something that

I have to do for myself. Besides, have you actually seen the examples for us, the backsliders? Have you been to churches lately?" Jeremy waited for his mother to answer. When she didn't, he continued his speech. "Preachers have wives and girlfriends. Everybody dating somebody else's spouse and single women, now they are a real example. Virtuous, ha? More like vultures."

"Now that's sort of true," DeAnna chimed in. "I see it at churches all the time. It's hard for men to repent and stay on track while learning the Word, with desperate women throwing themselves at them as soon as they walk through the doors. But remember Jeremy, they are not the standard for righteousness, salvation, or Christianity."

"You don't have to tell me that," Jeremy quickly replied.

"Ms. Dee, I'm tired, so I am headed home," Ma Phillips replied as she grabbed her purse and began walking towards the door.

"Okay, I'll take you," DeAnna said as she got up from her seat.

"No, that's okay, Myles will be here in a few minutes. He's gonna take me home and then he's going to pick up Malcolm and Johnathan. They're going to be here for a while, so you might want to order some pizza or something for them to eat."

"I guess I'd better get going too then," DeAnna hesitantly said. She was a little confused. *Maybe she thinks I should stay. Is she trying to set me up with one of Jeremy's friends*? She thought to herself.

"No, why don't you stay," Ma Phillips said and turned and winked at DeAnna. "At least until the others get here. Jeremy looks like he was enjoying talking to you."

"O…kay," DeAnna hesitantly said, even though she really felt that the invitation should have come from Jeremy instead of his mom, since it was his house. She felt as if she was being forced on him. "I guess, if it's okay with Jeremy."

"Sure, please stay. It's not every day that a man's mother, come home with a nurse for her blind son. I feel so special," Jeremy said and smiled, indicating to DeAnna that he was joking and not really upset with his mother for bringing her over. "Plus, you smell good."

"I am sure that I can give you some good tips about handling your blindness," DeAnna said, wanting to feel that she could be of some help."

"So, you've been blind before?" Jeremy joked.

"No, but I do have experience with helping the blind. My father was blind the last eight years of his life. I guess that's why I wanted to be your nurse."

"Wow, and I thought it was my boyish good looks," Jeremy said.

"Don't pay no mind to him Ms. Dee," Ma Phillips said as she peeped out the window. "He thinks he's a ladies' man."

"I don't think that," Jeremy corrected his mother.

"Anyway, Myles is here now, so I will see you later, Jerry. Ms. Dee, thank you for helping that stubborn son of mines. I'm sure you're going to be a great help to him with his condition."

"Blindness Ma," Jeremy said. "Why does everyone keep calling my being blind, a condition?" Jeremy asked and then paused. "Well, everyone except Ms. Dee."

"I'll see myself out," Ma Phillips said and quickly headed to the front door. "Condition or blindness, whatever you call it, you need help, and I think Ms. Dee is just the one for the job. Now you listen to her son and call me later," Ma Phillips said as she walked out the house and slammed the door behind her as if she was in a hurry.

"Okay," Jeremy yelled back as he slowly walked to the sofa and almost tripped over DeAnna feet.

"Sorry, Ms. Dee," Jeremy said. He eased himself back down on the arm of the sofa. "Why does she call you Ms. Dee?"

"On the day that I met her in the hospital, she kept calling me Ms. because she couldn't remember DeAnna. So, I told her to call me Dee," DeAnna explained. "I guess 'Ms.' just kind of stuck."

"Well, Ms. Dee, what is it that you are going to do to help me?"

"Well, when I ran into your mother, I told her that my father went blind. Well, she sort-of thought that I might be able to help you deal with your blindness," DeAnna said and then paused to find the right words. "My father wasn't born blind and had sight over 90% of his life, so it was hard for him to deal with it as well. And even though I couldn't change how he felt about being blind, I did a lot of things to help make life a little bit easier for him."

"Okay, so where would you suggest that we begin?" Jeremy asked.

"Well, I do think that you should do as your mom suggested and move some of your furniture. If you're going to be swinging a cane to find your way around your place, you don't need a lot of things cluttering up the room. You might knock down more things and break them. I would suggest large open spaces for now. The end tables and coffee tables are great but can cause some serious damage to the knees and toes."

"Thanks for the warning, but too late; been-there-done-that. Think I got the bruises to prove it," Jeremy said as he rubbed his knees. "What else?"

"I mentioned a cane earlier, I think you should get one."

"A cane, I am not some feeble old man."

"I know, but you can use it to feel for things, instead of waving your arms around feeling in the air like some confused mime."

Jeremy laughed so hard that his position on the arm of the chair became very uncomfortable. He slid down on the sofa beside DeAnna.

"Okay, makes sense, but I am not going public with a cane."

"Fine, that's up to you, but a blind handsome man usually gets a lot of attention from lonely women looking for some helpless man."

"I'm not helpless," Jeremy quickly interjected.

"I know that, and you know that, but they don't know that."

"Woman, you trying to pimp me out."

They both laughed again.

"Seriously, I do feel that you will regain your sight, but while you are going through your trial, test, or whatever it may be, you should make it easy on yourself. My father was a very strong man. The one thing I have never seen him do, was to show weakness and," DeAnna began.

"And asking for help is not a sign of weakness because it takes a strong man to realize that he needs help and even a stronger man to accept help. Is that where you were 'going' with that?" Jeremy asked, but did not wait for an answer. "Okay, I know that; have heard it all my life, so what else?"

"Well," DeAnna said as she scanned the room, remembering the last years of her father's life. "Pictures are nice, but until you are familiar with your surroundings, as to where everything is, you might want to either hang the pictures on the wall or put them away."

"You serious?"

"Yes," DeAnna said and started laughing as she thought about her father. "My father would walk into a room and start swing that cane trying to find the coffee table and knock all the pictures off the table. I remember coming home on my lunch break one day to check on him and there was broken glass and blood all over the coffee table and the floor."

"Blood and glass huh?"

"Yup! It was obvious that he was using that old cane, formally known as a stick, as his hands. He was trying to find the TV, so that he could listen to some game. He was only 100-feet away from the TV."

"Only 100-feet off," Jeremy jokingly repeated.

"Well, he knocked over a picture. Then he tried to clean it up and cut his hand. At some point, he got a glass of soda and set it down on the end table, on top of the broken frame. I am sure he must have cut his hand reaching for the glass of soda. I came home to find him asleep on the sofa with a pillow over his bloody hands."

"Was he trying to hide his hands?" Jeremy asked.

"No, he used mom's decorative sofa pillow to stop the bleeding."

"Are you kidding me?"

"Nope," DeAnna said and chuckled.

"Okay, pictures will be removed. What's next?"

"I don't have a little checklist in my hand, but I'll make one tonight if you want me to."

DeAnna and Jeremy suddenly stop mid-sentence when they heard the doorbell ring. DeAnna looked at Jeremy to see if he was going to make a move to get the door. She didn't want to just assume it was okay to answer his door.

"That must be your friends," DeAnna said when she heard the doorbell ring the second time.

"Yeah, it's them. Do you mind answering it for me?"

"Sure, I'll get it for you," DeAnna said, hopping up quickly. She opened it without asking who it was. "Come on in," she said.

"Who are you?" A woman asked and then stared at DeAnna as if to say, 'I am waiting for an answer.'

"Hi, I'm DeAnna. Are you here to see Jeremy?"

"Yes. I am Kimberly."

"Well, come on in Kimberly," DeAnna said, opening the door wide enough for the familiar woman to enter.

DeAnna could tell that Kimberly was checking her out. She wasn't sure who Kimberly was to Jeremy, but she remembered her from the hospital. She followed behind Kimberly as they both joined Jeremy. DeAnna took a spot on the love seat.

"Hi Jay," Kimberly said sounding like a giddy schoolgirl, addressing her crash.

"Hey Kiddo," he replied. "So, what've you been up too lately?

"Not much," she said as she moved closer to Jeremy on the sofa. "Now, who is Ms. Belvedere?"

"Who, DeAnna?"

"Oh, is there something you need to tell me?" Kimberley asked.

She pulled away from Jeremy and stared at him waiting for an answer. She instantly felt stupid when she realized that he couldn't see her playfully moving away from him.

"Get back over here girl," Jeremy said indicating that he did indeed feel her move away from. He playfully grabbed her by her arms and pulled her into his arms.

"So, tell me," she whispered in his ear. "Who's the beauty who answered the door?"

"You don't remember her from the hospital? She was one of my nurses. She's going to help me out around here. She's gonna help me deal with my "condition," Jeremy said using the universal signs for 'quote-quote' when he said the word *condition*.

"Oh, did I interrupt something?" Kimberly asked.

"No," Jeremy said. "Actually, maybe you can show DeAnna around the house, so she can decide how to redecorate for me."

DeAnna felt slightly ignored but decided to see herself as Jeremy's rehabilitation coach and not a friend or anything else.

"That sounds like a great idea," DeAnna said instantly accepting her role. Even if it was a role she volunteered for.

"Everyone is headed over," Kimberly informed Jeremy. "We are having a cookout."

"A cookout? Here, at my house?" Jeremy asked, sounding a little confused.

"Yes, it was your mother's idea. She said the guys are going to be moving furniture, so we might as well throw some burgers, chicken, and whatever else we'd like to grill, on the grill," Kimberly said, repeating exactly what Ma Phillips said to her.

"Sounds like fun," DeAnna said. "We can finish this another day."

"Oh no you don't," Jeremy said. "I need you here. If they see that I have a trained nurse by my side, they won't feel a need to drop in like this, unannounced."

"So, you just going to use a sister?" DeAnna playful asked.

"No, I wouldn't call it using you," Jeremy said.

"Well, what would you call it?" DeAnna questioned.

"It does sort of sound like using to me," Kimberly jokingly joined in.

"Oh, I see what's going on. Y'all just going to team up on a brother."

"That right," Kimberly said, leaning over and high fived DeAnna.

DeAnna still wasn't sure what to think about Kimberly and Jeremy's relationship. They seemed like sister and brother, but on the other hand, Kimberly seemed to hang onto his every word. She smiled at him with love and admiration in her eyes.

"So, remind me again," DeAnna said. "What is my role?"

"Come on DeAnna, let's see what is in the refrigerator. We can make a list of what we need for the cookout," Kimberly said.

DeAnna wasn't sure what to think, but she followed Kimberly to the kitchen. She admired the beautiful artwork hanging on the walls and the oversize candleholders. She could tell that Jeremy liked nice things. *Wonder why he's not married,* she's thought as she scanned the pictures to see if there seems to be a significant other, such as a girlfriend. When the doorbell rang, Kimberly looked at DeAnna without moving.

"So now I'm the maid," DeAnna said to herself.

"I'll get it," Kimberly volunteered skipping across the floor as if she was a twelve-year-old little girl.

"Who is it?" She yelled.

Kimberly didn't wait for an answer. She quickly flung the door open thinking it would be one of Jeremy's friends.

"Hi Kimberly," Latonya said, sashaying past Kimberly as if she had been invited in. "What are you doing here and where is Jeremy?"

As Latonya entered the living room, she looked up and saw Jeremy being escorted into the kitchen by a strange woman.

"Who's she?" Latonya asked, looking and sounding territorial.

"Oh, she is his rehabilitation specialist, coach, therapist," Kimberly said, looking at DeAnna and Jeremy and smiling at how comfortable Jeremy looked. "Or something like that," she said with a hint of mystery in her voice.

"Oh," Latonya said, her smile suddenly returning to her face. "I see, she's just his help. Hey sexy," she said, walking into the kitchen towards where Jeremy was standing, talking to DeAnna.

"Hey," DeAnna replied as if Latonya was talking to her. She walked Jeremy to the table and placed his hand on the chair, so he could feel his way into the chair.

"I wasn't talking to you. I was talking to my man, the one on your arm," Latonya said, a little annoyed that Jeremy hadn't said anything to her.

"I'm sorry, just a little joke."

"Well, it wasn't funny," Latonya said and then rolled her eyes. "Try to stay in your lane sweetheart."

"Latonya, what are you doing here?" Jeremy asked once he was seated and comfortable.

"Well, baby, I just wanted to see how my favorite man is doing," Latonya said as she walked closer to him.

"Your man," Jeremy repeated. "Oh, I'm your man now?"

"Excuse me, Ms..." Latonya said turning to face DeAnna. "Oh, I'm sorry, I didn't get your name. Jeremy, where are your manners? I know you are going to introduce us."

"Oh sure," Jeremy said as he turned towards DeAnna, without releasing her hand. "DeAnna this is Latonya. Hum. I guess you can say she was my girlfriend," Jeremy said in matter-of-fact tone.

"Nice to meet you Latonya," DeAnna said and extended her hand towards Latonya as Jeremy continued the introductions.

"And Latonya, this is DeAnna." Jeremy's tone softened when he said DeAnna's name. He didn't bother explaining who DeAnna was to him.

Latonya looked at DeAnna's hand as if she had a contagious disease. DeAnna got the hint that Latonya did not intend to play nice, so she slowly placed her extended hand on Jeremy shoulder.

"Well, DeAnna, I am here now, so you can show yourself out. We'll call you if he needs you and why don't you take little Kimberly with you. We need to be alone," Latonya said as she pointed to herself and then to Jeremy with her pointer finger and middle finger extended.

Like a broken tooth or a lame foot is reliance on the unfaithful in a time of trouble. Like one who takes away a garment on a cold day, or like vinegar poured on a wound, is one who sings songs to a heavy heart (Proverbs 25:19-20, NIV), DeAnna thought to herself. *This girl surely trouble.* DeAnna wanted to put Ms. Thang in her place but decided that it wasn't her job. *Besides,* she said to myself, *I'm not that woman any more. And she better be glad that I am not.*

Kimberly tiny-framed body sprung from around the corner and was face-to-face with Latonya. "You might be the boss of your house and your husband," Kimberly started and then paused for a second. "Oh, that's right," she quickly continued. "He finally left you, didn't he? Probably got tired of trying to get his pants back. Ms. I-N-D-E-P-E-N-D-E-N-T," Kimberly sang. "Do you know what I mean? So why don't you skip on over to your own house, in your own car, Ms. Bad..."

"Look, finding some boy to marry you, doesn't make you a woman little girl. Now go play with your friend over there," Latonya said.

"I'll show you who's a little girl," Kimberly replied.

Latonya turned to face Jeremy, hoping that he would validate her position as the woman in charge. DeAnna grabbed Kimberly by her arm and calmly guided her away from Latonya.

"Come on," DeAnna whispered. "Why don't we show her how real ladies act?"

Kimberly reluctantly obeyed DeAnna's request, but they walked out the front door. Kimberly was not quite sure where they were headed since she had been dropped off. She quickly stopped and looked at DeAnna as if she had an epiphany once they were outside on the front porch.

"DeAnna, that's your name, right?" Kimberly asked.

"Yes, that's right."

"What are we doing? Jeremy did not ask us to leave," Kimberly said as she motioned as if she was headed back inside. "Did you see his face? That woman is not in charge of anything."

"Yes, but nor did he stop her or stop us from leaving. Honey, take it from me, don't force him into making decision like that while under that kind of pressure. He's going to eventually get tired of a confrontational woman; especially, in a situation like this. If I was his woman, he wouldn't have to make a decision. He would show me that he wanted me, without me making him, but she jumped the gun on this one. I'm here to help in any way, but I'm sure she will not be willing to," DeAnna said. She could imagine the conversation going on inside. "Blessed is the peacemakers," DeAnna said and smiled.

"She doesn't scare me," Kimberly said.

"It's not about being scared. Let me tell you something, a boy might like girls pulling and fighting over him, but when a boy becomes a man, he put away childish things. At least that's what the Bible says. I can tell that Jeremy is not only frustrated with his condition; he's frustrated with childish women. Trust me, she's not going to get very far with him. I'm willing to bet she won't stick around long enough to help cook a meal or even un-thaw the meat for it."

"That's all well and good, but everyone is headed over here to help him re-arrange the furniture and we are planning a cookout, so I'm not leaving," Kimberly said and then laughed. "I can't anyway, my husband dropped me off."

They both laughed.

"But you are right, I forgot about the cookout," DeAnna said.

"Perfect timing," Kimberly said as she spotted Myles car pulling into the driveway, followed by Chris and Malcolm.

"Come on DeAnna, let me officially introduce you to everyone."

"No thanks, I think I should get going," DeAnna said.

As DeAnna began to slowly decline down the seven steps leading up to the two-story brick house, she heard the front door swing open.

"You can't see a good thing when it's standing right in front of you," Latonya said as she stormed out of the house. After a few seconds of thinking about what she'd just said, she burst out laughing, stopped dead in her tracks, turned around with her hands on her hips, and said, "Literally! For real, you literally can't see it," she said as she stared at Jeremy without any concerned for the hurt look on his face.

"Now you know that was a mean thing to say, Latonya-can't-keep-a-man Graham," Kimberly said and took a step towards Latonya ready to hit her.

"Well, baby girl," Latonya said facing Kimberly. "Half the fun is getting em' anyway. So, as long as I can get one, I'll worry about keeping one when I'm ready to keep one or I find one worth keeping."

"DeAnna," Jeremy said, uncertain if she was still there or not."

"Yes Mr., I mean Jeremy."

"I want to apologize for my uninvited guest's rude behavior. I should have stopped her. I was just not sure...."

"I understand," DeAnna said, as she winked at Kimberly.

"Rude," Latonya repeated as she hit the last step.

"Yes, rude," Jeremy said, realizing that he had had enough of her attitude and was no longer going to accept it. He was tired of the so-called independent women who sat in church Sunday-after-Sunday praying for a man and then when a man comes into their lives, they don't know how to let him be a man. He was tired of settling for pretty faces and the *I-can-have-any-man-I-want* attitudes.

"Well, you don't have to worry about seeing this woman ever again. Guess you cannot handle a woman who can think for herself," Latonya said as she headed to her car.

"Let me get that door for you," Malcolm said and opened Latonya's car door for her.

"See, he knows how to treat a real lady," Latonya said, smiling at Malcolm.

"Nah, the truth is, the quicker you are in, the quicker you can be gone," Malcolm said and closed the door behind her without waiting for her response. "Lord, forgive me for that," he said as he looked towards heaven. "I just couldn't resist." Malcolm headed up the step to join the others.

"I guess there's a silver lining after all," Jeremy said as he stood on the front porch feeling a warm breeze. "I don't have to see you again either, literally," Jeremy yelled to Latonya and then laughed.

"What's her problem?" Malcolm asked as he walked up the steps carrying a tool belt and a bag of groceries.

Kimberly grabbed the bag and began searching the contents. "She just realized that her looks can only get her so far and today it only got her two open doors and two closed doors. Thanks for being the one who opened one and closed it behind her. I opened the first one and let her in, Jeremy closed it on the relationship, for good I hope,'" Kimberly said.

"Well, she ain't all that no way," Myles said as he walked up the steps and grabbed the bag from Kimberly and headed into the house.

"Where's your trusted sidekick?" Jeremy yelled behind Myles.

"He is coming. He is getting something out of the car. Eric is on his way too. He just spent thirty minutes tracking down someone's husband." Myles said, glancing at Kimberly.

Kimberly turned her head as if to ignore Myles comment. "DeAnna, let me introduce you to everyone."

"Why don't we all go inside," Jeremy said as he slowly turned himself around and reach for the door.

DeAnna instantly placed her hand on top of Jeremy's hand and guided his hand towards the door knob. DeAnna's movement was so subtle and gentle; no one else noticed that she was helping him.

"Okay now, according to Ma Phillips, Mrs. DeAnna here is the overseer," Myles said.

"Ms. DeAnna," DeAnna said. "And you sure she meant me?"

"Okay sorry," Myles said. "Just thought a lovely lady such as yourself would have been snagged by some lucky man."

DeAnna could hardly contain herself. "Is he flirting with me?" She asked herself. She quickly surmised that he was just a charmer. She began to scan the room to figure out the best furniture arrangement. The living room was furnished with two oversized brown leather sofas. They were positioned in the middle of the room facing each other. A large coffee table set between the two sofas. As DeAnna continued to scan the room, she noticed four matching end tables. One was at each end of both sofas. *Wow, and I thought I loved an equal balance*, DeAnna thought to herself. She was shocked that there was only one matching loveseat in the corner. She could tell that Jeremy was a romantic guy. She scanned the array of candle holders decorating each end table and even the coffee tables. She had admired the ones on the wall earlier, hanging over the fireplace. She smiled as she imagined herself living in such a lovely home. The house was very spacious, but for a blind man, it would be considered too cluttered.

"Gotcha," a voice said, quickly snapping DeAnna back to reality. "Beautiful."

DeAnna recognized the face behind the camera. She recognized all the faces from the hospital, but still had not been formally introduced to anyone.

"I'm Eric. You must be DeAnna."
"Yes, the rehabilitation therapist. At least that's what I have been told," DeAnna said.

Eric chuckled as he scanned the faces of his friend, not knowing if DeAnna was joking or not. The smile on their faces gave him the answer he needed.

"Ma Phillips," they all said.
"You got it," DeAnna replied.
"That woman is going to make sure her baby boy is cared for," Eric replied.
"Are you licensed?" Eric questioned.
"More like experienced," Jeremy said. He had been sitting quietly in the corner of the room feeling left out in his own home.
"DeAnna leave all the heavy work to us," Johnathan said as he flexed his muscles like a schoolboy begging for attention.

DeAnna didn't remember him even entering the house. *He must have been the trusted sidekick who was getting something out of the trunk of Myles car or was it Malcolm,* DeAnna thought to herself. *Myles, Chris, Malcolm, Eric, and Johnathan* she said as she scanned the room trying to match the names with each of the faces. *Chris is the quiet one, looks like,* she said as she tried to size them up, but then realized that she was just the therapist and might not be around his friends that much. *Stay focused,* she told herself.

"Okay, for now I think we should reduce the..." DeAnna said and then paused. She didn't want to say clutter. She didn't want Jeremy to think she thought his place was junkie. It really wasn't, but she knew it might feel like a war zone to a blind man.

"Clutter," Jeremy finished her sentence. "Don't be scared to say it. I'm the only man I know with two sofas, four end tables, two coffee tables, four bar stools, a wet bar, a large stereo, computer, and two recliners all in one room.

"You forgot a huge TV screen," Johnathan reminded him.

"I didn't forget," Jeremy laughed. "I thought one of you would stop me from rambling."

"Well, I was going to, but well... look let's just get started. It's getting late," Eric said as he took the camera from around his neck and placed it on top of the refrigerator.

"Good point," Jeremy said. "I am sorry DeAnna. I am sure you have other plans tonight. A date or something."

Jeremy's word sort of faded in DeAnna's mind as her thoughts drifted to the past three Friday nights that she sat home all alone, wishing she was on a date or at the movie, or even bowling with a friend. All her friends seem to either be too busy to hang out on the weekends or resting up from the hard week's work. DeAnna was so tired of hearing, *'I'm going to just chill at home tonight and kick back and relax.'* Most of DeAnna's hanging buddies were single and it wasn't hard to figure out why. DeAnna scanned the room again trying to reposition things in her head. Hum, she thought to herself, *I wonder if they can hang the TV over the fireplace,*

"I think over the fireplace would be the perfect spot," Malcolm said as if he knew exactly what DeAnna was thinking.

DeAnna was concentrating so hard she did not hear what anyone was saying.

"What do you think?" Jeremy asked DeAnna.

"Oh, sorry. I didn't catch that. I was just thinking that mounting the TV on the wall would clear up a lot of space over there, and then you could move the sofa where the TV was. I can tell that you like all your things balanced, but for now you should open-up the room so that you can enter and exit the room without so much furniture to step around and try to dodge.

"So, you like that idea too?" Myles questioned.

"Yes, I'm a little surprised that it is not already mounted on the wall," DeAnna replied.

"Well really, it's just one of those projects on my to-do list," Eric said as he took the TV mount out of Malcolm's hand. "You see, I am Mr. Fix it, build it, hang it, move it, restore it, and even take a picture of it, in this group. Here's my business card," he said, handing DeAnna the card.

"You're a photographer too. I would have never guessed," DeAnna said with a smile, thinking about the picture he snapped of her earlier.

"Please don't get him started. That's the reason his 'to-do-list' is a mile long. He spends all his free time racing around the world taking pictures," Malcolm said as he placed the ladder against the wall. "Well, he used to, before he got framed. Oops. I mean nailed into marriage."

"Wait!" DeAnna said, suddenly thinking about where they wanted to hang the television. "You really want to hang it over the fireplace?" DeAnna questioned and then paused. She realized that she wasn't there to decide on the total décor of the room, but rather tips to help Jeremy cope with the blindness.

"Oh!" Jeremy said, suddenly remembering something. "DeAnna, can you assist me with something please?"

As Jeremy arose from his spot on the sofa, DeAnna joined him.

"There's a coat closet in front of the entrance," he said, walking in that direction.

DeAnna joined him at his side and gently guided him. She was careful not to get too close. She had been trained to be careful during home visits to be mindful of mistakenly touching or even appearing to be allowing herself to be touched inappropriately.

"Okay we're at the closet door," she said.

Jeremy reached out for the knob.

"Most doorknobs are about waist high. The edge of the door is about two inches in from the edge of the door frame," DeAnna explained. She wanted Jeremy to learn to open doors on his own.

Jeremy raised his hand to his waist and towards the closet door. He felt around with his hand until he found the edge of the door. He moved slightly to the right and found the door-knob with no problem. Jeremy smiled as he opened the door. He quickly realized that DeAnna was not going to do this for him like his mother or the other women would have, rendering him helpless and entirely dependent on them. *Not DeAnna, she is helping me to become self-sufficient and independent*, Jeremy thought.

"Look to the left on the floor," Jeremy whispered. He heard DeAnna exhale a soft awe and knew she spotted the mirror.

"It's so big and the frame. I love it," she said.

"Don't," he objected as he felt her bend down. "It is heavy."

"I got it," Myles said as he approached them. "Y'all watch out."

"Jeremy, I see what you are up to. You gonna get us to do all these projects you haven't had time to do," Eric said.

"Let me guess," DeAnna said. "You want that over the fireplace, don't you?"

"Yes," Jeremy quickly answered. "Don't you think it would be the perfect place for it? You were about to object to the TV being housed there any way, weren't you?"

"I was, but I thought I should just focus on your walking space, and not your wall décor," DeAnna said feeling like she had overstepped.

"Okay, let's just get started," Johnathan said. "We gonna be here all day and half the night as it is."

"You got a date too," Kimberly sarcastically asked as she began unplugging all the power cords from Jeremy's electronic devices.

"Yeah, I do. Is that so strange?" Johnathan asked.

"Really! What's her name?" Kimberly asked, staring him eyeball-to-eyeball.

"Well...um," Johnathan said, knowing he was caught in his lie.

"Just like I thought," Kimberly replied. "Anyway, maybe the TV should be on that wall."

"Maybe we should arrange things so that the back of the sofas will create a path to the front door when he enters from the kitchen," DeAnna said.

"Oh, that's a good idea," Myles replied. He quickly saw a vision of the path and understood the wisdom. "So, on this side, but with the back to the kitchen. That way when he comes down the hall, he walks straight to the back of the sofa. He will then know that he is in the living room. If he goes right, the path leads to the front door with no objects to bump into."

"Yes, that's the idea. Maybe an L-shaped chair arrangement," DeAnna said.

"I can see that," Jeremy hesitantly responded.

DeAnna removed her hair band from her wrist and pulled her long, thick, and wavy hair back into a ponytail as if she was getting ready to do some hard work. She began giving the guys instructions, and they obeyed as if she was the woman of the house instructing the hired hands.

Jeremy quietly retreated to his bedroom. Kimberly had felt his absence, as she glanced around. Her concern for Jeremy wasn't just because he was her brother's best friend. She felt responsible for his condition. She couldn't take away the sadness that seemed to have evolved. She quietly slipped out of the room, wanting to go to Jeremy's side, but she suddenly was afraid to face him. *What if he blames me?* She thought. She went to the bathroom and slammed the door closed. "I'm such a coward," she said. She flipped the stool top down and set down. She sat in the bathroom and tried to sort out her own feelings. *Why am I even here?* She asked herself. She suddenly remembered the reason that she was at Jeremy's. She was there to escape the reality that her marriage seemed to be falling apart. "No matter how much I try to be a good wife, Jason never seem to be quite happy with me," she muttered. She put her hands over her face as if she was trying to block someone from seeing her red eyes. "Lord help me. I don't want to think like this," she said. "This is not helping at all," she told herself. She splashed water on her face. "Enjoy the ones you are with," she said as she looked at herself in the mirror. "I'm trying," she said as if she was responding to someone else.

Kimberly decided to re-join the group. As she walked out of the bathroom, she noticed that Jeremy's bedroom door was ajar. She lightly tapped on the door, slowly pushed it open, and glanced in. Jeremy was laying across the bed, looking up towards the ceiling.

"Are you okay?" Kimberly asked.

"I'm fine," Jeremy replied. "Come on in, join me. I thought it would be better if I just stayed out of their way and let them do what they need to do," Jeremy said. He let out a tiny laugh. "My hearing has become so keen;

I can hear almost everything they are saying. I am just enjoying the listening," Jeremy said. "So, what are you doing, escaping the madness?"

"I guess you can say that," Kimberly said, not knowing what Jeremy had heard.

Jeremy patted the bed. "Join me," he insisted.

Kimberly walked around to the other side of the room, hopped on the bed, and positioned her back against the king-sized headboard.

"I'm sorry Jay," she said, unable to control her emotions. Tears began to flow uncontrollably.

"Look, I want you to know that I would go through this all over again for you," Jeremy said as he began trying to find her so that he could pull her closer. She matched his efforts and laid her head on his shoulder. "You are like my little sister. You might not remember this. It was some time before you dad passed. I think you were seven-years old. Or maybe it was right before your seventh birthday; I guess. Anyway, one day I was sitting on the porch with him and some little boy kept picking on you. He thought you were cute, but see guys are not as smart as girls, so we think hitting is the way to get girl's attention. So, he hit you and ran. Well, I threw a rock at that boy and yelled, 'leave my baby sister alone.'" Jeremy looked down at Kimberly and they smiled at each other. "Well, he will never hit you again. I told your dad that day, that I would protect you like you were my very own sister," Jeremy said. "I'll never forget that day. Your dad was talking to me about being a man and caring for and protecting the ones I love." Jeremy pulled Kimberly closer to him. "And I love you."

"So, that little boy, what happened to him?" Kimberly asked.

"You married him," Jeremy said.

"Are you serious?"

"Yup. His family moved shortly afterwards, that's why you quickly forgot him, but that was him. That's the boy who is now a man, who has liked you for a long time. I don't even know if he remembers that."

"He doesn't seem to like me so much these days," Kimberly said without thinking.

"I doubt that's true. If there's one thing I know, I know when a man loves a woman. Truly love a woman. I might not have ever felt it, but I know it when I see it," Jeremy said. He contemplated whether he should probe further. He felt that she might have wanted to talk but didn't want to feel that

91

she was intruding. He decided to help her make the decision if she needed to talk or not. He was determined to be there for her. "Something you want or need to talk about?" He asked.

"Well, seems that nothing I ever do is good enough. He doesn't say that, but that's just how I feel. He doesn't seem to want to talk and when I do say something, he always seems to act as if he doesn't want my advice or suggestions."

"Can I tell you what I think about something that I have observed?" Jeremy asked.

"Sure," Kimberly replied, anxious to hear what Jeremy had to say.

"You treat him like he's a child, as if he can't think for himself."

"He acts like a child sometimes," she said, defending her actions.

"But you married him, so you have to either give him the chance to grow up or let him go," Jeremy said not knowing what else to say.

"So, you're saying we should get a divorce?" Kimberly knew that Jeremy wasn't saying that at all. She was tired of hearing the same excuse.

"No, what I'm saying is, that men get scared too. The truth is, we sometimes want to be the head, but we don't know how, so we let the women take control, then we get mad when they do."

"Yeah and some women take it, whether you let them are not," Kimberly said as if there was some hidden meaning to her statement.

"So true," Jeremy agreed. "Kimberly, we have smothered you since the day your parents passed. You have had us making decisions for you. You haven't had anyone showing or teaching you how to be a woman or a wife."

"That comes naturally, right?" She questioned.

"Not always. Sweetheart, why do you think the divorce rate is so high? A wife is more than someone who cooks, cleans, and washes clothes. Kimberly, you want him to make all those decisions you are too scared to make them, and he wants you to make them with him. You both are afraid of being blamed when things don't work out. Sometimes, even the best efforts fail, but don't be afraid to try again. You come to us and we tell you both what to do. He's a grown man taking orders from his brother-in-law and us, your other big bothers. We know more about his business than he does."

Kimberly laid her head on Jeremy's lap like a child.

"What am I supposed to do? He won't..." she said but was cut off.

"Kimberly, even if you have to come up with a solution, let him make the final decision," Jeremy said.

"What do you mean?" She asked. She knew there was more to what Jeremy was saying and she wanted all the advice she could get.

"Have you ever come up with an idea and planted it in someone's head and made that person think he or she was the one who came up with it?" Jeremy asked.

"I used to do Ma like that," Kimberly said. "I used to call my brown crayon chocolate, the white one vanilla, and the pink one strawberry. I did that loud enough for her to hear me whenever I wanted ice cream. Ma would call my daddy and tell him to bring home that Neapolitan ice cream. She would ask me if I wanted brown, white, or strawberry," Kimberly said and then paused. "Oh, I get it."

"Listen to me, but not as your big brother or friend, but as a man who knows what a man wants or don't want. Trust me, no real man wants to feel that he cannot take care of or provide for his family. No real man wants to take all his advice from other men all of the time as if he knows absolutely nothing for himself," Jeremy paused to let Kimberly absorb what he had just said then he continued. "You know, I believe that's why it's so hard for us men to submit to a spiritual leader, but that's a different story." Jeremy wanted to help her understand. He could feel her desire to be a good woman and wife to her husband.

Kimberly saw Jeremy for the first time as a man. His words were so loving. She knew that most people saw him as a womanizer, but she saw a gentle, loving, and kind-hearted man.

"Why are you still single?" Kimberly asked.

"Wow! Where did that come from?" Jeremy asked.

"I guess all anybody ever sees is the fact that you seem to run from one woman to another. You have been called player, mac-daddy, and God knows what else. It's hard to believe that you ever think of the qualities to be a good husband and what it takes for a woman to be considered a good wife," Kimberly said.

"Well, I do. I just haven't found the right one yet. Sometimes people never factor into the equation that we keep messing things up because we can tell she is not the right one. It's better on them, the ladies, if they think it's us and not them. My self-esteem is not so fragile that it's going to be devastating to me if she calls me sorry, a player, a dog, or whatever. Truth is, many ladies don't get half as far as one might think. It's just going to take a very special lady for me. Do you know that other than my mom, Poochie, and now you, no other woman has ever been in my bedroom?"

"What about DeAnna?" Kimberly asked.

"Nope, she has not been in here. Now, she probably will in order to make sure I won't kill myself moving around."

"No," Kimberly interrupted. "I mean what about her as a potential mate?"

"She's probably only here because she needs the extra money," Jeremy replied. "I don't even know what she looks like."

"That's the beauty of it. If you fall in love with the spirit and the heart of a person, the looks shouldn't matter."

"I thought we were talking about you," Jeremy said as he stood up. "Come on, walk me back to the living room."

"Jeremy how am I going to learn to be a good wife without a good role model?" Kimberly asked as they reached the door.

Jeremy reached out for the doorknob, but Kimberly open the bedroom door for him.

"Don't do that," Jeremy said.

"What?" Kimberly questioned.

"There are things I have to get used to. I don't want to feel like an invalid."

"Sorry," Kimberly quickly said.

~

As Kimberly and Jeremy walked down the hall, Jeremy could tell that everyone was outside.

"Now your house has been re-arranged, shall I help you or not?" Kimberly asked.

"Well, I could get around when I knew where everything was. You figure out if I need help or not as we go, like DeAnna does. Only give me what you really think I need."

94

As Jeremy slowly walked past the entrance to the kitchen, he heard water running in the sink. "It's DeAnna," Kimberly said.

"I know," Jeremy quickly replied. "You're still here?" Jeremy asked as if he was surprised.

Kimberly wondered how he knew it was DeAnna, but she decided not to ask.

"Yes, I somehow got drafted into cleaning and seasoning the chicken and maybe steaks," DeAnna said as she turned to look at Jeremy. "And I think I'm supposed to make some hamburger patties as well."

"DeAnna, I am so sorry my friend did this to you," Jeremy replied.

"You don't have anything to be sorry about," DeAnna said. "We were waiting for you to re-surface and I kind of bragged about my famous burgers and…"

"You got drafted, trust me," Jeremy said. "Did the conversation by chance start with one of the guys bragging about Lesia's cooking?" Jeremy asked.

"Well, yeah. I think so," DeAnna hesitantly replied.

"Sorry, I actually think it was their idea that you make up the burgers and season the meat. They just tricked you into thinking it was your idea," Jeremy said. "Lesia is not that great a cook."

Kimberly smiled at Jeremy, but then she suddenly remembered that he couldn't see her smiling.

"Oh, Kimberly your husband is or was here. Myles introduced us," DeAnna informed Kimberly.

Kimberly's smile suddenly disappeared. She washed her hands and began helping DeAnna wash and season the chicken. Jeremy stood in the kitchen doorway. He wanted to join his friends but wasn't ready to let anyone see him tripping over furniture.

"Might help you if you started counting your steps," DeAnna said.

"What?" Jeremy questioned.

"Count your step. You should know how many steps from your room to your bathroom, your room to the kitchen, from the kitchen to the

95

living room," DeAnna said as she dried her hands. "Start with where you are now. Walk straight until you feel your feet on the carpet."

"One, two, three," he began counting. When Jeremy could tell that he was no longer walking on a hardwood floor, he stopped.

"I got this," Kimberly said as she smiled at DeAnna to encourage her to go help Jeremy.

"You sure?" DeAnna questioned.

"Yes, that's what you are paid to do."

DeAnna wasn't sure if she was actually hired to help Jeremy or if she was involuntarily drafted by Ma Phillips, but she was glad. She liked his family and his friends. They all had a strong friendship, which seemed so rare to DeAnna.

"Okay but let me know when you get it all clean and the fat cut off. I gotta hook it up with my special secret seasonings," DeAnna said loud enough for Jeremy to hear. She winked at Kimberly.

"Everybody's got secrets around here," Kimberly said under her breath as DeAnna walked past her and joined Jeremy in the living room.

DeAnna made a mental note- *Kimberly has something she needs to talk about,* she said to herself. *Keyword: Secrets.* DeAnna turned her attention back to Jeremy.

"How many steps from the kitchen doorway to the living room?" DeAnna asked Jeremy.

"Well, my feet hit the carpet at 12," he responded. "Now what?"

"Okay now walk forward and count the number of steps until you feel the back of your sofa," she responded.

When he touched the back of the sofa, DeAnna smiled. He wasn't walking like he was afraid that he was going to trip. He seemed confident.

"Okay, okay so now that you are in the living room, if you want to go out the front door turn right. The back of the sofa creates a path for you, so just walk straight. When you no longer feel the sofa, just keep walking straight until you feel that small section of hardwood by the front door entrance. You'll know that you're close to the door, so feel with your hands so you won't run into the door. Count your steps as you go," DeAnna said.

DeAnna watched as Jeremy obeyed her orders. He turned right and began counting.

"Stop!" DeAnna said as Jeremy reached the closet door. "How many steps?"

"You scared me sweetheart," Jeremy said and then laughed. "That was twelve-steps," he answered.

"You are standing directly in front of your closet door. Remember what I told you about most door knobs."

"Most are waist high and the knob is about one inch from the frame," Jeremy replied. He raised his hand up to his waist and felt until he found the door molding. He moved his hand inward about an inch. His hand landed perfectly on the doorknob.

DeAnna wanted to say, 'great job' or 'super,' but it sounded too childish to be saying to a grown man about something like this. She wanted him to feel like a man. She knew all too well how easily a man's sense of pride could be shot down. Foolish pride, her mother called it, but valuable to men nonetheless and she wasn't going to toy with it.

"Now continue going toward to the front door and count," she said, slowly walking behind him.

When Jeremy reached the front door without bumping into anything, he felt a sense of accomplishment. Such minor day-to-day acts had bought him much joy. "Sixteen," he said. "Twelve from the kitchen doorway to the living room, twelve from the living room entrance to the closet, and four more from the closet to the front door," Jeremy said, "Or sixteen steps from the living room, straight to the front door."

"You got it," DeAnna said. She couldn't resist the urge to clap and rush to give him a pat on the back. "You are such a quick learner."

"Nothing to learn," Jeremy said. "It's not algebra or trigonometry."

"Well true. I guess I should have said you're a gracious learner," she said. "I cannot tell you how many people would have resisted help until they'd practically burnt the house down, broken all the dishes or almost killed themselves," DeAnna said.

"Independence is one hard thing to lose. It's almost like losing your freedom," Jeremy muttered. "Okay, now what?" He said, determined to make the best of his time with DeAnna. He had accepted his condition as a temporary inconvenience and he had accepted that he would have to learn to deal with until his sight returns.

"Okay turn around and come back," DeAnna said.

Jeremy walked back. He walked sixteen steps to the living room's entrance. He raised his hand out and felt the back of his sofa. He was standing directly in front of the hallway, which lead to the kitchen.

"Okay, this is where you started," DeAnna replied.

"Ok, I think I got it," Jeremy said.

He reached out until he felt the back of the sofa. He then slowly walked around the sofa and began to feel on it. He felt the arm of the sofa. He patted the seat as if he was trying to find exactly where he wanted to sit. He began to feel for the coffee table with his foot.

"Wait! Where is the coffee table?" He asked when he didn't feel it.

"Well, it's there, but it's far enough away from the sofa, so you won't bump into it," DeAnna replied.

"But, I sit in front of the TV and eat. So, I'll need it close."

"You know what," DeAnna said. "I figured that. Now, since you have two coffee tables, I set the left side of the room the same as the right, but the coffee table is closer to, not only the sofa, but to the dining room entrance. So, when you leave the kitchen and come through your dining room, the coffee table is right there," DeAnna said, hoping that he would understand the set up.

"Oh, that does make it easier. So, if I am not eating, I can sit over here. If I am eating, I can eat over there and not have to worry about a place to set my plate," Jeremy said.

"You have a great layout by the way. I love the fact that your family room is kind of tucked away," DeAnna said.

"Thanks, that's what made me buy this house. A lot of people don't even know I have a family room. Well, I call it my den," Jeremy paused for a second and thought about all the plans he had for the family room. "I was thinking about turning it into my man cave."

"Really, I'm surprised," DeAnna sarcastically said. "Oh, I noticed from your family room that you have patio doors that lead outside to your deck. Does anyone use it during cookouts?"

"Nope. Most of the time they use the front door and walk around to the back," Jeremy answered.

"Oh, that's right your porch wraps all the way around to the back yard," DeAnna said as she remembered how much it reminded her of her grandmother's porch.

"Have you seen the deck?" Jeremy asked.

"No!"

"Well, the grill is sort of right there at the patio door because during the winter, I cook outside and…"

"I get the picture," DeAnna said. "The grill has to be right there at the door. You quickly slap the meat on the grill and then quickly dart back in the house. My uncle does the same thing."

"People got tired of trying to squeeze past a hot grill, so they just started walking out the front door and walking around to the back," Jeremy continued.

DeAnna gave him a disapproving look that he couldn't even see.

"Why does it seem that you instantly got quiet?" Jeremy asked.

"Oh," DeAnna replied. "I feel a little foolish. I was giving you the evil eye, as my mom called it, and was waiting for your response and then I suddenly remembered you couldn't see it."

"Don't feel bad, I didn't see it."

"I wanted you to see it," DeAnna laughed. "One day you will see it though. So now, do you want to go out back with your friends?"

"If you don't mind," Jeremy replied.

"Why would I mind?"

"You are my guest," Jeremy said then paused, "well they are too, for that matter, but I don't want to leave you here in the house doing all this hard work while I sit down and just enjoy. I don't want you to feel neglected."

"Its fine, I want to help Kimberly season the meat anyway. You can go and have some male bonding time. I probably need to get going soon anyway," DeAnna said, but she really had nowhere to go, except home, and nothing to do once she gets there, and knew she was going to wish that she was anywhere but there, once she was there.

"You're not going to stay and eat with us?" Jeremy asked as if he was shocked.

"No, I don't want to intrude any longer."

"Intrude, please they are the intruders," Jeremy said referring to his friends. "They just came in and took over. They re-arranged my house and planned a cookout without asking me anything. I'm surprised that they didn't re-arrange my bedroom."

"Oh," DeAnna said. "You haven't heard, huh?"

"Heard what?" Jeremy questioned.

"Well, the bedroom reconstruction began tomorrow after church," DeAnna said as she nudged him towards the front door.

"You are kidding, right?"

"Sorry, afraid not," DeAnna said trying to keep a straight face and avoid laughing.

"What's wrong with the bedroom? I can find my way around in there with my eyes closed," Jeremy said then paused for a few seconds. "But I guess I don't even have to close them now."

"Yeah," DeAnna said. "I was joking, but we do need to address the kitchen and dining room."

"So, are you coming back Sunday after church too?" Jeremy asked as if he had no control over who and when people came to his house.

"If you want me to. I don't want to be pushy. It really wasn't even my idea," DeAnna explained. She didn't want him to think she was creating reasons to come to his house.

"It's okay with me, you are easy to talk to. You're always welcome here," Jeremy said.

DeAnna guided Jeremy around the coffee table and towards the family room. She'd forgotten just that quickly what Jeremy said about not being able to use the patio doors because the grill was in front of the doors.

"What's up? Where's the meat?" Johnathan asked. He had strolled through the front door, yelling as if he was in a hurry to get the meat on the grill.

"It's coming, now stop yelling," Kimberly said. "I bet you don't even have the grill ready."

"Where's Jeremy?" Johnathan asked, while walking towards the bedroom."

"I think he's showing DeAnna the family room," Kimberly replied.

"Why?" Johnathan asked.

"I don't know. Ask him," Kimberly said as if Johnathan was getting on her nerves. "I think he might be going out back with you guys."

"Now, the grill is in front of the door," Johnathan said, responding to Kimberly as if her tone didn't bother him at all. He seemed accustomed to it.

"They'll see that. Just leave them alone," Kimberly said. She smiled when she heard Jeremy laughing. "He's probably enjoying the attention since those other so-called girlfriends act like he has a plague of locusts flying around."

"Yeah, I noticed that too. Women are a trip," Johnathan said.

"Some," Kimberly clarified.

"Okay, some women," Johnathan agreed. "They want someone to be there for them when they are going through tough times, but they are the ones that get going when times get tough and we need them."

Johnathan sat down at the table and waited for Kimberly to finish seasoning the hamburger patties. DeAnna and Jeremy reappeared from the family room and joined Johnathan in the dining room.

"Man, walking that slow will wear you out. I feel like an old man," Jeremy said to DeAnna. He felt for a chair and sat down.

"You look like an old man too," Johnathan said as he studied Jeremy's unshaved face, wrinkled tee shirt, and old sweat pants.

Jeremy ignored the comment as if he had not even heard it. He wasn't even aware that Johnathan was even in the house, until he spoke.

"I think I'm ready to go outside," Jeremy said.

"Hold on, I'll walk you out. I was just waiting to get the chicken. I don't think the hamburgers are ready yet."

"Give me one minute," DeAnna said.

DeAnna quickly ran into the kitchen and opened the cabinet over the black flattop range and began grabbing spices. She moved around Jeremy's kitchen as if it were her own. She checked the refrigerator for butter and then began looking around for a saucepan. When she found one, she put it on the stove over medium heat. She dropped a stick of butter in the saucepan. Once the butter began to melt, she lowered the heat. After the butter was completely melted, she began to dip one piece of chicken in the melted butter at a time and then placed it back on the silver-serving tray. She then sprinkled different seasoning all over the chicken.

"Okay," DeAnna said turning to Kimberly, who had taken a seat at the table. "The chicken is ready for the grill. How about the hamburgers, did you season them?"

Kimberly looked at DeAnna with a confused look. She did not know what she meant by seasoned. "I made them into patties" Kimberly said. She suddenly thought about the word seasoned. "Oh, you mean did I add salt and pepper. Yeah, girl I did that."

Johnathan grabbed the tray of chicken and headed for the front door. "Jeremy," he yelled. "Are you coming out with me?" He asked.

"Yeah, hold up," Jeremy said as he pulled himself up from the chair. He wasn't sure which way to turn. DeAnna could tell that Jeremy was a little confused and apprehensive about moving around with others watching. She knew that he didn't want anyone seeing him bumping into things.

"When you came in the dining room, you took the first chair at the head of the table." There was no chair at the other end of the table so DeAnna knew that Jeremy would be able to figure out exactly where he sat.

Jeremy smiled. He knew that DeAnna understood why he wasn't moving. *Straight through the kitchen is easier,* Jeremy thought to himself. So, he walked straight through the kitchen. "Thanks," he said when he went past DeAnna and felt her presence. When Jeremy got to the doorway which led to the hall, he knew if he turned right, it would lead him down the hall to his bedroom, so Jeremy turn left. He walked until he felt carpet under his feet. He turned right and was headed for the front door.

"Twelve steps to the closet," he said to himself. "Four more steps, I'm at the front door," he said as if he was singing a song.

"I'll get the door," Johnathan said as he patiently waited for Jeremy.

Jeremy's confidence began to quickly fade as he suddenly thought about the number of steps it would take before he tripped off the front porch. He slowly and carefully stepped onto the porch. He could still hear DeAnna giving Kimberly instructions on seasoning the hamburger. Jeremy wanted her by his side, but he didn't want to tell Johnathan what he was feeling. He knew that Johnathan would not let him fall or walk off the porch, but he also knew that Johnathan would not be as attentive as DeAnna had been. He wanted to go back inside.

"I guess it is a good thing you have this large wrap around deck," Johnathan said as he slowed down to make sure Jeremy wouldn't bump into anything.

"Why?" Jeremy question.

"Well, you don't have to walk down the steps and then around the house, only to climb back up steps to get to the patio table," Johnathan explained.

"I guess you're right," Jeremy said realizing that Johnathan was more aware of how complicated things were for him than he thought. Jeremy felt a little more relaxed.

"Might be a good idea if you would move the grill away from the patio door. Then you can go out through there," Johnathan said. "At least for now. I mean if you want to." Johnathan knew it had to be hard for Jeremy to have to keep taking orders from everyone. He didn't want to make Jeremy feel like a little boy being ordered around.

When Jeremy got to the back where his friends were, he could tell that they were having a serious conversation. They suddenly got quiet when Jeremy approached them and reached for a chair.

"I got it," Myles said as he pulled Jeremy's chair out for him. He did as he had seen DeAnna do. He placed Jeremy hand on the chair.

Jeremy felt the chair with his hand and then set down. "Now, what's going on?" Jeremy asked.

Malcolm glanced at Chris.

"Don't everybody speak at one time," Jeremy said. "If you're going to have a discussion about me, I would like to be a part of it."

"We were not talking about you. We'll talk about you to your face," Malcolm said without a hint in his voice that he might be joking. "We were discussing Jason."

"Oh that," Jeremy replied as if he knew what was going on.

"So, you know?" Chris asked.

"Well, I know he and Kimberly are having marital problems. She thinks he's cheating," Jeremy bluntly said.

"He is," Myles replied with more than a hint of anger in his voice.

"What?" I gonna..." Jeremy started, but was interrupted.

"Kill him," Chris finished Jeremy's sentence, but as if he was asking a question. "Man, what hypocrites we are."

"Do I have to remind you that she's your sister he's cheating on?" Malcolm asked. "And she is like a sister to the rest of us."

"So, Lesia's brother should have killed you?" Chris questioned Malcolm. "You think I don't want to kill him myself, but you all know that will turn Kimberly against all us. Then who will she have?"

"He's right," Johnathan said. "Besides, we all know that there is a reason why Jason is cheating. He's a good kid and that's just it. He's a kid."

"A married kid nonetheless," Jeremy said him. "They both are."

"There's more," Myles said as he took a sip of his cranberry juice.

"Please, don't tell, not a child," Jeremy said. When no one said anything, Jeremy knew the answer. "Poor Kimberly, she's not going to handle this well at all."

Jeremy could tell by the complete silence that as bad as it already was, there was still more to the story. He had completely forgotten about himself and his blindness. His fears disappeared and at that very moment, Jeremy wanted to go back inside and wrapped his arms around Kimberly. *She will need someone to talk to. A good woman. Someone who can make her understand why men do what we do. Someone with a good spirit and a loving and good heart.* Jeremy was so deep in thought he had not heard the conversation that the others were engaged in. "DeAnna!" Jeremy blurted out as if everyone knew what he was thinking or perhaps as if they all were talking about the same thing he was thinking about.

"No, Danielle," Myles said, not sure what Jeremy was talking about.

"Danielle?" Jeremy questioned.

"Yes, Danielle. She's the one that Jason was seeing," Myles said, looking at Jeremy who had a confused look on his face. "Why would you think it was DeAnna?"

"I had my mind on something else for a minute," Jeremy explained. "But you said, 'was seeing,' so it's over?"

"Yup, it's over. She was trying to use us to get to Kimberly," Myles said as he tried to figure out the short version of the story. "Seems that they had a one-night stand and supposedly she got pregnant."

"She's pregnant?" Jeremy questioned.

"Nope, not any more. She had the baby," Chris continued the story, where Myles left off. "The baby was pre-mature. She delivered after only five months.'

"Does Kimberly know?" Jeremy asked.

"We're not sure. She knows something, but we just don't know what she knows," Chris replied.

"How do you know all of this?" Jeremy asked.

"The little homewrecker-troublemaking friend of hers," Myles said.

"What does she have to do with this?" Jeremy asked.

The story kept getting more and more complicated. It was almost like a mystery. Jeremy shook his head in disbelief.

"Seems that she knew Danielle and had actually introduced Jason to Danielle. She was keeping tabs on Kimberly so that she could tell Danielle everything that was going on. She's been collecting the child support from Jason and giving it to Danielle," Myles said. "Oh, and get this," Myles continued. "This chick has been blackmailing Jason. Threatening to tell about the affair if he didn't give her money."

"This is not good," Jeremy said. "I'm telling you man, somebody is going to get hurt."

"Calm down Jeremy, she could walk up at any time," Myles said. "But why did you think it was DeAnna?"

105

"Oh, no," Jeremy quickly protested. "I didn't think it was her. I was thinking that Kimberly will need someone to talk to. She doesn't really have any friends."

"I think one of the ladies from church or your mom could help her through this," Malcolm suggested.

"Or Lesia," Johnathan said. "After-all, she knows first-hand how it feels..." Johnathan said, but his words faded as he scanned Malcolm's disapproving stare.

"But Lesia is or acts angry. It's not a good idea to have somebody giving advice about something that they haven't gotten over themselves. I was always told, never get counseling about a man from an angry woman. Two angry bitter women together, that's not a good combination," Chris replied.

"She's not that upset all the time," Malcolm said, defending his wife. "We have some good times too. More good, than bad."

"I think she needs someone who can be totally objective and someone who will not judge Jason. I was thinking DeAnna," Jeremy suggested. "She seems to have connected with Kimberly already. She's in there right now giving her cooking tips. Kimberly seems to really be comfortable with her."

"I don't think Lesia would be a bad choice," Malcolm said, still feeling defensive about how his friends seemed to judge his wife, but even though they didn't want anyone to judge Jason.

Everyone ignored Malcolm and continued to talk.

"Sounds good to me," Chris said. "If one of us talks to her, she'll just think that all men look out for other men. I don't want to see her hurt or divorced at the age of 21. I don't think we should tell DeAnna what's going on either. Let Kimberly tell her when she is ready. Let the bond build naturally. We just create the encounters if we need to."

"Oh," Jeremy said. "If you guys don't mind; I would like the grill moved. If during the winter, I want to cook out, I'll just move it back."

"We cannot move it now," Johnathan objected. "It's hot."

"It has handles on both sides and wheels. I think we can handle this without any problems," Chris said. "We just need to move it over about 6 feet."

Myles and Malcolm got up and walked over to the grill. Chris and Johnathan got up and move the large plants and the stainless-steel buffet table. Eric, who had been in the yard taking pictures, turned and began taking pictures of his friends moving the grill. The grill was moved in less than two-minutes.

"Now," Malcolm said as he took his seat, "we can finally go in and out without being watched by Jeremy's nosey neighbor peeping out the window."

"You know you enjoy being stalked by Martha Mary Robinson-Robinson," Myles joked. "Somebody needs to go on ahead and marry that woman, so people can finally forget that she married her first cousin slash brother.

"You know that woman didn't marry her brother. She just happened to marry somebody with the same last name," Johnathan said as he opened the sliding glass patio door. "But Martha Mary Robinson-Robinson is one good looking sixty-eight-year-old. Lesia better watch out, you know she wants you Malcolm."

"Somebody better check on that chicken," Jeremy said. "Or we all are going to be knocking on Ms. Robinson-Robinson door for something to eat."

"Hey, where are the hamburgers?" Myles asked. He grabbed the tongues that were hanging on the side of the grill and began turning the chicken over. "The chicken is almost done," he announced.

Johnathan reminded Myles to drip the chicken in the saucepan that DeAnna had prepared to base the chicken in.

"About time," Kimberly said as she stepped around the corner with the platter of hamburger patties. I have often wondered why you got that door blocked with that grill. I know why during the winter. The grill is on wheels, how hard is it to just move it."

Myles pointed to the buffet table. Kimberly placed the burgers down and went back into the house. Everyone seemed nervous when Kimberly was around. She could feel the tension. They were glad when she went back inside.

Kimberly sat down in the family room, isolating herself from everyone. She could hear DeAnna washing the few dishes that were in the sink. DeAnna had even done a little re-arranging to make sure everything that Jeremy really needed was within arm's reach. Kimberly smiled as she thought about the list that DeAnna had jotted down of a few simple meals that Jeremy might try to make. As Kimberly sat in Jeremy's family room, she flipped through an old photo album.

"Oh, I see they moved the grill," DeAnna said, walking into the family room. She took a seat.

"Yes! Finally," Kimberly said.

"Wow, this is a big room. Why doesn't he come down here much?" DeAnna asked, thinking there might be some hidden reason.

"He did at one time when they had game night and fight night, but when he got the flat screen TV, they started watching it up there," Kimberly said. She thought about a few times that it took Jeremy so long to get from the family room to answer the front door; they had to walk around to the back. "The living room is closer to the front door and you won't miss anything when you get up to answer the door. You know black folks, they don't believe in coming through the backdoor if they don't have to."

"You're right about that," DeAnna agreed.

"So," Kimberly began as if she could wait no longer. "What's up with you and Jeremy? I really don't buy this therapy story. He seems too comfortable with you floating around his house."

"I think he's using me to get his mom off his back," DeAnna jokingly said.

"Jeremy's mom has been riding his back since he was seventeen-years-old. Trust me, he didn't care then, and he doesn't care now," Kimberly said and then paused. She didn't want to give DeAnna a bad impression of Jeremy. "Don't get me wrong, he respects his mother, but he has always been the type of man who talks to whomever he wants to talk to, even if everyone else disapproves of the woman. People think he's a dog, but he's not. He has had a lot of girlfriends, that's true, but I can tell you this, none makes it past that living room. Some women even thought he was gay."

"Is he," DeAnna jokingly asked? "I mean, he is a handsome man, got a good job, some common sense, and intelligent. There's not a lot of single engineers lurking around. Well, not in this area."

"Ms. Latonya, the girl who was here earlier, she's been trying to hook him for almost a year. She thinks he's gay or married or he has a girlfriend. He's too nice to tell her to take a hike or maybe he likes having her around for when he has no one else but..." Kimberly paused. She could tell that DeAnna was itching to make a comment.

"So, Mr. Nice guy lets women run over him? A passive man, huh?"

"No," Kimberly said, trying to figure out the best way to explain him. "I guess you can say passive to a point. He tries to stay drama free, but when he gets mad you better watch out."

"Maybe he's afraid of being hurt."

"Maybe," Kimberly said, remembering the woman everyone thought he was going to marry. "He's been down that road, treated her like a queen and she..." Kimberly said then paused. Kimberly wasn't sure if she was telling too much of Jeremy's business.

"What?" DeAnna questioned. It was as if she was listening to a story and could not wait to hear the ending.

"Well," Kimberly said, sounding if something was really bothering her. "Jeremy once told me that people can't forget their past because other people won't let them. Here I am digging up his past and don't even know how to deal with my future."

DeAnna wanted to ask Kimberly if there was anything she wanted to talk about, but she didn't want to appear to be nosey, nor did she want to be pushy.

"Now back to you," Kimberly said. "You also seem very comfortable here yourself. You re-arranged all this man's furniture, been very attentive to his every need, and keep pretending you got to go, so he can ask you to stay."

"What?" DeAnna said. "Look, it just comes natural. My father was blind, and I cared for him for eight years."

DeAnna decided not to address the 'got to go, so he can ask you to stay' comment. She knew it was true. She didn't want to go home anytime soon.

"Can I ask you a question?" Kimberly asked. She knew that she could ask the question, but she needed a few second to build up her nerves.

"Sure," DeAnna replied with no hesitation.

"If you found out that your man was or had cheated, would you stay with him?" Kimberly sort of blurted out, needing to get it out.

"I don't want to sound like a hypocrite. You see my ex cheated and I left him without giving him the chance to explain, but I wasn't married to him and he wanted more than I was willing to give, so the decision was easy for me make," DeAnna explained.

"But," Kimberly said, feeling that a 'but' was coming.

"But circumstances are different for different people."

"So, your decision would have been different if you and he were married?"

"Depends," DeAnna replied.

"On what?" Kimberly questioned.

"Kimberly, we don't know each other, so I know it may be difficult confiding in a stranger. Well, the truth is sometimes it's easier, but if you don't want to discuss it with me, I'll understand, but I'm going to ask anyway. Do you suspect that your boyfriend is cheating?" DeAnna asked.

"Husband," Kimberly corrected her. "And yes."

DeAnna suddenly remembered that she had been introduced to Kimberly's husband earlier. She wasn't sure where he had disappeared to, but she knew that he no longer seemed to be there.

"Do you want to talk about it?" DeAnna asked.

Kimberly explained to DeAnna about all the hung-up calls that began a few months ago. She told her how someone would call and breathe in the phone and then hang up. A few hours later, the person would call again. Kimberly explained that she thought it was a bill collector hoping a man would answer the phone, since most of the bills were in her husband's name. After a week, the calls began coming in at night. Jason would answer, and the person would ask for someone who didn't live there and then hang up. "At least that's what Jason would tell me," Kimberly explained. She explained how Jason suddenly became pre-occupied. He began coming home later and later and claimed that he was working overtime, but there never seemed to be any additional money coming in. "He seems angry and frustrated a lot," Kimberly said.

"How does he treat you?" DeAnna asked.

"When he is there, he treats me okay. He seems mad with me sometimes for no reason. He tells me that he loves me and that he'll always love me no matter what, but…" Kimberly said, thinking of the conversation that she had with Jeremy. "Sometimes, I do feel as if I just cannot do anything right, so maybe he is mad at me, but just don't want to tell me. Maybe that's why he doesn't want to be home as much."

"Have you asked him if he is cheating?" DeAnna hesitantly asked.

"No, I'm afraid of the answer. He's a good man and…" Kimberly was almost in tears.

"Do you treat him as if he is a good man?"

"Sometimes," Kimberly paused and whipped a tear away before it could fall. "But…well, sometimes I just get so tired of having to make all the decisions. He acts like he's scared to make any decisions. Too scared it might not work out or something will go wrong."

"Has he ever tried to make a decision and when he did, it didn't work out?" DeAnna asked. She knew the situation all too well.

Kimberly looked at DeAnna as if she was crazy for even asking the question. "Yes, plenty of times."

"I am just wondering; how did you react?"

Kimberly took a deep breath as she began to think. "One time, Jason wanted to buy a used car from someone who lived a few houses down from where he grew up. He had agreed to pay the man two hundred dollars a month until he paid it in full. The man told Jason that they could have the title signed over after Jason paid the last payment. I told him to get the agreement in writing. Jason acted like it was an insult to have the man sign an agreement." Kimberly chuckled. "He said that he had known Mr. Johnson all his life and could trust him. He was trustworthy alright. After Jason had paid six hundred dollars, Mr. Johnson sold the car to someone else for two-thousand-dollar cash. When Jason asked for his money back, Mr. Trustworthy Johnson claimed that Jason had only given him three hundred dollars."

"What did you say?" DeAnna asked.

"I remember saying something like, 'Why didn't you have sense enough to get a written contract, so he could not sell it to anyone else? At the very least, get a receipt each time a payment was made," Kimberly stated. "So, you see why I stay so frustrated. I am sure you see why it's hard to trust him to make decisions."

"So how do you know to request that he get a contract or receipts," DeAnna asked as if Jason actions were no big deal?

"I have been taken advantage of before by someone that I trusted," Kimberly answered. "Besides, I watch Judge Mathis."

"I see. So, you learned by experience?" DeAnna questioned.

"Yeah and…" Kimberly words sort of faded. She realized the point that DeAnna was obviously trying to make was, 'we *learn from experiences*, she said to herself.

"Maybe that's just a lesson that he learned, but if that one bad experience called you to question, analyze, or simply not trust his judgment to make any other decisions, why wouldn't he just let you handle things?" DeAnna questioned.

"It's hard to trust him though," Kimberly said as she sat back in the chair.

"I know, especially when a lack of good judgment might mean that the lights could get turned off or the car gets repo'ed. Honey I've been through that too, but you have to start somewhere. Trust him with something small. Something you can live without if his decision turns out bad. And if it does, don't make a big deal about it, just pray and work though it together."

"Like what?" Kimberly questioned.

"Telephone, cable. I don't know. What can you go without a few days if he doesn't pay it? Find something that, if he doesn't pay it, it will be an inconvenience, but well worth the lesson. Believe it or not, a man's ego is a very fragile thing. If you don't stroke his ego and help him maintain his pride and position as head of the house, whether you like it or not, he won't have a desire to be there. Whether we like it or not, the fact remains that God created the man to be the head and we can't change it either. Keep this in mind," DeAnna said as she looked around to see if anyone else was listening. "You can lead a man without being the head of him," DeAnna stated.

Kimberly stared at DeAnna as if she had no clue of what she was talking about. "Lead without really being the head. Does that make you the leader or the follower?" Kimberly asked.

"Well, maybe this is a better way to put it, 'make the decision, but let him think he thought of it. Sometimes women are so busy trying to claim all the glory of being right or, as some would say, 'having their man in his place.' Many women don't even realize that the prize for being right or having their man 'in his place' isn't even worth the effort. Think about it, who cares if you found the house, got it financed, decorated it, if he feels that it is what you wanted, but you didn't care about living in it happily ever after with him. Some women put more energy into decorating the house than they do in building up the head of the house. Who's the one working to keep the house, him or her? It should be both."

Myles walked in the house with the tray of chicken. Kimberly and DeAnna gave him a look that said 'keep-it-moving, nothing-to-see-here.' Myles wasn't about to disregard the familiar looks. He quickly walked past the ladies and into the kitchen. "I'm coming back though," he announced. "I don't want anyone to think I am eavesdropping." He didn't even look at the ladies as he past back by on the way out. He looked straight ahead. When he reached the patio, he pulled the door open and then turned to DeAnna and Kimberly and said, "Carry on." He stepped back outside and closed the door behind himself.

The music that the guys were listening to outside was loud enough to be heard by Kimberly and DeAnna. It was also loud enough so the guys could not hear the ladies on the inside, nor could the ladies hear what the guys were talking about. Myles tapped on the glass patio door and waited for Kimberly to look at him before he pulled the door open.

"Hey, did y'all cook anything to go with the meat. We are about to send Johnathan and Eric to the store to get some potato salad, macaroni and cheese, and some chips, do you think that will be enough?"

"I have potatoes on now for the potato salad," DeAnna said. "I probably need to go check them," she said as she quickly returned to the kitchen.

"And I saw two boxes on mac and cheese in the cabinet, unless you are expecting some more people, I think that will be enough," Kimberly replied as she got up from the table and returned to the kitchen as well.

"Just checking. Oh yeah, there will be a few ladies joining us," Myles said and closed the door back.

DeAnna wondered who the ladies were and who they were coming to see.

"Probably Eric and Malcolm's wives," Kimberly answered as if she could tell what DeAnna was thinking. "They will probably only stop by to make an appearance." Kimberly rolled her eyes at the thought of them. She could tell that DeAnna had picked up on her mood change. "Long story," she explained before DeAnna had a chance to decide if she would ask about the mood change.

"Oh, I see," DeAnna said not wanting to ask any questions. She was just glad to know that the ladies that Myles announced who were coming, were not coming to see Jeremy. *Wait,* she thought to herself. *What does it matter to me, I'm just the therapist, rehabilitation coach, or whatever he calls me?* She thought to herself.

"Eric's wife, Tesha," Kimberly began as soon as she was sure that Myles was no longer at the door. "Acts young and… well sought of silly. Now, I know that I can act like a baby sometimes, but I am only twenty-one, but she's almost thirty-five. Anyway, she is too busy running behind her friends all the time to even act like a wife, but Eric loves her regardless of what she does. They have fun when they are out together, which is not often. Eric would probably be a couch potato if she would come home more. The kids are usually at their grandmother's house doing the weekend when it's their time to have them. Whatever understanding Eric and Tesha have, it seems to work for them, but she is not one of my favorite people. I definitely would not seek any advice from her. Had Tesha married any other man but Eric, she would probably be seeing Judge Maybelline or Judge Toler, I think that's the name of the that Judge on Divorce Court."

As for Lesia, she hangs with Tesha from time-to-time," Kimberly paused to think about her impression of Lesia. "Lesia, Malcolm's wife, well, she's okay. We don't really be around each other that much. She always seems to be working on some new project. She has very little time for Malcolm or anyone else. She seems to feel that because she's at home all the time that Malcolm should be right there by her side but spends no time with him when he is there. She feels that he should be happy just because she's not running the streets. She complains about everything. Like their three-bedroom apartment, but you should see it. It is almost as big as a house, but she acts like it is a matchbox. They have no kids, at least not living with them. Wait! Let me back up a bit, the kids are never really there because she doesn't want them there. She pretends she does, but she doesn't. They are Malcolm's kids from previous relationships, but they don't have any together. He has an eight-year-old little girl that he adores but doesn't see her that much. He never talks about his son and rarely visits him. It seems that if he says anything about his son, she gives him the cold shoulder and stop speaking to him. I think it has something to do with the fact that she didn't find out about his son until the night before their wedding. The little boy is the child of an affair he had after they had been dating for almost a year. So, you can imagine there was no marital bliss or wonderful honeymoon for them. Seem as if the child is a constant reminder of his infidelity."

"What's the story on the others, single, or married, what?" DeAnna asked. She was really only interested in Jeremy, but she didn't want to be so obvious.

"Well, the rest seemed to have declared their singlehood and wear it as if it were a badge of honor, but they all seem to stay on the prowl for the right woman. Myles is the romantic and gentle one, but he is the *one strike and you're out type* of man. Girl can you believe that at one time he had rules that he lived by for dating. He seems to view relationships and dating as if it's a burden. I think he wants to find the right one, but without dating. He wants to just get married," Kimberly said.

"And Johnathan?" DeAnna asked, pretending that she wasn't really all that anxious to hear Jeremy's profile.

"Girl, he is in a world all by himself. He preaches too much to ever find a woman. He takes Christianity to a whole new level. It's gonna take God Himself to bring a woman to him." Kimberly burst into laughter when she thought about all the blind dates that the guys had set him up with. "They set him up with a woman one time. Chris and Malcolm sat at the table beside him to try to determine what he was doing wrong. Girl, it took all of five minutes before he began analyzing the woman's entire life. One question after another. 'What church do you belong to? Who's your pastor? Do you serve in the church? How long have you been there? Are you a member or are you a full-time visitor? Do you pray? Do you pray to Jesus or to God? Do you pray to God in Jesus' name? Is your church a first and third service or second and fourth or do you go every Sunday? If you are a first and third, where do you go on second and fourth? When do you take communion? Do you take communion? What does communion mean to you?' That woman claimed that the Holy Spirit told her that she needed to get home immediately." Kimberly laughed so hard she almost couldn't finish the story. "Girl do you know that Johnathan had the nerves to say, 'wait I prayed about whatever it is, and the spirit is telling me that there's nothing wrong at home.' Then he asked her if she speak in tongues. She walked out and left him at the table before the food even make it from the kitchen."

"So, you mean to tell me, he asked all those questions on the first date?" DeAnna questioned.

"Yes, and he was just getting started," Kimberly replied. "If it had not been a blind date, he would have asked all those questions over the phone. One of his dates requested the meal ticket after drinking a glass of water. They had not even ordered. See..." Kimberly said and then paused. She wasn't sure how to explain him. "Well," she continued. "Johnathan is one of those people who can see the wrong in everybody else and most of the time, he's right, but he never looks at himself. He asked all the right question for a man who really wants a good Christian woman, but he asks them all at one time. He doesn't use the spirit of discernment or even wisdom to discover some things. I believe he is waiting on the perfect woman, who does not exist."

"Oh, I see," DeAnna said and then paused and looked at Kimberly as if she was waiting for her to say something else. "So how do you get along with the two wives?

"Well, that's a love-hate relationship. I guess we tolerate each other. They are older, but don't really act like they are, especially Eric's wife. She can be a little childish. Now, Malcolm's wife, well she goes along with it. I don't feel that comfortable getting any real advice from either of them," Kimberly stopped talking as thoughts suddenly evolved about her own marital issues. "Speaking of advice, what do you think I should do about my situation?"

"Well," DeAnna began and then paused to think about the best way to answer this question. DeAnna had been trained to help people find their own solution without telling them what they should do, but she wanted to give her feedback that would really make her think. "Okay, worst case scenario, if he is cheating, but is willing to stop to save the marriage, would you be able to forgive him?"

"No," Kimberly said without hesitation.

"Well, ask him if he is cheating. If he is, end the marriage. Cut your losses and move on," DeAnna said without hesitation. She wasn't expecting such quick response. She didn't really want to encourage Kimberly to end the marriage, but she knew all too well that a marriage without trust was almost pointless.

"What?" Kimberly responded. "Just like that, I'm supposed to throw away my marriage?" She questioned.

"Well yes, if you cannot forgive him, you're only going to torture yourself and him by staying. Unforgiven breeds bitterness. A marriage filled with un-forgiveness, bitterness, and a lack of trust is a recipe for disaster and misery. Is that what you want? If you cannot forgive him, I mean, if he is cheating, then you're not gonna to be able to trust him. Forgiveness is the foundation for building the trust back. And if you cannot trust him, you'll always wonder if he's with someone else every time he walks out that door. You'll be checking his cell phone. It can really drive you crazy. Actually, it'll drive you both crazy. He will wonder why you are with him, if you don't trust him. He'll probably think you want to do something to pay him back. He'll began to think that if you're going to treat him like a guilty man, then he might as well do it." DeAnna went on and on with the, *if this-then that.*

"Are you speaking from experience?" Kimberly questioned as she stared at DeAnna.

"Yea, afraid I am. I have been through it all. I have been cheated on and lied to night after night. I thought I was getting revenge on him, but I can tell you from experience, revenge and un-forgiveness hurts more than it does being cheated on. When they cheat on you, they hurt you, you have the choice to decide whether to live with them or not. When you go after your own revenge, you have to live with your actions. I had to live with what I had done. I was angry and bitter for a long time and trust me, he used it to do whatever he wanted to do. He would say, 'since you don't want me anyway, I might as well do this' or 'be with her.' Yes, he blamed me because I wouldn't talk to him, trust him, or forgive him.

"Wow, you just don't seem to be the type that would do that," Kimberly said as she stared at DeAnna.

"And I didn't think I would be that type either. Honey, when you don't know how to deal with pain, anger, and disappointment, it is hard to predict what you will do."

"So how do I deal with this?" Kimberly asked.

"First, you have to find out exactly what you're dealing with. Right now, it is just speculation and assumptions. You have to ask him a few questions, but before you ask him, ask yourself a few questions."

"Like what?"

"Do you love him? Do you believe in the marriage? Do you really want it to work no matter what his answer is? Then ask him, if he loves you, and if he says yes, ask yourself if you believe him. Does he believe in the marriage? This might seem irrelevant, but this is one of the questions you must ask yourself. Have you ever needed God's forgiveness, and will you need it again? If you can answer yes to all these questions, especially the last question, then you should at least forgive him. If for no other reason than the fact that God will not forgive you, if you cannot forgive your husband. Now that's reason enough right there to always forgive, whoever, for whatever. Even if you don't take him back, at least forgive him. God's word says forgive and you shall be forgiven. It also says that if you don't forgive, your Father in Heaven won't forgive you. If Jesus can forgive those who nailed him to the cross, hammed bolts through his hands, and placed a crown of thorns on his head, then we should be able to forgive anybody."

"Well," Johnathan said as if he was in church.

DeAnna and Kimberly was so immersed in their conversation, they did not hear Johnathan when he slid the patio door open and entered.

"How long have you been eavesdropping?" Kimberly asked.

"We were not eavesdropping. I was about to bring the hamburgers in and didn't want to interrupt the sermon, but I couldn't help but admire DeAnna's passionate speech on forgiveness. I mean, I've never thought about forgiveness like that before."

"Me either," Kimberly replied.

"Be careful DeAnna, I just might fall in love with you. A spirit-filled woman is a huge turn on," Johnathan jokingly said, winking at his friends. "Ain't that right?" He asked the others who had also heard the forgiveness sermon.

Myles glanced at Jeremy. He wasn't sure what type of relationship Jeremy and DeAnna had, so he declined to respond. He did not want to encourage Johnathan to continue. Judging from DeAnna's size, Myles knew that she would not have a chance with Jeremy if he could see her. Myles personally thought she was a very beautiful woman.

Kimberly wondered how much of the conversation the guys had heard. She wasn't sure how long Johnathan had been standing there with the patio door open. She hoped Eric and Malcolm had not heard what she said about their wives.

"Let's eat," Eric said as he entered through the front door followed by his wife, Tesha.

Good, maybe he was sitting on the front porch talking to his wife, Kimberly said to herself. Eric and Tesha often grabbed all the alone time they could get. Maybe not, she corrected her thoughts when she realized that Lesia was following behind them. *Tesha and Lesia must have just arrived together and Eric met them out front to carry the bags,* Kimberly thought.

"The ladies picked up some chips and dip," Eric announced as he sat the bag on the counter and headed back outside. He walked pass Kimberly and DeAnna and pointed towards the kitchen. "There are some paper plates in there too."

"DeAnna whispered something in Kimberly's ear and then the two ladies headed into the kitchen. DeAnna pulled her homemade macaroni and cheese out of the oven and turned the stove off.

"The oven has been on the entire time?" Kimberly asked.

"Yes, I had it on low heat, just wanted to keep it warm. I hate to reheat food."

Eric came back in the kitchen and pulled the paper plates out of the bag and handed them to Kimberly. He glanced at DeAnna and turn to introduce his wife and Lesia to DeAnna, but they had already made a quick exit out the front door. He knew that they were both avoiding the kitchen. He walked through the dining room and out the sliding patio door and greeted them as they rounded the corner. He ushered them both back into the house to meet DeAnna. Eric could instantly tell that Tesha was not too thrilled with DeAnna. Tesha seemed to oppose any woman that doesn't seem to have *independence,* or *don't-really-need-a-man,* stamped across her forehead. It was not hard to tell that DeAnna was what Tesha called an old-fashioned woman. As Tesha extended her well-manicured, ring on every finger hand to shake DeAnna's hand, Tesha made a point of clarifying DeAnna's position as the help.

"So, are you the rehabilitation specialists and the maid?" Tesha asked.

Lesia shot Tesha a look that said *don't start.* Lesia apologized for Tesha's comment and offered to help DeAnna in the kitchen. DeAnna explained that everything was ready.

"I guess you both can fix your husbands' a plate and Kimberly and I will fix the rest," DeAnna said as she grabbed the plates out of Eric hand.

"Honey do what you want to do, but they are grown men, let them fix it themselves," Tesha responded.

"I like DeAnna's idea better," Eric quickly interjected.

"Me to," Malcolm said as he smiled and looked lovingly at his wife.

"You should be kissing up to me," Lesia said as she rolled her eyes at Malcolm and waited for his objection.

Malcolm knew that if he did not fix her a plate, there would be an argument and he had a feeling that an argument was the excuse she was waiting for, to leave. *She is not going to get one today* he thought to himself.

"Okay, honey one plate coming up. What do you want?"

"Just fix your own plate. Don't worry about me. I'm not as helpless as you might think," Lesia said.

Malcolm was used to his wife's objections to his offers of assistance. He knew that it was her way of continuing to make him suffer. He preferred to keep their personal business and arguments private, but she had a way of making a point and showing off in front of his friends. They had become accustomed to her blatant disrespect to her husband.

DeAnna could not help but to think that if this was how she reacted in public with her husband, it was only a matter of time before she was going to completely push him out of her life. DeAnna fixed the plate for Jeremy and then one for Johnathan and delivered it to them.

"She really is the maid," Lesia said to Tesha as they watched in amazement as DeAnna placed Jeremy's plate in front of him. She appeared to be whispering something in his ear.

"Hamburger at eleven o'clock, hotdog at one o'clock, mac and cheese at three, potatoes salad at nine, and chicken at six. If you forget, the meat forms a Y. The plate is about 3 inched from the edge of the table, so if any food falls off the spoon it will hit the table and not your lap," DeAnna whispered in Jeremy's ear. She knew that he would not want anyone feeding him like he was a child.

"Thank you so much, you just don't know what this mean to me," he whispered in her ear. "I think I need to keep you."

DeAnna walked back into the house as quickly as she could. She didn't want anyone see her face lit up like Christmas lights. Lord, I hope he does really does want to keep me, she said as she entered the kitchen. Kimberly gave Chris and Myles a plate. Eric and Malcolm had fixed their own plates.

The guys offered to move over to make room for the wives outside, but the wives declined. They sat at the dining room table. Kimberly fixed a plate and headed to the family room. DeAnna made sure Jeremy had everything he needed then she went inside and fixed herself a plate. She hesitantly walked into the family room with Kimberly.

"He doesn't care," Kimberly said, sensing DeAnna's hesitation to eat in the family room.

"Why don't we just join the other ladies?" DeAnna questioned.

"Trust me, it's better if we don't."

"Come on," DeAnna said as she turned around and headed for the dining room. "Mind if we join you?" DeAnna politely asked as she set her plate down and pulled the chair out.

"No, by all means, have a seat. It is practically your house, or so it seems," Tesha said, rolling her eyes and staring at Lesia for back-up.

DeAnna wondered why they seem to be so territorial.

"Wait, tell me again, what did you say your name is?" Lesia asked DeAnna without acknowledging Tesha's comment or stares.

"DeAnna."

"Why do you look so familiar?" Lesia asked.

"I was Jeremy's nurse," DeAnna said.

"Oh right. Well, it's nice to officially meet you," Lesia said.

Tesha shot Lesia another disapproving look. DeAnna thought about what Kimberly had mentioned to her about the two ladies. It was easy to see that Lesia was probably a nice person but putting on her independent tough girl act as a camouflage for her pain.

I'm not in competition with these ladies, DeAnna told herself, but she was too familiar with women who had low self-esteem or women who, in order to deal with the pain of infidelity and so many other relationships issues, always seemed to view all other women as competition or a threat to their relationship.

"So, you change his bed pan?" Tesha teased.

"No, by the time he got to my unit, he was mobile," DeAnna replied.

"Lucky you," Tesha said, seeming disappointed that her attempt to insult DeAnna had failed.

"I'd like to think of it as a blessing for Jeremy," DeAnna replied.

"So," Lesia interrupted. "Do you like the nursing field, and do you meet lots of good-looking doctors?" Lesia asked.

"I can't tell you how many times I have been asked that question, but yes, I do meet a lot of good-looking eligible doctors."

Tesha could tell that Lesia was not going to go along with the mean girl routine. Lesia did not want to be mad with anybody other than her husband. She was quite tired of being mean to him. Lesia enjoyed taking to DeAnna. It was refreshing to talk to someone who didn't seem mad all the time or acted as if she hated men. Lesia realized that most of the time she had allowed Tesha to caused her to stay mad at Malcolm. Tesha was constantly reminding Lesia of why Malcolm should be kissing her behind. Lesia would go along with it as if it was a joke, but she was tired of going home and ending up having arguments about how she often tried to embarrass him.

Chapter 9

"Who in the world is calling me at this time of the morning?" DeAnna asked. She glanced from the ringing phone to the clock hanging on the wall? She looked at the caller ID, but she didn't recognize the number. She contemplated not answering it but decided it might be an emergency.

"Hello," she said answering the phone on the fourth ring.
"DeAnna, I need to talk to you."

It had been over two weeks since the cookout at Jeremy's and DeAnna had not seen nor talked to Kimberly, although she spent three days a week at Jeremy's house. DeAnna knew Kimberly's voice instantly and could tell that she was crying. She also knew that things had not gotten any better, nor had they got any worst, based on what she heard Myles telling Malcolm as they watched a movie at Jeremy's one night. DeAnna had cooked a home cooked meal and Jeremy could not wait to brag to the guys. Chris, Malcolm, and Myles were ringing the doorbell before the dinner plates had hit the table. Chris was on his way to work, so he took a plate to go. Myles and Malcolm stayed to be companions to Jeremy. As they talked and DeAnna washed dishes, she heard them talking about the fact that Jason was still working overtime, but just couldn't seem to keep ahead of the bills.

"Sweetie, what's wrong?" DeAnna asked in a soft motherly voice.
"I am so sorry for calling you so late or should I say so early in the morning, but I didn't know what else to do or who else to talk to."
"What's wrong honey, where are you?" DeAnna questioned.
"I've just been riding around. I can't stay home. I cannot go to my brother's house nor," Kimberly paused. "I hate them," she blurted out.
"Who sweetie? Who do you hate?"
"All of them, my no-good husband, my brother, Myles, I hate them all," Kimberly screamed in the phone uncontrollably.
"Why? What happened? Honey, where are you?"
"I was headed to Jeremy's house, but he's in it too," Kimberly said.
"I have no one, no mother, no father, no brother, no friends, and," Kimberly paused then finished. "And I have no husband."

"Kimberly, listen to me sweetheart. You're upset, and I don't want anything to happen to you, okay. Take a moment to calm down. Get yourself together. Breathe. Just take a few deep breaths." DeAnna listened to her breathing. "Okay, now come to my place."

DeAnna gave Kimberly the address to her apartment. She stayed on the phone with her until she heard Kimberly pulling in the driveway. She quickly ran to open the door for her. When Kimberly entered, she practically collapsed in DeAnna's arms. DeAnna noticed that Kimberly was driving Jeremy's truck.

"Come in," DeAnna said, ushering Kimberly into the living room and directed her to sit down. DeAnna got a white wash cloth out of the linen closet, wet it with warm water, and handed it to Kimberly. "Wash your face, sweetheart, and I'll put some coffee on. Are you hungry?"

DeAnna fixed a plate for Kimberly and placed it in the microwave. She already had a cup of coffee ready even though she wasn't sure if Kimberly liked coffee. When the food was warm, DeAnna gave it to her and sat down. She urged her to eat something first, to give herself a moment to think. Kimberly resisted at first, but once she tasted DeAnna's meatloaf, she couldn't resist trying the collard greens, the garlic potatoes with gravy, and the corn bread.

"I wish I could cook like this," Kimberly said, dipping the meatloaf in the gravy.

"Practice makes perfect," DeAnna said.

"Well, I would not know where to even begin," Kimberly replied. Her thoughts of food instantly faded. She placed her hand over her face and burst into tears.

"Oh, honey," DeAnna replied. "What's wrong? I can't stand to see you looking like this." DeAnna tried to fight back her own tears as she wrapped her arms around Kimberly and softly rocked her back and forth. DeAnna could feel Kimberly warm tears as they rolled down Kimberly's face and hit DeAnna's thin satin nightgown. Kimberly felt DeAnna's tears too."

"What's wrong with you?" Kimberly asked.

"Honey, I'm sorry, I just hate to see people in pain. My heart cries for you. Is there anything I can do to help you? Do you want to talk? When I went through my little ordeal with my ex, I prayed and praised a lot. The more I praised God, the easier it became. His goodness and mercy are our ever presence help. So even if you don't want to talk about it, we can pray."

"I just can't believe that they all knew. They all knew." Kimberly kept repeating.

"Who knew and what did they know? If you don't mind me asking?"

"They all knew about Danielle and Jason," Kimberly said with bitterness in her voice.

"What about them, and who is Danielle?" DeAnna questioned.

"Jason had an affair and they all knew. They even played ball with her at the gym."

"How do you know?"

"Jennifer told me."

"Who is Jennifer?"

"She is my," Kimberly paused to think of how to explain who she was to her. "Well, she was my best friend. She is part of the reason Jeremy got shot. She's known as a home-wrecker, which is the reason she's no longer my friend. Jennifer introduced Jason and Danielle, then she became my friend, so she could keep tabs on me and, I guess she kept tabs on Jason too," Kimberly explained.

DeAnna stroke Kimberly's hair as Kimberly told her about the affair. DeAnna could not believe that Danielle and her friend had the nerve to come to Kimberly's birthday party and pretend that they were at the wrong house.

"How does your brother, Myles, and the others all fit into this and why do you hate them?" DeAnna questioned.

"Well, yesterday, I took Jeremy's truck to make groceries for him, and when I was pulling out of the parking lot, I saw some girls waving at me. The windows are tinted so they could not tell who was in the truck, but I stopped. One of the girls got out and ran up to the truck. I put the window down. Boy, was she surprised to see me. The same girl that came to my house. She introduced herself as a friend of Jeremy's who played ball with him at the gym. She thought I was his girlfriend, so she quickly explained that nothing was going on between them. Then when I got home Jennifer, called and said that she had something to tell me. She told me that the girl I met, did play ball with the guys, but she was also the one who slept with Jason."

"Why did she tell you?" DeAnna asked.

"I don't know. I think Jennifer got jealous when she saw that I had Jeremy's truck. Jennifer is in love with him and Myles, but Myles can't stand her. He was the one who started the homewrecker tagline; I think. Jeremy is nice to her, but I don't think he likes her either."

"Okay, remember the questions I told you to ask yourself that day at the cookout?" DeAnna asked.

"Yes, and I did ask myself and I do want this marriage or at least I did before I knew the truth."

"Have you talked to Jason?"

"No, I waited for him to come home and by the time he did, I was so hot with him, I just left. I couldn't stand the thought of him telling me lies. I just…" Kimberly couldn't fight the flood of tears. "I hate them all. I wish…" she stopped instantly and began to cry uncontrollably.

DeAnna grabbed Kimberly's hand and prayed for her. She asked God to heal her broken heart and comfort her. She prayed that God would give her the peace that surpass all understanding.

"Kimberly, you don't have to decide now, but you need to think about your marriage. Is it worth saving? I have a feeling that your husband is avoiding you because he cannot face what he has done. He's probably punishing himself more than you ever could," DeAnna said and then paused and looked at Kimberly. "I'm willing to bet he's hurting too."

"Good, he needs to hurt just as much as I am. More!" Kimberly yelled.

"Why don't you sleep here tonight but call him and let him know where you are," DeAnna suggested.

"Why should I? He didn't call me to let me know," Kimberly angrily replied. "Oh, I almost forgot the best part. You're not going to believe this; I heard he has a child by her. No DNA test to prove it, but they say he looks like… just like Jason."

"Oh no," DeAnna said, shaking her head and brushing another tear away from her own eyes. She remembered the hurt that she felt when she found out about her ex fiancée's expecting girlfriend. Her first-born child, she always wanted with her man, was the child that was conceived without her. DeAnna silently questioned *'Why God? Why am I suddenly thrown into this? Why do I have to be reminded of the most painful part of my life?*

126

Why me? Why do I have to feel this pain all over again?' DeAnna heard a voice. She did not know if it was her own or if it was God, but she heard, *'Because you felt this same pain, you can feel her pain, she needs someone to truly understand what she is feeling right now.'*

"Do you love him?" DeAnna asked point-blank. She wasn't going to let Kimberly make the same mistake she had made when she let the love of her life go because her pride wouldn't allow her to forgive him. This was her second chance to save a marriage, even if it wasn't her own. "Do you love him?" She repeated with a firm, but loving voice.

"Yes! I love him," Kimberly said with tears rolling down her face as if floodgates had been opened again. "I know I don't always tell him or even act like it, but I do. I love him so much."

"Okay sweetie, it is gonna hurt to hear the true, but you are going to have to ask him and ..." DeAnna paused to make sure she worded her next statement just right. "You have to start being honest with yourself."

"Me, honest with me?" Kimberly questioned, sounding confused.

"Yes, you. It may not be right, but men sometimes cheat because of the things we do. Once again," DeAnna continued over-talking Kimberly's pending objection. "I know it is not right, and we get mad at them too and even if we don't cheat on them, we feel we would be justified if we did. We do other things to get back at them, like stop cooking and cleaning. We don't come home for long periods of time. We stop talking to them and even stop making love to them. Which is a sin too."

"A sin? Yeah right," Kimberly said, looking at DeAnna in disbelief.

"Well, actually the Bible calls it fraud. Now, of course that's for married people only. Single people should withhold it until they are married."

"I'm guilty of that, but why would I want to be with him, knowing he's been with someone else?"

"Believe me, I understand why, AIDS is taking too many people outta here. This is no time for playing games," DeAnna said. "But that's why you have to talk to him. Let him know why, no cookie or nookie."

DeAnna carefully explained to Kimberly that the fight for her marriage would not be easy.

"Even if he wants the marriage, he may be tempted to stray again, but temptation is not a sin and even though we don't like the fact that our man wants another woman, he can resist it. God will make a way of escape. You have to make it hard for him to want to lose you," DeAnna told her. She explained that the first step to recovery is talking. She explained the importance of having a heart-to-heart talk and being completely honest with her husband.

Kimberly checked her cell phone when she felt it vibrating. She knew that the only person that would be calling her at that time of the night was her husband. She quickly placed the phone on the table. She didn't even want to see his name on the caller ID.

"It's him?" DeAnna questioned.

"Yes, but I don't want to talk to him right now," Kimberly responded.

"Honey the fight starts now. The devil isn't giving you a head start. He going to use every bit of leverage he already has. Answer it and just let him know that you are okay. Tell him you need time to think. He's probably sitting home right now thinking the worst. He's probably thinking that you're either with another man or…"

"Good," Kimberly shouted.

"No, not good. First of all, if you want that man back, the last thing you want him to think is that you are with another man. Men cannot handle that as well as women can. If you want him back, you have to help keep the foundation that's left and rebuild a solid foundation of trust with what you have. Don't help him lose trust in you. I know he is the one who betrayed your trust, but don't make him think that you are betraying his. Pay back might seem like a good idea, but it's a costly one. This is not a game. It's a war and the devil is the puppet master of evil tricks. And trust me, payback never works out as well as we expect it to work out."

Kimberly wanted to object, but she knew it was pointless. DeAnna was not like most friends, who would tell you what you wanted to hear or who would be on your side if you felt justified in cheating on your husband because your husband cheated on you. No! Not DeAnna.

Kimberly looked down at the phone. She thought he would give up calling back by now, but he was calling again for the third time in ten minutes. She answered the phone and let her husband know that she was okay. He explained that he wanted her to come home, but she refused. He then asked where she was and if he could come to her, so that they could talk.

"You want to come here?" She repeated as she looked at DeAnna, hoping she would refuse. DeAnna looked at Kimberly and knobbed her head yes.

DeAnna was tired and sleepy, and wanted to go to bed, but she couldn't stand to see Kimberly hurt and she knew that Jason needed to be reassured that Kimberly was not with a man somewhere. "Give him the address," DeAnna whispered. DeAnna knew that being on neutral ground would make things easier for Kimberly, but perhaps a little uncomfortable for Jason. *It will probably eliminate their desire to yell or even curse at each other*, DeAnna thought to herself. She had never heard any of them curse, but she wasn't sure if it was because they were showing her respect.

Kimberly agreed to talk to her husband, but she didn't want to keep DeAnna up, so she told him to pick her up, and they could go somewhere to talk. Ten minutes later he was pulling up in the driveway. He did not even bother coming to the door; he blew the car horn. Kimberly instantly wanted to change her mind. *Why can't he get out and come to the door like a gentleman,* she thought. Kimberly decided to force him to come to the door by refusing to go out until he came to the door to get her. After honking his horn for the third time, Jason finally got out of the car and came to the door. He rang the doorbell. Kimberly couldn't move. She suddenly felt paralyzed. DeAnna went to answer the door and let Jason in. Kimberly quickly ran to the bathroom to wash her face. She didn't want him to see that she had been crying.

DeAnna introduced herself to Jason, then remembered that they had met at Jeremy's. She escorted him to the sofa and explained to him that Kimberly would be out in a few minutes.

"I've heard a lot of good things about you," Jason said to DeAnna as he flipped through a magazine that was lying on the coffee table. He was turning the pages so hard, he almost ripped one out of the book. "Can I ask you a question?" He asked DeAnna.

DeAnna stood in shock. She barely knew Kimberly and didn't know Jason at all, and now she felt like Mother Teresa or the marriage counselor to them both. *Maybe it was something simple*, she thought. *Might not even pertain to the issues between him and Kimberly*. "Sure," DeAnna hesitantly replied. She sat down in the love seat across from were Jason sat with his head down.

"How do you convince someone that you love them with your entire heart after you've hurt them beyond belief?" He asked without lifting his head.

"You have to make her, I mean them, feel that they're the only one for you and the only one that you love and want. You have to constantly tell and show her that no one has your attention the way she does. Women want to feel loved even when they have messed up or don't do the things you expect them to do. The same way men want their woman stroking their ego; a woman wants her man making her feel like she's worth sacrificing everything for. You just can't run to another woman when you're upset, disappointed, hurt, lonely, or intoxicated. Whatever the reason you use, nothing is ever a good reason to us. No excuse is ever good enough to run to another woman," DeAnna said without thinking.

"I get that, but I already messed up. I made one mistake, and it seems that I'm going to be punished for the rest of my life," Jason said, talking more to himself and not DeAnna.

"Who's punishing you?" DeAnna questioned.

"Well, I mean," Jason looked up. He didn't know and didn't want to answer the question.

"The longer you carry this around, hiding it, you are punishing yourself. You made a mistake; you need forgiveness, just like all the rest of us. Man, you first have to forgive yourself."

"I can't lose her," Jason said as he began rocking back and forth. "I am so sorry I hurt her. I love her more than life itself," he said as the tears began to form in his eyes.

Kimberly stood in the hall listening to Jason. She wanted to run to him and tell him that she didn't want to lose him either. She wanted to wrap her arms around him and tell him that she loved him too, but she didn't want to make things easy for him either. The loving feelings lasted about fifteen seconds and quickly faded. She instantly remembered what her mom used to say, 'don't let the devil steal your joy.' "I wonder if that includes your husbands too," she silently questioned. She slowly walked down the hall listening to Jason talk to DeAnna as if she were a marriage counselor.

"I'm not even going to lie like most men would and claim I was intoxicated. I wasn't, but I was hurt. It's hard always being compared to Jeremy and Myles. Oh, and let's not forget the perfect Chris. The quiet, humble man, who says little, but each word delivered with love and passion," Jason said with resentment in his voice. "How can I live up to all her big brothers?"

"So, you feel that you are expected to fill their shoes."

"Yep, I mean most of her life it's like she has had six big brothers and regardless of what they have done, they are all viewed as good men. They are some sort of the standard. Jeremy has this... Malcolm does that for his wife. Oh, and Myles the lover, who never seem to have a love for long, just makes me think he waited for her to grow up to," Jason paused. "No matter what they do, they are forgiven by her, but me... I'm a good man too, but because she's my wife, she cannot forgive me as easily. I don't... don't want to be compared to anyone. I am my own man. Yes, I know, there's a lot I have to learn, but..."

"But what?" Kimberly asked as she walked in the room.

Jason stood up and turned to face his wife.

"But I'm learning. Maybe not as fast as you might want me to, but I am learning," Jason said.

"What is there to learn? You mean to tell me someone actually has to teach you how to be a faithful husband?" Kimberly questioned and then paused. "Wait! Listen to me accusing you," she sarcastically said. She wanted him to admit it himself. She stared at him waiting and hoping that he would tell her that it was not true, that he had not cheated and that he was a faithful man.

"Look," Jason said as he gently grabbed Kimberly and pulled her down on the sofa. "I love you. I have never loved anyone the way I love you. I've loved you since I was old enough to know what love was-is, but sometimes you make me feel that I'm not good enough for you."

"No, I don't," Kimberly replied.

"Baby, I'm trying to tell you how I feel and even if you didn't mean to do it, you make me feel like I am not good enough. I cannot tell you how many times I have had to hear, 'Chris has a master's degree.' He's building a house from the ground up. When the house was built, it was 'Chris is going to do this for his daughter'...blah, blah, blah."

"I just hope that you would be inspired to look at your options. You're twelve years younger and by the time you hit 34 you –we can have all he has and so much more. Chris says that all the time, that you have so many options, so much potential and that he hopes you don't wait like he did."

"Maybe I don't want his life," Jason said and looked at Kimberly. "Did you ever think about that?"

"So, you want to live in that tiny house and pay rent for the rest of your life?" Kimberly asked. "Is that the master plan?"

"No, I don't, but baby I just don't see why we should have to move to only the beat of your drum, especially since I'm going to be the one who has to pay all the bills. It's like you want to do everything, but..." Jason paused because he felt himself getting angry. He promised himself that he would not get mad.

Kimberly stood up and put her hands on her hip as if it would somehow mean that she was serious. "And I want my own house. I want children too and you don't. Why? Or do you just want me to be step-mommy dearest to your illegitimate child?" Kimberly could tell that Jason was upset, but she knew she had reason to be mad as well. She was not going to let him play the innocent victim. "And don't change the subject this time, like you always do," she replied.

"Okay-okay, Kimberly, you want the truth, well sit down because I'm going to tell you everything. I wasn't ready to get married, but I didn't want to keep doing what I, we, were doing. I hated sneaking around with you and hoping your bodyguards wouldn't find out. So, I ask you to marry me. Then..."

"So, you really didn't want to marry me, just have legal sex with me?" Kimberly interrupted and asked.

"No, I mean yes. Well, I did want you to be my wife, but I wanted to wait a year or two."

"Oh, I see," Kimberly interrupted again. "So, you could run around a little before settling down. Sow your wild oats."

"No," Jason snapped.

"Really?"

"Now see Kimberly, this is why we have some of the problems that we have. Do you realize that you have no faith in me to do the right thing?" Jason paused to see if she would interrupt again before he continued. "And you won't even allow me to finish my own thoughts or sentences. I was going to say, I wanted to be more financially stable before getting married.

"And I have reason not to trust your judgment," Kimberly replied.

"You do now, but you didn't have faith in me from the beginning."

"Yes, I did," Kimberly replied.

"When? When have you ever had faith in me? You acted like you had to check every single thing I did with Chris or Eric," Jason paused. He pondered telling her how he felt about Jeremy and Myles. "You act like you were more in love with Jeremy and Myles than me. How do I compete with that?"

"They are like brothers to me,"

"And you look at them with so much love, admiration, and so much more respect. What man, what husband can handle his wife giving that to everyone, everyone but him?" He said, sounding like it was more of a statement than a question.

"I married you, so now why are you changing the subject to them," Kimberly said, hoping to get back to talking about the rumors of the baby."

"I'm not changing the subjects; you just keep interrupting me," Jason stated in a matter-of-fact tone.

"Sorry! By all means- finish," Kimberly said.

"As I was saying, I did and still do love you. It's just, I was not ready for marriage, but I wanted to do the right thing. I was not raised up to just fornicate. It was like disrespect to the one I claimed that I love, you. The Bible calls it defiling the body. We are where we are now, because I just got tired of being compared to one of them. I got tired of being treated like a child who could not cross the street without holding my mommy's hand. I work all day and when I come home, I get grilled about everything. 'Did you pay this? Did you pay that? Did you ever think to just simply pick up the phone and call to see if the bills had been paid? I mean you were not working. Baby, did you ever think to take the credit card out your purse and pay the bill yourself. We are in this together. I got so tired of coming home after working nine, ten, sometimes twelve hours a day and having to cook hot dogs or wait for you to cook something, anything. All you did for months was watch those Lyfetime movies. You know the ones that made men out to be wimps. A man working to put a woman in a beautiful home, so she can complain that he's never there. Men work 40, 60, or 80 hours a week to provide a beautiful life with nice cars, vacations that people only dream of, just to listen to their woman complaining. Is that what you want to be like? Never once have I heard any of those women say 'honey, I'll work full time so that I can help pay some of these bills. Or let's move into a small two-bedroom, 1500 square-foot home, so you can quit working at least one of the jobs that you're working and then we can have some quality time, other than the three vacation we take a year," Jason said trying to sound like a snobbish woman from one of the movies. "Stop living alone in that lyfetime fancy world of spoiled, self-centered, male-bashing women." Jason paused for a few minutes and studied his wife's face. "So, Kimberly, here comes the part that I guess you have been waiting to hear. I met Danielle at one of my friend's house. She gave me her number. I had it for three or four days, then one day, I came home late and you were out at yet another church function, nothing had been cooked and I remember telling you that I wanted to grab a movie and just snuggle up and hold you. I had already been feeling the distance and I was afraid of losing you. When I opened the door, and found an empty home again, I just got fed up.

"So, it's my fault?" Kimberly interrupted again.

Jason didn't say anything for a long time. He looked at the tears forming in Kimberly's eyes. He knew that he had to be honest. He had to get it out, even if it meant that it was the end of his marriage. He wanted to hold her one and kiss her one last time. He stood up and pulled his keys out of his pocket. He kneeled in front of Kimberly, grabbed her arms, and forced them around his neck. He wrapped his arms around her waist and held her tightly, as he squeezed her, he whispered in her ear that he would always love her.

"Just say it," Kimberly whispered.

Jason couldn't resist, he kissed his wife with all the passion that he had. Kimberly kissed him as tears rolled from her eyes and down her cheek. Jason released her from the kiss and wiped her tears away with his cheek.

"Just say it!" She demanded. "Just say it," she said a second time and pushed him away from her. "Just say it," she yelled a third time.

DeAnna slowly entered the room. Jason stood facing DeAnna. He didn't even remember her leaving the room. He looked at DeAnna with tears running down his face. He didn't care. "Can she stay with you tonight?" He asked DeAnna.

"Just say it," Kimberly said, as if she had no more energy in her body.

"Yes, Jason," DeAnna replied. "She can stay here, but it is not fair to leave her like this. She has a right to know."

"She already knows," Jason said as he looked down at Kimberly. He kissed the tear that sat on her cheek, refusing to fall. "She knows," he said again.

"She needs to hear it from you. Even though she thinks she knows, she still believes in you enough not to totally believe what others have told her. She needs you to help her begin to face this and learn how to deal with it. That cannot happen until she hears the truth from you. It's not fair to give other people the upper hand, by knowing something about her husband that she doesn't know."

"You're right," Jason said to DeAnna and then turned and looked at Kimberly. "I don't know what you've been told, but yes I was with Danielle one time."

"Why?" Kimberly screamed out. "Why would you do that to me? I never once looked at or even thought about being with another man."

"Honey that night," Jason paused to search for the right words to say. "I don't know why I called her, but when I got to her apartment, she made me feel wanted, welcomed, and," Jason paused to think if he wanted to finish telling his wife how another woman made him feel. "Well," he said deciding to get all the secrets out now. "And like a real man. She cooked for me, listened to me…"

"So, she gave you a meal and an ear and you gave her a child. Something you don't even want with me."

"I slept with her, okay! And even though it's not going to make a difference to you, I laid in her arms and I cried because I hated myself. I hated her. I even hated how you made me feel."

"So once again you're blaming me?" Kimberly asked. "You are…"

"Say it," Jason said as he shook his head. "Say it Kimberly. I was expecting to hear it from you tonight anyway. You think I haven't heard you tell your friends what a sorry husband I am?" The flashbacks raced to Jason's head of the many times he'd overheard Kimberly put him down. She would then jump up and give him a kiss when she realized that he had quietly walked in the house. "He acts like a little boy," Jason said to let

Kimberly know that he knew how she felt about him. "I pretended that I had just walked in and that I didn't hear you, but Kimberly I heard you. Heard you plenty of times. Now, so I won't be accused of changing the topic, let me go on. I only visited her one time. She treated me like I was a king. Why couldn't you have treated me like I really meant something to you? Other than just being your husband, seems you women like that title- my husband, more than you like having a husband. Why couldn't you just believe in me like she did?" Jason said as he slowly walked towards the door. DeAnna followed him.

"I am sorry; I didn't mean to…" Jason words faded as if he had no more energy to speak.

"It's okay," DeAnna replied. "She will be fine here for a few days. You did the right thing. If she takes you back, you won't have any secrets, right?"

Jason stop suddenly. He realized that the worst was almost behind him, but he had one more thing that he had to confess. "Do you mind if I keep you up for a few minutes longer? I have one more thing I need to tell her?"

"Sure," DeAnna said as she sighted. She knew that Jason had not told everything. "It may not seem like it now, but this could be a new and better beginning."

"You really think so?" Jason questioned, not sounding so sure.

"Yes, I do," DeAnna said as they turned around and walked back to the living room. "You made a mistake, but you have done more than most men would have. You're being honest. It might be hard to believe now, but eventually she will forgive you and you need to forgive yourself. Give her a little time but take this advice from someone who's been through it. Don't give up on her. Fight to the end. Make her feel that she's the only one and you are willing to do anything to be with her once again. We women love it when a man fights for our love. Even if she doesn't give it back- the love, give her all you have. Pray and trust God. God won't fix your marriage, but he'll definitely give you the tools you need to begin the reconstruction yourself. He's the master of love, seek Him for guidance."

Once Jason was back in the living-room, facing Kimberly and DeAnna had gone back to her bedroom, Jason looked Kimberly eye-to-eye. "Baby, I hope you'll find it in your heart to forgive me someday. I know that you did the best you knew how to do as a wife. And I had no right to expect so much from you; we were and still are both young. I am begging you to please, please don't make any hasty decisions." Jason paused to build up the nerves to finish. "I do have one more thing to confess. I have been working a lot of overtime, of course you know that, but the reason why you cannot tell, is because, I have been giving the extra money to Danielle to care for her...our... son."

Kimberly put her hands over her face and cried uncontrollably. She pulled her knees to her chest, rocked back and forth, cried, and moaned. Jason wanted to comfort her but decided against it. He knew that she probably wouldn't even want him touching her. Her sobbing grew louder and louder. DeAnna quickly returned.

"Jason, maybe you should leave now," DeAnna said in a soft voice. She hugged Jason with a tight motherly hug. He tried to control himself, but he couldn't. He cried too. "Don't worry," DeAnna whispered. "Trust God and pray. I'm gonna pray for you both. I'll talk to her and help her to understand that you are good man. I can see that, even if she can't right now. You just made a mistake."

Chapter 10

"Hello," Kimberly said, answering the phone on the third ring.

"Hey, beautiful."

"Hey," Kimberly replied as she wiped her flour-covered hands on her pink apron.

"What are you up to?" The caller asked.

"You are not going to believe this but, DeAnna is teaching me how to cook meatloaf," Kimberly said in a matter-of-fact tone and without a hint of friendliness in her voice.

"What! You?" The caller responded. "What y'all going to cook to go with the meatloaf?"

"Cabbages and stewed potatoes," Kimberly replied.

"I sure would love to be there to see you cooking."

"So, what's up," Kimberly asked the caller.

"Nothing, just checking on you."

"I'm fine," she snapped back in an annoyed tone.

"Good, let me speak with DeAnna."

Kimberly handed DeAnna the phone without saying another word.

"How's she really doing?" The caller asked as soon as DeAnna was on the line.

"I'm doing fine," DeAnna responded, indicating to the caller that she was not able to talk about Kimberly, since Kimberly was standing right in front of her face. "Give me a minute, let me go check my calendar," she said as she glanced at Kimberly and walked down the hall to her bedroom. When she got to her room, she eased the door closed. "She's fine," DeAnna said as she laid across her bed. I think she's coming around. They have been talking almost every day. I even heard her laugh at one of his corny jokes."

"Well, I want you to know that I really appreciate all you have done to help her. I can tell that you are a good influence on them both."

"Thanks. You know," DeAnna said and then paused. She wasn't sure whether she should ask or not. She didn't want to seem to be pushy. *What the heck*, she said to herself. "I really get a lot of advice from listening to my pastor. Kimberly is going to church with me this Sunday. You should come too," DeAnna said and then quickly said a silent prayer. *Please let him say yes, Lord.*

"Maybe I will," the caller replied.

That's better than a flat out-No! DeAnna said to herself. She tried to think of something else to say. She didn't want to hang up. "Oh, I'm planning something tonight and I could use your help."

"What?"

"I have been teaching Kimberly to cook, as she just told you. Well, I'm planning on inviting Jason over for dinner tonight," DeAnna paused to try to figure out how to ask for help without sounding like she had motives other than setting Jason and Kimberly up on a not-so-blind-blind-date.

"How can I help?"

"Well, I need a reason to suddenly leave, once Jason gets here," DeAnna said.

"Oh, so I'm gonna need your help tonight, huh?"

"Great minds think alike," DeAnna replied.

"Okay, well I think I can handle that. So, what time will I be needing you?"

"Jeremy, I will need you," DeAnna paused to re-gain her focus. The *words I will need you* sent chills over her body. "Uh, maybe around 6:30 will be a good time. Jason should be just getting off work; he'll be hungry and tired. I even got a great movie for them to watch while they eat and relax."

"So, you're playing matchmaker to a husband and a wife," Jeremy said, and laughed.

"Look, those kids are too young to end up in Divorce Court over one big mistake and a few pity ones."

"A huge mistake," Jeremy reminded DeAnna.

"Yeah, it was kind of a whopper, but not an unforgivable one."

"Okay, so I'll call you in a few."

"Perfect," DeAnna said.

DeAnna made another call and then returned to the kitchen just in time to see that Kimberly was panicking because something was burning. DeAnna grabbed the oven mitts and opened the oven door. The grease from the meatloaf was spilling over onto the bottom of the oven. DeAnna showed Kimberly that everything was smoky, but fine. She proceeded to show her how to make homemade gravy.

Kimberly followed DeAnna's instructions. She put the frying pan on the stove and set the heat on medium high. Once the pan was hot, she poured the grease in the pan. She sprinkled a spoonful of flour into the hot grease as DeAnna had showed her. She carefully stirred the flour around in the grease until it had turned dark brown.

"I've never heard of anybody letting the pan get hot before putting the grease in it," Kimberly said. "Most of the time people put the grease in the cold pan and let the grease and the pan get hot together."

"I got that tip from a famous chef who I saw one time at a cooking presentation at Wesleyan College. He cooked right one stage. We all got to sample his cooking. Chef Jerome Brown, girl that man is fine too," DeAnna said, watching Kimberly sprinkling salt, pepper, and onion soup mix in the gravy. Kimberly poured the water in the pan and lowed the heat. As the mixture changed a few shades lighter, Kimberly poured in chopped onions that she sautéed earlier. She slowly stirred the mixture until it was the perfect texture. DeAnna smiled at Kimberly as a sign of approval. Kimberly smiled back feeling a sense of accomplishment.

~

The phone rang, and Kimberly quickly answered it, then passed it to DeAnna, and continued to stir the gravy. After a few minutes on the phone, DeAnna turned toward Kimberly with a look of concern on her face.

"Okay, I'll be right there," DeAnna said.

"What's going on?" Kimberly asked, sensing that something was wrong.

"It's Jeremy. He needs my help," DeAnna said as she quickly grabbed her keys and her purse. "I'll be right back. Maybe I can get him out of the house and over here to taste your masterpiece."

"Why don't you pack it up and take it to him?" Kimberly suggested.

"No, I don't think that's a good idea, I need to get there ASAP."

"But, I cooked all this food," Kimberly tried to protest, but DeAnna didn't' stop heading for the door. "I don't want to eat alone."

"I'll be back in a few, Sweetie," DeAnna said. "I can't wait to taste it. It all looks and smells so delicious. Your mother would be so proud of you."

As DeAnna was about to grab the doorknob, the doorbell rang. "I'll get it," she yelled to Kimberly

"Jason. What are you doing here?" DeAnna yelled loud enough for Kimberly to hear, acting shocked to see him. "Kimberly is in the kitchen. Come on in."

Jason looked at DeAnna with a confused look on his face. He glanced at her purse and keys. "But I thought..."

"Jason look, I'll be right back," DeAnna said as she pointed to the kitchen. "Go talk to your wife. She just cooked a delicious meal and I have an emergency. I would hate for her to have to eat alone." DeAnna didn't wait for a response from Jason, she walked out and closed the door behind her.

"Wow, smells great," Jason said as he hesitantly walked into the kitchen. "You cooked all this?" Jason questioned, scanning the food.

Kimberly couldn't contain her excitement even though she wanted to act cool around Jason. She didn't want him to get the wrong impression, as if everything was okay.

"Yes," she replied with a smile on her face. "I cooked all of this. DeAnna has been giving me cooking lessons."

"Jason," DeAnna yelled as she re-entered the house. "I need your help. Do you know anything about cars?"

"What's up," Jason said as he turned to face DeAnna.

"My car won't start, and I need to get to Jeremy's right away."

"Why don't you take Jeremy's truck back?" Kimberly said as she grabbed the keys off the key hook on the kitchen wall. She tossed them to DeAnna. "I've been meaning to return it, but since he doesn't need it, I didn't see a real big rush. Selfish, I know, but I was sort of mad at him too."

"Are you sure that Jeremy won't mind?" DeAnna questioned.

"Mind! Are you kidding me?" Kimberly chuckled. "That man is practically in love with you."

"What?" DeAnna laughed, knowing it was a silly thought. "How can he be, girl that man can't even see me. I've only been around him a few dozen times."

"I guess it's now time for me, to educate you," Kimberly jokingly said.

141

"Has he said something to you?" DeAnna asked in a joking manner, but she was seriously wondering.

DeAnna laughed as she walked forward the door. She couldn't get Kimberly's statement out of her head. She knew that Kimberly hadn't spoken to Jeremy much in the last few weeks. Kimberly was still mad at everyone, but she did manage to talk to Jeremy a little bit when he called DeAnna.

"I can tell," Kimberly yelled to DeAnna.
"Jason don't let that beautiful woman of yours eat alone. I will feel so guilty. Please stay with her until I return."

Jason quickly agreed, and Kimberly did not object. Kimberly was about to fix herself a plate, but then she remembered that she wanted corn bread. She had never cooked any before but had already mixed the batter. She looked at the mixture in the bowl and considered making it without instructions from Chef Dee.

"Is everything ready?" Jason asked, not knowing what else to say as he walked back into the kitchen.
"Well, sort of. I was supposed to cook cornbread, but I guess we can just have loaf bread," Kimberly said and made a disapproving face at the thought on loaf bread.
"I used to watch my mother cook it all the time," Jason replied.

Kimberly looked at Jason with a look of disbelief on her face. Jason rolled up his sleeves as he walked over to the sink and washed his hands. He was about to erase the doubt from his wife's head and heart. He put the frying pan on the stove and poured the cooking oil in the pan. Kimberly wanted to tell him that he should have waited until the pan was hot before adding the oil, but she decided to just be quiet and observe. She wanted him to see that she trusted his judgement. Jason found a serving spoon and began to scope out a spoonful of cornbread batter and then dropped it in the pan. He turned them over to brown on both sides. They looked like miniature pancakes. When they were golden brown, Jason removed them from the pan and placed them in a bowl that he had lined with paper towel so that the oil would drain.

Kimberly fixed a plate for Jason and herself. They both went into the living room. She grabbed the movie that was on the table and put it into the DVD player. She laid the remote control beside her plate.

"Finished," Jason yelled.

He bought the small basket of cornbread and set it on the coffee table.

"What do you want to drink?" Kimberly asked. "Milk, water, tea, or water." Kimberly laughed. "I know," Kimberly said as she headed back to the kitchen to fix them both a glass of iced tea. She quickly poured the tea and then joined her husband.

"Maybe we should pray," Kimberly jokingly said. "This is the first time I've ever cooked a real meal. Unless hamburger helper is considered real food."

Jason grabs her hands and blessed the food. It was the first time they had ever prayed together. He said a very short prayer because he was ready to dig in.

"Well, baby let's see what you are made of," Jason said and with no hesitation, he quickly began digging in. They ate in complete silence and watched the DVD that DeAnna apparently left for them to watch. After watching about fifteen minutes, Kimberly was convinced that this whole dinner arrangement was planned. Jason's silence was not due to a lack of words, but because he was too busy eating. Kimberly could tell that Jason really liked her cooking.

"There's more," Kimberly said when she heard the fork scrapping the plate.

"Baby that was sooooo delicious. I have never had meatloaf that good before."

"DeAnna's recipe," she replied.

"Cooked by you, so that makes it even more special," Jason said, slowly turning to look into his wife's eyes.

Kimberly almost ignored Jason's compliment, but she remembered something DeAnna told her. She could hear her voice, '*keep on acting like*

143

you don't appreciate it when he compliments you or says something nice, and he'll stop doing it.'

Kimberly had made up her mind that she loved her husband and she wasn't ready to give up on him so soon. She decided she was going to start showing that she appreciated him. She wasn't ready to accept the child, but she knew she had to start somewhere.

The longer one resists, the longer the devil rejoices, so go on and wipe that silly little grin off the devil's face, and give your husband another chance," Kimberly remembered hearing DeAnna tell her ex-roommate on the phone one day. DeAnna's apartment was like the Underground Railroad for broken marriages. She told Kimberly that her last three roommates had all moved in doing troubled times in their marriages. She had convinced them all to fight for their marriages.

Kimberly smiled at Jason and planted a kiss on his cheek. "Thank you, I'm so glad that you stopped by and stayed to keep me company." She hesitated a moment, trying to think of something else to say. "This was nice; really nice," she said.

"There's no place else I'd rather be," Jason said, feeling more hopeful about his marriage then he had felt in weeks. He smiled as he watched Kimberly gather their plates and take them to the kitchen and set them in the sink.

"Need help with the dishes?" Jason yelled.

"No, I got it," she said thinking about the fact that he had worked all day. "Why don't you just relax; you've worked hard today," Kimberly said remembering that even though she had not been home in a few weeks, other than to get some clothes, Jason still came over and dropped off grocery money and/or gas money for her.

Kimberly looked at all the dirty dishes and quickly retracted her previous statement. "On second thought," she said looking towards her husband. "There are a lot of dishes here," she laughed. "I don't think we even own this many dishes.

"Okay! I gotcha," Jason said as he strolled up behind his wife and gently kissed her on the back of the neck. You are so beautiful," he said as he put his hands around her waist and slowly shifted her body from left to right, rocking her slowly.

"Why don't," Jason began, but stopped.

Kimberly slowly turned around to face him as if to object to his next statement.

"Why don't what?" She asked.
 "Why don't I wash, and you dry," he said and then laughed.
"Fine with me," she quickly agreed. "I know how you hate to dry."

They both laughed.

Chapter 11

DeAnna plopped down on the sofa beside Jeremy.

"I don't know how I'm ever going to repay you for all you've done to make this situation more manageable for me," Jeremy said as he felt DeAnna's presence beside him. He reached out to grab DeAnna's hand. DeAnna matched his effort and reached out and met his hand. Kimberly's statement floated around in her mind all evening. It gave her the courage she needed to allow herself to break down her walls and to be open to accept a new challenge, a blind challenge.

"So, what do you want to do?" Jeremy asked.

"A movie would be nice," DeAnna quickly said.

"Yeah right, for you," Jeremy replied.

"No, it can be nice for both of us," DeAnna said and sort of allowed the word 'us' to linger in the air. She liked the sound of it in conjunction with her and Jeremy's names. "I have an idea," DeAnna said as she looked at the clock. "Oh, wait!" She said remembering that she had not told Jeremy that she had driven his truck and if they went to the movies she'll have to drive his truck again. "Look, I should have called you before I left home," she said.

"What is it?" Jeremy questioned. He sensed the hesitation in her voice and quickly allowed his mind to begin to wonder if she was going to tell him that she had an old boyfriend waiting for her to come back home or wanted her to come over to his house.

"My car wouldn't start, and Kimberly suggested," DeAnna hesitated again.

"I can get Malcolm or even Myles to look at it for you," Jeremy said cutting her off before she had the opportunity to finish.

"Okay, good," she said knowing a car repair bill was the last thing she needed, but hoping the offer came with a discount.

"Have you been having problems prior to tonight?" Jeremy asked.

"No, but that's not what I wanted to tell you," DeAnna said. She was thankful for the interruption which helped her to build up the nerves to just tell him.

"Oh, I'm sorry," Jeremy said. "I have a nasty habit of doing that."

"Well, Kimberly had your truck and," DeAnna started and then stopped to take a deep breath. "Well, she suggested that I," DeAnna paused and said a quick silent prayer. *Lord don't let him get upset. He might think that one of his women might have seen me driving his truck and could get the wrong idea.*

"What is it?" Jeremy asked again.

"Well, Kimberly suggested that I drive your truck back over here," DeAnna finally said.

Jeremy waited, wondering if there was more.

"You're not upset, are you?" DeAnna finally questioned after a few second of silence.

"Upset, why would I be upset? I just didn't want to interrupt you again. I kind of thought you were going to say you wrecked it. Now that might have upset me."

"Well, I should have called you before I left home to at least get your permission. I mean, men are funny about their precious vehicles; it looks like you put a little cash into it. Besides, what if one of your female friends spotted it, with me driving it? You know they know your truck, make, model and tag number," DeAnna said.

"DeAnna, it's okay. Look! Yes, I do spoil myself and I get what I want. I work hard to have what I like and what was in my budget, but I don't idolize that truck. I might not do all I should do, but my mom raised me up right and not to idolize, worship, or praise anything or anyone, only God."

"I was hoping no one who knows you would see me," DeAnna said with a hint of relief in her voice. She was glad he wasn't mad.

"What? Are you ashamed to be associated with me?" Jeremy asked, sounding a little hurt by her statement.

"No-not at all. I was thinking about your women," DeAnna jokingly said.

"What women? Have you seen anyone coming around here trying to help me? I don't get along with fair weather people. I have been there plenty of times when my friends needed me. Now that I am down on my luck, I now see what I really meant to them."

"Latonya came back," DeAnna replied, but quickly realized it was not a good example to use, since she just wanted to see if things were really over between them.

"Funny you mention her. The only reason she came by was

147

because she wanted to keep my truck. She just wanted to profile and probably make some dude jealous. She said that I wouldn't be needing it for a while anyway, so what's the harm. She was not about to get my baby shot up."

"Your baby," DeAnna replied and then laughed. "I hear ya."

"Well, I don't have any kids," Jeremy said and then paused to think. "Or a girlfriend for that matter. So, now let's get back to your big idea about the movies."

"I was going to suggest that we go to the movies. There is a show starting at 8:30."

"So, are you going to be my eyes?" Jeremy questioned.

"No! Actually, I'm going to cover my eyes. We will listen to the movie and paint our own pictures and one day, when you have regained your sight, we can watch the movie again and see how well we paint pictures together."

Jeremy thought for a minute, then he began to laugh. "Ok, so you're going to go on a real blind date."

DeAnna laughed too, "I guess so."

"Sounds like fun. Shall I drive or you?" Jeremy asked. "After all, we are both blind tonight."

DeAnna had let her guard down completely. She knew that she had been totally welcome and accepted in Jeremy's world and in his heart, and she liked it there.

"Let me just change my clothes," Jeremy said as he got up and quickly and confidently walk to his bedroom.

DeAnna could tell that he no longer needed to count his steps. DeAnna washed the few dishes they used for desert and then she returned to the living room and folded the golden throw that she had used to warm her, almost frozen toes.

Jeremy kept the air on all the time. She did not complain. He knew she was often chilly, so he asked Kimberly to buy the throw just for DeAnna to use when she was there. She loved it.

~

As DeAnna closed Jeremy's truck door and walked to the driver's side and pulled herself into the big SUV, she felt good to be with him in public. They drove in silence most of the way and sang song together the other part of the way. They pulled into the parking lot of the local drugstore and parked. DeAnna grabbed the temporarily handicapped tag and placed it over the rearview mirror.

"I'll be right back," she said to Jeremy as she opened her door.
"I want to go in too," Jeremy said as he unbuckled his seat belt.
"Oh! Sure," DeAnna said, quickly turning the engine off.

She got out of the truck and walked around to the passenger side to help Jeremy get out of the truck. She was surprised to see that he had taken her advice and had gotten a cane. He'd gotten a black cane. DeAnna and Jeremy walked into the drug store arm-in-arm.

DeAnna whispered commands into his ear. "Shift left, shift right, okay now, step up."
"So, what are we here to get again, eye patches, right?" Jeremy asked as they quickly walked. Jeremy's body movements were perfectly in sync with DeAnna. He didn't seem to walk like a blind man at all. He could feel her gentle tugs when he was about to bump into someone, she pulled him closer to her. He understood all her movements and commands perfectly.
"Yup, you know those things that some women put over their eyes at night to block out any light," DeAnna explained.

DeAnna quickly walk to the cosmetic department. She skillfully maneuvered Jeremy around the few people who were wandering around the store. They were in and out of the store in less than five minutes.

"An all times record," Jeremy said, feeling the air on his face when they walked back outside. "I don't think any woman has ever been in and out of a store that quickly."

~

As DeAnna waited for Jeremy to climb back in the passenger seat, she heard a woman's voice yelling.

"Hey Jeremy," the voice said, getting louder.

DeAnna turned around and saw three women. They walked up to the truck and casually greeted DeAnna and then quickly turn their attention back to Jeremy.

"So, Jeremy, haven't seen you at the gym lately," one of the ladies said.

Jeremy didn't recognize the voice and he didn't want to do anything to reveal the fact that he couldn't see and didn't know who she was.

"Hi, I'm DeAnna, and your name is?" DeAnna intervened right on time. It was as if she could read Jeremy's thoughts.
"She's good," Jeremy whispered. *Only you could have set me up with her God,* Jeremy thought. "Thank you, God."
"I'm Danielle and this is Stacy and Jasmyne."

Danielle didn't seem to be the least bit concern with who DeAnna was; DeAnna wasn't really interested in who Danielle was either. The fact that Jeremy didn't recognize the voice was enough to let DeAnna know that Danielle didn't have a significant role in Jeremy's life.

"So, Jeremy, where have you been and what have you been up to for the last few months?" Danielle asked.
"Busy!" He replied knowing that Danielle was partly responsible for Kimberly's marital problems.
"Too busy for a quick game?" Danielle questioned.
"Look Danielle, the game is over. The only reason why you wanted to play games with us was to find out information about Jason. I guess you really did your homework, but you did the wrong assignment, didn't you?" Jeremy said. "You didn't get the grade you expected either."
"What's that supposed to mean?" Danielle asked.
"You thought Jason would one day join us or maybe you would somehow find out information about him from us."
"I got the address, didn't I?" Danielle snapped back.
"DeAnna, sweetheart let's go. Women like that turn my stomach," Jeremy said and closed his truck door.

On the way to the movies, Jeremy told DeAnna all about Danielle and her friends popping up one day at the gym pretending to be All-Star women athletes.

"So, you didn't know them prior to that?" DeAnna asked.

"Nope!" Jeremy replied. "Didn't even know that she knew Jason until they showed up at Kimberly's birthday party. They must have followed someone around."

"She's bold," DeAnna replied.

"Not really. She claimed she had the wrong address. If she was really all that bold she would have given her real name and the reason for coming."

"Bold enough," DeAnna stated.

DeAnna suddenly remembered that Kimberly was mad at him. She wanted to tell him, but he didn't want to betray Kimberly's trust.

"Did you know that she had an affair, one night-stand, whatever it's called these days, with Jason?" DeAnna asked.

"We had a sneaky feeling, but we weren't sure," Jeremy said. He thought about the fact that he'd gotten shot because of lies. "After what happened the last time a few lies got passed around, we thought it was best to keep our mouth closed until we were sure."

DeAnna pulled into the parking lot and decided not to park in the handicap park. She wanted to enjoy the long walk to the building, arm-in-arm with Jeremy. She wanted people to see her with this handsome man.

"Feels good out tonight," Jeremy said, slowly strolling to the building. "Are there any stars out?"

"There's plenty of stars out, but none seem to be shining through," DeAnna replied. She remembered her mother telling her that there are always stars in the sky even during the daytime, when we can't even see them.

"Funny thing about stars, they're always there waiting for a moment to shine," Jeremy said with a sadness in his voice as if the comment had another meaning for him.

"Are you waiting for your moment to shine?" DeAnna asked without thinking.

"I had a moment to shine, but..." Jeremy said, but he didn't finish.

As they walked into the movie theater, DeAnna saw a few people she knew. They also ran into a few people who knew Jeremy. They waved, but of course, Jeremy didn't see them.

"There is a guy waving at you to your right," DeAnna said as she smiled at the guy.

"This is a bad idea," Jeremy said. "I just don't want people knowing my business."

Jeremy made one of those 'Oh, I didn't see you looks and gestures. DeAnna placed her hand in Jeremy's hand as if they were a couple holding hands. She pulled their hands in the direction in which to wave and they waved to the guy together-hand-in-hand.

"No big deal. Don't be afraid to let people know you are temporarily blind. Real friends will offer understanding, love, support, and assistance, if needed. Of course, foes will rejoice in your downfall," DeAnna said as they continued to walk.

"And that's not good," Jeremy replied.

"No, but if they're not doing anything for you and you don't need them to make you happy, who cares what they think," DeAnna said. "Do you need them to make you happy?

"I need a good woman to make me happy?" Jeremy said with no hesitation.

"Well, I don't," DeAnna responded.

"I hope not. A woman can't do nothing for you," Jeremy joked.

"You got that right," DeAnna agreed as she looked at the movie menu to see what was playing.

"All jokes aside. I don't need a man to make me happy either," DeAnna said, wanting Jeremy to understand her position.

"Really?" Jeremy said feeling as if this was a hint to him that she did not need or want a man.

"That's right, you shouldn't want," DeAnna paused for a second and then continued, "or need someone to make you happy. You should make yourself happy."

"I feel ya!" Jeremy said feeling a little better about the possibility of becoming the significant other in DeAnna's life.

"I want someone to add to my happiness," DeAnna said and then paused to try to think of a better way to explain her happiness philosophy. "If you and I were together and I need you to be happy, then I would only be as happy as you are. So, if you're not happy, then I'm not happy. If you're not happy, I want to be able to share my happiness with you. If I'm not happy, I want you to be able to infect me with your happiness. So, we should each have our own individual sort of happiness and fulfillment separately, as well as a combined source of happiness, gained as a unified couple."

"So, DeAnna are you happy?"

"Yes," she responded without hesitation. "I can honestly and truly say, I am happy. Lonely sometimes, but happy nonetheless. Or maybe I should say, alone, and not lonely."

"Two please," DeAnna said to the cashier.

"What show?" The cashier asked.

DeAnna pointed to the list. "The fourth one on the list," DeAnna said not wanting Jeremy to know what they were going to watch.

"What am I paying for?" Jeremy asked.

"I got this," DeAnna replied. "I invited you. And I don't want you to know the name. I want you to guess."

"Well, a woman who cooks, cleans, and pays for dates. I think I'm keeping you," Jeremy joked.

"So, this is a date?" DeAnna asked.

"Sure, why not?" Jeremy replied.

DeAnna wanted him to feel excited about being with her, but she knew that this wasn't the typical date and he was at a huge disadvantage. They made a quick stop for popcorn and drinks.

"I got this one DeAnna and trust me you don't want to object this time," Jeremy said as he reached for his wallet.

"Okay," DeAnna said with no objections.

"Why don't you place your order first?" Jeremy told DeAnna. "I'm still thinking of what I usually get."

"Medium popcorn with butter and a bottle of water," DeAnna said and then tapped Jeremy's arm to indicate that she was finished ordering and it was his turn.

"That's it," Jeremy said. He could not believe her order.

"Yes, that's it for me. I prefer real food verses snacks."

"That's my kind of lady," Jeremy said and turned in her direction and smiled. "My kind of lady," he repeated and smiled at her again. "Now, first of all, Dee are you sharing that popcorn with me or do I have to get my own?"

"Share, of course," DeAnna replied smiling at the fact that he was comfortable enough with her now to call her Dee.

"So, make her medium size popcorn a large. You don't mind extra butter, do you?" He asked DeAnna but continued ordering without waiting for her answer. "And don't just put the butter on the top of the popcorn. I want it on all of it," he told the guy taking his order.

"Anything else sir?" The guy asked Jeremy.

"Oh yeah, I'm just getting started."

As if one large order of popcorn with extra butter and a king-size drink was not enough, Jeremy ordered a large order of Nacho chips with extra cheese, a king-size bag of M&M's and a Hershey bar.

"I'll start with that for now," Jeremy joked. "I got the Hershey bar for you Dee. Make sure you let the chocolate melts in your mouth and not in your hands," Jeremy said, feeling for the cards in his wallet, searching for his debit card. Jeremy handed the cashier his debit card and waited for DeAnna's response.

"I can tell you are waiting to ask," Jeremy said.

"Wow, you either have super powers or..." DeAnna said and then paused.

"Nope, I'm just really in tune to you. I can't explain how I know, but right now I know you are wondering how I knew which card was my debit card."

"And your senses are on point," DeAnna confirmed. "The Holy Spirit is awesome."

"Yeah, that what my mom would always say- the Holy Spirit. Kimberly help me with this one, but it was all my idea," Jeremy said with a hint of pride in his voice. "It was inspired by you. I asked myself, 'what would DeAnna do to help in this situation.' So, I asked Kimberly to chip the right corner of my debit card and the left corner of my Master card. Those are the two that I use to most. I've even learnt to feel the imprint of my name to know whether the card is upside down and not."

"Wow, I'm impressed. I've never really thought about that when I helped my father. Somebody would just simply take his cards and pay his bills for him."

"The other cards are all placed in my wallet in alphabetical order," Jeremy said.

"We're going to need some help with this," DeAnna whispered as the guy placed the popcorn, Nachos, drinks, and candy on the counter.

"Once we find our seats, I'll have to come back for the rest," DeAnna said, gathering what she could. She placed the candy in her purse.

"One of the ushers can help you," the cashier said, realizing from the conversation he overheard and the cane in Jeremy's hand, that he was blind. The cashier motioned for one of the ushers. He explained that they needed help. They placed all the items on a tray and the usher followed behind Jeremy and DeAnna.

DeAnna found two empty seats about midway of the theater. "Prefect," she said as she gently guided Jeremy, who had interlocked his fingers with hers. She liked the feel of his big hands holding hers. Even though he was blind, and she was guiding him, she felt protected and secure with him. She gently pulled his hand downward, indicating for him that they were at their seats and he could sit down. He released DeAnna's hand to feel for his seat and sat down with no problem. The usher waited until they were seated and passed DeAnna the drinks one by one to place in the cup holders, then he handed her the tray of snack. DeAnna placed the tray on Jeremy's lap.

"You're going to need a bib. There's a lot of cheese on the Nachos," DeAnna said, unfolding a napkin.

"Babies wear bibs, I'm a grown man," Jeremy replied.

"Yes, a grown man eating cheesy-cheesy nachos in the dark."

"Newsflash sweetheart," Jeremy said, grabbing a chip. "I've been eating in the dark for a while now, and I'm not talking about just since my little mishap either. You're the one who's going to need a bib. When I ask for butter, I mean, I want butter."

They both laughed as DeAnna pulled the eye patches out of her purse and placed them over her eyes. She feared Jeremy was right. It's one thing to eat in the dark when you can still see an image of the food; it was a totally different thing to see nothing.

"Well," she said. "There's no skill needed to eat popcorn. Once you find the bowl and your mouth, it is a done deal. No cheese dripping."

"Oh, so you aren't going to taste my Nachos?" Jeremy protested. "That's like an unspoken rule of dating, you have to eat from each other's plate," he said then paused. "I feel you smiling. I knew you wanted to taste."

They both laughed. DeAnna reached over and found the tray. She felt around until her hand touched his hand as they both reached for a Nacho chip. Even though DeAnna had held his hand more times than she could count, it felt different this time as their hands touched. As she grabbed a chip, he grabbed her hand and guided it to his mouth.

"Don't get scared, I'm not going to bite your fingers."

They both laughed again.

"So now, explain to me once again, what are we doing," Jeremy asked, feeling completely at ease and ready for anything DeAnna wanted him to do.

"Well, we're just going to listen to the movie and guess what the characters look like, what they may have on, what they are going to say next. When it comes out in DVD, and you regain your sight, we are going to watch it again someday and see just how wrong or how right we were," DeAnna said.

"It's a date, but the game will begin right after we finish eating these nachos."

Myles and Malcolm pulled up at the gym at the same time. They got out and greeted each other. As they stood in the warm sun talking and making polite conversation, they noticed Jeremy's truck.

"Maybe he got his sight back," Malcolm said as they both quickly began walking towards the building.

"He would have told us," Myles replied. "Besides, I talked to Ma Phillips last night and she didn't say anything about it. She did say that he has been spending a lot of time with DeAnna. Oh, and get this," Myles said. "They have even been to the movies together."

"The movies, to see what?" Malcolm asked.

"Nothing," Myles replied.

"Man, that's cold,"

"No, they went to listen, not see."

Chris and Eric pulled up. Myles and Malcolm stopped and waited for them.

"He's really been getting out a lot," Myles continued.

"Talking about Jay?" Chris asked.

"Yep, I think he's really falling for her," Myles replied.

"She's not his type," Chris quickly said.

"Man, are you crazy? He hasn't had a good woman like her since," Myles paused to think of the last good woman Jeremy was with, "Well, he has never had a good woman like that. She has a heart of gold and a beautiful spirit."

"I know that, but let's be real, as soon as he sees her, he's gonna dump her. You know how set in his ways he is about looks," Chris said as they started walking towards the building.

They were all silent for a few minutes. No one saw Johnathan pull into the parking lot, but he suddenly walked up behind them.

"Who died?" Johnathan asked, studying his friends' faces. "Look! Is that Jeremy's truck?"

"Looks like it," Eric confirmed.

When they walked into the building, they checked in at customer service to see if the basketball courts were available. As they walked through the double doors leading to the basketball court, the saw Jeremy sitting on the bleachers with DeAnna. They joined them.

"What's good Jay?" Myles asked.

"Nothing, I figured I'd come to hear you guys fuss," Jeremy joked.

"Hear you been getting around," Chris said.

"Yes, my personal assistance here refuses to believe that I actually like sitting at home alone, just listening to music, and twiddling my thumbs," Jeremy said as he rocked left and bumped shoulders with DeAnna.

"Sound like she knows you pretty good," Malcolm said.

Jeremy could tell by the sarcasm in Malcolm's voice that he was about to ask something crazy.

"What movie did you go see?"

"Which time?" Jeremy playfully snapped back. "I see you been talking to my mom again."

DeAnna was surprised to hear that Jeremy had been sharing their outings with his mother. She wondered if he had told her about the fishing trip and the carnival. They had so much fun that Jeremy declared that even when his sight returns, he was going back, and he was going to wear a blindfold. Jeremy enjoyed playing the guessing games and trying to tell what something was by its smell or shape. He admitted that DeAnna had made being blind more of an adventure than a condition.

"Well, I'm not sure what movie we saw, but one day I'll figure it out," Jeremy said. "But, y'all didn't come here to stand around talking to me. I'm just here to listen. Go play!"

"Alright man," Johnathan said, pulling himself off the floor.

"Now, time for our next adventure," DeAnna said as she looked at the guys warming up. "You played with these guys for years, so you know them, right?"

"Yeah, I know them pretty well," Jeremy replied, not sure what the new adventure was going to be.

158

"Good! Now relax, this is more of an activity, then an adventure," DeAnna responded as if she knew what Jeremy was thinking. "As the game starts, you will predict what they're going to do. I will tell you who has the ball and who's guarding who, and you take it from there. A tall skinny man just walked up to Eric."

"Does he have a large birthmark across his forehead and down the side of his face?" Jeremy asked.

"Yes," DeAnna replied.

"That Daniel, he comes here just about every day. Most of the time he just shoots baskets by himself. Then he goes upstairs to lift weights. I guess because we've always had enough players, he's never asked to play with us."

"Daniel has the ball now. He just threw it to Malcolm, being guarded by Johnathan," DeAnna said like a sports commentator.

"Johnathan hands, wow. They are everywhere. He is waving them up and down, like he's trying to flag down help," Jeremy laughed and then continued. "Malcolm has a frustrated look on his face like he wants to just say forget it."

"Yup!" DeAnna confirmed.

"Myles is somewhere with both hands on his head like he just can't believe what he is seeing. Eric is bent over, no wait, his hands on his knees huffing and puffing as if he just finished running a marathon. And ole Chris eyes are set on the ball as if he is hypnotized."

"Boy you sure got them down pack," DeAnna said. "Do you study women that way?"

"I try, but women are fickle," Jeremy said with no hesitation.

"That's true, but some men are too," DeAnna said. "But some things don't change, and you should know those things that are consistent in your woman. If you can take the time to study your friend's habits, you definitely should know your woman's likes, dislikes, and habits."

"I guess you would have to be in a relationship long enough to study her," Jeremy replied with a hint of sadness.

"True, most people learn sexual preferences of their mates before they learn anything else," DeAnna stated.

"Now you're talking," Jeremy confirmed.

"But that's out of order," DeAnna interjected.

"Yeah, I know, I was just having a little fun with you. I remember hearing my sister and her friends singing that little song when they used to jump rope, 'first come love, then come marriage, here come mommy with a baby carriage," Jeremy sang.

DeAnna laughed as she remembered thinking about the games she played when she was a child. She remembered singing that same song as she jumped rope. *Too bad we didn't sing the same songs as grown women,* DeAnna thought to herself.

"People just want to test the waters these days," Jeremy said as if he was reading DeAnna thoughts again.

"Yeah and the funny thing is, we keep swimming in the devil's pool. I mean, it looks all warm and inviting, but after the devil sees that you are hooked, and your relationship with God is not important enough for you to resist, he stops cleaning the pool, he stops adding chlorine, and it just feels dirty, slimy and nasty."

"Okay stop," Jeremy said, waving his hands in the air. "That's an image I don't want to imagine. I don't even want to think about it."

"Eric has the ball and is half-court, not being guarded," DeAnna said.

"He's gonna take the shot, miss, and then rush in for the rebound," Jeremy said matter-of-factly.

"Johnathan got the rebound," DeAnna continued without confirming whether Eric took the shot or not.

"He's going to dribble out mid-court, probably double dribble, be everywhere, because nobody's going to guard him. At some point, he's going to mess around and try to shoot, the ball is not going hit anything but the back wall and the floor," Jeremy laughed at the thought, then suddenly seemed a little sad. "I actually wish I could to see him right now," Jeremy said, more to himself than to DeAnna. "You're shaking your head. You cannot believe how accurate I am. You probably saying to yourself, 'I need a man who knows me like that," Jeremy said, imitating a woman's voice.

"So now you think you know me," DeAnna questioned him.

"No, but I am thinking that was a pretty good guess," Jeremy said and rock to the side and dumped her again as he had done earlier.

"Johnathan just hit a 3-pointer, nothing-but-net," DeAnna said.

"Are you serious?" Jeremy asked.

"Yup!"

"Wow," Jeremy said, shaking his head in disbelief. "I guess he bought his 'A' game today,"

"Guess so," DeAnna replied.

"So how was work today?" Jeremy asked DeAnna. "Any crazy patients wanting their bed pan change every twenty-minutes so that they can get a good look at you?"

"No, but I did get a patient that thought I was Grace Jones."

They both laughed.

"What," Jeremy said. He had an image running through his head.

"Yeah, I thought that was funny since I have long hair and skin brighter than the sun.

"Maybe he thought you were ..." Jeremy's attention was suddenly drawn from DeAnna and back to the game as he heard a loud smack.

"Foul," Myles yelled. "I know you felt that way over there, didn't you Jay?" Myles questioned

"Let me guess, Johnathan?" Jeremy questioned.

"You know em," DeAnna confirmed.

"He really does have some anger issues. I think that he needs counseling," Jeremy joked. "I think he had a bad childhood. Growing up in the home with some real sanctified, fire baptized, Baptist church folks can do some damage to a child," Jeremy said, sounding like a Baptist preacher.

"You need to man up," Johnathan said.

"That wasn't no baby tap," Myles said.

"See, I told you, that man is going to be a child abuser one day," Jeremy yelled.

"The Bible says, spare the rod, spoil the child," Johnathan replied.

"Spoil me," Myles said. "I have need of some spoils right now."

"Don't get him started please," Chris said, throwing the ball in the air, giving up on the game.

"Chris is walking off the court. Myles is going to sit down. Malcolm just became a one-man show. Its break time now, so Chris is going to run for his phone."

"I guess Daniel's standing on the court looking lost as if he doesn't know what to do," Jeremy said, showing that he even knew the habits of his friends doing half-time. "Eric probably is going to head over here in a minute."

161

"Or in a few seconds," DeAnna corrected him. "Here he comes."

Eric sat down on the bottom bleacher, but without saying a word. Jeremy was not used to Eric not talking. His silence spoke volumes to Jeremy.

"What's wrong Eric?" Jeremy asked. "You are kind of quiet today."

"Ah, it ain't nothing, just have a lot on my mind."
"Wifey?" Jeremy asked.

Eric was hesitant to talking in front of DeAnna. He often talked to his friends about his marital issue, but never in front of strangers. He really liked DeAnna. *Maybe a woman's perspective is exactly what I need*, Eric thought to himself.

"Nothing really," Eric said, not knowing where to start. "It's just that I am kind of tired of her complaining all the time, about everything, nothing, or anything. Sometimes, I don't even want to come home. All she does is yell at the children, the TV, her friends and I just hate going home."
"What's wrong with her?" Jeremy asked.
"I think she's dissatisfied with something, but what, I just don't know," Eric said. He looked at DeAnna, expecting her to have an answer.

DeAnna waited for confirmation that Eric was soliciting her advice.

"Why do females fuss so much?" Eric asked, looking directly at DeAnna.
"Different reasons," DeAnna hesitantly replied. She wasn't sure if this was a rhetorical question or if it was an invitation for her to join the conversation. "Some people or women fuss or complain all the time to get attention," DeAnna continued. She suddenly felt that Eric was soliciting her advice, so she continued. "Sometimes, it's to show that they are unhappy. If they grew-up in an environment in which dissatisfaction was showed by fussing, they do and act what they know to do, whether it's right or wrong."
"Well, I know it is not how she was raised," Eric said. "Her mother is an easy going, good spirited, and loving woman. She always finds the silver lining."

"Maybe she can't find the silver lining," DeAnna replied. "Have you ever felt like every time you put your best foot forward, someone or something seems to step on your toes?"

"Yep, all the time," Eric replied.

"Some people forget that they got other toes left and another foot," DeAnna paused. She waited for Eric to explain more about his situation. He didn't seem to want to talk, so DeAnna continued. "It just seemed like every time I got excited about something good, something would spoil it. You ever felt that way so much that you begin to expect it?" She asked.

"Yup, Jay remember when we used to say something then get in fear and say knock on wood?" Eric asked Jeremy.

"I still do that," Jeremy responded.

"That's the devil that has you in fear, because God is not the author of fear," DeAnna said. She rocked to the side and bumped Jeremy. "And your wife, well maybe she's afraid that if she shows that she is happy, that she'll have to knock on wood too. Maybe she thinks the devil may come and steal her happiness."

"I never thought about that," Eric said. "But, I still think there something else going on with her."

"Life and death are in the power of the tongue," DeAnna said as she looked at Eric. "I used to press my hair out with the flat iron. It would be so straight and pretty, hanging half-way down my back. Every time I did that, older men would love it," DeAnna stated. "It would be so shiny and black. Wouldn't you know it, every time I pressed it out, it would rain. So, I stop pressing it out and simply pinned it up, in a ponytail mostly. I hated it. It took me a long time before I realized that I had faith in what I believed. I gave those words power. The more I confessed it, the more I believe it, the more power I gave to it, and that's why it happened more and more. So, I stopped saying it," DeAnna said. She remembered what her Pastor would always say, *Faith is an action word.* "I had to change my actions too. So, I started pressing my hair out more. I knew it wasn't going to rain every day. The more I did it, the more days I went with long, pretty, straight hair."

"I see," Eric grunted. "Guess that's like washing your car and then a bird does a drive by. Or as some guy say, as soon as I wash my car, it rains. You expect it to happen, then you're surprised when it does."

"Right," Jeremy agreed.

"Okay, I get that. Now what does that have to do with her fussing and complaining?

"Maybe she just has to have more victorious days, so she can expect good things to continue to happen. Maybe the complaining is to draw your attention to her. So, the next time she's complaining, walk over to her, sit down, don't say a word and just listen. Just stare at her. She's going to wonder why you're staring. Tell her that you were just waiting to tell her how much you miss her and love her, but you wanted to allow her to finish talking first. Eric, if you do that for a week, I bet when you come home, she will be quietly waiting each day to hear those words."

"That won't work with her," Eric said,

"Expect it to work, Eric. Just try it and see. Oh!" DeAnna said, suddenly remembering something. "Try this one day. Take her around someone who is as negative as she is. Than express how frustrating it is to be around negative people like that."

"Is that the best way?" Eric asked.

"No, the best way is to talk to her. Find out what's going on with her and what complaints she has about her life. Oh, and find out what she is willing to do to change what's not working for her."

"She's tired of seeing all her friends get what they want, like a house, but she can't have it too. She often says that she doesn't want one like they got because it's tiny and over price. Which is true, but I bet if we got one she would love it, tiny or not."

"Probably, but sometimes you have to learn to appreciate what you already have before you are get or are given more," DeAnna said, talking more to herself than Eric. "Have you guys discussed buying?"

"No, she hints around and say stuff like 'I'm tired of this 2-bedroom dump.'"

"Wow," DeAnna and Jeremy said in unison.

"I mean she keeps running up the credit cards. She doesn't help with hardly any of the bills," Eric paused to calm down. He could feel himself getting upset. "But yet, she wants to increase our debt with a large mortgage."

"My Pastor tell us all the time that God is not going to give you a three-bedroom house, if you can't keep your two-bedroom apartment clean. Same goes for the bills. If you can't pay the bills you got, why would you create more? Do you think you would even qualify for a loan now?"

"It's borderline. They would probably tell me I have to pay off some debt first."

"Does she know that?" DeAnna asked with an idea cooking up in her mind.

"What do you mean?" Eric questioned.

"Have you ever talked to her about the debt-to-income ratio?"

"Not really, I mean she knows that we are behind in some bills."

"If you think the root of her dissatisfaction is her life and she want a house, let her see that she is making things worse for herself. Take her to a mortgage company," DeAnna paused to think of what Eric would need. "Get a recent copy of your credit report and a month worth of check stubs or your tax return from the last two or three years. Tell the lender that you want to see if you pre-qualify and if not, ask her what you need to do to improve your chances. They're probably going to say reduce debt, pay off some cards, and increase your income. Maybe that's what you will be told. Then ask your wife if she is willing to do what it takes. If she is serious about wanting a house, she will help you more. She will feel good about being a future homeowner. If she is not serious or if she's not willing to help, she will stop complaining about her present condition."

"You know what," Eric said with a quizzical look on his face. "That just might work. Thanks, doll," Eric said as he jumped up to join the guy who were headed back to the court. "Jeremy," Eric yell when he was halfway down the court. "She's a smart woman. I see why you hang out with her so much."

"Why didn't you go to college for counselor?" Jeremy questioned.

"Don't know, never thought about it, I guess. This stuff is not that hard to figure out. Watch other people. Listen to people. Sometimes people have the answer to their own problems, if they would only listen to the advice that they give others."

"Oh, I see, and you know that's true," Jeremy said. "I used to get so upset to hear guys fussing about how some dude was dogging his sister or mother out, yet the very same dude would be dogging his girlfriend around."

"That's it," DeAnna replied. "We know the right thing to do, we just have to do it."

"That example about washing the car and then the bird does a drive by, Eric was on point with that. That happens for real. After I wash my car, I start looking for em.' I guess I need to stop that, huh?" Jeremy questioned.

"People need to realize that our faith should work for us and not against us. Stop expecting the worse; start expecting the best. Faith in a thing can breathe life. The Bible says faith is the substance of things hoped for, evidence of things not seen. So, basically think positive. Let your faith be the evidence for the things which you think does not exist. Hope for the best," DeAnna said. "No, correction, believe and claim the best."

"Is that what you do?" Jeremy asked.

"I do now," DeAnna replied. "Most of the time, anyway."

"You didn't always?" Jeremy questioned.

"No, I had to learn," DeAnna said, matter-of-factly.

"So, you are self-taught?" Jeremy questioned.

"Well, yes and no. I did learn a lot from my experiences, but I got a lot of information and clarification from my pastor.

"Yeah, about your pastor. You know, I really enjoyed the message I heard that time I went with you. I would love to go back soon. His very image has changed the way I think about preachers, pastors, and bishops, and other titles which I once doubted."

"Really?" DeAnna replied.

"Yeah, I mean you always see the old, pop belly, unmarried, poor looking preacher. Makes you think that the only reason they are for Lord, is because they have nothing else to do. For them, it's the only place they feel important. Some of them even look like they are hopeless. Truth is, that sort of repulse most people, well me anyway. Makes me ask- is that all God has to offer us?" Jeremy paused to see if DeAnna had any objections. "Look, in most churches, you see either married men being forced by their wives to go, or men who can't get a woman, so they play all holy and claim they are waiting on the Lord to send them a woman," Jeremy said.

"You know something, in some cases, you might be right. But a spiritual revelation is going on because that's not how God want people representing him. Men often follow women, right? Many women are getting tired of being cheated on, beat up, talk down to, or ignored by their boyfriends or husbands. They are now running to the church. Now to be honest, some are just going from being street harlots, to being church harlots. I wanted to say the other word, but I have to be spiritually correct," DeAnna joked. "Truth is, the men are now going to church looking for good women and sometimes they end up running straight to the harlot. Spirits know like spirits. Men looking for a good woman sometimes give up and they just settle for the so-called fine woman. He simply prays that God changes her. Praying God will make her a good woman, make her have eyes for only him. But that same man does nothing to change himself. Yeah, some even put on a show, yelling, speaking in tongues, and pretending that they are so holy. But…"

"That's funny because, all the women I have met, I met them in church and they were nothing but hypocrites. I've gotten more action from them, then the ones that didn't claim to be a good church going, Bible toting, word quoting," Jeremy paused to think if he had covered it all. "Oh, and let's not forget, tongue speaking, fire baptized, Holy Ghost Christian woman."

"That's probably true, but if they are in the right church, and are really being taught, they will change. Their actions will convict them. I mean, now truthfully, not everybody is going to change overnight. But if the pastor is concerned about helping his members, he's going to give them a message that will help them find themselves."

"Let me stop you for a second. How and why would they do that, when they, the pastor themselves, has a wife and a girlfriend and a few outside kids and one on the way. He is not going to teach on family values, adultery, fornication, good relationships, or commitment."

"No, probably not. The members aren't going to be taught at every church. I've always been leery of churches that have all these extra classes that teach those messages. I wonder why the pastor is not teaching them. The extra classes being taught by their ministers and assistants should be to confirm the word that's being taught by the pastor already. Some people are allowed to be comfortable in their sin. They got a packed house every Sunday. People will flock to comfort when they are not ready to change and is not in any danger of being convicted or having to change," DeAnna said, thinking of the many churches that she visited that only talked about salvation, but never mention how to live a save the life.

"Yeah, they are comfortable alright," Jeremy replied. "I can testify to that. Just a bunch of hooping and…"

"When the overseer doesn't feed the flock, they perish, or they are spiritually dead, but now my healing…" DeAnna suddenly stopped talking. Memories evolved that she didn't want to think about.

"Finish. Your healing what?" Jeremy questioned. "It's not time for the benediction yet. We were just getting started."

"That's a story for another time, but now back to my pastor. What is it that impress you about him?"

"One, he's a real man. He doesn't look and acts like a punk. He doesn't stand in the pulpit acting like he is better than the people he serves. He's just real. I mean when he said, 'all men really want is a naked cheerleader,' I almost ran up there and gave him a high-five and invited him to play a few games with us just to hear more."

"Now you know he was referring to a husband and wife, right?"

"I know, but that's real. People need to know more than how to get Saved. They need to learn how to live a saved life and he tells it like it is, the word."

"Yeah, he does that." DeAnna thought about his message about overcoming roadblocks. "You know I have some CDs that you might like."

"I can honestly say that I wouldn't mind following in his footsteps. He's cool. I saw him on the basketball court a few years ago, but I would never have guessed that he was a pastor. I could tell that there was something different about him. He was competitive, but he didn't seem to get upset like the other guys. He didn't fuss, cuss, or curse. You know the type that stands out, but still fit in- sort of."

"Yeah, I know the type. It's almost as if God warns you. 'That's my son whom I am well please with; don't try nothing," DeAnna laughed as she talked.

"Well, you are welcome to come anytime. Maybe the next time you go, you can actually meet him."

"What?" Jeremy questioned in total disbelief. "So, he let strangers just come up to him without an appointment?"

"Yes, he doesn't act like he's some big-time celebrity, who's too good to greet the people that he serves. We are a family."

"Wow see that's a real man. I would have thought that after the service is over, his armor-bearers would escort him out through some side door. Especially, since y'all have such a large congregation."

DeAnna thought about the times when she was a little girl, and the preacher used to stand in the back of the church to greet the members as they left.

"I got a question for you," DeAnna said to Jeremy.

"Okay shoot," he said without hesitation.

"Have you ever asked God to restore your sight?"

Jeremy thought about DeAnna's question for a long time. She thought he was ignoring the question.

"Yes, I have," he finally said. "And I guess I thought that he didn't hear me or didn't answer my prayers because I am..." Jeremy paused to think of how to explain what he thought.

"You're what?" DeAnna softly asked.

"I guess because I haven't been living right. Well, at least in the past. For the last seven or eight months, I can honestly say that I have not been drinking, which I never really did that anyway. I have not been with a woman since my accident. Sexually, it has really been well over a year..." Jeremy paused. "Well, it's easy to reframe from women, when nobody wants you."

"I'm sure that somebody would love to have you. I mean you're a little rough around the edges," DeAnna joked. "But you're a good man."

"Not really," Jeremy protested.

"I believe you are. Nobody is perfect, but my heart is telling me that you, my friend, are really a good man. You will eventually do the right thing. As I mentioned earlier, change isn't instant. Change is a process, except for in a few miracle cases, nobody changes overnight. Nobody changes all bad habits or sinful behavior at once. Some sin, we don't even know is sin. Like worry, that's a sin."

Jeremy pondered DeAnna's question for a few minutes.

"Back to your question. I did ask God, even begged him. Prayed day-after-day while in that hospital bed, while at home lying on the floor, after I tripped in the shower, after turning the cold water off first and feeling that hot water hitting my skin."

"Did you believe that he would restore it for you?"

"The first time I asked, I believe that I would be able to see again instantly, but then," Jeremy said and then paused.

"You didn't get it right away; so, you asked again, right?"

"Well yes," Jeremy said, shocked that DeAnna knew what he did.

"Have you ever asked one of your friends to do something for you?" DeAnna asked.

"All the time and I knew that they would do it, if they could."

"So, if you call Malcolm and asked for a ride somewhere and you tell him," DeAnna paused briefly, "Let's say you tell him you got a doctor's appointment at three and need a ride."

"He's going to be at my door at two- o'clock," Jeremy replied.

169

"Well, what if it's 1:50 and you have not heard from him. Do you call and say can you please take me to my appointment?

"No, I'm going to ask him where he is, or if he is on the way. Or if his car broke down," Jeremy replied. "I might even just say, what's up?

"Why wouldn't you ask him if he can take you?"

"Well, because I know if he said yes, then he's going to do it unless something came up."

"So, basically you only need to ask him once because you know he's going to do it, so then you just wait on him to do it."

"Yeah!" Jeremy said as if it was a no-brainer, "That's right."

Jeremy suddenly realized what DeAnna was getting at. 'Faith that He will do it,' Jeremy said, more to himself than to DeAnna. 'Kind of like what you told Eric about having faith for the wrong thing. We must have faith in God to do what we have asked of him. We have to say the right things and believe what we confess and expect.

"Ask once," DeAnna confirmed. "I've always been told that, then thank Him as if you've already received it."

"I understand all that, but still I have been so far removed from God that..."

"But he still loves you," DeAnna softly said.

"You know what's so funny?" Jeremy said as he turned towards the court where his friends played. "Johnathan preaches to us all the time and it always seems to me, I mean I know he's speaking the truth but, I don't know... it just gets on my nerves, then I feel a little guilty because it is the Word of God."

"I know. You've heard people say that presentation is everything. Johnathan will probably tell you about the story of the prodigal son. He would try to convince you that you need to return to your father's house," DeAnna said.

'What would you say now," Jeremy asked

"Now that story is great, and I would use it to too, then maybe follow up with an example."

"Like what?

"When I used to work with an after-school program, I had a few kids who were bad. When I say bad; I mean bad. Their parents would make sure those little rascals were at school every day just to get them out of their hair. It seemed we spent more time working with the troubled kids then the good kids. Trying to save them, from themselves. We gave them three times as much attention as we gave those that seem to have it all together. When their bad butts began to conform and try to be good, we praise them for every little effort. It mades us try harder to get him or her one step closer to their goal. We were often harder on the kids who acted twice as good, whenever they made the simplest mistake. 'They should know better,' we would say.' We expect better since the good ones had always given us the best," DeAnna explained.

"Is that fair though?" Jeremy asked.

"Maybe not, just how it is. When you know better, you do better. People expect better from you."

"Guess God is really going to enjoy rejoicing when I return to Him. He's going to kill the fattest cow, throw a party, and drape me in the best robe."

DeAnna was impressed and Jeremy could really tell. She was speechless.

"Yes, I know the story," he said not giving her a chance to respond. I was raised in the church. And as you probably know, train up a child in the way I should go and..."

"Yes, I do know you were. I can tell."

"Well darling," Jeremy said trying to sound like a Texan. "It's been fun as always, but let's find something more exciting to do."

"Well, I got somewhere to go tonight," DeAnna said.

"Oh, I'm sorry I didn't mean to..."

"No, it's okay," DeAnna replied and then paused. "Now of course you are welcome to come with me. It might actually be fun."

"What?"

"I'm in charge of a singles' group at my church. We are having a group meeting or group discussion."

"So, a group of unhappy single women dogging men out, uh..." Jeremy sarcastically said. "Oh, that's right its Christian women, so you all will be spiritually analyzing their failed accomplishments. Sounds real fun, but..."

"You know what you're probably right. That's how it's been before, but I'm in charge now. Well just for tonight. But I understand. I just felt a man's perspective would be so enlightening. Usually the leader seems to question all your thoughts. She seems to talk to you and acts as if you're just stupid for thinking the way you do or did. She's so busy flexing her Biblical knowledge, that it is hard to be honest. Oh, and that belittling fussing tone is just ridiculous. Most of the singles dropped out."

"So why is she still in charge?"

"Now that's the million-dollar question."

"So, is there going to be anyone there tonight?"

"Maybe two or three people. I did ask a few people to come just to support me."

"How long is it?" Jeremy asked.

"It supposed to be an hour; normally it last thirty minutes." DeAnna said.

"I guess it wouldn't kill me to go, as long as I can wear my shades," Jeremy said, thinking of all the extra attention DeAnna had been giving him.

"Okay by me," DeAnna said, shrugging her shoulders.

"Why don't you take me home, so I can get ready? You can pick me up later."

"Ok, but…"

"Don't worry," Jeremy said, "Kimberly told me that your car quit on you. You are my personal assistant, and I can't have you caught riding the bus. Now, can I?"

"Actually, that's not what I was going to say. But I think catching the bus could be fun."

"Are you serious?" Jeremy questioned.

"Yes, I'm serious." DeAnna said.

"Maybe another day darling, during the daytime."

"Isn't it always night time for you anyway?" DeAnna questioned.

"You know what? I can tell day from night. When I open my eyes, I can actually see the light. I think," Jeremy said.

"That's good," DeAnna said, but her heart began to feel heavy. She was afraid that it would all end once he could see.

"So, we gonna wait?" Jeremy asked, referring to riding the bus.

"Your call. I understand if you're too chicken to ride a bus with me."

"Chicken, please. I'll ride a bus," Jeremy said with his chest out.

"Okay then, I'll meet you at…" DeAnna said and then paused. She had not figured out all the traveling arrangements.

"Why don't we go to your place, you change, then we can go to my house, I change, and we leave from there," Jeremy suggested.

"Sure," DeAnna agreed secretly rejoicing as she envisioned her nosey neighbor, Gina, peeping out the window and seeing DeAnna enter her apartment with Jeremy on her arm.

Chapter 13

"Hey honey," Eric said as he dropped his tool belt on the floor by the closet door. Tesha glanced at her husband, then at his tool belt in its usual spot on the floor.

"Hey, how was work? Did you call the plumber today?" She asked without waiting for him to answer the first question.

"No, I was…" Eric tried to answer his wife's question, but she cut him off.

"Well, you need to call someone. I have had to clean water out the bathroom floor twice. Oh, and you need to tell Mr. Peeping Tom over there to stop looking at me. I'm so tired of him. He makes me sick."

"I can't tell that man who to look at Tesha. Has he touched you?"

"No, but I am tired of him staring at me. It's creepy."

"The man is a little," Eric hesitated, trying to decide the best word to use. "Well slow," he said, not wanting to say anything that might be considered mean or cruel about his neighbor's disability. "So, leave him alone,"

"So, you don't care about my feelings?"

"Honey please, can I come home just one day without…"

"Without what?" Tesha asked.

"Just forget it," Eric replied.

"Without my mouth? You just like all the other men who don't want to hear…" Tesha stopped talking, realizing that Eric had turned his back to her as if he was no longer interested in the conversation, so she turned her attention back to the television.

Eric hated conversations which included the phrase, 'just like all the other men' or when she stated what other men think. He would often tell his wife that he's not 'other men' and if she constantly thinks about what other men think, maybe she should be with other men.

"Tesha," Eric yelled from the kitchen. "What's for dinner?"

"Whatever you cook," she yelled back.

"Even when she only works part-time and is home half the day, she still can't fix a meal," Eric murmured.

Eric thought about Jeremy. He had never really been envious or jealous of any of his friend's relationship because they all had challenges. Jeremy's relationships always seem superficial. He always had the model type women who were too pretty to do anything except get their nails and hair done and sit around and wait to be served. Myles never seemed to want to seriously commit to anyone. Malcolm and Lesia were always in a 'break-up to make-up state.' Johnathan often ran women away playing judge and jury in the name of the Lord. Chris was always sort of secretive about his relationship issues and rarely introduced the latest fling. They all thought Chris was single more often than not and was still secretly in love with his baby's mama. "But Jeremy seemed to have struck gold with DeAnna," Eric said as he slammed the refrigerator door shut. "Ain't he blessed? '*She is beautiful, loving, caring, practical, God fearing, and seems to genuinely care about other people's happiness,*' Eric thought to himself. Eric began to think about the conversation he had with her at the gym. The advice that DeAnna gave seemed to make so much sense at the time, but Eric found it hard to be nice to someone who fuss all the time about anything and everything. He went to the bedroom and closed the door. He could hear Tesha fussing at the television. He laid across the bed and flipped the television on.

"Divorce court," Eric muttered. "You trying to tell me something God?" Eric asked as he turned the volume up.

"And what did you do to make things better?" The Judge asked the plaintiff in one of the cases.

"What have I done?" Eric asked himself.

He thought again about what DeAnna had said to him earlier at the gym. Eric got off the bed and joined his wife in the living room. Tesha looked at Eric as if he had done something wrong. He grabbed her feet and pulled them into his lap.

"Now, what are we going to eat?" He asked. "Maybe we can order something." He could tell that she was shocked that he was massaging her feet.

"Fine with me," Tesha said, staring at her husband, wondering if he was up to something.

"You order, I'll pay," Eric said.

"Fair enough," Tesha said. She glanced around for a phone book since her cell phone was dead. "The usual?" She asked. She found the phone book under a pile of newspaper on the table.

"Yeah, that's good," he replied.

"Eric, what's up with you?" Tesha asked as she dialed the number to the Chinese restaurant.

"Nothing, I just want us to be okay," he replied.

"Do you really?" She questioned.

"Yes, I really do."

"You sure there's not someone else you would rather be with?" She questioned, as if it was a question she had been waiting to ask.

"Is that what you think?" He asked. He could not believe what he was hearing.

"Well, sometimes I think that," she said in a softer tone.

"So, is that why you've been so fussy lately?" Eric asked. "More than usual."

"No!" Tesha shouted and then realized that she had been thinking about it a lot when he came home later than usual. "Well, maybe."

"If I was seeing someone else, I wouldn't rush to come home to you every day," Eric said and then paused and waited to see if she had a response. He thought it was a great opportunity for them to hash out some issues. "Baby, I love you, but it's not but so much a man can or is going to take."

"I guess my defense is up because I thought," Tesha said, then paused. She really didn't know how to explain what she was feeling.

"Well, let them down. I am yours and you need to realize that you and only you, has my heart," Eric said trying to sound romantic.

"Well, sometimes when we are out together, I see you looking at other women and..." she started but was cut off.

"And I've seen your eyes straying some too," Eric informed her. "But I'm not worried about a five-second glance. They cannot love you like I can."

"And you're the one I want," Tesha said, feeling convicted.

"Likewise," Eric responded leaning in to kiss her.

"What do you want to drink?" Eric asked, thinking about something he heard DeAnna telling Kimberly. *If you want a friend, show yourself friendly. If you want a compliment, give a compliment. If you want a woman to serve you, serve her.*

"Wow you really gonna do something for me?"

176

"I do stuff for you all the time," Eric responded.

"What? When?" Tesha snapped back.

"Excluding paying the bills," Eric sarcastically replied. "You always asking me to pick up stuff on my way home from work, I do it. I even run your bathe water. Oh, and let's not forget all the times..." Eric words seemed to fade as he looked at her and realized that she seemed no longer interested in finishing the conversation.

"Where is the food? These people are slow," Tesha began to fuss. "I knew I should have told you to go get it. We are going to be watching and waiting all day."

Not even been ten minutes, Eric said to himself, thinking about how long Tesha had gone without fussing about something. *It has only been about five minutes since she'd ordered the food*, he thought. "Some things never change," he muttered.

"You say something?" Tesha asked, looking for an argument.

"No baby," Eric said, and went back to the master bedroom. He flipped through the channels. 'Consistency is the key to break through, he heard ringing from the television.' "Hey!" Eric said, recognizing a familiar face sitting in the congregation of one of the most well-known televised churches. "That's DeAnna's church," he said. He listened intensely to the message from the pastor.

'Things are not going to change just because you try something one time. You have to work at it. If we would chase our wives now as hard as we chased them before we got them and treat them like we treated them before they gave in; I'm telling you husbands, there would be less fussing and more loving. Yeah, y'all going to want to come straight home after work. You going to be racing your coworkers to the time clock. Running around here like a crackhead looking for his next fix. Wives, I have not forgotten you all. Y'all got some nerve to be mad at him. Y'all need to fix your hair and nails like you did when you were dating. And what happened to that good smelling body wash. Some of y'all use to smell like Victoria secret done told it all. Now you just smell like you took a drive by bath. Let's get real.'

The message was so captivating that Eric didn't hear the doorbell.

"Hey what'cha doing in here," Tesha asked. "I need money to pay for the food."

Eric glanced up at his wife, standing in the doorway. He saw her mouth moving, but he was so engulfed in the preacher on the television, that he didn't understand what she was saying.

"Who's that," Tesha asked as she glanced at the TV.

"I think he's DeAnna's pastor," Eric said without taking his eyes off the television.

"DeAnna who?" Tesha asked as if DeAnna was some woman that Eric might have been seeing.

"DeAnna, Jeremy's girlfriend," Eric replied.

"Girlfriend?" Tesha questioned, sounding offended. "You mean the help, don't you?"

"Help," Eric responded and chuckled. "She is not the maid, if that's what you are implying. Why do you insist on calling her that or the hired hand? I heard you telling Lesia that. It was funny then and it is funny now. And you both know that Jeremy is falling for her. How many hired hands or maids do you know go on dates with the boss and drive the boss' truck?" Eric asked.

"Why are you defending her?" Tesha asked, sounding upset. "And plenty of women date the boss. I know you have heard of ladies who sleep their way to the top."

"Defend her? Honey what are you talking about?" Eric asked and then quickly paused. He could tell that he was getting frustrated again.

"You pay the man," Tesha yelled.

Tesha stood in the doorway with her hands folded, staring at the television wondering what is his fascination with this preacher. After a few seconds of watching, she flipped the television off and followed her husband. Eric paid for the food, placed the bag of food on the counter, and grab a plate out of the dish rack.

"Honey," Tesha said, walking into the kitchen, determined to finish the conversation about DeAnna's status. "Do you really think Jeremy has fallen in love?"

"Well, maybe," Eric said not ready to get into another mini-debate about someone else's love life. He was sure that there was more to it than just concern for Jeremy's relationship status.

"What do you think of Ms. DeAnna?" Tesha asked, confirming Eric's suspicions.

Eric wanted to ignore the question because he knew it was a trap. He was in a no-win situation with this question. If he told the truth and admitted that she seems like a very nice, Godly, loving, and caring woman than Tesha would start shooting off one question after another: 'Do you wish you had met her first. Is she what you really like? Do you want me to be like her? So, what, you like fat girls now?' If he said, 'she's just alright,' Tesha would say he's lying and must be hiding something.

"It doesn't matter what I think," Eric said. He smiled to himself for coming up with a good answer so quickly. "What matters is that I think that he seems happier with her then he has in a long time."

"You think so?" Tesha said, spooning food out of the container and dropping it onto her plate as if she was upset about something.

"Have you noticed that in all his relationships, he was the one that always seemed to try to convince others that they were so happy? The women for example, Tanya, Latonya, Latonja, whatever her name was, she would always say negative stuff about him. Yeah, sometimes she was kind of joking, but I just wonder if he was trying to convince us that she was happy or himself. She was trying to keep him under control with threats and insults. I remember she said, 'He knows better than to cross me.' Really, I remember thinking. 'If he so happy with her, why would he think about crossing her?" Eric paused and poured gravy over his rice. 'If he wants me, he is going to have to come better than that," Eric said, imitating a woman's voice. "Seems to me that he was struggling to paint pictures of a happy couple that didn't exist."

"Must have been hard work?" Tesha said, licking her spoon.

"Work?" Eric said. "Yes, work and that's exactly what it was, hard work. I know they say anything worth having is worth working hard for, but it just seems to me that if you work hard to be happy, then looking happy should be the product of the hard work and not work itself.

"I guess you're right, Mr. Professor. How does he seem to work hard with the…?" Tesha stopped mid-sentence, she didn't want to call her the help. She knew she appeared to be jealous or envious of DeAnna and she didn't want him think that. "DeAnna," she said, smiling at her husband.

"Seems like a very special friendship which allows him to be himself. He seems to just be, as they say, going-with-the-flow," Eric said. "Seem that things are forming naturally without any pressure what-so-ever."

"Well, I don't know about all that," Tesha couldn't resist saying. "I'm not around him that much. Seems to me that he's always with her as if she is keeping him all to herself in the house somewhere, I guess. Almost like she doesn't want anybody else seeing them together."

"What?" Eric said, looking Tesha with a confused look on his face. "They are always out in public somewhere, the movies, fishing, they were even spotted at a carnival."

"What is a blind man doing at a kiddy carnival?" Tesha questioned.

"The man stayed locked up in the house until she started coming around," Eric said.

"Maybe she's trying to keep him from his friends," Tesha persisted with her attack on DeAnna's motives.

"No, I don't think so," Eric hesitantly said. "At first it may have seemed like that, but the truth is, he just didn't want us around fussing over him, worrying about him, and doing stuff for him that he had to learn to do for himself. DeAnna, well she came along and helped him re-gain some of his independence."

"Okay now," Tesha said, warning her husband. "I see you're just going to keep on praising the miracle worker, but I'm telling you, she's trying to make him dependent on her, so he won't need y'all."

"I don't know about all that, all I know is, he seems to be changing for the better and it's all good. He's going to church and seems to see things differently."

Eric smiled as he thought about the day at the basketball court. He realized that Jeremy didn't seem concerned at how much attention DeAnna was giving to him while discussing him and Tesha's relationship issues. Most of Jeremy's girlfriends were always begging for so much attention from other men that it made Jeremy uneasy. Jeremy trusted his friends, but he didn't want them to think that his lady didn't truly want him.

"He cannot see anything," Tesha said and then instantly noticed Eric staring at her. "Oh, I'm sorry, I didn't mean to sound mean or insensitive to Jeremy's condition," she said.

180

He continued to look at her with a look of disbelief.

"Come on now, that was a joke," she said knowing Eric was really concerned about Jeremy's blindness, even though they all had lighten up about it and truly believed that he would re-gain his sight. "It's just made me so frustrated that you continued to praise the work of the help."

"Let's just eat," Eric said, grabbing his plate off the kitchen table. Headed to his usually spot on the sofa in front of the television. He sat his plate down and headed to the DVD stand.

"What movie do you want to watch?" He asked.

"Doesn't matter," Tesha said. "I'll see what's on the movie channel," she said as she flipped through the channels.

"I want to ask you a question," Eric began as he sat down on the sofa beside her. "Why don't you act the way you did when we were dating?"

"And how was that?" She asked him.

"You used to call me all day just to hear my voice," Eric said as he scooped up a spoonful of chicken and rice. "Well, at least that's why you claim you would call me all the time."

"Most of the time when I did call you," Tesha said, turning to face him square in the eyes. "You would say that you can't talk."

"True, but only if you called and I was not on a break. You could have at least called during my lunch break," Eric laughed, indicating to Tesha that he was not trying to start an argument. "You would call fifteen minutes after I get to work to ask if I left gas in the car. The car would be right outside, all you had to do was go check it for yourself. Baby, I knew you were calling just because you missed me." Eric laughed again. "I miss that."

"I don't remember doing that," Tesha said, then paused to think if she remembered ever doing that. "I might have done that a few times," Tesha laughed.

"Nine times in one month," Eric said, matter-of-factly.

"So, what you do, count them?" Tesha asked.

"Yes! As a matter of fact, I wrote it down."

"Are you serious Babe?" She asked.

"Yes, you have called me at work about fifteen times over the last year. I wrote the first one down just as a reminder to ask you why you called. I taped it to my desk. You called again one day and again I jotted it down as a reminder to ask what you called about. I think I thought you were just calling for... well... foolish reasons and I just wanted to ask. "I wasn't actually trying to track your calls; it just seemed to happen."

"Well you use to call me on your break too, then you stopped," Tesha replied.

"When I did call you, you would spend more time telling me about what your friends were doing. I wanted to hear about you, not what Lesia and Malcolm were going through," Eric said and then took a sip of his drink. It isn't like Malcolm wasn't going to tell me anyway. I really didn't need to hear it from you too."

"Well, I didn't have anything else to say," Tesha replied. She was ready to change the topic or just watch the movie.

"You could have just said, 'Hey, baby I don't want anything. I just called because I was thinking of you." Eric said.

"Look why are we talking about this now anyway," Tesha asked, annoyed with the conversation. "You want me to act like DeAnna, catering to her man, bringing him his plate, cleaning up behind him. I'm not your mama, help, or the miracle worker."

"So, you want me to work, keep the yard and the cars clean, take out the trash, pay the bills, but it's too much for me to ask for you to fix me a plate of hot food?" Eric questioned. "Now, I am not saying you gotta bring it to me, but it would be nice if you would just fix it for me."

"It's a two-way street," Tesha replied, turning to face him again. "Sweetheart!" She said and then started back eating her food as if the conversation was over.

Eric knew that Tesha wasn't going to admit that she had not made thing easy. He wanted to push a little deeper but decided that he needed to let things go for now. *Consistency might be the key to break through* but knowing when *to let it go is a demonstration of wisdom. There are other ways to make my point*, he thought.

"You know honey," Eric said after a few minutes of uncomfortable silence. "This guy on my job is always inviting me to come to his church."

"And?" Tesha asked with a mouth full of food.

"I think we should go," he hesitantly replied.

"Let me guess what church he goes to. DeAnna's church, right?" Tesha asked and then turned the volume down on the television. She looked at him as if she was ready to go to war over her husband's seemingly fascination with DeAnna.

"Something wrong with that?" He asked.

"Do you want to go because he asked, or because you might get a chance to see her?" Tesha questioned. She then dropped her spoon in her plate as an indication of her dissatisfaction.

"Why is everything always an argument with you?" Eric asked and dropped his folk in his plate as she had done. "I'm really trying, but this is getting old and I'm getting tired of it. I can't take much more of this. I need some peace in my life."

"So, what are you saying?"

"I am saying that I am getting tired of arguing with you," Eric said as he picked up his plate and walked back to the bedroom.

"Do you want a divorce? Is that what you are saying?" She yelled.

Eric didn't answer, he was not going to argue anymore.

"I just told her earlier that I love her and only her," he said to himself. He moved their wedding picture on the nightstand to make room for his plate. "She seems to need 24-hour reassuring about our relationship," he said. "I'm not going to keep defending myself against her self-defeating imagination.

"Do you hear me?" She yelled down the hall to the bedroom. "Huh?" She asked as she entered the room and smacked him on his leg.

"Yes, I hear you, but you're gonna have to figure this out for yourself. I'm not going to keep answering the same question repeatedly," Eric said and grabbed his plate and sat it in his lap. "You figure out what you want, because if I leave you, you gonna be the one who pushes me out."

"So, you're blaming me because you're not man enough to handle your business."

"What business am I not handling? Please tell me, because I get so sick of hearing women saying we ain't handling something but can't never tell us what it is we aren't handling. Maybe we just get tired of jumping through hoops like a circle show dog."

"Women? So, are other women telling you the same thing?" Tesha questioned.

"Look, if I cannot have peace in my own house," Eric said, staring at Tesha looking like she was daring her to say something else.

"Then what?" She asked.

Eric resisted the urge to throw his plate of food across the room. He stood up with his plate in his hand and walked up to his wife and looked her in her eyes, kissed her forehead and said, "Then I don't need to be here." He walked out of the room with her following behind him. He tossed the plate of food in the sink.

"Wow, you just like your sister, walk away from your marriage," she said as she watched Eric searching for his keys. "Y'all show ain't like your parents."

Eric knew Tesha was trying to make him feel guilty about leaving. *Not this time*, he thought. "I'm outta here," he said and walked past Tesha and out the front door. He wasn't sure where he was going, but he knew that he needed to calm down. He pulled out of the driveway. He thought about his sister, Betty, but decided against going to her house. They were not close, but she stayed with Eric and Tesha for a month after she left her husband. Eric felt as if Kimberly was more of a sister than Betty. He decided to go see how Kimberly was doing, so he headed to DeAnna's house where Kimberly had taken up residency. He knew the general area that she lived in, but he was not exactly sure which apartment was DeAnna's. He was about to call Kimberly when he spotted Jeremy's truck. He smiled and turned into the apartment complex.

Chapter 14

"What's up sis?" Eric said as Kimberly held the door open.

Kimberly had not made up her mind if she wanted to stay mad at the guys or not, since she had forgiven her husband, but she had decided to be civil to them all. "Not much, just getting home from work," Kimberly said as she closed the door and escorted him to the living room.

"Home," Eric said, looking around at all the pictures, none of which showcased Kimberly.

"Yes, for now this is home," Kimberly clarified.

"So, speaking of your husband, how are you two doing?" Eric asked as he sat down.

"Well, I wasn't speaking of him, but things are really looking up. I am coming around," Kimberly said and then paused. She plopped down beside Eric and laid her head on his shoulder. "But it's hard accepting the fact that I am a step-mommy," she said rolling her eyes.

"I would love to say that Jason is a jerk," Eric said as he faced Kimberly. "It would be easy to say that you should divorce him. But as a man, I know just how easy it is to stray," Eric said hoping that he wasn't offending her. He didn't want her to push him away and stop talking. "I'm not saying that it's your fault; what I'm saying is that we all need to learn to communicate better. We need to know our spouses' likes, dislikes, and what not to do to push his or her buttons," Eric said, thinking about how Tesha seemed to know exactly what to do to push his buttons, but she didn't seem to avoid them.

"Well," Kimberly said, staring at Eric. "That sounds sort of personal. Tesha pushing your buttons, huh?"

"I can't tell you how many buttons that has been pushed just today."

"Guess communication wasn't flowing for you and her today," Kimberly said.

"Oh, we communicated, it just wasn't the good kind," Eric said getting up and slowly walking towards the window. Seems that all she wants to do is fuss and complain about everything."

"Sometimes, the only time you listen to people is when they fuss," Kimberly said.

"What?" Eric said, staring at Kimberly as if she'd said something he had never heard before. "What do you mean?" He asked with a confused look on his face.

"Yes Eric, I can remember plenty of times that she asked you to do something and she would have to ask four or five times. You've even treated me like that a few times when I stayed at your house when my parents we out somewhere. I didn't know if you were mad at me or just not aware that I was talking, but I would get so mad. I would start screaming at you."

"What?" He asked, sounding clueless.

"I thought you were just a very angry man. Especially, after my parent's accident and I was around you more. I remember crying one time and calling you a jerk. I thought you didn't like me," Kimberly explained.

"What, please, like you?" Eric joked. "I couldn't stand you. Chris had you thinking and acting like you were some little princess. He paid us to like you." Eric turned to face her and smiled, indicating that he was only joking. "You know Johnathan often said that I act like David."

"David who?"

"David in the Bible. He said David got distracted with other things."

"Well, are you?" Kimberly asked.

"Sometimes I am, but I think it's because I," Eric paused to think. "Well, I know I need to..." Eric paused again as he thought about the peace he felt when he was watching DeAnna's preacher on television. "Just forget it," he said. "Oh, hey DeAnna," Eric said when DeAnna entered the room. "I didn't know you were here. I didn't see your car."

"Yeah, I know. It's in the shop. Trying to see if it is possible, for me to extend the lifetime. God knows I don't want a payment," DeAnna said as she grabbed a can of cranberry juice out of the refrigerator.

"I was surprised to see Jeremy's truck parked outside," Eric said trying to figure out who actually had it, Kimberly or DeAnna. *Prior to his accident, Jeremy wouldn't allow any woman to drive his truck*, Eric thought. "Nice day like this and a nice ride like that, I would be rolling."

"Well, I don't want him to feel that I am using him," DeAnna said, thinking about all the stuff she needed to do, but since she didn't have his truck to run her errand, she decided not to push her luck.

"Trust me, he knows when he's being used and when he's simply helping out a friend," Eric said.

"Is that right?" DeAnna replied as she peeped out the window. "It is a nice day, so what brings you here?" DeAnna stared at Eric and then at Kimberly. She could tell that Eric was there for more than just to check up on his so-called sister.

"Well, just checking on Kimberly," he said, smiling at Kimberly.

"Looks like she should be checking on you," DeAnna replied.

"Me," Eric said. "I'm good; I'm here to make sure Kimberly is okay."

"Well, besides being betrayed, cheated on, lied to, and laughed at," Kimberly said, smiling back at Eric. "Oh and made an instant mommy without labor pain. Other than that, I'm fine."

"You are gonna get through it, I promise you that," Eric said as he faced Kimberly and smiled. "He really loves you and although I am mad at him, I understand more than I care to tell you about why we men get stupid for a minute and do what we do."

"What? So, you on his side," Kimberly questioned. "I can't believe this. I guess all that sister stuff is just talk."

"Kimberly look, I'm so sorry," Eric said as he took her hand. "I know we did not make things easy on Jason."

"I don't follow you," Kimberly said, looking confused.

"Well, I was thinking about how often we came over and acted like we were in control. A man has to be the man in his own house. Who would want their wife's brother and friends coming in like they own everything?"

"So, you're the blame now?" Kimberly shook her head in disbelief.

"Sort of," Eric confirmed.

Kimberly sat back on the sofa and thought about something similar Jason said. She realized for the first time that Jason was not just trying to make up an excuse for his behavior.

"But still, he could have talked to me," Kimberly said

She thought about the many times that Chris and all the other guys would come over and walk around like they were at home. Jason never bonded with them, like they bonded with each other, no matter how hard they tried to include him. They would tell Jason what to do, like he was a kid. *Why he didn't just man up to them*, Kimberly thought.

"People tolerate a lot from their mate's family," Eric said.

"He knows that you all are literately, all the family I have," Kimberly said. She seemed to be finally, but slowly putting the pieces together. "He took it all just to keep peace while suffering himself. I didn't make things easy for him, always acting like my brother and y'all were my heroes," Kimberly said, flowing in tears. "He was my real hero and I pushed him away."

"It's so easy to push someone away without even realizing it," Eric said as he stared at Kimberly. "I am so sorry Kimberly."

"When and how did you come to this revelation?" Kimberly asked, not knowing what else to say.

"I guess I was thinking about what a home really is."

"Huh?" Kimberly questioned, looking confused. "Please explain?"

"A home is your comfort zone. The place where you should be able to be free to do whatever, well whatever that's legal to do. It should be the one place where a man should feel like a king."

"You're really pushing it," Kimberly said as she glanced at DeAnna. "A king, huh? What do you think DeAnna?"

"Well, I think the man should feel like a king in his own home. He should be the head, that's what the Bible says."

"What does the Bible say about a woman who fusses all the time?" Eric asked without thinking.

"A what?" DeAnna questioned as if she hadn't heard Eric correctly.

Eric looked at her, knowing that she heard him. He patiently waited for her to answer.

"Basically, that type of woman breaks her house down. But a better question to ask would be, 'Why is she doing it, and how does one stop the destruction?" DeAnna said. She had a feeling that there were more to the questioning and a story behind them.

"And how does she change it?" Eric added.

"Funny," Kimberly said as if she was about to begin a sermon. "Men want to be the king, the head, and the boss, except when it comes to making decisions to change things."

"Change what?" Eric asked. "And how exactly?" He desperately wanted to know since he felt the problems stemmed from his wife.

"If you want the marriage to change, you have to change the way you relate to your wife," DeAnna explained.

"So, I have to be the one who plays the peacemaker. Well, I have tried that," Eric said, feeling as if he was being double teamed by Kimberly and DeAnna.

"You tried once, and it didn't," DeAnna began, but Eric interrupted.

"More than once," Eric interjected.

"Twice, three times, four, maybe more," Kimberly chimed in.

"Well, yeah," Eric said.

"When did the destruction of the relationship begin?" DeAnna asked.

"I don't know. Maybe over the past two years," Eric responded.

"Oh," DeAnna said, as if Eric had said the magic words. "So, it wasn't overnight or as a result of simply three or four incidents?" She asked.

"Nope!" Eric replied, knowing where DeAnna was headed. "It happened gradually."

"Well, it may be a gradual process for your marriage to completely heal. It may take longer to fix then it did to break down. Hopefully, it won't. If you both want the marriage, I am sure you can make a huge turn around in no time."

"Hum," Eric said, staring into space as if he was waiting for a response to fall from heaven.

"What are you and Tesha doing Sunday?" DeAnna asked.

"Nothing, as usual," he replied.

"Why don't you and Tesha join me at my church," DeAnna asked as she winked at Kimberly. We are having a group relationship meeting," DeAnna paused. "Well, a group discussion is a better title for it."

"A discussion group?" Eric questioned. "I think I will pass. That is not my cup of tea."

"Is your marriage your cup of tea?" Kimberly asked, but didn't wait for a response. "Apparently not. If you are not willing to do something about saving it."

"Okay," DeAnna interrupted. "If you change your mind, we would love to have you and Tesha. I am sure that Jeremy would love some male company. Another male's point of view would really help him out. The last one he attended, not long ago, he got attacked. Last meeting, I was just stepping in, now they have put me over the single's group and I am praying it will be a big success," DeAnna said without thinking.

"I guess if Jeremy is going, I might go too," Eric said and then remembered how Tesha hated being around a group of women. "But I cannot make any promises about my wife."

"Fine!" DeAnna said and began to name others who might be there in addition to the church folks. "Kimberly, Jason, Jeremy, you, and maybe Tesha. I am so excited."

"If Lesia goes, I am sure Tesha will too," Kimberly said. "Those two can actually teach a class or two, but Lesia needs a lesson on getting pass the past. They give really good advice sometimes, even if they don't follow it themselves."

"Well, I think that happens more than one might think," DeAnna said. "I know you have heard the expression, "Easier said than done.""

"Whoever coined that phrase should be a Pulitzer Prizes winner," Eric said. "So, what time is the gathering?"

"From 6-8 p.m., but we can stay as late as we like or leave when we feel no one else has anything to talk about. I hope we have a good time. It used to be at 2 pm, but that just seem too early, people wanted to go home and relax a little, get something to eat, and take kids to the sitter. Besides, I think night time changes people's personality. During the day they think about everything they need to do, and they are in a "lets-just-get-this-over-with mode. I try to plan it for a time that fits the group. Too many people plan stuff based on what is good for two or three, then they don't understand why no one want to attend," DeAnna explained.

"So," Eric asked, interrupting DeAnna's. "Will there be any food there?"

"Well no, we had not planned for food, but I can try to get the pastor to spring for pizza. Its last minutes though," DeAnna said. "But snacks, now I am sure we can do that."

"What about daycare for those with kids?" Kimberly asked, making sure DeAnna had thought about everything.

"You know what, I have been saying that more people would come if we eliminated all excuses like daycare, dinner, and transportation. Some people would come just to get away from the kids. There are people in the church who would be willing to watch other people's children, now that their children are grown. Some people need a break from the kids, other than when they are at work," DeAnna said. "We just have to form a list of those who can help and what they can help with." DeAnna said, talking non-stop. She was glad to express her ideas to someone who seemed to understand.

"It seems like so many people in the church acts like they know everything and no one else knows anything but them. They act as if a title made them all knowing."

"Add food, and I know Johnathan will come," Eric interjected. "Oh, and Chris too, if there are single ladies there."

"This is not a pick up joint," DeAnna jokingly said, shaking her head.

"I know that, but so what if people come for the wrong reason and then end up learning some valuable information," Eric said.

"Well," DeAnna said thinking about the fact that she wanted and needed single men to entice the lady to want to join.

"Look," Eric said. "DeAnna you really give good advice and all you need is the opportunity to show your pastor what you are made of. Some people talk down to people and I know one thing, offended people are not going to receive well from people who talk down to them. You have what it takes to help others. Besides, the more the merrier and the more men, the more ladies. I mean if they know that men will be there," Eric said. It was as if he really had to convince her to invite the others.

"You are probably right," DeAnna responded.

"I know that I am," Eric replied. "You know, I was just telling Tesha earlier that I wanted to go to your church."

"Really?" DeAnna asked. She was shocked.

"You'll love it." Kimberly replied. "I have been a few times. I even got Jason to agree to go. The pastor is awesome."

"Yeah, I know. I saw him on TV and man was that brother real."

"So, why not join us for morning service too," DeAnna asked.

"I might. Is Jay going?" Eric asked.

"As a matter of fact, he is," DeAnna said, sounding like a proud mother announcing that her child was going to college.

"Hum," Eric said. "Let me see what magic I can work."

Chapter 15

Eric glanced in the sanctuary of the crowed church, searching for Jeremy and DeAnna. He spotted Kimberly and waived. The usher escorted Eric and Tesha to the empty seats that Kimberly had been saving for them.

"Thanks," Eric said as he sat down.

The usher smiled. Eric didn't bother telling the usher that he was thanking Kimberly for saving the seats.

"Man, I thought you had changed your mind," Jeremy said after DeAnna whispered in his ear and told him that Eric was sitting to his left.
"I almost did. Tesha thinks something is up," Eric explained.
"Why?" Jeremy asked.
"I'll tell you later," Eric said as he turned and smiled at his wife and then back to Jeremy. "We're acting like kids, talking in church," Eric said. He smiled at DeAnna who looked as she was about to say, 'shhhhh.'
"Today's lesson, Sisters." Tesha heard the pastor say.

"You are not going to keep that man if you keep on nagging, fussing, and complaining. You're going to run him to a strange woman. We're going to see what the Bible says about strange women in a few minutes," the pastor said.

Applause and Amen rolled throughout the sanctuary. A few men clapped their approval.

"Now men, the Bible does say, 'it's better to dwell in the corner of the roof-top than in a large home with a nagging woman," the Pastor said.

Again, the Amens rolled throughout the church.

"But, now listen men. It's talking about the roof of your house. Don't go to Ms. Jones' house… that's where some miss it and go to the wrong house.

The Amens echoed throughout the church from the women.

Kimberly looked at Jason. "You got that? Stay in the corner of your roof top."

They turned back and continued to listen to the message.

"Let me flip the script again. Women, learn to treat your man like the king of his house. One of the reasons why men run to other women is because the other woman allows them to have total rule over her house. What man is going to want to come home to disrespect when he is being treated with love and respect at her house. Now! Let me clarify something for you. Lust and love are not the same thing, but men feel loved when women treat them as if they cannot live without him. Men, you should not try to dominate that woman either," the pastor said.

"I guess that's why DeAnna serves Jeremy," Tesha whispered to Chris. "She's trying to make him her king."

"Ain't nothing wrong with that," Chris replied, squeezing Tesha's shoulder. "I wanna be the king of my house too."

"Great," Tesha replied. "Another DeAnna fan."

~

"I didn't think you were coming," Eric said to Chris later, as they stood in the church lobby after service, waiting for DeAnna to finalize plans for the single's event scheduled for later that evening.

"Man, I came because I heard there are some fine woman at this church," Chris said.

"I heard the same thing," Malcolm said as he walked up behind Chris. "But I also heard that it's hard to break them down. They don't fall for the mind games and lines that the average women fall for."

"Well, I'm not the average man," Chris replied, feeling ready for a challenge.

"That's true," Jeremy said, joining his friends, "You got no game."

"What's up player?" Chris said to Jeremy.

"Player? I've been played and now played out," Jeremy replied.

The lobby was crowded with people standing around talking. A few women stared as Jason, Chris, Malcolm, Jeremy, and DeAnna, standing in around waiting for Tesha and Kimberly to return from the bathroom. DeAnna could tell that a few of the women were checking the men out. When Tesha walked out of the bathroom, she glanced around and admired the lobby and the beautiful flowers that decorated the service desk.

"They do everything first class here," Tesha said to herself as she spotted the oversize armchairs.

"Hey Dee," a slender woman yelled as she approached.

When everyone turned in the woman's direction, she waved and quickly began to run her hand down the side of her own dress as if she was smoothing it out. DeAnna knew that move all too well. She had seen so many women use the smoothing out the dress as a 'check out my curves' move. She knew that the lady called her name with the hopes that the men standing with her would turn in her direction too. DeAnna pointed Malcolm and Chris in the direction of the men's room just in time to avoid Sister Stacy O'Neill's lurking eyes.

"I see we have new visitors," Sister Stacy said as she approached DeAnna.

"Yes, we do," DeAnna said, quickly trying to decide if there was a quick escape or not. DeAnna decided to be polite and to introduce everyone. "This is Eric and over by the service desk," DeAnna said pointing to Tesha, "is Eric's wife Tesha and the lady walking with her is Kimberly. Jason here, is Kimberly's husband. I know you've seen Jeremy here with me before." DeAnna didn't bother explaining whether Malcolm or Chris had wives lurking around or not since they had gone to the bathroom. "Everyone this is Sister Stacy."

"Nice to meet you all. I certainly hope that you all felt so welcomed that you will come back again," Sister Stacy said.

DeAnna could almost feel the spirit of disappointment floating in the atmosphere. She knew that the words 'married man' was floating around somewhere in Sister Stacy's head. It was a word that a lot of single Christian women hated to hear, especially if it was associated with good-looking men in a church environment. As Stacy was about to leave, Chris and Malcolm returned from the bathroom.

"Oh," DeAnna said as Chris and Malcolm approached. "Sister O'Neill, this is Chris and Malcolm, they are also first-time visitors here. And hopefully, they will return as well. I'm expecting them to join us tonight at the single's meeting to give us the male's perspective.

"Hello," Sister Stacy O'Neill said, staring at Chris. "I hope you will join our discussion group. Us single women could really use some good advice from intelligent men. She waited a few seconds to see if they agreed. "I mean we need someone to educate us on how to satisfy our man. Well, at least someone to teach us what to do when we know how to turn one on, but not keep him turned on."

"I understand that," Chris said, perking up. "And what better way to educate women on a good Christian man."

"Get the good book," Tesha chimed in and then burst out laughing.

"Yes, the good book does give us a lot of excellent advice," DeAnna said. "But the problem is, most people need help understanding the word."

"True," Chris said as he noticed several other women staring. "So, when is this discussion group, I'll be glad to offer all the advice that I can."

"Tonight," DeAnna said, feeling that she might have a good turnout.

"Tonight?" Sister O'Neill asked. "I thought it was today at 2 p.m.

"Well," DeAnna said, noticing a few eavesdroppers. "It's already been a long day for most of us and when we get to go home, freshen up, relax a little, eat dinner, and take the kids to a babysitter we feel…"

"I know that's right," Sister Gina White said, desiring to be a part of the conversation; therefore, she didn't even let DeAnna finish her sentence. "I'm sick of dragging my children behind me, hoping they sit quietly. I think it is a great idea DeAnna that we get to go home and rest. I'm definitely going to be here."

"Good," DeAnna said. She felt good that she wasn't the only one feeling the reservations about the daytime meeting. She had been trying for months to explain that maybe the singles would come, if they got some freedom from their children at night-time. She knew that it would be a better time to hold a meeting.

A few of the other eavesdroppers felt comfortable and joined the discussion in the lobby. They all agreed that 7:00 p.m. was a better time.

"My youngest son is eight and will be fed and enjoying cartoon network for at least two hours. And my seventeen-year-old will be on the phone, no one will miss me," Christina Milton said as she extended her hand. "Hi, I'm Christina, my friends call me Chrissy and I look forward to picking your brains tonight," she said as she shook Chris' hand.

Chris stared at Christina contemplating if he wanted to give her his name. She was definitely not his type. Chris could tell that she was the all-eyes-on-me type.

"Well, I may see you there," he said. He decided not to give his name. He didn't want her acting like she knew him when they got to the meeting. *Chris, you made it*, he could hear her say when he walked through the door. It was still a strategy used by blockers, trying to warn other women to back off. He was not about to fall victim to that trick.

"Didn't catch your name," Christina said, staring into Chris' hazel eyes.

She scanned his tall medium built body and tried to see if he had a ring on his finger. Chris hand was resting in his pocket.

"She's good," Chris said to himself. "Or at least she thinks she is." Chris played with his hand in his pocket for few seconds and then extended his hand.

"Sorry, where are my manners? My name is Christopher," Chris said, smiling as he studied Christina's disappointed look.

DeAnna stared at Chris' hand and the shiny, wedding band that suddenly appeared on his otherwise, empty ring finger.

"Okay Chrissy," Chris said with a grin on his face. "We look forward to seeing you tonight." He knew the word 'we' suggested that the wife would be with him, even though it was a single's meeting.

"Sound good," Chrissy said. She then made some excuse to leave, said goodbye, and quickly headed straight out the door.

DeAnna scanned the room and smiled as she admired the set up. She did not want people sitting around in uncomfortable fold-up chairs. She had managed to convert the church's kitchen into what looked like an over-sized living room with a 58-inch flat screen TV and DVD player. The folding tables which normally occupied most of the space in the kitchen, were folded up to allow for three oversized sofas, two recliners, and some padded chairs. DeAnna had decorated the floor with a beautiful earth tone multi-colored area rug in the center of the room. The sofas which were placed around the border of the rug, created a small intimate space.

DeAnna really wanted the participants to feel as if they were at home. She had lit candles around the room to really give it that intimate feel. She thought it would really make people feel open to converse like they would if they were at home with their friends and family and not just with a group of strangers, discussing their business. She smiled as she thought about the bond that could form from the group gathering. *We will no longer be just familiar faces who we waved at,* DeAnna thought to herself. *We will have a bond.* She became lost in thoughts. The door flew open and startled DeAnna.

"Oh, Brother Fred," DeAnna said after catching her breath.

"Sis, where do you want this cart?" Brother Fred asked, scanning the room for the TV.

"Oh, I almost forgot about that," DeAnna said looking for an outlet. "I guess over there," she said, spotting an outlet at the kitchen center isle work station. "Prefect," she said, realizing that everyone would have a better view of the television.

"You got it looking real nice in here," Brother Fred said as he scanned the room a second time. "Just like home. I feel like parking my young bones on that sofa, flipping on the TV, and just relaxing with a slice of Dani's famous honeybun cake." Brother Fred said.

DeAnna smiled. "That's exactly how I want it to feel, like home. People tend to let their hair down at home. Oh, and yes, that's one of Dani's famous home-made sweet treats and you are welcome to take a slice."

"Thanks, and yeah, you right. People do let it all down and out at home," Brother Fred said, shaking his head in total approval. "Real nice.

Well, you young folks go on and have a good time. Wish I could stay, but gotta get on home and begin my second job."

"What that?" DeAnna questioned.

"Oh, you done heard this before, plenty of men got these titles. I am Mr. fix-it, go-get it, stop-it, or go buy it."

"Sounds like you love it," DeAnna said, watching Brother Fred face light up as he talked.

"Well, baby girl, I do. Make me feel needed," Brother Fred said then paused for a few second thinking if he wanted to say more or not. "Young women these days always talking about they don't need a man. Act like they can do it all by themselves and they treat them like they are not needed. So, the man drifts away from her. Then when he meets someone that does need him, he feels wanted and needed. He starts to spend more time with his girlfriend than he spends with his wife."

"Um,'" DeAnna said, wishing Brother Fred would join the group.

"So, Brother Fred, what about these men that don't want to do nothing for his woman?"

"What about 'em? They boys; they ain't men. Simple as that," Brother Fred said. "Now, I do believe in balance; she can't have a man running around doing every little thing that she can do for herself. Like he just a puppet."

"Yeah, that's true too," DeAnna agreed.

"A man wants to feel loved and appreciated, but not used. Ya feel me?"

DeAnna laughed. "Yeah, I feel ya."

"My grandkids keep me hopped."

"You mean hipped," DeAnna managed to say after she caught her breath from laughing.

"I musta' missed a few lessons," Brother Fred said laughing too.

"Don't worry, the way these kids change Ebonics from month-to-month, we will always be students trying to keep up with them, but you got it."

"Thanks, Sister Dee. Now, I hope you take a few pictures, so Pastor can see what you did to this kitchen. People hear about this and you will have a packed house next month. Especially, if you really make this feel like home and have a home cooked meal."

"You know I thought about that," DeAnna said with excitement. "I wanted us to cook together as a group activity. I bet we will have so much fun cooking together."

"You got really good ideas. We need to start having fun together. Too many church folks come, hear the word, go home, and forget about each other until Bible study or the next church service," Brother Fred said.

"I hope Pastor will be pleased," DeAnna said as she looked around.

"Well, your heart is in the right place and you ain't trying to do something just to be seen, like most folks. Too many people want to claim that they called to the ministry or either some are given a title just to keep them as a member, so they tell the members that they called. They prepare for a week then they up in front of some congregation preaching they trial sermon and ain't got no more anointing than a little bit. Just repeating what they heard someone else say. Then they got minister on their license tag and in the signature line of every e-mail, *Minister this, Deacon that*, acting like they created some ministry class when all they do is copy everything someone else done said. If theys' called, God will give them their own special gift. When you're called by God, you will work without a title. When you are called, the anointed is in your walk, your talk, it's so much a part of you, ya don't have to announce it to the world. You know, you don't see God tagging stuff and announcing Himself, but you know He's there. You know His work without Him always telling you He did it. These so-called ministers will only be seen at church with Windex, if someone is looking, but think they are too good to wash a window otherwise. Hum, but Jesus washed feet."

"Brother Fred, you said a mouth full," DeAnna said, agreeing with everything he said.

"So, what you saying? I'm talking too much. I didn't mean to carry on like that."

"No-no. Brother Fred that's one of those expressions the young people use when they are 100% in agreement with what you are saying, and you said everything that needed to be said."

"Oh okay. My grands have not taught me that yet, I guess I will have to take your word for it."

"You can trust me," DeAnna replied.

"I do," Brother Fred said and quickly looked around. "Well, I see your guest are beginning to arrive, so you enjoy and don't forget to take pictures."

DeAnna's heart fluttered as she stared at Jeremy, Malcolm, Chris, Tesha, Lesia, and Kimberly entering the room, followed by Christina and two of the other church members.

"Wow! DeAnna, you really got it feeling like home in here. I love it," Christina said.

"You said a mouth full, "Brother Fred chimed in before DeAnna had the chance to thank Christina. Brother Fred headed for the door. "You folks enjoy your party,"

"Thanks, we will," DeAnna said, laughing at the seventy-two-year old man who acted as if he was about 45 years old and still trying to stay hipped. DeAnna quickly turned to her guest. "Help yourself to a snack," DeAnna said as she checked on Jeremy, who had taken a seat. DeAnna whispered something in Jeremy's ear. He rubbed his stomach as if he was ready to eat.

"Okay," Jeremy replied with a smile on his face.

DeAnna fixed a plate for Jeremy and sat it down on the table in front of him. Kimberly sat down beside him to help him if DeAnna was too busy.

"What's up?" Kimberly said to Jeremy.
"I'm good kiddo," he replied.
"So, we are back to that Kiddo stuff?"
"Oh, sorry old habits die hard."
"So they say."

Jeremy could sense that Kimberly was upset about something. Although his senses had become much stronger, he wasn't sure if Jason was with her or not. It was hard for him to sense the presence of his friends when he was in large groups of people and in public places. He smelt so many different colognes, lotions, perfumes, and even food. The smells seem to blend together.

"Okay everyone, let's get started," DeAnna said.

Kimberly sighed. Jeremy wanted to give Kimberly a comforting pat on her back, but he felt a little uneasy about reaching out.

"Okay, we're going to do a quick ice breaker," DeAnna announced. She paused when she noticed the door creeping open.

"Come on in," DeAnna said to the unknown person behind the door.

Kimberly held her breathe and crossed her fingers. She hoped the person behind the half-opened door would be her husband. They all, even Jason, had agreed to support DeAnna since she had been such a blessing to them all. Even Tesha and Lesia had warmed up to DeAnna and had even called on her for a shoulder to cry on and some advice.

Two tall women walked in, winked a hello at DeAnna and quickly found a seat. The tall stout woman headed straight for the sofa. Kimberly watched as the 6 feet 3 inch, 350-pound woman slide in the small empty space on the sofa. As she wiggled from side-to-side and forced her way back in the sofa, Malcolm watched as if she was part of the entertainment.

"Comfee," Malcolm said as the woman exhaled.

The woman lifted her body a little and pulled her dress down. "You talking to me?" The woman asked when she noticed Malcolm staring at her. She continued to fix her clothes.

"Yes, I am," he replied.
"Oh well, I am now," the woman said.

DeAnna smiled. She had a feeling deep down in her spirit that she was in for an interesting night. She was shocked that Lesia did not react at all to the attention her husband was giving to the woman wiggling on the sofa. DeAnna quietly thanked God for the gathering and her supporters.

"Okay," DeAnna said, smiling at her new friends and church members. "Now, let's get started."

"Sorry, I'm late," someone said before the door was even opened wide enough for anyone to be seen. Kimberly smiled as the door opened wide enough and Jason walked in.

"Baby, I am so sorry; I got delayed. Please accept my apology," Jason said as he lowered himself down onto one of the bean bags across from Kimberly.

"This is DeAnna's gig; it's not mines. Apologize to her," Kimberly replied.

"I know," Jason softly said. "But I'm here for you." Jason quickly turned and faced DeAnna. "No offense Dee," Jason said, glancing at Dee. "I mean Sister DeAnna."

"None taken," DeAnna said and smiled. She winked at Jason, indicating that his response was prefect. "Okay," she said and turned to her guest again. "I want everyone to take the next ten minutes to get to know each other," DeAnna said as she nodded hello to a few other people who entered.

"Cool," Myles said, looking at the room décor. He held the door open for the ladies who were close behind him. He stared at the five-foot four inches, one hundred and twenty-five-pound woman who entered with him.

"But," DeAnna continued. "You can only spend about thirty to forty second with each person. In that time get as much information as you can."

"Easy enough," Myles said.

"Then we will introduce each other to the group, sharing what you learned about someone else." DeAnna continued. "And while gathering information, you cannot tell the same thing to different people. So, if I tell Jason that like peanut butter in my ice cream, then I can't tell Kimberly the same thing. Got it? Then when Jason introduces me to the group and he tells what he learned about me, other can share what they learned too," DeAnna said.

"Oh, I get it," Myles said with a devious grin on his face.

"Let's get started," DeAnna said.

The participants began to talk to each other. DeAnna sat down beside Jeremy as soon as Kimberly got up. DeAnna set an old fashion timer and sat it on the table. She watched as the men gravitated to the women and the women seem to head for whoever was closest. The alarm went off.

"Times up," DeAnna yelled. "Now it's time for the introductions. Everyone have a seat."

As soon as everybody was back in their seats, Myles yelled out, "I want to go first."

"I can always count on you to be the star of the show," DeAnna said to Myles.

"I'm here to make you happy darling," he replied.

"Okay, let's start with the person to your right," DeAnna said and pointed to Sister Regina. "Why don't you stand so everyone can see you?"

Regina quickly stood up and turned toward Myles as if she couldn't wait to hear what he could remember about her.

"Regina has been married once," Myles said.
"She has two children," Chris chimed in.

The group quickly understood the flow and continued to move around the room clockwise. DeAnna quickly realized that the ice breaker was going to take longer than she thought, but everyone seemed to be enjoying. They were comparing notes. The ten-minute icebreaker lasted over thirty minutes in order for everyone to stand and be introduced. They talked to each as if they had known each other for a while. DeAnna was glad that the activity took so long. Starting the topic about relationships and dating was harder than she thought. Kimberly was the last person to stand. Regina was the last person to give a piece of information about Kimberly.

"Kimberly wants to become a nurse," Regina stated.

"What?" Jason asked. He was pleasantly surprised. "I never knew that. Well, what do you know; I learned something new today."

"And Dee, I mean Sister DeAnna," Jeremy joked. "I learn more about everybody else than I know about myself."

DeAnna could tell that Jeremy was battling with inner feelings.

"I guess that's all I wanted to say," Jeremy said. He really had more to say, but he changed his mind.

"Why do you guys do that?" Sister Jackie asked, staring at Jeremy, not realizing that he couldn't see her looking at him.

"Do what?" Myles questioned as if Jackie was addressing him.

"I mean why do you clam up when you try to express your feelings. Like Ray Charles just did," Jackie said as she stared at Jeremy wondering why he had shades on.

"Well sweetheart," Myles began, ready to defend himself, Jeremy, and all other men. "It's not always a good idea to carry your feelings around on your shoulders and I definitely wouldn't express all my feelings in a crowd of strangers. Some women are quick to make fun of what they don't know," Myles said as he thought about the Ray Charles joke. He wanted to put her in her place and let her know that Jeremy is blind, but he knew that Jeremy didn't make announcements about it. "You know, like someone who has sensitivity to bright lights might be cracked on for wearing shades."

"Sorry about that," Jackie quickly said, sounding sincere.

"So, you wouldn't be affectionate in public?" Christina questioned.

"Depends," Myles said, quickly rising. He pulled Christina off the sofa. "I will hug you," he said as he gave her a friendly granny hug. "I will hold your hand," he said, grabbing her hand and swinging it back and forth like they were two kids skipping across the schoolyard.

"We going to play hopscotch too," Christina joked.

"We could," Myles responded. "But seriously!" Myles said as everyone laughed. "Men get a bad rap either way."

"Explain!" DeAnna said. She was excited that the conversation had already involved with little effort from her. DeAnna hated when facilitators spent most of time talking about what interested themselves, and never considering what the group wanted to talk about. She hated it even more when the facilitator acted like his or her opinion was the only one that mattered.

"If we cry, we are seen by some female observers as being too sensitive, or the loving boyfriend, husband, or friend etc., or whatever else y'all call us."

"I agree," DeAnna said. "A sensitive man has my heart always."

"Until," Myles interrupted, pointing his finger upward. "Until you get mad. Then we become wimps, punks, or big babies."

"I definitely agree with that," Jason said.

Kimberly stared at Jason, objecting to his comment, but she quickly removed her negative facial expressions. *Allow him to be open to express himself freely, without the fear of retaliation,* she could hear DeAnna saying.

"Have I ever made you feel like a wimp, punk, or even a big baby, sweetheart?" Kimberly asked, smiling at Jason.

"Well Baby," Jason hesitantly said. "You have made me feel less than a man sometimes, but..."

"Yeah and I bet you did something to deserve it," the tall stout woman said in a joking tone before Jason could finish his sentence.

"Don't start Jessica," the skinny tall woman said.

"Start what-the truth?" Jessica replied.

"No! Judging prefect strangers because of what your husband did. Not all men are dogs and not all women who want a man with an 850+ beacon score, a good job, and a nice..." the woman paused "well you know, not all of them are gold diggers."

"You forgot a clean criminal history, not even a speeding ticket, college degrees, a 5000-square foot home, and a white picket fence," Jessica said as if it was a regular conversation between the two of them.

"Baby, you don't want just a man, you want God," Jackie replied.

The group laughed.

"I know that's right Sis," DeAnna said. "Now, I can work with you on anything but God. You gotta have God in your life, if you want me there."

A few Amens echoed around the room from the women. They whispered a little among themselves. DeAnna could tell that even though not many of them spoke, they all seemed to be enjoying themselves.

"Amen," Michael Nelson said as he entered the room followed by Johnathan. "May I join you? Sounds like you about to praise the maker and creator."

"Sure, we are glad to have you," Jessica said. She rolled her eyes as Michael pulled out a fold up chair from the small kitchen table and sat down.

"I'm Michael Nelson," he said. "Heard that there was a single's meeting here and thought I'd see if I could get a few tips."

"On what, Mrs. Nelson? Oh wait; you want tips on how to be a married man. You're still married, aren't you?" Jessica asked.

"Depends on who you ask," Mr. Nelson said as he laughed.

"Okay, why don't we ask Sister Nelson," Jackie replied.

"Go ahead and when you get the opportunity to talk to her, please let her know that her husband left home about an hour ago. You might can get a word in between *'Lord I love you'* and *'Lord there ain't no man like you,'*" Mr. Nelson said, upset but trying to hide it.

"Sounds like you got a good ole praying woman, whose giving honor where honor is due," Johnathan said, sounding like he was a shy schoolboy trying to defend himself against a bully, but was too scared to really speak up loud enough to truly be heard.

"I understand that," Michael said as he extended his hand towards Johnathan. He politely shook his hand and introduced himself.

"Now, what I was saying," Mr. Nelson started to say then abruptly stopped. "Oh, I am so sorry Ms. Dee," he said as an afterthought. "I came in and took over didn't I."

"Well," DeAnna said trying to be careful not to offend Michael nor discourage the conversation. "Brother Michael, it seems that you are about to give us some insight that might lead us into a new topic of conversation. Are there any objections?" She asked the group.

"Sister DeAnna, before we change the topic again, I would like to say that I don't think there's anything wrong with the sister knowing what she wants in life and what she wants out of her man," one of the ladies said.

All the women and most of the men agreed. There were a few men who looked as if they were pondering the comment and still trying to make up their minds.

"I don't either," DeAnna hesitantly replied, "but we have to stop excluding men on the basics of he drives a Honda, and not an Escalade. If we allow God to lead us, he'll take us to our spiritual mate and we can strive towards some things together."

"Girl, sometimes it seems that God is moving too slow. I'm tired of being single," another lady said.

"Have you ever watched people walking or jogging around the track and by the time one person has been around one time, someone else has already been around twice. Now, it appears that the person in front is leading, right? In reality, the person behind is ahead because he's already been around one time and walking around another time. Ladies, God has already been around one time, done all He is going to do, and is just waiting on us to catch up," DeAnna said. "It's your move, our move, but before we move, we need to make sure we have prepared ourselves."

"That's right. Once you get married, it ain't no more 'my bed,' it is 'our bed,' ain't no more 'my house' it's 'our house,'" Michael Nelson said.

"I want a man, not a husband," Sister Jackie replied.

"So, why waste perfectly good husband material on a woman who only wants someone to pay for her two-piece meal and maybe give her a laugh or two," Tesha interjected.

"That's the problem, too many men and women want the marriage, but not the commitment of being a wife. I mean, I love God too and I pray and fast, but ain't there such a thing as too much praying?" Michael Nelson asked.

"What!" Regina asked as if Michael Nelson had just cursed God.

"Okay, I'm sorry; I might not be as saved or righteous as the rest of you," Michael said. "But personally, if all you got time to do is pray, why bother getting married, having kids, or working for that matter?"

"You got a point there," Christina a.k.a Chrissy replied.

"I've dated a Christian woman once and she prayed morning noon and night. If she wasn't working or sleeping, she was praying. Once I asked her if it was raining outside and she had to stop and pray about the rain watering the flowers, washing away the pollen, and how God clothed the Lillie's of the field, blah, blah, blah," Eric said. "I had taken a shower, put my PJ's on, and was almost asleep before she answered."

"That's what I'm saying about my wife," Michael said, sending a disapproving look at Jessica. "I love God and I pray just like the rest but is there such a thing as too much prayer when you are ignoring your mate all the time."

"Are you serious?" Tesha asked.

"Yes, I am," Michael said without hesitating or staring at Tesha for an answer.

"Maybe," Tesha said, searching for an answer. She could hear the desperation in his voice. "But maybe that's what it takes for her to get through."

"God didn't bring me a wife, to simply pray. I could have just stayed single," Michael said as he scanned the room to see if anyone would offer a rebuttal.

"I agree, if you have to pray that much, you don't have time to do anything else. I mean does she pray while the pastor is teaching? Does she pray while stuffing her mouth with the food that God blessed her with? But now, the million-dollar question is, did she pray before she decided to get married, because it sound like she does not understand that a married woman, cares for the things of the world to please her husband; at least that's what I was told the Bible says. And besides that, God wants us to live our life and have a life of balance," Jeremy said.

"Good points," DeAnna said, smiling at Jeremy. She was surprised at his response.

~

The discussion group went from topic-to-topic, hitting high level of participation to mild lows. DeAnna considered it a huge success. The past discussion groups she had attended, had been nothing more than an opportunity for the host to broadcast a well decorated personal and professional resume. The host would keep such tight control over the group that the participants were often told what they should and should not feel, without the host even trying to first understand the participants' perspective or situation. DeAnna remembered too many nights of wanting to just be free to feel what she felt and be able to express it without feeling judged, even if someone did give her a Biblical solution. After almost two hours, the conversation hit a high note, and it was almost impossible to come back down.

Why do men cheat, had drawn a division between the men and the women with Myles and DeAnna straddling the fence and playing mediator and peace maker.

"So, what it sounds like to me is, women want to know why men cheat, but yet you don't want to accept the man's reasoning," Myles said and then paused long enough to scan the women's faces. "So, it seems that you don't really want to know why; you just want another reason to dog men out, put all men down because of what your man or ex man did, and then complain."

"There is no justification for cheating," Kimberly said.

"That might be true for you, but to the cheating party, they don't feel they have to have a good enough reason for 'you' as long as it's good enough for them," one of the men stated.

"What?" Kimberly asked, looking as confused as the other women.

"I think I get what you're saying," DeAnna replied. "So, when a man or a woman cheats, then at the time, they feel that they don't care what happens if they get caught, whatever reason they chose to do it, is good enough for them to do it, even if their mate doesn't think so."

"Not the best logic to have, but yes that's what it amounts to," Myles said. "When in the heat of an argument, that's normally when he walks out; he's not thinking at the moment. What you ladies have to learn to do is calm down enough to make him want to stay or least not feel like he has to leave just to get any peace."

"You mean get a piece," one of the ladies sarcastically said.

"So, what you're saying," Tesha questioned as she turned to face her husband, "is that we should act like the men are perfect and do no wrong and…?

"No," Myles interrupted.

"What he is saying is, you don't need to point out every mistake. We already know we messed up and we don't need to be remind every five minutes. Either you are going to forgive or you're going to keep living in the past," Jason said.

"Right!" All the men in the room agreed.

"Oh, I get it. So, we say nothing, then you think it's okay to do it again and again," Tesha replied as if the conversation was a sore spot for her.

"No," Eric said, looking at his wife.

"I'm speaking for me, I don't know about nobody else," Jason said as he looked at Kimberly. "I love my wife and if I messed up before, I'm not saying it's right, but I won't allow her to punish me forever or remind me constantly of my mistake. I love you," he said, turning to face Kimberly, "To remind myself of what I almost lost; that's all it takes for me."

"Aww!" Everyone said in unison.

Kimberly was happy that Jason didn't admit that he was a cheater in a room full of strangers. She didn't want everyone to know that she had been cheated on. Kimberly knew exactly why Jason had used the word 'if.' She winked at him and smiled.

"Well, the pain doesn't stop just because you're sorry or claim that you're sorry," Lesia said.

"Starting an argument whenever someone walks in the room or always making accusations, doesn't stop the pain either," Malcolm replied.

"But it feels good for a minute to watch him squirm. Besides, if you're the one who messed up, you should be in the hot seat for a minute," Tesha said, staring at Malcolm.

"That always seems to amaze me," Crystal said, pulling herself up from her seated position. "I was married for over seven years before I realized that my attitude was actually causing more damage to our marriage then his cheating."

"So, you stayed with him, then why are you here in this meeting," Tesha asked, flashing Crystal a fake smile.

"Well, as I stated, my attitude did a lot of damage to my marriage," Crystal paused to get herself together; she did not want to cry over her husband again. "I have been separated now four years, but technically we are still married."

"A bad attitude will run a man away," Jeremy said. "But if I can just go lay down without a woman following behind me trying to be right or keep trying to make her point, I would not feel a need to leave. If I don't leave, the less chance I'm going to make a stupid mistake that I'll have to spend the rest of my life regretting, begging for forgiveness for, and trying to make up for. Truth is, I'm not going to keep begging for forgiveness."

~

As the discussion group ended, DeAnna made sure that no one left offended. She wanted everybody to see that this was an opportunity to learn from each other, express themselves, but also fellowship. Everybody helped DeAnna clean up and get things in order. Jeremy and his friends waited outside of the building while DeAnna locked up. A few of the ladies stood around still engaged in conversations with DeAnna about ideas for the next meeting. Jeremy had instructed Myles to go ahead without him. He patiently waited for DeAnna. DeAnna had become more than his unpaid private nurse, or the person he called on for help; she had become his best friend.

As the group walked towards the parking lot, and each headed to his or her own vehicle, DeAnna wondered why Jeremy wasn't headed towards Myles or one of his other friends' car. As she approached Jeremy's truck, which she had been driving for weeks even when he wasn't with her, she was shocked to find him waiting to open her door.

"Dee that was the first time I've actually enjoyed discussing and debating relationship issues in a co-ed group," Jeremy said as soon as he sensed DeAnna's presence and opened the truck door for her. "I guess once we better understand each other and accept the fact that men and women handle difficult situations differently, maybe relationship won't be such a struggle."

"So true," DeAnna replied.

Jeremy closed her door and walked around to the passenger side and got in. He had become skillful at finding the handle and opening the door without hitting himself in the face. He had become quite good at managing the everyday chores that he had taken for granted.

"Thanks for waiting for me. I thought you were going to ride back with your friends and talk about us women," DeAnna joked.

"No problem. I waited for you for a reason. I wanted to talk to you," Jeremy replied and then quickly paused as if he had forgotten something. "Oh, DeAnna, I wasn't thinking. I should have asked you first if you could drop me off at home. I just assumed that... well... I mean."

"Jeremy, it's cool. I am happy to do it. I needed some company tonight anyway," DeAnna laughed. She thought Jeremy was really joking. *He allowed me to use his truck since my car is still in the shop. Then he refused to inconvenience me when I decided to leave early to set up for the singles' meeting. He even insisted that he ride with Myles, so he wouldn't slow me down. Now, now he's apologizing for asking me for a ride home.* DeAnna smiled at him. As they pulled off, DeAnna waved goodnight to the night usher who always made sure that the ladies were safe.

"So, what do you want to talk about?" DeAnna asked as she drove toward Jeremy's house.

"Wow, what a night," Jeremy said, ignoring DeAnna's questions.

"Yeah, it was, and I want to thank you," she said.

"Me? What did I do?" Jeremy asked.

"Your friends came to support you, not me. If it wasn't for the fact that some new male's face a.k.a- your friends had not popped up at church today, half of those women would not have been there."

"Well, Babe," Jeremy said as he turned towards her. "I'd love to take credit, but Kimberly came because she wants to support you, and Jason came because he was trying to please Kimberly. Good move on his part. Tesha and Lesia have both benefited from your excellent advice. They would not come for me anyway, they don't even like me. They say I'm stuck on myself. They came for you. Well, Lesia probably came because she knew Malcolm is a flirt. A harmless flirt, but a flirt. Dee, you are good at giving advice and dealing with people."

"Experience is a good teacher. I've been hurt a few times and it taught me some valuable lessons," DeAnna replied.

"Yeah, I hear you, I'm learning too," Jeremy replied, sounding like there was some hidden meaning behind his words.

"So, what do you want to talk about?" DeAnna asked again.

"You and…" Jeremy started, but lost the courage to finish.

"Me and what?" She questioned.

"Me," Jeremy muttered.

"You want to talk about you?" She questioned.

"Yes, and you," he said and paused. He wanted to just spit it all out and get it over with, but the words seem to get stuck in his head.

"Okay, I'm not sure what you are…" DeAnna began to say but was cut off.

"Dee, I'm really not sure about my feelings, but it appears that the things that seemed to be so important to me before," Jeremy paused again.

Dee knew that he didn't like to think about the shooting, but she wanted to hear what he had to say.

"Before the accident," she said trying to help him fill in the blanks and get to his point.

"Well, yes and before you," he continued.

"Wow, it amazes me how trials can change your perspective on life. I discovered that people don't always accept you for you."

"That's not what I'm trying to say," Jeremy said, hoping DeAnna was not taking his comment the wrong way. "

"What I'm saying is, sometimes the people who like you when you are doing for them and looking after them…" DeAnna said then stopped mid-sentence. She realized that she had made a huge leap in the conversation and assumed that this was some sort of *I don't need you anymore conversations.* "I'm sorry, why don't I just let you finish," she said as pleasantly as she could.

"Well, I guess it hurts when people walked away, but" Jeremy paused for what seemed like the hundredth time.

"It's probably not a good time for you to be making any life changing decisions," DeAnna said, hoping to just end the discussion, which seemed like an end of 'me and you' discussion.

"Look, I know what I feel... look just forget it," Jeremy said.

"What?" DeAnna asked.

"Forget it. Maybe you are right. Now is not a good time," Jeremy said, sounding like a little boy who had just been told to go to his room.

"A good time for what, Jay?"

"Oh really, now I'm Jay. Thought you liked Jeremy better," Jeremy replied.

"Sorry Jeremy," DeAnna said, realizing they were having their first disagreement as a couple, even though they were not really a couple. She chucked a little at the thought.

"You're frustrated with me, aren't you?" Jeremy asked, hoping that he wasn't about to lose his private nurse and best friend.

"No! Why would you ask or think that?" DeAnna questioned, trying to control her voice.

"Because," Jeremy started and then took a deep breath. "You never call me Jay unless you're trying to control your temper with me."

DeAnna smiled to herself knowing that she had been discovered. She was a little frustrated. She'd secretly loved him for months, but she wanted him to want her too. She didn't want him to only want her out of a sense of desperation and loneliness. She was all too familiar with women who swooped in when the man was at his lowest point. They pick him up, dust him off, and make him feel loved, cared for, and wanted. When he realizes that he wasn't really in love, he leaves after he is all polished and renewed. *Too many people confuse love with* gratitude, DeAnna thought to herself, wondering if that's what Jeremy was feeling. *Some desperate women often seek out men when they are most vulnerable and clinging to dear life, but I am not one of them*, she thought.

"Why would I be frustrated with you?" DeAnna finally responded to him. "You haven't done anything. You have been a wonderful boss."

"Boss! Is that what you think of me?" Jeremy questioned. "I thought you and I were friends."

"Joking, but yes we are, and I value that friendship. You have given me something to do after work and before church. You have replaced..." she said.

"So, all I am is something to do?" Jeremy quickly replied.

"No, I didn't mean it like that," DeAnna said feeling even more frustrated. She wasn't sure how to respond. She didn't want to reveal that she loved him, only to find out he didn't love her the same way.

"I know Sweetheart. I'm just joking," Jeremy replied.

DeAnna could not help feeling that he wasn't joking and that somehow the conversation took a wrong turn and it would take a minute to get back on track. *I think he likes me, but what if I am wrong,* she thought to herself.

"Want to get something to eat. The chips, dip, and cookies were delicious, but in case you haven't noticed, I'm a grown man," Jeremy said, hoping to break the tension he felt between them.

"Yes sir, I definitely noticed," DeAnna said, smiling and giving him a quick up and down glance. "I got some great leftovers, barbeque chicken, mashed potatoes, green, and..."

"Please darling, let's just go. My mouth is watering and step on it," Jeremy ordered.

"You got it,'" DeAnna said, smiling to herself.

~

DeAnna turned the radio on so she wouldn't have to make polite conversation. She wondered how Jeremy really felt about her. Her brain was racing. She thought about a life as a wife to a man who had never seen her. She wondered if he knew that she was not one of the perfect size five women that he normally dated. *Could he ever really love me,* she thought to herself. She knew that he had been lonely since his accident and had not been out with anyone other than her. She had been careful not to have any physical interaction, other than the times she helped him get in and out of the car or buildings.

As she pulled in the parking lot, she was shocked to see Kimberly's car.

"What's she doing here?" DeAnna asked.

"Who?" Jeremy asked.

"Kimberly."

"After that meeting, are you surprised?" Jeremy said. "She's now realizing that she's not the wife Jason expected."

"Yeah, I guess so," DeAnna hesitantly said. "But until we are honest about our desires, weaknesses, disappointments, and expectations, we will never be truly fulfilled, nor can we completely satisfy our mates," DeAnna said as she parked and exited the truck as quickly as possible and helped Jeremy out.

"That's true," Jeremy said continuing the conversation as DeAnna walked beside him, holding his hand. "But it takes some time before people can be honest about their own shortcomings."

"It's not always about pleasing or meeting expectations, sometimes just to know that someone is willing to do it and even want to do it for you, outweighs all the disappointment."

"Wow, that's true also," Jeremy said, feeling a sudden sense of encouragement.

As DeAnna and Jeremy climbed up the steps, Kimberly came rushing out of the apartment with a plate in her hand.

"Kimberly," DeAnna said. "Girl, what are you up to?" She asked as Kimberly came zooming pass her.

"Gotta feed my man a home cooked meal," Kimberly said as she shot a devious smile to DeAnna. "And face it, you are the best cook I know."

"Now you know you cannot fool that man," DeAnna yelled.

"Yeah, I know, but he'll appreciate the fact that I am willing to do anything to feed him. Oh, by the way, the meeting was great. I enjoyed it. It was actually very informative," Kimberly said as she quickly got in her car.

"Goodbye," Jeremy and DeAnna said, waving to Kimberly even though she was halfway out of the parking lot.

DeAnna escorted Jeremy up the steps and into the apartment. She took a good swift of his cologne. *Wow*, she thought to herself, *he sure does smell good.* "Well Jeremy, I guess I better assess the damage of Hurricane Kimberly. We might have to order in or go out to eat."

"Fine with me," Jeremy said. "But make it snappy, a brother can't last long off of three oatmeal cookies and twelve chips."

215

"So, you counted the chips," DeAnna asked and laughed at the thought of a grown man counting potato chips.

They both laughed as DeAnna scanned the refrigerator to see if there were enough left over for two people. After careful review, she determined that there was plenty of food for one of them and perhaps both if she rationed out the portions.

"What's the damage?" Jeremy asked.

"Category five," DeAnna reported.

"Ok, let's head out before it gets too late," Jeremy said, patting his back pocket. He wanted to make sure he had his wallet. "Why don't you call that Chinese restaurant on Fairview?"

"Oh… ok. Dine in or take out," DeAnna asked as she looked at her watch to see if it was midnight yet. "9:45, good."

"We can decide later; just call to order so they can go ahead and be making it," Jeremy replied.

DeAnna grabbed the keys and her purse off the counter and retraced her steps back to the living room. She hooked her arms onto Jeremy's and made a quick exit. When they got in the truck, she called and placed their order. Once again, to avoid the silence, DeAnna turned the radio up and they listened quietly to soft romantic music. They pulled in the parking lot, parked, and quickly entered the building.

As DeAnna and Jeremy waited for their food, DeAnna heard a familiar voice.

"Well, well, well, if it ain't my old ex, Ms. Dee," a familiar voice said.

DeAnna looked at Chad, her ex-boyfriend, commonly known to her friend as DeAnna's common-law husband.

"Hi Chad. How have you been?" DeAnna asked.

"I'm doing exceedingly well. I'm engaged and expecting my first child next month," Chad announced.

"That's wonderful," DeAnna said, hoping he would quickly leave.

"So, who's this? One of your home-care patients you're using to get over me."

"No," DeAnna replied, but Jeremy didn't give her a chance to finish.

"I'm her boyfriend," Jeremy said. "Please to meet you."

"Yeah, whatever man. She's just using you to make me jealous. I bet she pretended she really had a taste for Chinese. She knows I come here all the time," Chad arrogantly said.

"Wow that's interesting Chad, I've been here hundreds of times and this is the first time running into you here, but at any rate we were in the middle of something very important, but hey, nice meeting you Chad," Jeremy said as he turned to face DeAnna and smiled.

"Likewise," Chad said, leaving the restaurant without ordering.

"Why did you do that?" DeAnna asked.

"Dee, I'm sorry. I could hear the arrogance in his voice. I couldn't resist," Jeremy said and then waited for DeAnna's response.

After two minutes of complete silence, DeAnna burst into laughter. Jeremy quickly joined in.

"Okay, I owe you for that. He really thinks I'm sitting around crying and waiting for him."

"I could tell," Jeremy said. He was unable to resist the burning urge to ask a question. "Are you?"

"No, absolutely not. I never wanted him back. I just..."

"What?"

"At first, I just wanted him to suffer. I wanted him to feel the same pain that he caused me, but..."

"What?" Jeremy asked.

"Well, I realized that my time was too precious, and I didn't want to waste any of my energy on him."

"So, you just let him put you down," Jeremy asked.

"Look, I will be the one who has to give account for every word I say to him," DeAnna said then paused for a few seconds. "Besides he's the one that's obviously concerned about what I'm doing."

"That's for doggone sure," Jeremy said. "And with good reason," he muttered, but loud enough for DeAnna hear. "Dude didn't even get his food."

As Jeremy and DeAnna waited for their food, they enjoyed polite conversation and the relaxing atmosphere. They sang the words to the familiar songs that played on the jukebox.

"I know that you've been talking about me. Why, I'm the flyest chick. Ran across your girl the other day. She thought she was cute, kinda funny by the way. Walked right pass me with a smirk on her face. I know she kinda petty, betta tell her I don't play (Aye). But imma cool kinda chick. Real smooth kinda chick. All the boys down the block wonna kick it with a chick. Hey, me and some girls don't ever seem to mix. When they see me, eyes be gleaming! Flip their hair. Roll their eyes, switch their hips. Talkin' loud acting real coincident. Girls please, you can beat it. I'm on a level so high in the sky. You can't see me. I know that you've been talkin' bout me. Why, I'm the flyest chick. Just ask about me. Girl don't be jealous. Don't hate, I won't take your man. I got my own, you safe."

"So, you a cool kinda chick?" DeAnna asked Jeremy and laughed.

"Nah, but it sounds like jDenea' is taking the music world by storm," Jeremy said and then paused. "You know who else is a cool kinda chick?" Jeremy said and then started singing a few more lines before answering. "You!"

Chapter 17

Jeremy plopped down on the chair and turned the TV to the music channel. He was in the mood for some soft romantic music. He laid his head back and began to imagine himself as a happily married man. He had enjoyed his large 4-bedrooms, 3200 square-foot home, but suddenly it seemed too big for him. He turned one room into a study, another into an exercise room, and the other into a storage room, but as he sat with his eyes closed, he could see one decorated in pink, purple, and green, with everything a little girl would want. He imagined a brass canopy bed and ruffled curtains. In the other room, he could see Tonka trucks and football jerseys.

Jeremy could almost smell perfume floating though the house. The smell was so pleasant and familiar. He felt a presence in the house. He actually thought someone was there. "God, it's almost like she's here," he said aloud. "I'm tired of being lonely. I have never truly felt complete. Lord, I know it's going to take more from me to be the man that you want me to be, but I need your help. She won't..." Jeremy paused. He began to wonder why when the smell of perfume was in air so strong, that it instantly made him think about God. "God, it might sound crazy, but I think I love her. How can I love her, someone that I have never seen? Someone I've never romantically touch. I've never kissed or held her, but Lord I can't stop thinking about her."

Jeremy was on his knees crying out to God. For the first time in his life, he felt free to allow himself to be completely honest with God.

"Lord, I'm sorry for what I've done to your daughters. I've lusted, fornicated, and taken advantage of women who, themselves were hurting and didn't understand what they were doing, well a few anyway. Some of them were just as bad as I was, but that still doesn't excuse my actions. God, I know they entrust their hearts to me and I didn't protect it, but God please give me this chance to prove my faithfulness to you and to your will. Lord, I'm so sorry for what I've done. I promise you that I've learnt my lesson. Just allow me to be a whole man. Lord, restore what the devil has stolen, and God I promise you, I claim and believe that I am the man you will have me to be. Lord, your word says that by Jesus strips I am healed, so I am healed, and my heart and vision is restored.

Jeremy heard the phone ring. He quickly and skillfully emerged from his knees and grab his cell phone from his pocket.

"Jeremy this is me, Kimberly. I need your help," Kimberly cried.

"What is it kiddo. I mean Kimberly," Jeremy said detecting that something was wrong.

"Jason, he's going to kill her."

"Kill who?" Jeremy questioned, realizing that he did detect fear in her voice.

"I can't reach anybody else," Kimberly said without answering Jeremy's questions.

"Kill who Kimberly?" Jeremy asked again.

"Danielle," Kimberly yelled. "He found out that the baby is not his and he is so mad, I can't calm him down."

"Is he still there?" Jeremy asked, praying that he was.

"Yes. I hide his car keys. He's looking for them and yelling at me."

"Baby, he loves you, ignore the yelling, but it's time to stop calling your big brothers. Time to be a woman. You're going to have to make him understand that he can't throw his life away because she lied. He has to understand that his love for you has to outweigh his hatred and anger for Danielle about what she's done," Jeremy calmly said.

"He has been giving her so much money that it left us struggling," Kimberly said.

"I understand, but listen carefully, that doesn't matter right now," he helped care for a child. God will bless him for that. Do you want to see your husband once a week on Sunday behind bars because that's what revenge will get him? Listen to me. Or do you want to rejoice that you now have the chance to give him his first child. You prayed to God and said don't let this child be my husband's. He prayed the same prayer, so now just rejoice. Most people don't get that lucky or should I say blessed. You play, you pay. Look at what happened to David, in the Bible. His child died. And remember the child is the one that needed him more than either of you realized. He acted like a man. Be proud of that. All the secrets are out, and you guys are getting back on the right track. This battle is over, now claim the victory of the war. It's time to rejoice."

"Jeremy, I love you," Kimberly said.

"Go love on him. You got what it takes to soften his heart," Jeremy said and hung up without saying goodbye.

"Jason stop," Kimberly yelled as he searched the house like a mad man. "Now Baby, listen to me, if you want to leave, leave. I'll give you the keys, but if you do, know this, you and I are over. I will not visit my husband behind bars. If you don't love me enough to let it go and pour all your energy into making our marriage work, instead of getting even with some conniving woman, then here," Kimberly said and threw the keys towards him. "Baby, if you are looking for a reason to see her again, then go and don't come back. We will be okay without you. I will not bring my baby to prison to see his daddy behind bars,"

"Behind bars! What are you talking about; I'm not going kill nobody? I won't even put my hands on her. I just want to give her a piece of my mind." Jason said. He was confused.

"Baby don't, you need to keep all the mind you got," Kimberly joked.

Jason shot Kimberly a serious look. "I'm not in a joking mood."

"Look Jason, do you think Jeremy intended to get in a fight and end up blind? No, he didn't. Baby one thing leads to another, somebody stays too long, pushes too hard, and the next thing you know, somebody's hurt. 'Oops' doesn't fix it. Why don't you just chalk it up to preparation?" Kimberly said realizing that Jason missed the earlier clues.

"Preparation for what?" Jason said as she sat down on the arm of the sofa.

"Preparation for the son or daughter that you and I are going to have together someday," Kimberly said, massaging her husband shoulders.

Jason smiled at the thought. Kimberly knew he misunderstood exactly what she was saying, so she grabbed his hand and placed it on her stomach. She moved from standing beside him, to facing him.

"Are you serious?" He asked.

"Yes baby. You are a real daddy," Kimberly said.

Jason looked at Kimberly. "I don't know what to say. I thought," he stopped. "Well, I thought God was punishing me for what I did. I didn't think he would trust me enough to give me another child."

"Why would you think that?" She asked.

"Because he trusted me with you and I betrayed you and Him," Jason replied.

"You made a mistake and I forgive you and you said that you have forgiven yourself, so trust that God has forgiven you too. So now it's time for you to forgive Danielle," Kimberly said. "And you know that's very hard for me to say; I don't want to forgive her. I am not as saved as DeAnna..."

"Baby, I hope you don't get mad," Jason hesitantly said. "But I have to be honest. I'm not just mad about the money. I love my son... I mean Danielle's son. I felt as if my heart was being ripped out of my body, when..."

"Jason, I know. I hear the hurt in your voice, but that's how I know you are a good man, a real man, and how God knows that even if you made a mistake; He can trust you to do the right thing. He knows we are not perfect. You did the right thing for that child and at the expense of almost losing me. Now, until I found out I was pregnant, I hated you for that. Then I realized what a wonderful father you are going to be. I know that nothing or no one will ever come between you and this child," Kimberly said as she sat down beside Jason." You loved a child you thought you created from a one-night stand, so how much more will you love a child created out of love."

Jason slide down off the arm of the sofa and laid her head on his wife's stomach. He began to silently sing the words from the song coming from the radio, a radio that he didn't even know was on. Kimberly began to sing the song to him.

"I can explain the way I feel. Baby sit down for a minute let me make this right. I think its time I confronted you. Tell you what's been on my mind for 'bout a month or two. Things get strange when heavy on the brain. Tip-toeing around. Things just ain't the same. Look right at each other, but never say a thing. I'm mad at you, you're mad at me but we don't say a thing. I don't say a thing. You don't say a thing. We don't say a thing. Uhhhhhh, Baby please, Ba-baby please let's work this out. Baby please. Ba-baby please let's work this out. Put our pride aside and baby please let's work this out. We can work this out. Let's work this out...You cheated, I cheated. Now let's make a deal. Be loyal from this point, and let our hearts heal. Stand together through the stormy weather. Try to understand one another. With our hands together, we can make it through. We can make it better. Baby we're not through. Baby we're not through. We're not through."

"Nope, we're not through, Baby. You are my good man," Kimberly whispered in Jason's ear.

"Do you really think I'm a good man?"

"Nope," Kimberly said and then paused to see his reaction. "I know you are a good man."

"Do you really forgive me?" He asked.

"I can't say that it doesn't still hurt when I think about it, but I know that you love me and no matter how hard I tried to stop loving you, I can't," Kimberly said.

"So, you tried," Jason asked.

"Yeah, I did. I was so hurt, I wanted to hate you, but I couldn't."

"Okay, okay! Let's not go back down that road. Let's leave the pass in the past. We have to get ready for little Kimberly or little Jason."

"Baby, I do choose to forgive you," Kimberly said as she leaned down and kissed him on the forehead.

Chapter 18

"Excuse me Ms. I have been waiting for five minutes. Do you think you can stop gossiping, put the phone down, and assist me?" Tesha asked, as she stood at the receptionist window in the doctor's office tapping her nails on the counter.

"Okay, give me one minute please," the receptionist said, holding up one finger.

"Can I speak with your office manager?" Tesha demanded.

"Baby, calm down," Eric said.

"Calm down," Tesha repeated. "I am so tired of unprofessional women making it bad on the rest of us."

"And the ones who act professional are overlooked or are said to be arrogant. But you know what I'm tired of?" Eric questioned.

"What?" Tesha asked then waited three seconds for Eric's response. "Tell me please. I can't wait to hear this," Tesha said turning to face her husband. She was more upset about him getting upset with her, than she was with the gossiping receptionist.

"I'm tired of hearing you complaining all the time about nothing. I am tired of you fussing at the TV, the cashier at Walmart because she is moving too slow, the mailman because he didn't come the same time he did the day before, or the little lady driving too slow in front of you. You are the one with road rage not her, but you act like she's wrong for being on the road. You are the hazard," Eric shook his head. He was feed up. "Baby has fussing at the TV ever made the actors change their script and do what you think they should. If you want them to do what you think they should do, then sweetheart, why don't you write, produce, and direct your own movie. Since everything seems like a remake of something else these days, I'm sure everyone is ready for something new. Besides, at least you can make some money to yell at everybody, because right now all you are doing is getting on my last nerve and once that nerve is gone, I will be gone too."

"So, you want to leave?" Tesha asked. She noticed a few people listening and she was not about to let Eric make a fool of her. "Well, go then. You don't have to be here with me."

Eric didn't want to leave his wife stranded at the doctor's office, so he gently placed the car keys in her hand and turned and walked out the door.

"May I help you?" the receptionist asked Tesha who was watching her husband disappear out the door.

"Your timing is just perfect," Tesha sarcastically said. "I have an appointment; I am sure I have missed it since I've been waiting for twenty minutes for you to get off the phone," Tesha said, although she knew it had not been that long.

"Your name please," the receptionist asked without any reaction to Tesha's nasty attitude and comment.

Tesha's mind drifted to her husband's comment as the receptionist checked her in. She knew that she had pushed him too far this time. She wondered where he was going, if he called someone to pick him up, and if he would be out all night. *Lord knows, I know I need to stop fussing so much, but I am just so tired of feeling like I am never going to have anything. I'm so dissatisfied with the way my life is going right now. Lord, I need help. I know it's not good to compare yourself to others, but it is so hard seeing everybody have what you want,* Tesha thought to herself as she waited for the nurse to return her insurance card.

"Number 14," a nurse said.

Tesha walked towards the nurse who had called her number. She followed her to the examination room for her yearly checkup. She noticed that the waiting room was crowded with women. "Wow wonder if all these women are single?" She said to herself. As Tesha walked, she surveyed the ring finger of as many women as she could. A few women had on what appeared to be engagement rings and a few had on wedding bands. "Guess Eric felt uncomfortable being the only man here," she said to make herself feel better about him leaving. "He wasn't leaving me, he was leaving the situation," Tesha said as she realized how often Eric had escorted her to her doctor's appointments. Most of the times, he would sit in the waiting room, but she was happy that he came. "Never really seen other men with their wives," she said. She began to think of how often he had supported her and accompanied her to events that turned out to be mostly an all-woman's event, with a few men escorting their beloved mates.

"The doctor will be in, in a few minutes," the nurse said. She finished taking Tesha's blood pressure.

"Okay," Tesha replied.

"See your husband is not with you this time," the nurse said.

"No!" Tesha said. "Well, he was here, but he left. Guess it took a little longer than we expected."

"Oh, I see," the nurse said. She entered Tesha's blood pressure and temperature in the file. "Well, you are a very lucky woman."

"Thanks! I guess I am," Tesha said, regretting she had sent him away. *Lord, I have got to do better*, she muttered to herself.

Tesha was glad when the examination was over. She was ready to see her husband. She wasn't sure if he was going back to work or not. He had taken a half of day off, so he could go with her. He had done so for years. Sometimes, Tesha would tell him not to because she didn't want him using up all his sick or vacations days.

~

As Tesha headed out of the doctor's office, she thought about apologizing to the receptionist. She knew it was the right thing to do, but she kept walking. "I'll be nice to her the next time," she said to herself as she walked past the receptionist's desk, headed for the front door.

"Excuse me Mrs." Tesha heard the receptionist say but wasn't sure if she was calling her or someone else.

"You left your debit card," the receptionist said to Tesha.

"Oh, thank you," Tesha said to the receptionist as she handed Tesha the card.

"Look, can I ask you a question?" Tesha asked.

"Sure," the receptionist replied with a smile.

"How do you remain so polite when," Tesha paused to think of how to say what she wanted to say. "Well, with women like me acting so mean."

"Well, most of the time, I just tell myself that they aren't really mad with me. They are probably going through something or releasing some pinned-up anger that they have about something their husband did or didn't do or something the kids did, you know," the receptionist said with an understanding look on her face. "I guess I am an easy target. I'm at work and I'm probably not going to respond negatively, well at least not if I want to keep my job that is. I cannot say that I am this polite off the job. We all go through things."

"Wow honey you're better than I am," Tesha said as she smiled at the lady for the first time in the ten years that she had been a patient there.

"God gives you the grace that you need for every situation. Just ask him and he'll help you through it. We must learn when He is trying to help us. We have to be sensitive to His help," the receptionist whispered as if she wasn't supposed to be talking about God. "Anyway, gotta get back to work. You have a great day."

"Okay, you do the same," Tesha replied and headed out of the office. "Grace to handle this, is what I need right now Lord," Tesha said. "I really messed up this time."

~

Tesha drove straight home thinking that Eric would probably be there packing. She knew she had made it easy for him to want to leave. She thought about the conversation at the single's meeting they had attended to support DeAnna. She knew that it was time to swallow her pride and do as DeAnna would say, *be the peacemaker*. "Eric," she yelled as she entered through the back door. "Honey are you here?" Tesha quickly ran to the bedroom. Nothing looked out of place. Eric had not been home. *Good*, she thought. *Maybe he'll cool down before returning home*. Tesha decided to clean up the house to keep herself busy.

She changed into her gray sweatpants and one of Eric's t-shirt. She slipped on her gray bedroom shoes. *Maybe I'll cook too*, she thought. She went to the kitchen and took a pack of ground beef out of the freezer and placed it in the microwave to un-thaw. "I hate using the microwave to un-thaw ground beef, but that's the quickest way," she stated as if someone was listening to her. She was determined that she was going to make Eric see that she really wanted her marriage. Tesha fixed the bed and sprayed a little perfume under the sheets. She picked up all the clothes off the floor. She placed candles on the dresser and the nightstand. She cut the lights off and watched the shadows from candle lights dancing on the wall. She smiled as she went into the living room and began picking up empty soda cans and glasses. She dropped the cans in the recycling bin sitting beside the back step. She placed the dirty glasses in the dishwater. She finished cleaning up the living room and then washed the dishes.

After the house was clean, she started on dinner. She began seasoning the ground beef with diced peppers, onions, Italian breadcrumb, eggs, and meatloaf mix. She turned the oven on to preheat then searched the refrigerator for a head of cabbage. "*Oh, that would be good too,*" she said to herself, and then she grabbed a bag of potatoes and placed them in the sink. *That's good,* she thought, m*eatloaf, stewed potatoes, and cabbages*. She placed a pot of water on the stove for the cabbages and sprinkled crushed red pepper in the water. She chopped up ham bits and added it to the water. She cut the cabbages up. Once the water with the chopped ham bits began to boil, she added the chopped cabbages. She began peeling the potatoes and cutting them into small pieces. She dropped them in another pot of water.

Eric likes the taste of onions, but he doesn't like to bite into them, so instead of dicing the onions up for the potato, I'll cut it in half and dropped it in the pot with the potatoes, she thought. Tesha usually didn't bother to cook the onion in any of her food at all. It always seems to be too much trouble for him to have to pick it out. She was determined to please Eric this time. *He has always gone the extra mile for me,* she thought. *Now it's my time.*

The aroma began to fill the house. Tesha began to think back to the days when Eric would help her cook. He would peel the potatoes. She would chop the cabbage up as if she was going to make coleslaw. Tesha lowered all the burners to medium-low. She wanted the food to be hot when Eric got home, but not over cooked.

She decided to take a quick bubble bath and put on the silk night gowns that she had ordered from a lingerie party. When Tesha returned to the kitchen after she had bathed and changed, she checked the food and turned everything back to medium-high. She glanced at the clock every ten minutes. It was almost six p.m. and she had not seen or heard from Eric since he'd left the doctor's office earlier that day. The food was done and was quickly getting cold. She blew out the candle and plopped down on the sofa for the 100th time. She tried to be understanding about how she must have made him feel when she told him to leave and said it loud enough for everyone in the office to hear. She remembered DeAnna's pastor saying that men hate public humiliation and disrespect from their wives, Boos, wifey, or girlfriend. She tried hard not to be mad, but as the time slowly ticked away, she found it harder and harder not to be mad and not to think the worst.

"He's just mad," she told herself. "He's doing this on purpose. He wants me to worry. I'm sure he's just trying to teach me a lesson. Probably over one of his friend's house," she said to herself as she put the food in containers and placed it in the refrigerator. "Never again," she told herself. "All this hard work for nothing," she said. She sat down on the sofa and began flipping through the channels a few times. "Another male bashing Lyfetime movie," she thought as she stopped on channel 109. She tried to pretend that she didn't care that it was now going on 9 o'clock and she had no clue where her husband was. She refused to call around looking for him like he was a twelve-year-old runaway child.

Tesha fell asleep on the sofa. When she woke up and realized that she had been sleep for almost an hour, she quickly ran to the bedroom to see if Eric was home yet. "Okay," she angrily said. "That's what he wants to do, I can do it too." Tesha began to get dressed. As she combed her hair, tears ran down the side of her face. She had never cheated on Eric, but she was going to make him pay for leaving her. "I don't need him," she yelled as she washed her face and reapplied her eyeliner and lipstick. She threw the lipstick down so hard that the top cracked. A steady flow of tears ran down her freshly applied makeup. Waterproof eyeliner was not in her budget, so she had to wash the black strings of tears off her face and reapply her makeup again. She grabbed her mascara and applied three coats in order to darkened and lengthen her eyelashes.

Tesha stormed out of the bathroom and into her bedroom and plopped down on the bed with her vanilla-cherry lotion in hand. She applied lotion to her hands, feet, the back of her neck, and her shoulders. She sprayed on perfume as the finishing touch. She dabbed a little behind each ear and on her neck. "Wait a minute," she said to herself as she massaged lotion on her chest and stomach. "I've always loved the smell of this lotion," she said to herself as she looked in the mirror. "Now," she said to herself "I need to find a blouse that reveals more than I should, but not too much," she said to herself as if she thought Eric might be listening to her as she dressed to play a seductive woman. She found her black sheer blouse and put it on carefully trying not to mess up her hair or makeup. "If he can do it, well so can I," she said as she grabbed her purse and headed for the front door.

When Tesha got to the front door, she heard keys jingling in the lock. She quickly strolled over to the door, peeped out the window, and then unlocked the door for her husband. "Oh, baby thank God you're home," she said. She kissed and hugged him as if he was a solider returning home from war. She was still angry with him, but she resisted every feeling and desire in her that wanted to fuss him out. "Baby, I'm so glad you're home. Are you okay? Are you hungry? I made you dinner."

"Yeah, I'm ok," Eric said, practically pushing her away from him as he walked into the living-room. "We need to talk," he said, turning to face her. "I just can't do this anymore."

Tesha thought she knew exactly what he wanted to talk about. She often wondered if he had another woman.

"Don't tell me, you got someone else, right?" She asked.

"Why is it that, the only thing you women think men are capable of doing, is another woman when we are not happy at home?"

"I'm sorry," Tesha said not wanting to upset him anymore than she had already done. "I didn't mean…"

"Yes, you did. You seem to think or act like the answer to all men's problems is a bottle, a woman, a jail cell, or a joint. Like that's what we need to fill the void."

"Well," Tesha hesitantly said. "When you give us reason to think that, what do you expect?"

"I don't give you reason to think that," Eric calmly said. "Oh, wait did I look at another woman? Like you looked or stared at another man. So, I should think that you were headed out to cheat tonight, right? I mean the way you are dressed, who knows. You don't see me running around here feeling insecure when you stare at…."

"I don't stare at other men," Tesha said, cutting him off.

"What do you call it then?" Eric asked as he stared at his wife. "What is it called when you look at a person for five minutes; someone that you don't know, but you stare as if you are interested in knowing him?"

"Five minutes," Tesha said. "Please! Look it's late, the food is cold."

"Looks as if you have a hot date, don't let me stop you," Eric said.

Tesha looked down at her ensemble, she had forgotten all about her plans.

"So, who were you going out with?" Eric questioned.

Tesha busted into laughter. She laughed so hard, Eric could not help but join her. He didn't know what was so funny, but seeing her laughing was music to his ears, especially after all the fussing he was used to hearing. Once she calmed down, she managed to tell him that she was going to go to the bar and let a few men hit on her just to pay him back.

"For what," Eric questioned. "If I wasn't there to see it, how is that pay back? What would it have accomplished?"

"It would have made me feel better about what I thought you might have been doing to entertain yourself," Tesha replied.

Eric shook his head and then started chucking. "Well, after walking for an hour, I called an old friend from school. A male friend."

"Why?"

"Well, to be honest, I knew what my boys would say, and I wanted to be around someone who wouldn't try to make me go home and talk it out. Don't get me wrong, it's a good thing that my boys don't try to encourage me to cheat or anything like that, but I wanted to be around someone that wouldn't feel comfortable enough to ask questions. Who could tell that I was upset and just needed to chill?"

"So again, why?" Tesha asked.

"Okay, I knew that if I decided that I wanted to cheat, he wouldn't try to stop me. Crazy, I know."

"What? What the heck kind of friend is that?" Tesha asked.

"No friends at all, baby."

"So, please tell me why you would turn to someone like that?" Tesha asked.

"For the same reason, you women hang around other women that cheat, have sugar daddies whom they are using for rent money, or because he got a nice house," Eric said. "Look, the truth is, I wasn't thinking at the moment. Just wanted to be around someone who wouldn't…"

"Wouldn't care that you are married and would hook you up with someone. I just cannot believe you," Tesha replied.

"What? Say it," Eric said wanting to know if she was going to call him a name or accuse him of something more than what he had told her he did.

"I don't have to say it, you just did," Tesha said and turned away from him.

"No, Tesha. I didn't. I didn't say anything really. Look, I realize that even though I was mad enough to do it, if I wanted to; I really didn't want to. I love you and no other woman is going to solve my problems."

"What problem is that?" Tesha asked.

"That I love my wife, but I don't like the way that she acts most of the time. And I don't want to be with a woman that acts the way she acts, but I do love her," Eric said, looking into her eyes. "I cannot change you either."

"But, I can change me," she said.

"But are you going to?" He asked.

"I'm trying, but you just don't notice my efforts. Part of your, our, problem is my small efforts are often overlooked, then I get mad and I stop trying," Tesha said as she stared at Eric.

"Like what?" Eric asked.

"Today, I thought about apologizing to that receptionist," Tesha said, then she realized he wasn't even there to see it, if she had.

"Did you?" He asked.

"No," she answered.

Eric didn't say anything. He just stared at her, saying to himself, *then why bother telling me.*

"Every action begins with a thought. You got to start somewhere, right?" Tesha said. She remembered that she did talk to the receptionist. "I asked her how she could be polite to someone like me. So, I did at least acknowledge that I was wrong. Sort of."

"What did she say?" Eric asked, but he seemed uninterested in hearing the answer.

"She said that most of the time, she knew that people weren't mad with her, but rather at themselves or their spouse or something else. Oh, and that they were just taking it out on her because she was an easy target. She also said that it's her job to be polite and she wanted to keep it."

"Well, I guess that's true," Eric said.

"Sometimes, I act that way, so you will notice me," Tesha said.

"I do notice you," Eric said, smiling at Tesha. *I noticed a lot more than you give me credit for. Like the fact that not only did you cook, but you seasoned the potatoes with onions and then you pick the onions back out for me. I know that you have been doing that for a long time. All because I hate to bite into onions, but I like the taste.*

"How can you tell that without even taking the lid off the bowl?" Tesha asked, smiling back at her husband.

232

"Well, I see peelings and cooked onions in the trash can," Eric said, looking around the room. "I also noticed that you cleaned the house. Got it smelling really good. You even have on that vanilla-cherry lotion that you like. But I bet you don't know that it has been discontinued."

"No...but...how...?" Kimberly became speechless.

"I went to get you some one day and I was told that it had been discontinued. So, I bought cases of it."

"Aww baby, that is so sweet," Tesha said and then kissed her husband, but she knew that the battle was not over. "Sweetheart, did it ever occur to you that I would do more things for you, if you acknowledge the little things that I do. I mean sometimes you act like I don't work, but housework is work."

"I know that housework is real work, but it doesn't help pay anything else in this house," Eric said, matter-of-factly.

"See," Tesha said ready to give him a piece of her mind.

"You know what?" Eric questioned as he began to realize that the war was not over yet, but he needed to call a truce. "I want to taste those cabbages and potatoes and..."

"Say no more. I'll warm you up a plate. We can finish this dispute later. Let's just call it a truce for tonight. Our marital problems didn't happen overnight, and we aren't going to solve them all in one night either," Tesha said, remembering how often she heard other people say that.

"You're right about that," Eric said, licking his lips as if he could already taste the meatloaf.

"I forgot to tell you, we have an appointment tomorrow," Eric said.

"Oh yell. An appointment for what?" She asked, placing the plate in the microwave.

"It's a surprise," Eric said, taking whiff the food.

"I know you hate for your food to be warmed up in the microwave, but its late and after all that cleaning, Baby, I'm too tired to stand over the stove; besides, after you come strolling in here, you should just take what you get," Tesha jokingly said and then started laughing.

"Fair enough, and I am sorry for making you worry."

"I accept, but now about this appointment. You know doggone well I hate surprises, especially if I know there's a surprise waiting. Its better if you just not tell me that you're going to surprise me; just surprise me," Tesha said as she waved the plate of food in front of Eric's nose before sitting it down in front of him. "Your turn."

233

"Your will find out tomorrow," he said, looking at her with a devious smile on his face.

"Okay then, you will eat tomorrow," she said smiling back at him. She playfully waved the plate pass his nose several times.

"Okay, I'll tell you, but first the plate."

Tesha placed the plate in front of him.

"Your turn," she said.

"We are going to talk to Mrs. Norma," Eric replied.

"Who is Mrs. Norma," Tesha asked. She suddenly didn't like the surprise.

"She's the loan officer who's going to try to pre-qualify us for…" Eric paused and looked at Tesha. She placed a spoonful of potatoes in his mouth. He chewed them as if he had not eaten in days. "Baby, this is delicious," he said.

"Stop playing with me, what are we trying to pre-qualify for?" Tesha asked. "Another car?"

"You are the one that stuffed my mouth. I was about to tell you," Eric said. "A house," he quickly stated. He had a sneaky grin on his face as if he was joking and holding back the truth.

"What! Are you serious?" She asked as if she didn't believe him.

"Yes. I'm serious.

"I'm so excited," Tesha said, patiently waiting as Mrs. Norma keyed information into the computer.

"Okay," Mrs. Norma said, looking up from the computer screen. "Well you do have some work to do, but it's really not that bad. Your debt-to-income ratio is a little too high.

"What does that mean?" Tesha asked.

"It means that you have more debt than your income can pay for basically, and based on that, it appears that you cannot afford a mortgage," Mrs. Norma replied.

"What if we find a house with a payment around the same amount that we are paying for rent now?" Tesha asked.

"Well, the problem is, it still appears that your debt outweighs your income. I can suggest a few things that would give you a better chance of qualifying for a house, maybe in about a year or two," Mrs. Norma said.

"Two years," Tesha yelled.

"Or sooner," Mrs. Norma quickly replied. "Now, it all depends on how hard you are willing to work at reducing your debt or..."

"Or what?" Tesha asked looking at her husband.

"Now, please understand, I'm not saying that there is anything wrong with a woman who doesn't work. I have been praying my husband would get a raise large enough for me to quit my job," Mrs. Norma said trying to soften the blow. "But if you had more income and you used it to pay off the credit cards and saved some money for a down payment of about fifteen to twenty percent of the total cost of the home, we could get you in a home a lot sooner."

"I thought you said something about a hundred percent financing and no closing costs," Tesha said as if all hopes of home ownership without it was impossible.

"Well yes, for qualified buyers, but..." Mrs. Norma said, but was cut off by Tesha.

"I know," Tesha said. "Our debt is too high, and I need a job."

"Now, I'm sure that I can find some programs that would qualify you for down payment assistance, but you have to at least reduce your debt and or increase your income," Mrs. Norma replied.

"You're saying, if we reduce the debt and you find a down payment assistance program, you think we might could qualify for a loan, hopefully in a better neighborhood?"

"Well, to be honest," Mrs. Norma said. "I can get you in some nice homes, but the mortgage is going to be a few hundreds more per month than what you are paying now."

"So, I need a job," Tesha said, looking at her husband, expecting him to say something.

"Mrs. Norma, thank you for your time," Tesha said, pulling her purse straps onto her shoulder. She extended her hand to Mrs. Norman. "Nice to meet you," Tesha said, shaking her hand.

"Nice to meet you as well. Listen, many couples leave my office in worse shape than you and in six months to a year they are back. That two-year range I gave you is for those that aren't seriously willing do what it takes. So many are just trying to see what they need to do but aren't serious about doing it."

"Well, thank you once again," Tesha said, glancing at her husband, indicating that it was time to leave.

As soon as Tesha was in the car, she began questioning Eric.

"Why did you just sit there?"

"Baby, what did you want me to do?" Eric asked Tesha. "What did you want me to say? I have a good job. I can't work two jobs, unless you think I'm never supposed to sleep or ever see you again," Eric said, not knowing if his plan had worked or failed.

"I know that," Tesha said. She reminded herself that she was trying not to fuss so much. "It's just that, well it seems like she was judging me."

"Judging you?" Eric questioned. "No, she was only assessing the situation. That's her job. I'm just glad she was honest with us, instead of making us think we could get a house, running our credit, bringing down our credit scores with inquiries, only to try to place us in a bad neighborhood, or put us in a home only for us to be foreclosed on six months later. She did everything she could and was supposed to do. Now, we know what we need to do if we really are serious about being homeowners."

"Why does it seem like it's my fault that we can't get a house," Tesha said as she looked out of the window.

"Your fault?" Eric questioned. "What are you talking about?"

"The credit cards, I was the one who insisted you get them. I ran them up and if I had a job, I could pay them off. They really aren't that high," Tesha paused and waited for Eric to say something.

Eric was secretly smiling. *Its working* he thought to himself. *She is finally seeing the light.*

"Or," Tesha said. "You could get a loan to pay off all the credit cards and have one payment instead of four or five or six."

Eric shook his head. "Nah, that's not going to help. They are not looking at the number of payments; they are looking at the total amount of money that's going out."

"But, if you can have one payment that's less than the payment of all four combined," Tesha said as if she just knew that this would work.

"That's true," Eric said appearing to be considering it. He didn't want Tesha to think that he already knew that they would not prequalify for the loan. "But the one thing we do not want to do right now is to run our credit. Each time it's pulled, it lowers the credit score."

"Yeah, that's true. You're right," Tesha replied. "I forgot about that."

"We also need a savings account," Eric said thinking about all the time that Tesha would withdraw everything out of the savings account, all except the minimal twenty-five dollars required to keep it open.

"We have a savings account," Tesha informed her husband.

"Let me rephrase," Eric said, smiling at his wife. "We need to start saving."

"So, we have our work cut out for us," Tesha replied.

"Yep, we do if you want a house," Eric said.

"So," Tesha said, quickly turning to Eric. "Am I the only one of us who wants this?" She asked.

"No, I want it too, but sweetie, there's only so much I can do."

"Okay, so what you're saying is, I'm the problem?" She asked.

"No, I'm not saying you are a problem. What I'm saying is, you can be the solution," Eric said ready to give up on the conversation.

"We both can be the solution," Tesha replied, determined to make her husband admit that there's something that he could do too.

"Well, I plan on keeping my job," Eric said then silently prayed that she would just talk about something else.

"And we can also reduce some expenses," Tesha said then tried to think of what they could cut down on or just cut out. "Like eating out all the time."

"I agree," Eric said. "You get no argument from me.

"No going out with the guys and picking up the tab," she said. "No more cookouts every other weekend, unless everyone chips in."

"Ok, no more shopping sprees, spa treatment, or trips," Eric chimed in, noticing that everything that she wanted to cut out, were things that he typically suggested or did.

"By no trips, you mean no vacations?" Tesha asked.

"Not for a while. Let's look at the bigger picture, home ownership," Eric said, hoping Tesha would understand that they would have to make some real sacrifices if they want a house.

"No trips ever?" Tesha asked.

"No, I mean no more of the big ones like the Bahamas," Eric said and then paused to think of a time frame. "For at least two years. We have enjoyed and done more than most of the people we know. The truth is, if we never take another trip in order to enjoy a home, fine with me," Eric said.

"You know what baby?" Tesha asked. "We have enjoyed trips at the expense of home ownership and now we got credit card debt and it's all my fault. I could have said 'no.' All that money spent on trips could have been the down payment we needed for a house. I guess we were not thinking; well, I wasn't thinking."

"Baby, I could have said 'no' too, so if it's anybody fault, it's both of ours, but let's not think about that now. Maybe it just wasn't our time and now it is," Eric said.

"But you did it because you wanted to make me happy, and I have been blaming you all this time and…"

"Stop! Tesha, as long as we work hard, we can still have everything we want," Eric said and then paused, suddenly thinking about something he needed to tell her. "Look, I was going to tell you this later, but since you are blaming you, I have to tell you about a decision I made. We are going to make a sacrifice on a regular basis and we will start now. It may mean that it's going to take longer to come out of debt," Eric stopped and looked at Tesha for a few seconds before finishing. "Baby as head of this household, I will not waiver on this one," he said with a hint of pride in his voice.

Tesha looked at Eric afraid to ask what he was talking about.

"It's time to get my house in order," he continued.

"Okay, I'm listening." Tesha said expecting to hear something about the kids.

"I, and hopefully you too, will serve the Lord," he said with his head and chest out as he pulled in the driveway and turned the engine off. Eric turned to face his wife. "I made a vow to myself and God. I vowed that ten percent of everything that I bring in will go to Him. After reading in Malachi about tithes and offering and something about robbing God, I realize that there are two types of giving that is expected. I will give an offering too. I vowed that I would be obedient to His Word. Baby, I know you grew up in church and got burnt out with church folks, but it's not about them. I know you got tired of going every Sunday, but I know now that there is no real success and happiness without God and attending church in the place that God orders us to go. The Bible says, 'He set the member in their set place,' or something like that. I'll google it to get the right verse if you need me too," Eric joked.

Tesha kissed her husband with all the passion in her body. It was just something about him taking charge and stepping up to be the Godly man she dreamed about when she was sixteen. "Baby, I love you more at this very moment then I did the day I married you. I realize that you have made a lot of sacrifices for us, for me, and I'm going to spend the rest of our life showing you that I love and appreciate you. I am looking forward to going to church, sitting beside my mighty man of God. I think sometimes us spiritually immature woman get tired of going to church alone, not realizing that it our time with God that's more important and not whether someone is beside us or not, but knowing you are there as the king of our house, I know I'm going to enjoy it even more."

"Baby, one more thing," Eric said.

"Okay now, let's not push it. This is just too much for me to handle at one time," Tesha said, grabbing the car-door handle as if she was not going to listen. "What is it Eric," she said as she turned to face him.

"I'll get the car door for you, but just hear me out," he said. I don't want no secrets between us. I'm going to let you know now that I joined DeAnna's church a few weeks ago. I can't make you join, but I would like for us to serve under one roof, in the same church. Now, I know you love your home church, even though you never go, but..."

"But, I love my husband more and I'm going where goes," Tesha said and reached for the handle again.

"And," Eric said, not finished revealing his secrets.

"Wow, there's more," Tesha sarcastically said.

"Yes, I know you keep up with my bank account," Eric said as he reached for his handle as if he thought he would have to make a quick exit. "So, when you see that there is about two-hundred and fifty dollars missing, I want you to know that I started tithing already."

"But your check is only…" Tesha started adding figure in her head.

"I know," Eric said cutting her off. "I know what you are going to say, but I paid for two weeks that I missed. Dee said I didn't have to because I repented for not paying and God doesn't expect back pay. She said I just need to start from now and go forward, but I wanted to do it."

"It's your money, besides the interest God pays is better than the Credit Union, that's for sure," Tesha said. She was tired of talking.

"So, we're in this together?" Eric asked, surprised that Tesha had been so agreeable to everything.

"Yes, and Monday morning I'm going to get a job," she said with confidence.

Eric laughed, "You mean you're going to start looking for job, right?"

"I haven't been out of church that long, Bible basic 101 says, speak those things that be not, as if they are. By faith, I am going to get a job and after I pay my tithes and offerings, I'm going to take the rest of that money and start paying off those credit cards. We are getting our house, baby."

"I hear you, babe," Eric said as he got out of the car and quickly walked around to open Tesha's door.

"In nine months, we are going to give birth to our dream home," Tesha said. She had made up in her mind that she was going to really push hard and beat the odds. *Two years is too long to be pregnant with a dream,* she thought.

Eric laughed as he pulled his wife into his arms. "With God all things are possible," he whispered in her ear. "And I hope you still feel the same about me when I say this.

"Lord, when does it end," Tesha said as they strolled in the house arm-in-arm. "Just said it."

"I want my kids with me on a regular basis. I am tired of feeling like I have to sneak to see them," he blurted out.

"Sneak! So, you've been to Rochelle house?" Tesha asked. The loving feelings had instantly faded.

"No! She brings them to the park, sometimes to McDonalds, and I meet them there," Eric answered.

"How long has this been going on?" Tesha asked

"That doesn't matter. One weekend a month and a few park visits from time-to-time is not enough for me. You act like it's etched in stone that they can only be with us one weekend out of the month," Eric said as sweetly as he knew how. He didn't want to skip three steps forward with his wife only to be kicked five steps backwards.

"That's the arrangement you had when I met you," Tesha said as if she had nothing to do with when the kids came over.

"I know, and it was that way because I was out of town the other weekends and working a part-time job, but even then, I would stop by doing the week," Eric clarified.

"Look, the only time she lets you see them is when she needs a babysitter. She just wants to use you, and I'm not going to let her use me," Tesha complained.

"Even if she does need a babysitter, who cares if it means I get to see my kids more. You claim that you love them as if they are your own children, yet you don't seem to want them here other than the one weekend a month," Eric replied.

"That's not true," Tesha objected.

"Baby, I think you hate," Eric paused. He remembered Tesha once saying that she doesn't hate anyone, she just dislikes a few people. "I mean you dislike Rochelle so much, you allow it to hinder your relationship with our children."

"You just don't understand," Tesha said as a tear rolled down her cheek. "She made me..."

"Tesha, babe, I do understand, but you have to keep in mind she was before you and I met. She got hurt, too. We all were very immature then," Eric said. He paused and looked at Tesha as she pulled the leftovers out of the refrigerator. "She's a better person now, we all are."

"So what? You want her back. Is that what you are saying?" Tesha slammed the bowl down on the counter. "You want one big happy family with her?"

"That's not at all what I am saying," Eric said. "I just can't spend my life hating the mother of my children. I want my kids to know that their parents like each other, and I want God to know that I know how to forgive and walk in love. I want the family with you. Rochelle is very sorry for what she put you through, but you cannot blame her for the miscarriage. The doctor said that…" Eric said then paused and pulled Tesha into his arms.

"I know Eric, I know," Tesha said as the tears flowed freely. "But now I may never have a child because…"

"Baby, do you trust me?" Eric asked.

"Yes," she replied.

"Do you trust God?" He asked.

"Yes," Tesha said, wiping a tear away.

"Well, trust this, God will give me and you a child."

"How do you know?" Tesha questioned Eric. She could tell that this was more than just faith talking.

"I wasn't sure until you said, "in nine months we will give birth to our dream home. A dream home is not just brick and mortar. It's what's included in the whole home package. God, me, you, our children, and that include the ones you and I will have together."

"Our kids," Tesha said in disbelief.

Eric kissed Tesha again.

"When you said birth to a dream home, I heard God say 'children' at the same time you said home. I honestly actually never imagined or even thought I would truly hear from God."

Tesha smiled at Eric and he smiled back her. They warmed up the leftovers together in silence but feeling connected to each other's spirit.

Chapter 20

"Who's calling me this early?" Chris said, rolling over and looking at the clock on his phone and then the caller ID. "Jeremy." I hope nothing is wrong." He quickly answered the phone. "Hey Jeremy, what's up?"

"Chris, man something strange is going on," Jeremy said.

"What are you talking about? What's strange," Chris asked as he got up and started putting his clothes on. He wasn't sure whether he needed to head to Jeremy's or not.

"Things just seem blurry," Jeremy calmly said.

"Blurry? So, you can see images, but they are blurry?" Chris asked.

"Yes," Jeremy said.

"Your sight is returning. Oh my God. Have you called DeAnna?"

"No," Jeremy said. "I don't think I want her to know right now. If my sight does return, I want to surprise her."

Chris was not sure whether he should warn Jeremy about DeAnna or not. He hoped that Jeremy had learnt something from his unfortunate accident, but he wasn't sure. Chris thought the world of DeAnna, but he just wasn't sure Jeremy knew just what he had in her. He wasn't sure if her size would be a deal breaker for Jeremy, just because it wouldn't be one for him.

"Look man, maybe you should at least go to the doctor," Chris said. "Let them examine your eyes or whatever they need to do."

"I already set up an appointment," Jeremy said.

"Who's taking you?" Chris asked.

"I was going to call a cab," Jeremy replied as if it was no big deal.

"A cab! You mean you'll actually be seen riding in a cab?"

"Why not," Jeremy questioned.

"Man look when is your appointment," Chris asked.

"He can fit me in whenever I get there," Jeremy replied.

"I'm free until twelve. I can be there in thirty minutes," Chris said as he began to undress so he could take a shower.

"If you want to, but really I have been practicing this independent thing for a while now and it's really not that bad."

Chris laughed. "Okay, I'll drop you off and you can take the cab back if you need to, but if you need a ride, Malcolm is off today."

"Well, he probably has something to do if he took off," Jeremy said knowing Malcolm rarely ever takes days off.

"Nah, he said he just wanted a break," Chris replied.

"I'll keep that in mind. I'll hear you when you get here," Jeremy said.

"Man, you are funny. Bye," Chris said and hung up. "Hear you when you get here. Funny! I guess that's blind for 'see you when you get here.'"

"Maybe if I get him there early enough, he'll be finished by ten and then I can take him home," Chris said.

Chris thought about how Jeremy's blindness had really affected everybody. Chris didn't have a lot of close family members and he was single. He has a four-year-old daughter whom he saw five or six times a year when he visits his family in Georgia. He loved her more than his own life but worked so much that he couldn't visit her as often as he would like.

Naija's mother, Kristen, didn't seem to care if Chris ever came to see his daughter or not, as long as the checks were there each month. If Chris forgot to send the check, she would call him and fuss as long as he would let her. She'd threatened to go to Child Support Enforcement more than he cared to remember. Chris sent her almost a thousand dollars a month for Naija', but nothing ever seemed to be enough for Kristen.

Chris showered, dressed, and quickly walked down the hall. When he got to the accent table by the door, he grabbed the small envelope that was on the table. He glanced at the picture of Naija' and then opened the closet door and grabbed the small overnight bag. When Chris arrived at Jeremy's house, Jeremy was outside on the porch. Chris blew the horn and jumped out of the car. Jeremy was halfway down the steps by the time Chris reached him.

"Take it easy Champ," Chris said, grabbing Jeremy by the elbow to guide him. "Why you got sunglasses on?"

"My eyes feel a little funny from the light when I opened them. I think it is because everything's still feels blurry," Jeremy explained.

"But other than that, you feel ok?" Chris asked.

"Health wise, I've never felt better," Jeremy said as if something else might be wrong though.

Chris open the car door. "Remember you in my car now. Not your big truck," he reminded Jeremy.

"How could I forget that, Mr. Lowrider," Jeremy said, but instantly felt that something was different.

"Oh, that's right, I forgot to tell you," Chris said as he looked at his watch. "Just get in and I'll tell you on the way."

Jeremy lowered himself into the car. Chris considered helping Jeremy with his seat belt, but he knew that Jeremy liked to do things for himself.

"Ok," Jeremy said when he heard Chris car door close. "Either you raised the seats, the tires, or this is another car."

"Wow, man you are good," Chris said.

"Nope, I ain't that good," Jeremy quickly replied. "I just know that I'm not sitting as low as I normally am in your Vet. Seems roomier too."

"Man," Chris said as he pulled off. "I sold the Vet."

"What, the chick magnet," Jeremy replied as if he was shocked.

"Yep," Chris said, waiting for Jeremy to start the 20-question game.

"Why?" Jeremy asked.

"Well," Chris sighed. "I was on the phone with Kristen one day."

"Who?" Jeremy hesitantly asked. The name sounded familiar.

"KK, Naija's mother."

"Oh okay, Naija's mother," Jeremy repeated.

"Well, she was fussing because the child support check was late. Now, I sent her five-hundred dollars two weeks prior, so it wasn't like she didn't have anything, right?"

"Right," Jeremy replied.

"Well, I was a little upset and Dee heard me fussing after I got off the phone," Chris said then paused, wondering if Jeremy might get jealous.

"Dee who? My Dee, I mean DeAnna," Jeremy asked, sounding a little concerned.

Chris chuckled a little before he answered, "Yeah, your Dee. It was that night we all went over to Kimberly's and Jason's," Chris said and then suddenly remembered that Jeremy wasn't there. "Oh, that's right, you didn't go. We were helping them paint the baby's room."

"Oh yeah," Jeremy said hoping he had not appeared to be jealous. "I remember hearing something about that."

"Well, it made me a little sad when I thought about the fact that I would probably see little Kimberly or little Jason grow up," Chris paused and swallowed the lump in his throat. "But not my own child. Then Kristen called fussing."

245

"That girl's crazy," Jeremy said. "She's getting more than she would if you were under court order and she don't even have sense enough to keep her mouth shut."

"That's the same thing Dee said," Chris said, thinking about how DeAnna and Jeremy seemed to be on the same wave length with each other. "Anyway, it ain't even about the money. What gets to me is the fact that my daughter is growing up without me and I just know Kristen is not spending it all on Naija' either."

"Nope, what's a four-year-old doing with six-hundred dollars a month? Her mom doesn't even work, so she is not using it on day care. The child is out of pampers, man..." Jeremy said as if it was just ridiculous.

"More like, almost a thousand dollars," Chris hesitantly said.

"What? Man are you serious?"

"Yep, that's why I don't understand why she gets mad when one check is late. I send about three hundred dollars a week sometimes more," Chris slammed on brakes to avoid a dog. "Sorry, a dog ran in front of the car. Anyway, two weeks prior to be being late, I sent five hundred dollars. After talking to 'your Dee,' I called CSE and asked to sign a VSA.

"What's that?" Jeremy asked.

"A Voluntary Support Agreement," Chris proudly said.

"Wow, man I don't blame you. You can set up a savings account for her with what you'll probably save," Jeremy said.

"Man, you and Dee think alike," Chris said without confirming that DeAnna had told him the same thing.

They both laughed.

Kristen has not worked since Naija' was born; she is getting some support from someplace else," Chris said as he glanced at a text from Kristen. "She uses my money, well Naija's money, to pay her cell phone so she can text me," he laughed. "But won't send me a school picture that I paid for, but I bet she gets her hair done."

"Yep, you pay child support and adult support," Jeremy replied.

"Well, she had her fun off me," Chris said with more excitement in his voice. "The order was set and now I am ordered to pay three hundred and ninety-five dollars a month."

"Man, I know she wishes she had kept her mouth shut," Jeremy said as if Chris was telling a lyfetime story and he was enjoying it.

"Yup, because they made the order retroactive from the day I filed. I had already sent over eight hundred dollars before they gathered all the information they needed from Kristen, so technically I didn't owe for two months. I will say this, when I told them what I was sending and bought in the proof, Kristen didn't even try to lie, like most women. She admitted I had paid her the money."

"But now that doesn't explain why you sold the Vet," Jeremy said.

"I'm getting to that," Chris said. He took a deep breath as if he was getting ready for round two. "Dee said something else that got me thinking. She said that I should get an attorney and ask for joint custody."

"How is that going to work with you in North Carolina and her being in Georgia?"

"Well now, Kristen now has physical custody and we both have legal custody. I'll get Na' on holidays and summers when she starts school," Chris paused as he thought about his pending trip. "But until then, I can have her six months out of the year."

"That's a long time," Jeremy said.

"Yeah, but I don't think the six months is going to happen because she really needs time to adjust to me. She starts Pre-k, so she'll be in school this fall."

"Pre-k," Jeremy said as if it was a joke.

"You know Kristen is just doing that so she can stop me from getting her for the entire six months. See, when she's with me for the six months, I don't have to pay child support." Chris smiled as he thought about how much DeAnna had helped him. What had seemed like a huge bother and a costly venture helped him more than he had expected.

"So, you have already been to court," Jeremy questioned.

"Nope," Chris said.

"So, how do you already have joint custody?" Jeremy asked as if he was totally lost. He still was not sure what all this had to do with Chris selling the Vet.

"Dee knew an attorney in Georgia. He drew up the agreement and since Kristen could not afford an attorney, she signed the agreement. It was presented before a Judge, and he signed off on it and it's now a court ordered custody agreement," Chris said and then hesitated. "I think that's what it's called.

"Wow, that's great," Jeremy said.

Jeremy was happy for his friend, but he suddenly felt lonely as he thought about Chris spending time with Naija', and everyone else married or dating.

"That's not even the good news," Chris said, interrupting Jeremy's thoughts.

"There's more," Jeremy asked, thinking it was about the Vet.

"Yep, I am flying to Georgia today and I'm bringing Naija' back with me. She's going to be with me until she starts head start, pre-K, whatever."

"Kristen hates that, doesn't she?" Jeremy asked.

"Well, I agreed to still send her some money, despite the order."

"What?" Jeremy questioned as if Chris was crazy for doing so.

"One thing I can say, even if all the money is not being spent on my princess, she does live like one. Kristen has the apartment looking good. She has a car that she has to pay for, but it benefits my daughter. I don't want her to lose that. No telling when an emergency might come up and she need to get Naija' to the doctor and don't have time to wait on a bus, a friend, or even the ambulance."

"Well, I guess you a man now," Jeremy jokingly said.

They both laughed again.

"I guess I am," Chris said and laughed. "It's really not even about the money with every man."

"Who's gonna keep her while you're at work?" Jeremy asked. "Have you thought about that?"

"Yep, the same way women who work does it, I'm going to do it. I found a day care, which is open 24 hours. And between Lesia, Kimberly, Tesha, and Dee, somebody knows how to braid hair. If not, there is a hair salon on every corner. I sent Kristen extra money to get Naija' hair done before I pick her up, so I'm good for least two-weeks."

"So, I guess no more overnight guest?" Jeremy laughed.

"Nope, but I stopped that months ago," Chris said, feeling proud of himself. "I wanted something more than a jump off chick. I want a wife. Pastor said the reason why we don't see wifey is because we aren't husband material yet. When women say there 'ain't no good men, they aren't just insulting the man that dumped them, cheated on them, or lied to them. They are talking about those of us who wanted to play the husband role, without being a husband," Chris said and then paused. He began to think about something he heard the pastor say. *How would you feel if your daughter married someone like you?* "I'm going to focus all my efforts on being a good dad. Its parks, dolls babies, Chuck E Cheese, and no more Vet for me. One day Naija' will say, 'I want a man just like my daddy.' I want to smile when I hear that. The way I was going, that would have been a death sentence, if she ended up with someone like the old me."

"Man, you're 'bout to make me cry," Jeremy said and then laughed. He was proud of his friend. "Chris that's some grown-man stuff for real. No joke. I hear Eric and Tesha are going to have Eric's kids every other weekend now," Jeremy said as his mind drifted again. "Kimberly and Jason will be parents in about three months." Jeremy paused and thought about his own life. "Wow, so much has changed in such a short time. *What has changed for me?* He thought to himself, "Me, nothing," he muttered.

Chris knew exactly why Jeremy said, 'Me, nothing.' He heard the sadness in Jeremy's voice when he talked. Chris had heard it for months whenever someone would share good news to Jeremy. Chris knew that Jeremy was overjoyed for his friends, but he also knew that Jeremy seemed to feel that his life had changed for the worse.

"You just don't see it yet, but trust me, a lot has change for you," Chris said. "I think it's because of what happened to you, that we all realized how much we had taken for granted. I looked at you one day and I realized how strong you are. You don't even act mad at the guy who shot you."

"Mad! Man, I wanted to kill him," Jeremy said and then paused. He didn't want to cry another tear over this situation. "I was sitting in church one day and I asked God to erase the memory of his face because if I saw him, I was going to kill him. It was then that I realized being blind, saved my life."

"What?" Chris asked, sounding confused.

"If I had left the hospital with all that anger and rage in me and was able to go looking for that guy, I would either be dead or in prison." Jeremy paused again. "Dee asked me one day if I thought I was better than God. I said, 'no.' Then she asked if I had any of God's power, would I use them? I said, 'yes.' She told me that God forgives, and unless I thought I was higher than God, I should too. She said I had the power to forgive, just like God."

249

"Powerful and true," Chris said as he thought about his love-hate relationship with Kristen.

"Then she said, you have the power now, use it," Jeremy said.

"Jeremy, you know that the man who finds a wife has favor from God," Chris said as he pulled in the parking lot of the doctor's office.

"I heard that before," Jeremy replied.

"Do you believe that he gives that favor when we find her," Chris asked. "Or when you marry her?"

"Good question," Jeremy said. "I guess once a man realizes he wants to marry her and acknowledge that he has found his wife," Jeremy replied.

"Perhaps he receives her in his heart as his wife, regardless of the ceremony. Some men might be married but acting single and have never received her as his wife and still don't have that favor. Others might have it-the favor-from the time he knows she is his wife."

"Hum,' Jeremy said, pondering what Chris was getting at.

"Well, we're here," Chris said, not wanting to push the conversation any further. He wanted Jeremy to just ponder the thought. "Do you need any help?"

"What parking space are you in?" Jeremy asked as if that's all the help he needed.

"The first handicapped park on the left," Chris said hoping he had explained it correctly. "You are directly in front of the office door."

"I got cha," Jeremy replied.

Chris always parked in the same park, if it was free.

"Jeremy?" Chris called out then hesitated. He wasn't sure if it was the right time or thing to say, but he felt in his heart that it was true. "Thanks."

"For what?" Jeremy asked before he closed the car door.

"For allowing your favor to flow down and rain on me, I mean us."

"What?" Jeremy asked, but he had a clue what Chris was talking about.

"Never mind. Don't forget to call Malcolm. He's taking me to the airport at 11:30, if you finish before then, call and you can ride with us, if you feel like it. I got to go pick up a few things for Naija' right now. It's a little after 8 a.m. now."

As soon as Jeremy was inside the office, Chris called DeAnna.

Chapter 21

"Hey Chris, what's up?" DeAnna asked.

"I want to take you to breakfast," Chris hesitantly said. He wasn't sure if he was doing the right thing. "I have something to talk to you about."

"Okay, we can meet at the diner off Winsted. I'm almost there now," DeAnna informed Chris. She knew he lived close by.

"I'll be there in five minutes," Chris replied.

When DeAnna arrived, Chris was already there. She waved and headed to the table.

"Hey Dee," he said as he pulled the chair out for her.

"Hey Chris. You look serious, is anything wrong?" DeAnna asked as she studied his face.

"First, I just want to thank you for the advice and the attorney."

"Did she take care of you?" DeAnna asked, hoping she didn't sound as if she expected Chris to tell her his business.

"I'm leaving today to go pick up my daughter. I'll have her for a few months. And I'm not going to lie or play like it's all cool. I'm scared. I mean, what if she gets sick or..."

"You will handle that when and if that happens," DeAnna said and smiled at Chris. "You are being the man and the dad that she needs you to be. This little girl will never wonder if you truly love her. Just think about that."

"I know, and I have you to thank for that. It's not that men don't want to do it, some of us just don't know how. All I kept thinking was, who is going to keep her while I'm at work. It never crossed my mind to put her in daycare or to pay someone to do her hair."

"That's understandable, but at least you didn't wait until she was 18 and then try to figure it out," DeAnna replied. "No looking back."

"I also want to know if you will help me with something else. I know that you didn't expect everybody pulling on you like this when you agreed to help Jeremy, but..." Chris paused. He wasn't sure what to say. "You are more than just Jeremy's friend, you are our friend too, Dee," Chris said.

"You know; I finally feel like I have true friends. I never really felt like just 'the help.' Well, at least you didn't make me feel that way."

"I have been going to church and getting these feeling about things. For some reason, I don't feel that it was ever part of the plan for you to be the help or just Jeremy's friend."

"Really?" DeAnna asked.

DeAnna had heard stories similar to this before. She didn't want to get excited because some guy thought she was great for his friend, then the friend walks off into the sunset with someone else.

"Look Chris, I know where you are going with this and I have to stop you. I've been down this road; I've been burnt and learnt."

"You learnt how to help everybody else learn to trust God, have faith, and be patient, while you locked your heart away from all men."

"I'm not locking it away," DeAnna replied. "I'm just waiting for him, whoever *him* may be, to accept me for me."

Chris simply smiled at DeAnna as she talked. He wasn't buying her 'waiting on God speech.' He'd heard so many women say that, but many seemed to be waiting with so much doubt that a man could truly love them, that they had a closed spirit while they so-called, '*waited on God.*' Chris often felt that there was no point in God sending a man to them, until the woman truly believed that someone could and would truly love her.

"DeAnna, you have one of the most beautiful spirits that I have ever seen, or shall I say, felt. I can't tell you how I wish I had met you before Jay met you, but I know it happened as it should have happened. I've never seen Jay so happy and confident. He seems more confident now without his sight, then he did with it. Well, around you that is. He has never been like that around any of the other women. He acted like he was Mr. Confident around us, but he wasn't keeping it real. Now? Wow! He has allowed you in a place no woman has ever gone."

"Where is that?" DeAnna asked.

"DeAnna, in his heart." Chris paused. Do you think that the only reason that the women haven't been around is because they were only using him in the first place and he no longer has anything they want? Nah, the truth is, he pushed them away. He always does before he gets too close. I think he wants them to like his image, but he doesn't want them close to his heart, his dreams, or his fears," Chris said. "I think he's afraid to regain his sight because he thinks he will lose you. He's afraid if he does get it back, you won't want him."

"Wow, he tells me about his dreams all the time. I remember him telling me about the…" DeAnna paused. She didn't want to betray his trust. "I guess I better just keep that a secret between him and I." DeAnna said. She liked the way *'him and I'* sound together. She smiled at the thought of knowing that she knew something the others didn't know.

"That's what I'm talking about, no one, not even any of us has heard his heart," Chris smiled at DeAnna. "Dee, he loves you, but…"

"What is it Chris. I'm a big girl; I can take it," DeAnna said, sensing that there was a big 'but.'

"I'm not sure if I should say this or not," Chris said and then paused to think it through.

"What?" DeAnna pleaded.

"Dee, Jay has changed a lot since his accident, in so many ways. Thanks to you. Well, thanks to God for blessing Jeremy with you. But in the past, he was one of those guys all about images and looks." Chris prayed that he had not hurt DeAnna's feelings, but he did not want her to hurt worse later if Jeremy rejected her.

"Oh, I get it. He likes the model type. The size-2, salad eating, cracker snacking, body-no brain type chicks."

"Dee, I'm sorry," Chris said, wondering if he had made a mistake. The logic sounded good in his head, but now his heart hurt for DeAnna.

"Why would you tell me that he loves me and then tells me this?" DeAnna softy asked, not wanting anyone else to hear her.

"Well, it might sound crazy, but I don't want you to give up on him. He might have some problems accepting your size at first, but he has never felt true love and I know him. He has waited too long; he is not going to give up on it too easy. But I guess the secret is safe for now." By the look on Chris' face, DeAnna could tell that there was more.

"What?" DeAnna asked. "You said all of that, might as well let the whole cat out of the bag."

"He's at the doctor's office now," Chris said, staring at DeAnna. "He woke up this morning and he could see images."

"Oh my God that's great," DeAnna said. She waited to see what else Chris had to say.

"The images are blurry," Chris continued.

"That happens at first, so this is some great news," DeAnna replied.

"Dee let him tell you, okay? Don't tell him that I told you please. Whatever happens, I hope you will stay in all of our lives. I don't know many people here. I was always the shy one, but I have come to really love you like a big sister and I want you to be a godmother to Naija'."

"I won't, I will, and I would love to be her godmother," Dee said as her eyes filled with tears. "Chris are you sure? What if?"

"Yes, I'm sure. No matter what happens. If there's anyone around her who I know will teach my little princess how to be a Godly young lady, it's you." Chris handed DeAnna an envelope.

"What's this?"

"I asked Naija' how she wanted her room decorated and she sent me this picture," Chris laughed. "This little girl texted me this, in-boxed, and e-mailed it to me. I want her to feel like she's at home and not just at daddy's house."

"You are going to be okay Chris."

"You said that you always wanted to be an interior decorator," Chris said as he looked at DeAnna for confirmation that he had heard right. "I remember hearing that, right?"

"I can't believe you remember that."

"Nope," Chris laughed. "I forgot you said it, just as soon as you said it, but Jeremy reminded me one day. He asked me if his place was too masculine. He said he was going to have it re-done when he goes back to work. Said he was thinking about paying you to do it. He wanted your dreams to come true."

"Are you serious? He remembered that?" DeAnna asked, staring at Chris. "Wow, I mean, he said... wow," she said not sure what to say.

"Take it from me," Chris said, staring into DeAnna eyes. "No man is going to allow someone to affect him like that, then just walk away over..."

"Over excess weight. You can say it," DeAnna said.

The waitress came to the table, took their orders and left.

"DeAnna, we have trusted so much of what you have told us. No matter what the situation looks like at first, hang in there a little while longer. Trust me this time. I know him. Just as Cain and Able were brothers so is Jeremy and I."

"That not really a good example," DeAnna said, shaking her head. "Cain was the first person to commit murder and he killed his brother, Abel," DeAnna said and smiled.

"You're right, bad example," Chris said, shaking his head too. "But you know what I mean. And even if you can't trust me, trust God. 'You shall reap, if you faint not.' Those are your words to me when I first started this custody issue. Besides God's workman, you too are worthy of double honor. I don't think it's just for preachers, leaders, and pastors. Look at all you have done in just our small circle and in the single's group."

"Wow, now I'm really impressed. You've been paying attention in church," DeAnna said and winked at Chris.

"Yep, I have. So now back to my question. I want to know if you will help me with Naija's room. I don't mean right now. Naija' will be here for two weeks, then she'll go back home for a few days for her family reunion. When she comes back, she should be comfortable with everybody else. Maybe, just maybe, the two of you can find some time to shop."

"Okay, that sound like a plan," DeAnna said.

"Oh and let me know your fee so I can start saving up. I got my child support reduced, sold that gas guzzling Vet, and saved on my car insurance, so I should be okay."

"Okay," DeAnna said.

"Hold on a minute," Chris said to DeAnna and then answered his phone. "Hey Malcolm, what up?"

"Jeremy is finished at the doctor's office, and he has already gone," Malcolm said.

"Gone! What, did he call a cab?" Chris asked, looking at DeAnna.

"I guess so, he's not answering the phone." Malcolm replied.

"Not cool Jay," Chris said. "Ok, thanks for letting me know."

"What's going on?" DeAnna asked.

"Jeremy left the doctor's office. I guess he called a cab," Chris said as if he was talking about an eight-year-old child.

"And what's wrong with that?" DeAnna asked. "He hates being chauffeured around. Y'all make him feel like a child sometimes."

"He could have at least called to let us know," Chris replied.

"After he gets where he's going; he's going to call. He probably left a message on his home phone just in case," DeAnna said. She didn't want to say in case he got lost.

Dee called Jeremy home phone and keyed in his pin to check the messages. "He's going to his mother's house and then he's going to," DeAnna paused. She wasn't sure who the message was referring to. "He's going to see his old girlfriend," DeAnna said and then hung up the phone. "For future reference, don't make him feel like it's an incontinence to help him. That's why he does that, he doesn't want to bother you," DeAnna said and then grabbed her purse and walked out of the diner, upset.

"DeAnna wait," Chris yelled. He placed twenty-dollars on the table to cover the food that they never received." He ran behind DeAnna. "Wait Dee," he said as he grabbed her and turn her to face him. "Is that what faith is? Trusting God only as long as everything looks like it is going your way. Dee, I know what I'm talking about. I was just like Jeremy, maybe even worse. Naija's mom was the first big girl I ever dated. I love, I mean loved her so much."

"What happened?" DeAnna asked.

"She didn't believe that I or anyone could truly love her, but I did. I didn't believe I could love at all, at first. She seemed to have a better time flirting with me, than being with me. I guess she just thought I just wanted to sheet rumble," Chris said and laughed. "As soon as I really started falling for her, she pushed and pushed until I was gone, then she became bitter and I left, came back to North Carolina. Dee don't push him away. Let him figure it out. Let him accept what he is feeling. He might just be as confused as I was, but..."

"What if he pushes me away?" DeAnna asked.

"He probably will at first. Just give it time. I mean if you love him, at least understand and even appreciate that he loved your spirit. Just keep your spirit." Chris paused. "I'm not as good at this as you are, so just think about what you would tell a woman in this situation who was trying to accept a man who was too skinny whom she fell in love with. Jeremy knows that the devil will always disguise God's blessing, then we walk away from the best things."

"I will try to remember that. Oh, and by the way, the way you talked about Naija's mom," DeAnna paused and smiled. "You still love her."

"Dee please, let's go back in and eat. I got a plane to catch in a few hours and I hate eating alone."

DeAnna smiled and locked arms with Chris' and headed back into the restaurant. She noticed a few women staring at her. Chris notice that they were staring, and he gave them something to talk about, he kissed DeAnna on the forehead. He didn't want to over-step his boundary since he was certain that she was Jeremy's woman, even if it had not been officially established.

"Thank you," DeAnna said, realizing that he was officially showing that he was not ashamed to be seen with her, no matter who was looking.

"So, tell me, what is the purpose of Jeremy's messages on his own voicemail?"

"Well, if something happens such as he falls or get lost, someone will to be able to retrace his steps," DeAnna said and then paused. "Like now, if I couldn't find him, I would check with his mom or the old girlfriend," DeAnna said and then paused, "If I knew who she was."

"Smart, but why not just tell someone?" Chris asked.

"Well, it's really just a backup plan. If he calls to tell you, but he doesn't reach you or the message box is full. Or if he doesn't really want anyone to know where he is going unless, it's an emergency. He probably didn't want you to stop him or talk him out of taking a cab, so he didn't want to call you or Malcolm."

"Oh, okay I get it," Chris said with a confused look on her face.

"If he called you and left a message with you; you would have instantly gone to get him as soon as you listen to the message. Even if he said, he didn't need a ride," DeAnna explained.

"Yep, you're right, that's what I would have done," Chris said with no hesitation.

"Soooo."

"Wow, you are going to be a great auntie," Chris said, thinking about the emergency plan DeAnna would be able to help him with.

"I hope so," DeAnna said with a hint of doubt in her voice.

"You will," Chris said. "You'll be a good auntie, this I know, 'cause the spirit tells me so, my little girl will be so blessed because her auntie is the best," Chris sang in the tune of the Christian children's song 'Jesus Loves Me.'

"Wow, now you know the church does need some more men in the choir, maybe even someone to write their own songs," DeAnna said as she clapped for him. "So, Chris did you ever think about getting back with Naija's mother?"

"Kristen," Chris said, informing DeAnna of her name. "Yup, I did. I even asked her to marry me, but she thought it was because of Naija'. She just didn't believe that anybody could truly love her."

"Well, sometimes," DeAnna said and then paused to gather her thoughts. "For some women, especially those who have been passed over and overlooked all of their life, or just used by guys, it is not so easy to believe that a man who can have any woman he wants, truly wants her."

"I know you have heard it all before. Everybody has the right to like who and what they like, but generally a real man is going to pick the woman that pleases his spirit over, the one who only pleases his eyes. Especially, when it comes to who he marries. A man who has a beautiful, spirit-filled, God-fearing woman, who makes him feel loved, who strokes his ego, and appreciate him, eventually those will be the attributes that matters most, not her weight," Chris said, speaking from personal experience.

"So, what would you rate me, eighty or twenty," DeAnna jokingly asked. "My feelings don't hurt easy."

"DeAnna you are about a ninety," Chris said without hesitation.

"Stop," DeAnna said.

"No, I'm serious. See weight is not a big issue for me. Now, I do have limits, as long as she is not sloppy, dress nice, and smells good, I can handle it. DeAnna you always look good, you cook, clean, work, and you are a God-fearing woman with a good heart. A virtuous woman, who can find?" Chris said, pointing at DeAnna. "Jeremy did, I know that."

"Thanks Chris," DeAnna said. "You just don't know how that makes me feel,"

After they finished breakfast, DeAnna went to work and Chris went to Malcolm's house.

"Hey Ms. Dee," one of DeAnna's coworker said with a huge smile on her face. "Looks like one of the patients was well pleased with your bedside manner."

"Girl what are you talking about?" DeAnna asked and then paused when she looked at the desk at the nurse's station. "Those are for me?" She questioned, completely shocked. She'd never gotten flowers at work before. She grabbed the small card attached to the beautiful arrangement of flowers.

"That is the biggest arrangement I have ever seen. They looked really expensive," Karen, the head nurse said. "Somebody has really been a good girl."

All the women on the floor and that shift acted like sisters. Karen and DeAnna were as close as sister could be.

DeAnna opened the card slowly. The others anxiously waited to hear what it said. DeAnna was afraid to read it. Karen snatched it from her and read the card. Karen knew that DeAnna wouldn't get mad at her for reading the card. They had often done things like that to each other. "I want to see you," Karen read the note, sounding like a man. "Will call you late, signed, me."

Everyone laughed.

"Well," Karen said. "There's no name on the card, so who are you going to be meeting later, Ms. Lady?" Karen asked.

DeAnna knew that the flowers were from Jeremy. *So, he wants a real date, huh,* she thought to herself. Her mind started racing. *I wonder if he went to see his old girlfriend and now they are back together. I wonder if he's going to let me know he doesn't need a personal assistant anymore. Oh my God, I still have his truck, and haven't even thought about checking on my car lately. He might ask for his truck back. Lord, I have to get myself together. I spend so much time helping others, I haven't been handling my own business.* DeAnna became overwhelmed with thoughts. She grabbed the daily log to see what rooms were occupied with patients. She strolled away, still deep in thought and left her flowers at the nurse's station.

DeAnna had the best day and the worst day all in the same day. All her patients were friendly and able to go to the bathroom on their own, without assistance, but she felt like she needed assistance. She was so nervous about meeting Jeremy that every time she thought about it, she felt like she was going to vomit. A million new questions ran through her head. *What if he can see me and don't like what he sees. What if he wants to see me to tell me he's engaged? What if all he wants me to do is decorate his house. Why hasn't he called me by now?* As DeAnna finished up her final round, she thought about what Chris said about not believing.

When DeAnna returned from her final round, she checked her cell phone for the thirteenth time that day. *Well maybe he thinks I'm not off work yet. I know what I'll do. I'll go home, take a long hot bubble bath, put on something nice, and just wait.*

"So Dee, was he the guy that sent the flowers?" Karen asked.

As close as they were, DeAnna had not told Karen much about Jeremy. She really didn't want anyone knowing that she was crushing on an ex-patient, a blind patient at that.

"He who?" DeAnna asked.

"The guy that just left here," Karen replied. "I thought he was here to pick you up. He went down the hall that you were on. You were coming out of 419; I pointed to you. I told him just don't go into the room with you. I knew that was your last bed check and you would be headed out, so I thought he was just going to escort you out."

"You didn't see him?" Karen questioned.

"Nope, didn't see him," DeAnna said.

"Well he just left. He's probably out there somewhere looking for you. He couldn't have gotten that far. He was walking with a cane," Karen said.

DeAnna rushed downstairs and out of the hospital in time to see Jeremy getting in a cab. Right before the cab pulled off, Jeremy look back. DeAnna was sure that he looked in her direction. "I guess he got his sight back," DeAnna said as she slowly walked to his truck. She sat in the truck crying. She felt that the blind romance was over. As a flow of tears rolled down her cheek, rage filled her heart. She took a few deep breaths to calm herself down. She started the engine and headed home. She wanted to take him his truck back but decided she would call someone to come get it. "God! How could this happen to me," she asked, not sure what was really happening. "I tried to be the Proverbs 31 woman that you told me to be and I'm still alone. I did everything right or best that I could, and I couldn't even get a blind man. God why? Why let me fall in love, if he was never going to be mines? Why do I keep putting my heart out there only to get stepped on and thrown away as if I'm nothing? Not even worthy of an explanation." She talked to God all the way home.

~

DeAnna walked in the house and placed the flowers on the table. She started to throw them in the trash but decided to keep them. They matched her home decor perfectly. DeAnna didn't want to allow Jeremy to have the upper hand. She decided to call him. She was surprised when he answered the phone.

"Hey," Jeremy said. "How was your day, Hun?" Jeremy asked, not feeling brave enough to call her honey.

"'It was good. Someone sent me a beautiful arrangement of flowers," DeAnna said as if it was no big deal.

"Wow, you must have been a good girl," Jeremy said.

"Not good enough evidently," DeAnna said.

"What do you mean by that?" Jeremy asked.

"Nothing!"

"I had another doctor's appointment today. I thought my sight was returning," Jeremy said.

"Oh yeah, why did you think that?"

"Well, I saw images or figures, but they were blurry," Jeremy said and then paused. "Then everything went black again."

DeAnna felt a little better. *Maybe he didn't see me today*, she thought. "So, what are you up to tonight?"

"Well, Tamela ask me to help her with a business plan. She's finally going to start a business."

"Okay, well I guess it's better late than never," DeAnna said. She wasn't sure who Tamela was, but she decided not to ask.

"What about you?" Jeremy asked.

"Well, I thought I was going on a date," DeAnna said, throwing a hint. "But I guess it was wishful thinking."

"It will happen for you. DeAnna you are a beautiful person."

"How do you know, you can't see me," DeAnna said. She felt as if he was giving her the *old push off.*

"I don't have to see you, to know you're beautiful. I can feel your beauty. I might have lost my sight, but God opened my eyes, my spiritual eyes."

"Is that right?" DeAnna said, not knowing if he was flirting with her or just trying to give her some encouraging words with a soft push off.

"Yep, that's right! "Jeremy said. "Look, I got another call. I'll check back with you later. Okay"

DeAnna felt like something had changed between her and Jeremy. He didn't seem to need her as much. "He seemed to be saying bye to me," DeAnna said as she listened to the dial tone for a few seconds after Jeremy hung up.

Chapter 23

Weeks passed and DeAnna and Jeremy had been spending less and less time together. They called each other a few times during the week, but they both became exceedingly busy. DeAnna had found great comfort in spending time with Naija' and Jeremy was preparing for court. The man who shot him was charged with attempted murder. Jeremy seemed to want to be alone with his thoughts.

Everybody's life seemed to be changing. Tesha and Eric had started attending church together. Chris was enjoying his life as a single dad. Kimberly and Jason were preparing for the arrival of their first child. Myles was dating on a regular. Johnathan was just Johnathan, too spiritual to get a woman, but he was getting a little closer to dating. He was at least having longer phone conversations with women.

DeAnna felt blessed to have met them all, but she felt like she was intruding in Jeremy's life whenever she attended one of the group events or gatherings. When they were together, they interacted like a couple. Jeremy relied on her and seemed to want all the attention he could get from her, but he didn't seem to reach out to her at any other times. She decided to limit her interaction with them as much as possible. She thought it would hurt less to be rejected, if she voluntarily withdrew from him. The group went to DeAnna's church, all but Johnathan. He had his own church. Jeremy didn't come as regularly as the others, but he was there from time-to-time. He would ride with Chris or Malcolm. Even Myles would pop in every now and then during special events.

~

"Chris look, I'm wondering if I could take Naija' shopping today. Won't she be going back to Georgia tomorrow? I want to get her something special," DeAnna asked as they walked out of the sanctuary, after one Sunday service.

"Sure, she'll love that. She loves her Auntie Dee."

"I love her too," DeAnna said.

"I can take her now," DeAnna said then realized that the mall wasn't open yet. DeAnna often forgot that they were out of church by 11:30 a.m. each Sunday. "Or I can come to your place later."

"Why don't you come by later," Chris said. "I promised her that we would have lunch and ice cream after church. You are welcome to join us."

"Sounds great," DeAnna said. "You two enjoy your daddy-daughter time. Those times are priceless."

DeAnna went straight home after church and fixed a snack. She had just enough time to eat and clean up her apartment before it was time to go pick up Naija'. DeAnna wasn't sure if it was best to call Chris or just get out and ring the doorbell. *He might have company,* she thought. *Nah, he has not been seeing anyone since Naija's had been there*, she thought. She decided to go to the door. She had always hated it when guys pulled up and honk the horn. She took a deep breath and headed to the door. She rang the doorbell.

"Who is it," she heard Chris yell.
"Auntie Dee," DeAnna yelled back.
"Hey Auntie Dee," Chris said, opening the door.

When she stepped inside to wait for Naija,' she saw Jeremy sitting beside some strange woman. The woman had her hand on Jeremy's lap. DeAnna had a strange feeling that Jeremy's sight had returned.

"Hey Dee," Jeremy said without looking in her direction.
"Hey Jay," DeAnna said, looking at the woman.

Jeremy knew that any time DeAnna called him Jay, something was wrong. He looked in DeAnna's direction. The woman looked at DeAnna too. DeAnna's heart felt as if it had fallen to her feet.

"Hey, little princess," DeAnna said to Naija' as she entered the living room clutching her favorite doll.
"Hi, Auntie Dee. I am feeling good and I'm ready to hit the mall."

DeAnna was amazed at how mature Naija' sounded. She looked like she was four-years-old, but when she spoke, she sounded like she was at least ten-year-old. Chris always referred to her as a mini version of her mom.

"Well, let's go then," DeAnna said, thankful for a way of escape.

"She has already eaten and had dessert," Chris said as a warning to DeAnna so Naija' wouldn't try to trick her into getting more ice cream.

"Okay," Dee said. "I'll call you when we are headed back."

"Daddy, I want to go to Auntie Dee's house for a little bit and watch TV with her, so she won't be lonely. Can I?" Naija' asked.

Everybody glanced at Naija'. She sounded as if she had aged ten years in the last two minutes. DeAnna was a little embarrassed.

"It's up to Aunt Dee," Chris said. "But we got a big day ahead of us tomorrow."

"Oh yeah, I forgot I'm going back to my Georgia home for a few days. I wish you could come with me too," Naija' said to DeAnna.

"Me too," DeAnna said, truly wishing for a way to escape from North Carolina for a while. "I've never been to Augusta, Georgia, but for now let's just hit the mall."

"Ok, we can talk about this later," Naija' said and then hugged goodbye to Jeremy and said goodbye to his lady friend.

DeAnna wanted to scream and cry all at the same time, but she calmly waved goodbye and walked out. She knew that Jeremy couldn't see her wave, but she knew his friend saw her.

"What's wrong with Uncle Jay?" Naija' asked as she climbed into the back seat of the car. DeAnna wanted to change the subject. "Oh, Aunt Dee, I have to use the booster seat because I'm so tiny. My daddy got one in the new car. You know, he sold that other car."

"I know honey," DeAnna said as she contemplated calling Chris to tell him she needed the booster seat. "I like his new car."

"I like his new car too," Naija' replied.

"He got it just for you," DeAnna said, rolling her eyes at the thought of having to face Jeremy again. "Sit tight sweetie. I'll get your booster seat."

Dee was about to knock on the door when it opened, and the young lady stormed out.

"You wouldn't know a good thing if you could see," the unknown woman said, bouncing down the steps. She sounded like Latonya, same lines, attitude, and all.

"Don't try to stop her Chris," Jeremy yelled. "Let her go."

"Chris, I'm sorry to interrupt," DeAnna hesitantly said. "But I need Naija's booster seat."

"Oh yeah," Chris said and stepped back in the house and grabbed his keys off the table by the door. He pointed the keys toward the car and hit unlocked. "It's unlocked," he said to DeAnna.

DeAnna could tell that Jeremy was upset. She wanted to stay to make sure he was okay.

"Is he okay?" She whispered to Chris.

"You know it just seem like something died in him that day he got his sight back temporarily. He started dating again, but he didn't seem happy.

"Most women our age do not want the burden of a blind boyfriend," DeAnna softy said then paused and waited for Chris' response. "But why do I have a feeling that you expected this?" DeAnna asked when Chris did not respond.

"Well, I guess I did sort of expect it, but he had to see for himself. I know it probably hurt you when he stopped calling you for help. But until a man knows for himself that he has the best, he'll always wonder if there is better available. It's better that he finds out this way, now"

"I don't follow you," DeAnna said.

"Remember what I told you the day we had breakfast," Chris said.

"Okay whatever," DeAnna said, heading to Chris' car. She grabbed the booster seat and quickly headed to her own car. She strapped the car seat down and Naija' in. She quickly left. She turned the radio on and they sang songs all the way to the mall.

~

"She's cute," DeAnna heard someone say as she and Naija' walked out of the shoe store.

"Thanks," DeAnna said, turning around to a familiar voice. "Bobby," she said as she quickly reached out to hug him.

"In the flesh," Bobby said, looking DeAnna up and down. "I haven't seen you in years."

"Don't I know it?" DeAnna said, noticing how handsome he looked.

"Well, you look good," Bobby said. "Is she your little beauty?

"Thank you, but no," DeAnna said, looking down at Naija'.

"My daddy name is Christopher E. Jacobs and my mom's name is Kristen K. Nelson.

"Wow aren't you a smart young lady," Bobby said, smiling at Naija'.

"I'm not a lady yet," Naija' corrected Bobby. "I'm a child and this is my Auntie Dee."

"She's my friend's daughter."

"So DeAnna, I heard you were about married," Bobby said as if it was more of a question than a comment.

"I was headed that way," DeAnna said. "But didn't make it down the aisle, not even the wedding dress isle to get the dress."

"What? You mean some clown let you get away?" Bobby said.

"I guess he did," DeAnna said.

"So, you're dating her dad now?" Bobby asked.

"You don't waste no time, do you?" DeAnna said and then laughed. "No, I'm still single."

"Do you think there's a chance that we could get together later and catch up on old times?" Bobby asked.

"Nope, you don't waste any time," DeAnna said, laughing. "Okay, but it'll have to be after seven. I got a movie date from five to six at my place and then I must take my little date home," DeAnna said as she looked at Naija'.

"I'm going back to Augusta, Georgia tomorrow," Naija' said and then got distracted when she noticed the soda machine. "Auntie Dee, I'm thirsty."

"Ok, sweetie why don't we go get something to drink," DeAnna said and then turned to Bobby as if to say goodbye for now.

"Mind if I join you?" Bobby asked before DeAnna had a chance to say goodbye.

As they walked to the food court, DeAnna was deep in thought about what Chris told her. *You shall reap if you faint not. Fainting does not always mean falling out and throwing a temper tantrum. It could mean giving up on what God is preparing for you and settling for the next best thing, after all your hard work to get the best,* DeAnna thought. She thought about the fact that even Naija' could tell that Jeremy wasn't happy.

"What do you want to drink, Naija'?" Bobby asked.

"Lemonade please, with a little bit of ice."

"Yes ma'am," Bobby said to Naija' and then turned to DeAnna. "What about you DeAnna?"

"I'll just have a cup of water," DeAnna said, watching Bobby as he walked off to get the drinks.

"Hey Dee," Lesia and Tesha said as they approached the table where DeAnna and Naija' were standing.

"Hey Lesia, Tesha. Where's your other half," DeAnna asked.

"He's somewhere around here," Tesha said, looking around as if he might pop up. Lesia didn't say anything about Malcolm's location.

"Here you are DeAnna," Bobby said, handing DeAnna a cup of water. He sat Naija' drink on the table that they were standing beside. "And here is your lemonade, lite on the ice," Bobby said.

"Thank you," DeAnna and Naija' said in unison.

"Bobby," DeAnna said. "This is Lesia; Lesia this is my high school sweetheart Bobby. This is Tesha; they are married to best friends.

"High school sweetheart," Bobby protested. "DeAnna was the love of my life. The one I was crazy enough to let get away."

"So why did you do it?" Lesia asked.

"Do what?" Bobby questioned.

"Why did you let her get away?" Tesha chimed in.

"Well, after graduation, I moved to Atlanta, went to college, and made the dumb mistake that dudes make in college, if you get my drift."

"Yea, we get where you drifted to," Lesia said and then laughed.

"The things our boyish actions cause us to lose and then when we are grown men, we spend a lifetime regretting."

"Wow! So, Bobby are you married?" Lesia asked.

"Hey Baby, what happened to you?" Malcolm asked as he walked up and placed his arm around his wife's' neck.

"Oh, I ran into DeAnna and her high school sweetheart, Bobby, a.k.a, the college drifter," Lesia said and then introduced Bobby to Malcolm.

"Nice to meet you," both men said to each other in unison.

"But baby that's college draft pick," Malcolm said.

"Not him. He was a college drifter." Lesia said and laughed as they started walking away. "Dee, see you next Saturday at the baby shower."

"Oh yeah, I almost forgot about that," DeAnna said and waved goodbye to Lesia, Tesha, and Malcolm as they headed toward the exit.

"Bobby, it was nice meeting you. Hope to see you again," Malcolm said then turned and walked off.

"Same here," Bobby said.

Bobby and DeAnna sat down at the table with Naija'

"So those are your friends." Bobby asked, trying to make small talk.

"Sort of," DeAnna said, not knowing if she wanted to talk about it. "It's a long story.

"Well, I don't want to keep you from your niece. Why don't you take my number and call me when you are free tonight?" Bobby suggested. "I will be headed to Atlanta tomorrow for a two-day business conference."

"Wow, we might be on the same plane," Naija' said.

"We might," Bobby jokingly replied.

"Auntie Dee has never been to Georgia."

"Really, that too bad." Bobby said. "Why don't you come with us," Bobby asked. "I'm sure your niece here would love for you to come."

"Her dad's going with her." DeAnna said. "Besides, I have to work Wednesday night."

"So, you'll be off from now until then?" Bobby asked.

"Yes, I am, but I thought a friend," DeAnna said then paused. "Well never mind… yes, I'm off," she said, resisting the urge to talk about what plans she thought she would have with Jeremy when she scheduled those days off, but yet she never even got around to asking Jeremy.

"Tell you what Dee," Bobby said as if he had everything worked out that fast. "I have some free time. I can get you a round trip ticket."

"And where am I going to stay?" DeAnna asked.

"We'll get a room," Bobby quickly answered.

"Now wait a minute, I ain't that type of girl," DeAnna said, giving Bobby the evil eye.

"We will not share a room Ms. DeAnna. You are always worthy of the royal treatment. It's been a long time since high school, but I know that you are still the lady that I fell in love with."

"Auntie Dee, are you and Mr. Bobby going to Atlanta with us?" Naija asked.

"No, I don't think so. Maybe another time, but for now we need to get home, so we can watch our movie," DeAnna said. She didn't want to discuss going off somewhere with a man in front of Naija'. "Bobby, I'll call you later."

"Sounds good my love," Bobby said.

Dee smiled, remembering how much she loved Bobby in high school. She loved him so much she wanted to marry him. "Thanks Boo," she said, remembering how much he loved for her to call him 'Boo.'

~

"Auntie Dee, why Uncle Jay don't drive?" Naija' asked.

"Well, sometimes he doesn't see things clearly and he doesn't want to hit anybody or cause an accident," DeAnna said, carefully avoiding the word blind.

"Is that why he always looks sad?" Naija' asked.

"Maybe!" DeAnna said, remembering that Naija' had mentioned this before. *He must be sad a lot, a four-year-old child has noticed*, DeAnna thought.

"Well, I like it better when he smiles and tell stories," Naija' said.

"Oh yea! What type of stories?" DeAnna asked as she drove Naija' back home.

They had watched part of the movie that Naija' picked out, but then Naija' began to get sleepy. DeAnna decided to take her home early so that she could get plenty of rest. She knew that traveling could sometimes be very tiring for a child.

"Fairy tales about a blind man that kept bumping into things and the nurse that helped him see the invisible," Naija' explained.

"What did he say about the nurse?" DeAnna asked. She felt as if she was prying, but she wanted to know if Jeremy said anything that would indicate that he fell in love with his nurse.

"He said that she took him to the movies and put on blindfold, so she could be blind like him," Naija' said. "Oh, and that she smelled good all the time."

"What was her name?" DeAnna asked.

271

"Her name was..." Naija' was trying to think of her name. "Oh yeah he called her his Angel."

"What happened to Angel?" DeAnna asked and then realized she was asking too many questions. She didn't want Naija' to go back and tell Jeremy about all the questioned she asked.

"She went back to heaven because she thought she had a date."

"Dee didn't ask any more questions, but Naija' talked all the way home. When DeAnna got to Chris' house, his car was gone. She pulled out her phone and called him, just as she was about to leave a message, the front door open. DeAnna walked Naija' to the door.

"Hey Uncle Jay," Naija' said when they got to the steps.

DeAnna instantly looked up. She was not expecting to see Jeremy. They stared at each other, making eye-to-eye contact. DeAnna loved the fact that Jeremy didn't act like most guilty men, who avoid speaking and eye contact.

"DeAnna," Jeremy said then paused to get his thoughts together. "Look! We, I..." Jeremy said, stumbling over his words.

"Look," DeAnna said, determined that she was not going to allow him to open old wounds that she thought had completely healed. She knew that Jeremy had not done anything wrong and he had not made her any promises. They were friends and even though she thought what they had was leading to a relationship, he hadn't promised her anything.

"You don't owe me an explanation," DeAnna said, letting him off the hook. She wasn't sure how good his vision was, so she made sure to keep a pleasant look on her face. She smiled at him and then bent down to kiss Naija' on her forehead.

"I know, but..." Jeremy said.

DeAnna was shocked that he said that. *I know*, she repeated in her head.

"Look Jeremy, I have a plane to catch in the morning, so I better get going," DeAnna said, sounding as pleasant as she could. She turned and walked down the steps as quickly as she could.

~

DeAnna cried all the way home. When she turned into her park, she leaned her head back on the headrest and let the tears flow. She kept hearing his words, *I know*. "Why didn't he feel he owed me an explanation," she asked God. *There was something special going on between us. I knew it and he knew it too,* she thought. "I've got to get away from here," she yelled. Dee thought about Bobby's invitation. "I told Jeremy that I had a plane to catch and even though I said that as a means of escape, that is exactly what I am going to do," she said. "Georgia, here I come." She rambled through her purse and found the business card that Bobby had given her. "Why not?' She asked herself. "I'm single," she said as she dialed the number and waited for Bobby to answer. She knew if she waited and really thought about it, she would change her mind.

"Hello beautiful," Bobby said.

"Hey Bobby. Question! Do you still want company on your plane ride tomorrow, well if they have any available seats?"

"Are you serious, Dee Dee?" Bobby asked.

"Dee Dee, now I have not heard that in years," she smiled as she thought about how much she used to love to hear him call her Dee Dee.

"Yes, if it's not too late and if there is a seat available," DeAnna replied.

"Not at all. Actually, I'll be leaving on the company plane," Bobby said.

"Company plane? Wow, you got it like that, huh?" DeAnna said.

"Well no, not usually," Bobby said.

"So, is it going to be okay for me to ride?"

"When I called the office to get my travel plans and was told that the company plane would bring me back, I asked about guest. They said yes, since the plane would be empty other than me and the pilots. I asked just in case you said yes. You can even bring your niece and her dad."

"Are you serious?" DeAnna asked in total disbelief.

"Yep, I'm serious. I've got a little pull with the boss," Bobby said as if he was joking. "Actually, they have been considering letting people lease it out for private trip. So, this is like a test run, I guess. They dropped a group of businessmen off this morning, and since I had to come back anyway, it's cheaper to fly me back then pay for a ticket."

"Wow, I've never been on a private plane," DeAnna replied

"So DeAnna, are you going to allow me to take you out for a drink or movie, it's only 6:30," Bobby said and waited for DeAnna response. "The night is still young."

"Well, we have a plane to catch in the morning," DeAnna said as she looked in the mirror at the mascara tracks on her face.

"The good thing about a private plane is, we do have some flexibility to decide what time we want to leave," Bobby said. "Well, to a certain degree," he corrected himself. He remembered that the receptionist told him he needed to check with the pilots, so they can check with the flight patterns of other planes.

"I think it's scheduled now to leave at 12:30 p.m."

"Well in that case, I guess we can meet for drinks," DeAnna said. "But just no alcoholic beverages."

"Why don't we meet at our favorite spot on Memorial Drive?" Bobby said. "Oh, and you might want to call your friend, to see if he wants to cash in his tickets and ride with us."

"Okay and I'll see you in twenty minutes," DeAnna said. Her heart felt funny. She felt as if she was cheating on a man who didn't even want her. "Jeremy, your loss," she said as she rushed in the house to wash her face.

As she rushed back out, she called Chris.

"Hey DeAnna, what's up?" Chris asked.

"Have you reserved or purchased your ticket yet," DeAnna asked.

"Oh my God," Chris yelled. "She is going to kill me. "I forgot. Great! Kristen is going to think I did this on purpose. I can hear her saying…"

"Calm down," DeAnna said. "I have a solution. Have you ever flown on a private plane before?" DeAnna asked.

"Private plane?" Chris questioned. "I don't know any millionaires, athletes, entertainer, or mega preachers, so nope."

"Well, one of my friends is in town for a business meeting. He is headed back to Georgia tomorrow and we have been pre-approved to hitch a ride with him," DeAnna said as she started the engine.

"DeAnna don't play with me," Chris said. "You are a lifesaver for real. I just cannot believe my luck."

"I'm shocked too, but it is not luck. It's God," DeAnna said thinking it was the perfect timing for this opportunity. She really needed a quick get-a-way. "The flight is scheduled to leave at 12:30 p.m.

"Wait, so you going to Georgia too?" Chris questioned.

"Yep, just for a few days. I have to get my head straight," DeAnna replied in a soft wounded voice.

"Yea!" Chris replied knowing what DeAnna was referring to. "Jay told me that he stuck his foot in his mouth tonight."

"Wow, didn't waste no time, did he?"

"What?" Chris asked, not sure what DeAnna was referring to.

"Playing innocent," DeAnna said.

"You really should have let him explain."

"Well, he didn't feel he needed to explain, so I guess my feelings don't matter." DeAnna said, knowing that Chris was going to tell Jeremy what she said.

"They matter DeAnna," Chris said. He wanted to tell her everything that was going on but knew that it would mean betraying Jeremy's trust. "It's his own feeling he's careless with right now."

"Let's talk about this another time, maybe at Jeremy's wedding," DeAnna said. "I have a date and I need to make sure that I'm looking good," DeAnna said. She wanted to give Chris something to tell Jeremy. "So, I'll call you tomorrow. You might need to get a refund for your tickets. Oh, that's right you never got them. Anyway, kiss my niece good night for me."

~

DeAnna wanted to be excited about meeting with Bobby, but she kept thinking about what Chris said. "What does he mean, he's careless with his own feelings?" DeAnna really didn't want to sit in a restaurant. She wanted to do something exciting and different, something that would not remind her of or even give her the time to think about Jeremy. When she pulled into the parking lot of the mom and pop restaurant, she wondered if Bobby was inside waiting. She didn't know what type of car he was driving. She looked to see if she saw a rental sticker on any of the cars. She didn't see him or anyone else sitting in either of the three cars in the parking lot. The restaurant was not in the best neighborhood, so she was hesitant to get out of her car. Immediately she began to think that it was a bad idea meeting him there. "God has not given me the spirit of fear," she said. As she was about to open her door, her cell phone rang.

"Bobby, where are you?" DeAnna asked without even looking at the caller ID.

"It's me, DeAnna," the caller said.

"Oh, Jeremy I'm sorry. I thought you were..." DeAnna hesitated.

"Bobby, I know. Sorry to disappoint you," Jeremy replied.

DeAnna couldn't tell if he was serious or joking. She wanted to give him a piece of her mind. She chuckled to herself as she thought about the concept. She suddenly remembered her pastor saying, 'Don't ever give someone a piece of your mind. You need all the mind God gave you.'

"What's so funny?" Jeremy questioned, sounding a little annoyed.

"Nothing, Look, I'm meeting someone in a few," DeAnna said.

"I really miss you and just want to talk to you," Jeremy said.

"Oh hey," DeAnna said as Bobby tapped on her window. "Jeremy can we do this another time?"

"Sure," Jeremy said and quickly hung up.

"Prefect timing," DeAnna said to Bobby. She really didn't mean it. She really did want to talk to Jeremy. She thought about how many relationships ended over a lack of communication. She didn't want to lose him only to find out later that he was trying to build up the nerve to be open with his feelings for her. She wasn't sure if he was only reaching out to her because he was lonely. "Maybe he's jealous," she said as she unlocked her car door and waited for Bobby to open it.

"Hey, *pretty in black*," Bobby said as soon as DeAnna stepped out of the car.

"I thought that was *pretty in pink*," DeAnna jokingly corrected him.

"Well, why limit it to just pink?" Bobby replied.

"You're just a regular charmer, aren't you?" DeAnna said, secretly wishing it was Jeremy that was giving her the compliments.

"If you say so," Bobby replied.

DeAnna and Bobby walked into the restaurant. They both looked around as if it were their first time there.

"Place has not changed one bit, has it?" Bobby asked.

"Nope, there's the same old broken-down chair that Steven Brown broke in the 10th grade," DeAnna said.

They both laughed as they walked toward an empty table. DeAnna looked at how gloomy the place looked.

"Bobby, I need to be honest with you, tonight I just really want to do something that keeps my mind from thinking too much," DeAnna said and then paused to think about what she wanted to do. "I really need to laugh."

"Is everything okay?" Bobby asked. "You're not sick, are you?"

"No, I'm not sick," DeAnna replied.

"Breakup to make up," Bobby started singing. "Or did you lose your best friend?"

DeAnna chuckled.

"Nope, no break up. I do think I may have lost a friend, but I don't want to talk about it or even think about it. I just want to laugh."

"Well, this place doesn't seem to have anything worth laughing at, but I have an idea. Do you mind riding with me to my parents' house?" Bobby asked with a sneaky look on his face.

"Your parents' house?" DeAnna questioned. It didn't seem like the type of fun she was looking for. She wanted to go bowling or shoot pool.

"Is that a problem?" Bobby asked. He didn't want to do anything to upset her. They had been friends long enough for her to know that he would never do anything to hurt her.

"No, I haven't seen them in years, but I thought they bought a house in Florida," DeAnna said.

"They did, but we kept the house her to use as our summer home. Summers in Florida are scorching hot."

"I can imagine. I've never been there either, but I hear it an oven," DeAnna said. "But what are we going to do there, at your parent's house?"

"You'll see," Bobby said with a grin on his face. "And don't worry, I will still respect you in the morning."

DeAnna gave him a long hard serious stare.

"I'll be a good boy. Dee Dee, your friendship has always been important to me. I won't try anything. I know that you are very serious about your Christian values. I'm a saved man myself and I am serious about my relationship with God, all jokes aside. Don't be fooled because I joke, I'm saved, but not dead. I like to have fun. DeAnna, even if it took me years to get back here to see you; I respect our friendship too much to ever do anything to destroy it."

"Ok," DeAnna agreed. "But I'll just follow you there."

~

When Bobby and DeAnna entered the house, DeAnna laughed as soon as she saw the picture of Bobby sitting on the wooden mantle. She walked in and immediately began looking at all the pictures on the wall. Bobby began to search a stack of books. He found his old high school yearbooks and placed them down on the coffee table. He motioned for DeAnna to join him as he gently pulled her down to the floor beside him. They sat with their backs against the sofa and began flipping through the year books. They laughed at DeAnna's 9th grade FBLA picture.

"Girl, you know you want those pigtails back," Bobby said with a serious look on his face. He could only hold the look for five seconds before he burst out laughing.

"I know you ain't talking, train tracks," DeAnna said pointing to Bobby's choir picture with his braces looking like they were about to pop off his teeth.

They both laughed so hard they cried. They pulled out a book from elementary school. DeAnna got so comfortable that she kicked her shoes off. They talked about all the old school gossips, their relationship as boyfriend and girlfriend, and their outfits during senior spirit week. They talked for hours. DeAnna had not laughed and cried that hard in years. She had completely forgotten all about her problems with Jeremy. She wanted to stay longer just to reminisce more, but she knew she had to pack and get ready for her last-minute plans.

"It's getting late," DeAnna said, glancing at her watch. She was still laughing and crying all at the same time.

"Wow, it is late," Bobby said when he looked at his cell phone. "We can do some more catching up on the plane," he suggested as he pulled his body off the floor.

Bobby waited until DeAnna had put her shoes back on and then he extended his hand toward her. She smiled and placed her hand in his hand

and he helped her up. As they walked toward the door, DeAnna saw a picture that she had never seen. It was a picture of her and Bobby sitting on the bleacher at the homecoming football game. It was framed and hanging on the wall by the front door. She wanted to ask Bobby who framed the picture and why, but she decided to let some memories stay buried. She remembered enough about that night. He used that night to make her feel like the homecoming queen.

Bobby walked DeAnna to her car. "I need to know if Princess Naija' and her dad are going to travel with us. The pilot has to file a report of all passengers," Bobby said, as he opened her car door. "Oh, and I'll need their names."

"Okay," DeAnna said.

Bobby moved in for a kiss, but DeAnna turned her head slightly to the right and the kiss landed on her cheek. "Bobby, I'm sorry," DeAnna said. I'm just not ready…"

"It's cool. I know I just can't expect to pick up where we left off."

"It's just that…" DeAnna said, trying to find the right words.

"You don't have to explain. I should have known that a beautiful woman like you wouldn't be available," Bobby said.

"It's not that," DeAnna said then paused. She didn't know how to explain that she was in love with a use-to-be blind guy, who she thought loved her until he saw her. But she wasn't even sure if he saw her. "I'll tell you all about it tomorrow."

"Okay, but really Dee you don't owe me any explanation."

DeAnna smile and said goodbye. Bobby closed her car door and watched her drive off.

Chapter 24

"Bobby," DeAnna said, as she, Chris and Naija' approached the plane. "This is Chris and I know you remember little Princess Naija'. Chris, this is Bobby, my high school sweetheart."

"Nice to meet you," Chris said, shaking Bobby's hand. "Thank you so much for allowing us to fly on your private plane. This is an experience of a lifetime."

"Well, it's not my plane, I wish it were, but it's my boss'. It's actually my first time on this plane too, and you are welcome," Bobby said. "Any friend of Dee Dee is a friend of mine.

As they boarded the plane, DeAnna looked around as if she had never been on any plane.

"Wow, this is awesome. I've never even seen the inside of a private plane," DeAnna said.

"Me either," Naija' said and quickly selected a seat by the window. "Look daddy," she yelled as she looked out of the window. "It's Uncle Jay and some other man. He's waving goodbye."

"Jeremy," Chris questioned and quickly moved to the window seat across from Naija'. "What is he doing here?" Chris asked, looking in DeAnna's direction.

"Whose Uncle Jay or Jeremy," Bobby asked. "Is he going with us because I need to let..."

"No!" Chris quickly interjected. "He's probably just coming to say goodbye to Naija'."

"Well, we have about ten minutes before we take off," Bobby said. He turned to DeAnna.

Chris knew that Jeremy was not there to say goodbye to Naija'. He had already said goodbye to her. Naija' jumped up to meet Jeremy as he slowly headed towards the steps. Chris followed her and headed down the step to meet him.

"Hey dude, what's up?" Chris said as he skipped down the steps towards Jeremy to stop him from boarding the plane. The guy who was escorting Jeremy stop and pulled Jeremy's arm indicating for Jeremy to stop.

"Where is she?" Jeremy asked.

"We already on the plane and are..." Chris tried to explain.

"I figured that, but I need to talk to her," Jeremy replied. "Just help me up the steps. I will only be a minute."

Chris turned around trying to quickly figure out what to do. He saw DeAnna standing in the doorway.

"We are about to take off," Chris said.

Jeremy continued to climb the steps. The steps were a little blurry, so he mis-stepped a few times. Jeremy eventually stopped looking down and looked up. He systematically stepped upward and climbed the steps one at a time.

"He can come aboard," Bobby said. "The pilot said there is a ten-minute delay, we will be departing at about 12:45."

"That's not a good idea," DeAnna said to Bobby. "He doesn't need to be here."

"Why? What's wrong with him saying goodbye to his niece? Am I missing something?" Bobby asked as he stared at DeAnna.

"Well," DeAnna said, not knowing what to say.

"I want to give Uncle Jay another hug," Naija' said when Jeremy walked onto the plane. "I want him to see me now, just in case he goes blind again before I get back."

"What is she talking about?" Bobby asked.

"Jeremy was temporarily blinded and now his sight has returned," DeAnna whispered to Bobby. "I'm not sure how long or even if he has his full vision. My understanding was that the images he saw or sees were still blurry, but I guess he can see full figures clearly," DeAnna said, hoping Jeremy got the hint.

"Wow, awesome. Let her see her Uncle," Bobby said as he headed towards the door where Chris stood talking to Jeremy. "We can call for an attendant if he needs help back to the building."

I've got to see her, Bobby overheard Jeremy say as he walked up.

"She's waiting for you," Bobby said, escorting Jeremy back as if he was a flight attendant.

Naija' hugged Jeremy when he bent down and hugged her and kissed her on her forehead. When Naija' saw her dad take his seat, she joined him. Bobby smiled and thought the moment was over, until he saw Jeremy approach DeAnna.

"DeAnna," Jeremy said. "I need to talk to you."

"Can't it wait until I return," DeAnna said. She remembered that she didn't want to totally push him away. "I think we are about to take off. I will only be gone for a few days," she assured him. "We can meet and talk then, when I return, okay. We can talk about anything you want to. I can even tell you all about my trip."

"Please Dee. What I need to say is very important. If I don't do this now, I may never do it."

"Jay, I mean Jeremy, we are about to leave," DeAnna said in the sweetest voice she could manage. She didn't want everybody to hear what he had to say to her. She wasn't sure if he was going to tell her that he just didn't love her the way she wanted him to or he loved her 'but.' She wasn't even sure if he knew that she loved him. "If it's really all that important to you, you will be able to say it later. I know you, you will not give up on anything that you really want. I love that about you." DeAnna said, hoping he got the hint- *she loved him.*

"Dee, it can't wait, I need…" Jeremy said and then realized he was getting a little too loud. "Sorry," he quickly said.

"Look," DeAnna said, feeling confused. She was happy that he was pursing her, but angry he seemed to have walked out on her at the hospital. "Jeremy, you should have said what you needed to say that day at the hospital," DeAnna said in a lower volume, but in a harsher tone.

"What are you talking about?" Jeremy asked.

"The day you came to the hospital and left without speaking to me. I guess I didn't meet your…" DeAnna statement faded.

"Dee, it's not what you think. Baby, please let me explain."

"You can explain when I return from my mini vacation," DeAnna said. "I need a moment to myself. I need to think. She was glad that Bobby was talking with the pilot and didn't hear Jeremy call her baby. "I think you should leave now," DeAnna said and looked at Chris. "Do you need help Jeremy getting back down the steps?" DeAnna asked, looking at Chris.

Jeremy didn't want to leave her, but before he could say anything, he heard a tiny voice in his head say, *'it ain't over until God says it's over.'* He wasn't sure if it was a word from God, or if he was hearing the words to the last song he had listened to before getting out of the cab.

When Chris got up to help Jeremy, Naija' followed him. She hugged Jeremy again. DeAnna watched the affectionate exchange. She couldn't help but to wonder if she would ever have a child of her own someday.

"DeAnna, please call me as soon as you get back," Jeremy said.
"I'll remember to do just that when I get back home," DeAnna said.

She didn't want to completely shut Jeremy out. She remembered Chris saying, 'you will reap if you faint not.' She had heard her pastor say that so many times, it was more like confirmation when Chris said it. *Maybe my harvest is on the way,* she thought.

Jeremy took one last look at DeAnna before he existed the plane, escorted by Chris. He looked at her as if he expected to never see her again.

DeAnna walked into her hotel room, dropped her bags at the door, and immediately did a swan dive onto the large king size bed. "Oh, this feels so good," she said as if she was trying to convince someone to join her. She rolled from her stomach to her back and stared up at the ceiling. She immediately began to think about Jeremy's plea to talk to her. She really didn't want to let her guard down any more. "The Bible does say 'guard your heart, for out of the heart flows the issues of life. Too many women get hurt when they are not careful with their heart and I am not going to be one of them," DeAnna said as she glanced at an old message from Jeremy. *Keep it closed too tight, you might miss out*, she thought. "Lord, I just can't take any more disappointment," she said.

DeAnna thought about the many lonely nights she spent hoping, wishing, and praying that God would send her a man, a husband. She prayed that he wouldn't be unemployed or have four kids and three baby mamas. She was tired of getting hit-on by married, unemployed, unsaved, or as she often called them, the uncircumcised Philistines. "I know that there're plenty of good men out there," she said and then sighed. "It just doesn't seem that any of them are interested in me. Now, I am in the A.T.L, let's see what's here to help me forget Jeremy," she said.

DeAnna looked at the open Bible on the nightstand. "Lord, tell me why it feels that if I want a man, I'm might have to settle. Settling just ain't me. I want the man of my dreams? I want who I want and who wants me; I want us to want each other," she said and then began thinking about Bobby. "What's wrong with Bobby? He's nice looking, kind, considerate, single, and he accepts me as I am. I wouldn't be settling, would I? Would he?" She asked herself.

DeAnna looked at the clock. It was only two p.m. She wanted to get out of her room and see Atlanta, but she didn't want to rely on Bobby. She didn't want him to feel obligated to her. "I know," she said when she began flipping through her contact number. She dialed a number and patiently waited.

"Hello," she hesitantly said.
"Hey you! What are you up to? You out sightseeing yet?"
"Nope," DeAnna replied, sounding disappointed.
"Good!"

"Why is that good? Is there a thunder storm?" DeAnna asked.

"Well, I'm headed to your room as we speak. As a matter of fact, five…four… three… two…one…," he said, sounding like he was doing the New Year's count down. DeAnna heard a knock at the door. She jumped up off the bed, ran to the door, and peeped out the peep hole. She opened the door with a big smile on her face.

"Hey Chris," she said in the phone and then looked at him standing in the door. They both hung up their phone. DeAnna opened the door wide enough for Chris to come in. When Chris took a step, DeAnna saw Naija' hiding behind her dad.

"Where is Naija', Chris?" DeAnna jokingly asked. "I thought I heard her laugh, but I don't see her. I am going to be sad if I don't see her."

"Don't be sad Auntie Dee. Here I am," Naija' said and laughed.

"I thought you would be home with your mommy," DeAnna she as she tickled Naija'.

"I called her as soon as we landed, but she has not called me back," Chris said. "So, I thought we could take a nap then head to Decatur Mall, but somebody," Chris said and then paused. He scooped Naija' up in his arms as if she was as light as a feather. "She is too wide open, for a nap. This child askes one hundred questions a second. And boy does she love some Jeremy. Uncle Jay this, Uncle Jay that," Chris said, then suddenly realized that it might not be a good idea to talk about Jeremy, so he quickly changed the subject.

"I know the feeling," DeAnna said as she sat down on the bed. She quickly realized how her response must have sounded. "I didn't mean that I love Uncle Jay, I mean Jeremy," DeAnna said. She was getting caught up in her words and was quickly revealing a truth that she didn't want to admit, at least not at that time. "I mean, I am too excited to take a nap too."

"So," Chris continued. "I thought I'd see if maybe you would like to join us. I could rent a car, or we could call a cab."

"Well, I don't know. Bobby is…" DeAnna stopped mid-sentence, remembering Bobby said had a business meeting the rest of the day.

"I just hate for you to spend all day looking at the wall and never get to visit the Underground or the MLK Center. I thought that I was going to have to take Naija' to Augusta, but I don't know. So, I have more time on my hands than I thought. You did say you'd never been to Atlanta, right?"

"Nope, never been here before," DeAnna answered. She thought it might be best to get out, so she wouldn't just lay around in her room and talk to herself the rest of the day and night about Jeremy.

"Okay, let's go. I heard Bobby tell you that he will be back around 7 p.m. for dinner. We will be back in plenty of time."

"Well okay. Let's go," DeAnna said. She slipped her shoes back on, grabbed her cell phone and purse, and followed Chris and Naija' out the door.

Once they were in the lobby, Chris made a phone call immediately after reading a text message. "We'll be waiting," he said to the person on the phone. Chris stopped and pointed to a sofa in the lobby of the hotel, indicating for DeAnna and Naija' to have a seat. He sat down beside DeAnna. They looked as if they were a happy family.

"Okay," Chris said once he was off the phone. "Let's walk one block down and find someplace to eat. My cousin will pick us up in about an hour. They headed out of the hotel and began walking downtown on Peachtree Street.

"What do you want to eat Dee?" Chris asked. "Have you ever eaten any goat meat?"

"Goat meat? Absolutely not," DeAnna said.

"I had some Daddy," Naija' said. "It's really not that bad."

Chris laughed at the expression on DeAnna's face. They continued to walk downtown. DeAnna felt Naija' grab her hand. She looked down and smiled. *Wow, if anyone saw us, they would think that we are a couple*, she thought to herself.

"So, I'm guessing this is the reason why you were so anxious to leave Atlanta, huh?" DeAnna heard a woman say. She thought the woman was talking on her cell phone, so she kept walking and didn't bother to turn around to see what the woman looked like. DeAnna noticed that Chris had stopped walking. DeAnna felt Naija' release her hand, so she stopped. She thought that Chris had stopped to sample something.

"Mommy," Naija' yelled.

"Hey sweetheart. How is mommy's baby?" Naija' mother asked.

"Mommy," Naija'," said folding her arms and looking at her mother as if she did something wrong.

"Oh, I'm sorry. How's mommy's big girl?"

"I'm good. I missed you," Naija' said as she turned to her dad. "But my daddy has been taking good care of me and Auntie Dee has been helping him."

"Kristen, this is my friend DeAnna; DeAnna this is Naija's mother, Kristen," Chris said, looking as if he'd just gotten catch cheating.

"Nice to meet you," DeAnna said and extended her hand towards Kristen. DeAnna was surprised that Kristen shook her hand.

"Nice to meet you, whoever you are," Kristen replied. "So, Chris," Kristen said, then released DeAnna hand from the handshake. "I guess you finally decided to take a little family vacation, huh?"

"What makes you think that?" Chris asked, expecting things to turn for the worse.

"Well, you usually fly in and fly out the same day, but this time you bought your friend."

"Well, sometimes you just have to take a little time for yourself. Ain't that what you've always told me?" Chris said knowing that Kristen was expecting clarification of DeAnna's status as girlfriend, finance', or just friend. Chris had fallen for the trap one too many times. He wasn't going to give her the satisfaction of an explanation this time.

"So Dee," Kristen began, instantly realizing that Chris wasn't going to give her the answer that she wanted. "Is this your first time in Atlanta or do you live here?" Kristen asked hoping that DeAnna lived there. Kristen knew Chris well enough to know that he would not be able to maintain a long-distance relationship.

"This is my first time," DeAnna said. She could tell that Kristen really didn't care about her travel history. DeAnna was very good at figuring out other women. "Which really makes this trip even more special to me," DeAnna said. She wanted to see how Kristen was going to react. DeAnna had already figured out that Chris still loved Kristen. Now it was time to see if the feelings were mutual.

"Oh, more special. I see," Kristen said.

DeAnna could hear hurt in Kristen voice. She wasn't sure if Kristen was just hurt because she lost him or hurt because he seemed happy without her. She knew all too well that sometimes women don't want the man back but hate to see him happy and making someone else happy; especially if he never tried to make her happy. DeAnna knew that women often felt that a cheating man didn't deserve to have anyone else. Not until the woman cheated on is in a new relationship, is happy again, or had cheated back on him. DeAnna wasn't sure where Kristen stood, but she was positive that if she spent some time with her, she would know within an hour whether or not Kristen was still in love with Chris.

Chris knew that Kristen had begun to generate ten thousand and one questions about why this trip was so special to DeAnna. He wasn't going to give her the opportunity to rake DeAnna over the coal; especially after all DeAnna had done to help him.

"Look, why don't we walk back to the hotel and get Naija' things. I'm sure she's ready to go home," Chris suggested.

"No Daddy, I want to go to the mall with Auntie Dee. Can we please, please go to the Underground? Mommy can go too?" Naija' said, looking at Kristen. "Right mommy?"

Kristen really just wanted to take Naija' and go home. She didn't think she could handle being nice to Chris and his girlfriend, but she didn't want to act ugly in front of her daughter. She was really trying to release the bitterness and un-forgiveness. She did want to ask DeAnna a few more questions to see how she would respond.

"Well, I guess that will be okay. It's just a few blocks over and since Aunt Dee is going to be in your life, I guess I better get to know her," Kristen said trying not to sound jealous. She didn't really want to be there but didn't want to disappoint Naija'.

Chris wanted to object. He knew exactly what Kristen was thinking. Chris looked at Dee.

"I don't see any harm in Kristen tagging along," DeAnna said.

Chris could tell that DeAnna knew exactly what was going on and that she was up for the challenge. "Well, if it's okay with DeAnna and Naija'," Chris said, smiling at them both. "Then it's okay with me."

Kristen was not happy with Chris' response, but she wasn't going to let it show. "Let's get to stepping," Kristen said, quickly grabbing Naija's hand and skipping ahead of Chris and DeAnna. They laughed as they skipped.

"We can get something to eat there," Chris said to DeAnna as they slowly strolled behind Kristen and Naija'.

"Good," Dee replied. "My stomach will be singing a song after a while. "DeAnna's hungry this I know, because her tummy tells her so, the tummy grumbles you will see. It will say, will you please feed me," DeAnna sang to the tune of *Jesus loves me.*

Chris busted into uncontrollable laughter. "So, is that equivalent to growling?"

"Yea, it sounds so barbaric or animalistic to say growling," DeAnna explained.

They both laughed as they looked at Naija' and Kristen, who had stopped skipping and were resting with their hands on their knees as if they were catching their breath.

"She heard the laughter," Chris said.

"She's pretending to be tired, so we can catch up and she can hear what we are saying," DeAnna said. "They will start back if we get too close, but they won't skip too far out of hearing range.

DeAnna and Chris both laughed again.

"I guess since you provided such luxurious accommodations to Atlanta," Chris said and smiled at DeAnna. "I guess I can at least purchase some tasteful note to feed your song bird."

"You will not get an argument out of me," DeAnna said, watching Naija' and Kristen skip forwards four or five steps and then backwards two. When they were close, Naija' grabbed DeAnna hand. "Auntie Dee, you and daddy are rotten eggs because me and mommy got to the newsstand before you".

"Well, let's see who gets to the mall first, so we can get something to eat, before DeAnna's rotten egg starts singing," Chris said and started laughing again.

"Mommy," Naija said, suddenly remembering something. "I came home on a big plane." Naija' talked about the plane ride as they all strolled the rest of the way to the mall together.

"I know sweetheart. Your daddy told me," Kristen said, knowing she had not talked to Chris since they had arrived, but she had listened to the messages he left. She wanted DeAnna to think they had been talking.

"Did you know, the plane had a lot of room on it to walk around? It had a sofa, just like a house has and about four or maybe three skinny TVs and movie players. Oh, and I got to talk to the pilots."

"Oh, you did? I bet that was fun," Kristen said, looking at Chris.

"Yes, it was fun. It was a pirate plane," Naija' said.

"A pirate's plane?" Kristen questioned. "What's a pirate plane? Did it have pictures of pirates on it or something?" She asked.

"Well, it was only us, no one else on the plane. Oh, and Mr. Bobby."

"Oh, you mean a private plane," Kristen said, correcting Naija' "Not a pirate's plane."

"Yea, I think that's what the pilot said," Naija' confirmed.

Kristen slowly turned and looked at DeAnna. *She doesn't look like she got it like that*, Kristen thought to herself. "Well, I am sure that was very exciting. I've never been on a private or a pirate's plane before. Maybe one day your mom will find herself a rich boyfriend with a private plane," Kristen said.

"Maybe Auntie Dee's friend can let you ride too; like he let me and daddy ride. He is very nice."

"Yea! Maybe," Kristen said, looking at all the food choices as they walked pass the different food stand and restaurant.

Kristen was quiet the rest of the way to the famous Underground Mall. Thoughts raced through her head. *This Negro has the nerve to be flying around on a private plane but reduced his child support obligation. Seems to me he wants the good life for himself, the whole while he's trying to cheat his daughter out of the life that she's gotten used to.* The more Kristen thought about DeAnna and Chris flying style, the madder she got. As they descended the steps that lead to the entrance to the mall, Kristen spotted one of Chris' old friends. She tried to avoid eye contact, but it was too late.

"Is that Jack Spencer?" Chris asked, as they got closer.

Kristen quickly tried to move closer to Chris. She wanted Jack to think they were still a couple. "Oh good," she said when a little girl suddenly ran up behind Jack and diverted his attention. Kristen suddenly realized that this little excursion/mission was not a good idea. "I'm sort of tired," Kristen said, feeling badly. "Maybe you can do this another time since DeAnna has a private plane. Y'all can come another weekend and we can play one big happy family then," Kristen said.

"Well, that sounds great, but I'm not sure how much longer I'll..." DeAnna started to say but was cut off.

"You'll what, be with Chris?" Kristen interjected.

"No, that's not what I was going to say. I'm sure that Chris and I will have a lifetime together," DeAnna said, glancing at Chris and smiling.

"Oh, I see," Kristen said as she turned to Chris. "Is that right?"

"If she says so," Chris said, not knowing what else to say.

"If she says so," Kristen repeated Chris' words. "You mean to tell me you don't know."

"Look," Dee said realizing that Kristen was getting very upset.

"No, you look," Kristen said. She just couldn't take it anymore. "I'm not sure it's a good idea for you to be spending time with my daughter, treating her like she's your child, if you and Christopher are just playing house."

"Playing house? What are you talking about? We aren't playing house." Chris said. "She doesn't live with me. She has her own place. As a matter of fact, she's never even spent the night with me at my place or hers."

"Oh, I guess you are one of those holier than thou chicks. Saved, sanctified, and saving the sex until marriage, huh? Good old southern Christian woman, right?"

"Sounds good to me," Chris said, turning to DeAnna wondering what she was about to say, "Dee, you are not sure how much longer you will...?" Chris began, but was cut off by DeAnna.

"Well, I don't know about the holier than thou, but yes I am saved and no, I don't believe in sex before marriage. I do practice celibacy, if that's the answer you were after. I am not ashamed of that. I didn't always, but I am glad I didn't stay on the road that I was on."

"Wow Chris," Kristen said, turning from DeAnna to Chris. "I see why you got to have a woman on the side."

"What are you talking about now?" Chris asked Kristen.

"The last time you were here, remember that?" Kristen asked.

"Yes, I remember and?" Chris said." What about it? Say what you got to say. That's been what, six or seven months ago? Maybe even longer than that."

Dee knew exactly what Kristen was trying to do. Like most women who realized that she still loves their ex or her baby's daddy, yet don't want to admit it, Kristen was trying hard to plant a seed of doubt in DeAnna's head. She wanted DeAnna to believe that she and Chris had attempted to get back together and even had been intimate the last time he was there. *Joke's on Kristen, since Chris and I aren't even a couple,* DeAnna thought. DeAnna pretended not to hear the comment.

"Oh, let's head to the food court before we head back, I have not eaten a real meal since breakfast, I'm starved," DeAnna said as she looked at Chris for approval.

"Can we go somewhere that has chicken strips?" Naija' asked.

"Sure," Chris replied.

"Good, because that's exactly what I got a taste for," DeAnna said.

Kristen grabbed Naija's hand and walked towards the food court. She was hurt, but she didn't want to give them the satisfaction of knowing that she cared enough to be hurt. Chris and DeAnna followed behind them but walked at a much slower pace. As they walked, Chris and DeAnna let out a simultaneous snicker.

"You are a mess," Chris whispered.

"And you are loving it," DeAnna said.

"So, it shows?" Chris asked.

"Yes, and she still has feelings for you?" DeAnna told him.

"I don't think so, I think it's just one of those things," Chris paused. "You know when you don't want a person, but you don't want no one else to be happy or have him or her."

"Trust me, she still wants you," DeAnna said, remembering how often Chris told her to trust him when they talked about Jeremy's feeling.

"But she has a boyfriend," Chris said.

"Someone to help her, that's all. Sugar daddy maybe," DeAnna said as if he was insufficient and irrelevant.

"Well, maybe it's for the best that she keeps thinking you and I are together. That way, she won't have false hopes that she and I will be together."

"You know when you told me about her that day at the restaurant," DeAnna said and then paused to give Chris time to think about what he said that day. "Well, I might be wrong, but you sounded like you still love her."

"Well, I think I was probably," Chris couldn't think of what to say.

"Probably what?"

"Tired and sleepy," he quickly said.

"You know, you could have simply said that you don't love her,'" DeAnna said.

"Yea, I guess," Chris said. "Guess I just didn't think to say that."

"You still can say it now," DeAnna softly said.

"Even if I do, things are so complicated now. She has someone and I'm not going to move to Augusta or Atlanta. Besides, I just can't deal with that attitude."

"I can't say I blame you, but people change," DeAnna said, thinking about all that they had just put her though. "I'm actually impressed with the way she's handling herself now. I really thought that she would have cussed and cursed the both of us out by now."

"If Naija' wasn't here, she probably would have," Chris said.

"At least she has some restraint about herself. Maybe having a child has changed her. She does seem to do what's best for Naija', that a big plus. Even if it means holding her tongue."

"Yea, but for how long?" Chris asked.

"A few more buttons and it's over," DeAnna replied.

"What do you mean?" Chris asked.

"If you or I push a few more of the right buttons, she'll either prove that she has changed, or she'll prove that she's the same old ghetto-acting, finger-snapping, got-to-get-you-told, baby-mama you remember."

"Trust me DeAnna," Chris said, shaking his head to say, *'no don't do it*. "You don't want to go there. Her bite is much worse than the bark."

"Okay," DeAnna said as she walked up beside Naija' and Kristen. "If you say so. You know you really make it easy for me to want to please you," DeAnna said to Chris and smiled.

He looked at DeAnna as if he had no clue of what she was talking about. He suddenly looked at her and then quickly glanced at Kristen. He was suddenly expecting a war to start. DeAnna looked at the menu but decided she wasn't ready to order just yet, so she let Chris order first. She walked off as he ordered. As Chris ordered he got the hint and realized that DeAnna was going to push some buttons regardless of his objections.

DeAnna saw a few things she liked at a nearby vendor's cart. She decided to get them after she'd ordered her food, but she had not decided what she wanted to eat. She looked some more and thought about what she wanted to eat. She looked at a few key chains and other items.

"My treat," Chris said, walking up to the vendor's cart.

"You sure?" DeAnna questioned as she held up a key chain.

"Sure, you know I owe you," Chris said. "Let me pay for something."

Kristen turn to see if Dee and Chris were talking to each other.

"You owe who," Kristen asked, looking at Chris.

"Well, I was talking to Dee, but I got you and Naija' as well."

"Oh, that's so sweet, like always," Kristen said, smiling an obviously fake smile. "But suddenly, I'm not hungry. I'm on a diet. I finally got a good reason to lose some weight."

"You can get grilled chicken," DeAnna suggested.

"No, I ate some yogurt this morning," Kristen said and then ordered Naija's chicken strips.

"Yogurt, this morning, you probably burn those calories off walking out your front door. You know, starving your body will have the opposite effect that you are trying to achieve," DeAnna said. She knew all about diets and starving the body.

"And what do you mean by that?" Kristen asked, as she stared at DeAnna plus-sized body.

"Well, when you don't eat, your body thinks you're starving it, so it holds onto everything you do eat. It's better to eat six small meals as opposed to three large meals. Not eating at all, that's not good. I heard that on one of those doctor shows."

DeAnna decided what she wanted to eat and left the vendor's cart to order her food. After DeAnna placed her order, Kristen ordered for her and Naija. Kristen seemed to have appreciated the advice and ordered grilled chicken with a diet soda. As Kristen waited for her food, she visited a few nearby vendor's cart. Chris agreed to bring everyone's food once it was done, so the ladies found a table and sat and waited for Chris.

"Dee," Chris said as he approached the table where everybody was sitting. "I got you two bottles of water; I thought I heard you say that your mouth was dry as we were walking over here. You can keep one in your purse for the walk back."

"Thoughtful as always," DeAnna said. She placed the bottle of water in her pocket book.

Everyone began grabbing their food off the tray. They all seemed to be starving and ate like they had not eaten in days, all except Kristen. She nibbled on the food that she had finally decided to order. She ate as if it wasn't good or she wasn't hungry. Kristen heard Chris telling DeAnna that their ride got delayed, but they could take a cab back, so she wouldn't be late for her business dinner. He told her that he was so hunger that he had another order of food coming. Kristen watched them so hard that she got sick to her stomach.

"Look, I thought I could handle this," Kristen began. "I mean Chris you and I have been over with for a while, shortly before Naija' turned two, I think. And well, you know my situation," she said. "The truth is, it was hard for me to move on." Kristen's eyes begin to water. She slowly placed a small piece of chicken in her mouth and began to chew it. Chris wondered if she was going to finish what she had to say.

"Hurry up and eat Naija'," Kristen said after two-minutes of silence. "We need to get home. We have a big day tomorrow. We're going to a family cookout."

"Can Daddy and Auntie Dee come?" Naija asked.

Chris could tell that Kristen didn't want to disappoint Naija.

"No baby, not this time. Daddy and Aunt Dee will be on a plane headed back home tomorrow. We have to work," Chris said.

Kristen looked at Chris and quietly whispered, 'thanks.'

"Wow, tasty," DeAnna said. "How's your grill chicken Kristen?"

295

"Better than I expected," Kristen said. "Thanks for suggesting it."

Kristen looked at Naija' and then at Chris. "Look, I can't pretend that I'm not uncomfortable. I only agreed to come along because I wanted to pretend that you two being together doesn't bother me, but the truth is," Kristen began, then paused for a long time before she could finish. "Well, it does bother me. It bothers me that you acted like I wasn't good enough because I was or am a big girl and then you come here with a big girl and treat her like she's the queen of Egypt."

"Now, wait a minute," Chris said. "Once and for all, I want you to get this. Your weight never bothered me. You compared yourself to all the girlfriends that I had before you and you decided you weren't good enough for me. I tried to convince you that I loved you."

"I never doubted that you loved me," Kristen said. She was getting confused about what she was feeling now and what she felt in the past.

"Then what?" Chris asked, softening his voice. He didn't want to upset Naija' or make Kristen feel any worse. "Kristen, I wanted to make you my wife."

"Yea! So, you say. I was your fallback woman. You only wanted me because no one else wanted you."

"Oh, is that what you thought?" Chris smiled and shook his head indicating that was not true.

"Naija' why don't you and I see if we can find me a neck pillow for the plane ride home and I have to get you something special," DeAnna said and then turned toward Kristen "Do you mind Kristen?" DeAnna asked.

"Why not, you'll probably be her new step-mommy," Kristen said.

DeAnna could hear the pain in Kristen's voice. She glanced at Kristen as she waited for Naija'.

"Chris tell her," DeAnna said as she waited for Naija'.

"Tell me what?" Kristen asked DeAnna.

"Kristen, y'all need to talk," DeAnna said, grabbing Naija's hand.

"No, why don't you and I talk," Kristen said to DeAnna. "Let Naija' and Chris find your neck pillow. If you're going to be a part of Naija's life, I need to know you," Kristen said "Chris do you mind? Don't worry, I won't tell her any of your dark secrets."

"I'm not concerned about what you tell her. Nothing you tell her is going to change what she and I have," Chris said. He was a little upset, but he was ready to deal with this once and for all.

"Wow, confidence," Kristen said. "That the Chris I know. So, let's talk than Ms. Dee."

Chris looked at DeAnna. She shrugged her shoulders as if it didn't matter.

"Fine with me," DeAnna said, looking at Chris for a sign indicating that he didn't mind her telling Kristen the truth.

~

"Kristen, before you start, please just let me say that I commend you for how you are handling this whole thing. I don't know if I could have been as cool as you are about hanging out with a man you obviously still love very much and another woman," DeAnna said.

"What are you talking about still love? Please!" Kristen said, not ready to admit to anything.

"Just let me finish and I promise you, you'll see things in a different light," DeAnna replied.

"By all means, finish, but please let's make this quick," Kristen said. "I have to head home. I got some cleaning to do."

"When you first spotted Chris and I together, Kristen, I could tell that you went through so many different emotions. Maybe jealousy, I understand, it's normal. You see your ex-boyfriend/ex-fiancé with another woman, walking in public, they all holding like one big happy family, it could cause a flood of emotions. I'm sure you saw yourself in that picture, but then you realize that I'm a big girl, you probably thought you weren't good enough for him so, 'How could he?' You ask. After all, I'm big like you-right?"

DeAnna could tell that Kristen was about to interrupt.

"Wait, a few more minutes, please. It will all make sense, I promise. Since you didn't know who I am to Chris, you said to yourself, why not ask a few probing questions, hang out together, and see just how well Chris and I knew each other. I could tell by your questions. I could also tell that you are a great mom and you want the best for her. You could have really flipped out and embarrassed all of us, including yourself. You didn't do that. Kristen, I see pain in your eyes, but I also see love when you look at Chris. I know love when I see it and I think that you do love him."

Kristen eyes filled with tears. "Yes," she said with a forced smile and tears rolling down her face.

"I guess we both love him," Kristen said.

"Kristen, Chris and I are just friends. You see, I was Jeremy's nurse when he was in the hospital. That's how I met Chris and all the other friends and family. I was recruited by his mother to help him with his recovery. I was with Jeremy so much that people thought we were a couple. I have now met coworkers, ex-girlfriends, and everybody in between."

"Oh my God," Kristen said then slapped her hands over her mouth as if she was trying to avoid saying something.

"What?" DeAnna questioned as she looked around as if something might be happening behind her.

"You're in love with Jeremy, that's what?" Kristen said, shaking her head as if she was coaching DeAnna to say yes. "Yep, I know love when I see it too and your eyes lit up as you talked about him."

"Chris and I were just pushing your buttons. If you had acted ghetto, wild, rude, disrespectful, etcetera, I would have never decided to tell you what I'm about to say. It might be wrong for me to say this, but I think Chris still loves you too. I'm sure of it."

"Nah, I don't think so," Kristen said.

"If he didn't, he would not have allowed me to talk to you right now. He would have just let you keep thinking whatever you want to think about him and me. I mentioned to him that I thought that he still loved you and…" DeAnna said and then paused, she looked at Kristen to see if she was interested to knowing the answer.

"So," Kristen asked after a second of silence. "What did he say?"

"Well, put it like this, he didn't deny it. He just said it wouldn't work because he is not moving to Atlanta and you have a boyfriend."

"What? Well," she said stumbling over her words. "Never mind," Kristen said feeling a little strange.

"Look," DeAnna said and then paused to think of what she wanted to say. "I don't want to give you any false hopes and I probably should not have said anything at all."

"So, does Jeremy love you?" Kristen asked.

"That's where the story gets a little bit more complicated, but I think he does, and Chris says he does, but well, that is another story. Kristen, I guess I owe you an apology."

"I owe you one too."

Kristen and DeAnna both said, 'I'm sorry' at the same time.

"I do think Chris is right," DeAnna said.

"About what, that Jeremy loves you?" Kristen asked and smiled.

"I think you make your weight an issue. To be honest, everyone has the right to like what he or she likes, so if a guy doesn't want you because of your weight, it's his right, but it's also his loss. Truth is, there is something about everyone that the spouse or mate might not like, but for Chris, weight doesn't seem to be the deal breaker. If you are unhappy with it, do something about it. One thing I do know is that men might not like plus-size women, but they seem to dislike a woman with a lack of confidence even more.

"I don't think I should have to lose weight for a man," Kristen said.

"Now, I know exactly how you feel. I've been down that road a few times. I may have even pushed a few men away myself, comparing myself to other women. I've been on every diet there is. Finally, I decided to just trust God to bring me a man who will love and appreciate me. At one time, I wanted to lose weight too, for him. I'm not one of these oversized ladies claiming they love how they look, then as soon as insurance kicks in, they under the knife. But God will send me the right one. The one that will help me if I want him to and love me, if I don't."

"I hear that," Kristen said.

"You shouldn't have to lose for him, as you said, but since he never asks you to, don't, but if you feel it's a problem, maybe you should do so, for you."

Kristen sighed as she began to clean her trash up.

"I think we should find them, so we can leave?" Kristen said as she realized it was later than she thought it was and she had a two-hour drive back to Augusta."

"Oh yeah, you said you had some cleaning to do."

Kristen and DeAnna cleaned the table, and then headed towards the main entrance.

"Look DeAnna, I appreciate you telling me all that you did. I think that's the first time I ever had a sho' nough grown woman throw down like that," Kristen said and then laughed. "It's time us ladies stop fighting over men and learn to talk, huh? I really don't know how things could ever work out between us though."

"Even if it doesn't, just know that you are beautiful, and you don't have to settle. Have confidence in the fact that God made you and that qualifies you for fashion model status; so, don't compare yourself to others. I mean, if you like fashion model status, fine. Personally, they look too plastic," DeAnna said and then laughed.

"If you say so," Kristen said, then let out another huge sigh of relief. "There they are," she replied. "Oh, speak of the angels."

"I say that same thing," DeAnna said and then laughed. "I always hated that 'speak of the devil.' I am not calling my friends and loves ones the devil, even if they act like it," DeAnna said as she and Kristen laughed again.

"So, I guess you told her the 'secret,'" Chris said, once he noticed that both Kristen and DeAnna were smiling.

"Yeah, thought I'd tell her before we all began to qualify for some stereo type of an angry black man and angry black women, who had to resort to eye-rolling, neck-jerking, name-calling, four-letter-word-using folks who then resorted to violence as a mean of settling their differences."

"It wouldn't have gone that far," Kristen said. "I'm determined not to instill that type of anger and bitterness into my daughter. I don't want her to do it, so I don't want to demonstrate it. I grew up in that type of environment."

"So, we all good?" Chris asked.

"I guess. You are my baby's daddy and I promised myself that I would always speak positive about you to her and around her," Kristen said.

"So, what about when she's not around? How do you speak about me then?" Chris asked.

"Do you really want to go there?" Kristen asked as she playfully hit him on the shoulder."

"Why not? I love it when you got me on your mind," Chris said as he scooped Naija' up in his arms. "Ain't that right sweetheart?" He asked Naija'.

"What are you talking about Daddy?" Naija' asked.

Chris kissed Naija' and ignored her question. He turned back to Kristen and cleared his throat.

"Now, I just need to hear what you think about your baby's daddy."

"Maybe we should meet for dinner outside the presence of innocent ears and I'll tell you everything you want to hear," Kristen replied.

"It's a date," Chris said as he smiled to himself. "I can't wait to hear what you have to say about me."

DeAnna glanced at Chris with a quizzical look on her face. She didn't know whether Chris was joking or not. He often acted as if he was joking, but sometimes he was actually very serious. The walk through the mall was more enjoyable than the walk to the mall. DeAnna watched, matchmaker Naija', doing her magic as she grabbed her mommy's and daddy's hand and then lifted her feet, so they could swing her. As DeAnna watched what seemed like the prefect couple, a tear rolled down her cheek without warning. She was sincerely happy because she knew that she was watching a new beginning of another happy relationship, but once again felt that her turn was nowhere in the near future.

"Naija', sweetheart do you want some desert?" DeAnna asked. She grabbed Naija' hand without giving Naija' a chance to respond. "How does ice cream sound?"

"Yummy," Naija' said.

DeAnna and Naija' quickly walked off and head towards the ice cream cart. Chris looked at Kristen and motioned for her to sit down. He grabbed his phone and began checking his messages.

"No problem, I almost forgot I ordered pizza too," Chris yelled to DeAnna. "I got to wait here anyway until they bring it to me."

As soon as DeAnna and Naija' was gone, Kristen looked up at Chris.

"Chris look, I'm sorry I jumped to the wrong conclusions about you and DeAnna," Kristen said, still not fully convinced that nothing had gone on between them. She couldn't figure out why DeAnna was in Atlanta with Chris, if Jeremy was the one she liked.

"It's okay," Chris said without looking up from his phone. "I guess we kind of painted that picture."

"Ya think!" Kristen remarked in a sarcastic, but playful tone.

Chris stood against the wall where Kristen sat checking his messages while they waited for DeAnna and Naija' to return. Kristen was a little annoyed that Chris would not even look at her, while at the same time she tried to imagine a life with her one true love.

"Let's talk now instead of waiting for a dinner date," Kristen asked.

"What's on your mind?" Chris asked as he slid in the booth across from her.

"You actually," she replied.

"What about me?" Chris asked.

"You and Dee," Kristen said with an attitude.

"Me and Dee, why?" Chris asked, thinking it had been explained.

"It's just hard to believe that you two are not a couple," Kristen said and then paused and stared at the vendor's carts for a few seconds. She turned back to Chris and stared into his eyes. "I cannot remember a time when you have treated me the way you treat her. You act more like her man, than her friend."

"When did you ever give me a chance?" Chris questioned.

"What do you mean by that?" Kristen asked, feeling insulted.

"I mean you and I were both young and immature when we first started dating, so we both did some stupid stuff, but eventually I grew up and realized that it was time that I be a man."

"A man. You call getting me pregnant being a man?"

Chris looked at Kristen. He could not believe that she would say something like that.

"You're not seriously going to sit there and pretend that you getting pregnant was a solo act, involving only me, are you? If I recall correctly, you were right there with me-a willing participant," Chris said as he grabbed Kristen hand and looked her in her eyes as if he was going to say something profound. "I am sorry if getting pregnant, hindered your plans, but I was only part of the blame. And 'No,' that is not what I call being a man. Being a man was when I realized that I had a child on the way, you know when I decided to go back to school because I wanted the best for you and Naija'. It had nothing to do with you not being good enough for me. Second of all, you were always acting so suspicious of everything I did. I couldn't even treat you like I wanted to. I remember trying to surprise you with a night out with your friend. Do you remember that?" Chris asked.

"No," she quickly replied.

"Yes, you do," Chris responded.

"I hate when you do that," Kristen said, rolling her eyes at Chris.

"What?" He asked.

"When you try to make me remember things that I don't or people I don't know. You remember Candi and them?" Kristen said trying to imitate Chris' voice. "When I say no, I don't know them, you say 'yes you do, they use to live over there by the school."

They both laughed. Chris knew Kristen was right.

"Anyway," Chris said, determined to finish telling his story. "I told you to meet your friend Lori at McDonalds over by the Rec Center. You said you were tired. I told you it was important, you said you had a long day and just needed to relax."

"I remember that day," Kristen said smiling at Chris. "I never did go. Then a few days later Lori and Chanel told me that they won a free Spa day with a full body massage, facial- the works."

"I told them not to tell you, but I had booked that for you and Lori, but since you refused to cooperate; I let Lori have it. I guess she invited Chanel. I was so mad at you. Even after I told you that I had something special for you, you kept asking 'what hoe you trying to sneak off with," Chris said, trying to sound like Kristen.

"Well, you cannot say that you didn't give me reason to. I heard about…" Kristen said, and then stopped mid-sentence.

"You heard what you wanted to hear, or shall I say, you believed what you wanted to believe," Chris replied. "Most of what you heard wasn't even true."

"So, you think I want to hear that the love of my life, the guy I've loved since seventh grade was messing around?

"Wait! Seventh grade?" Chris questioned. "We didn't even know each other then?"

"You might not have known me, but I knew you. You used to come down every summer to visit your cousin."

"Wow," Chris said. "Summer vacations in Carolina as a child.

"Look Chris, I know that you and I have had a long and bad history together, but we do have a daughter. I know where you're going with this conversation Chris and to be honest, I left Carolina because I could not deal with seeing you happy. I know that sounds selfish, but it is, what it is. And when I saw how attentive you were to Dee's every need, even her gut got your attention. My stomach could hold up a sign that says, 'I'm hungry, I'm starving, feed me now,' and you would ignore it."

"That's because you were always talking about your weight and concern with your calorie intake. I mean when I say let's get something to eat, you'll get upset and start crying and say I was trying to get you fat, or keep you fat," Chris explained.

Kristen dropped her head, feeling embarrassed to hear him talk about weight. Chris reached across the table and gently place his hand under her chin and slowly lifted it until her eyes met his eyes.

"If your weight bothers you so much, then we could have worked on it together. If you were happy with it, then act like it. Men like confident women. That's why it is easy to be with Dee, because she doesn't act like she is ashamed of who she is."

"All holy and sanctified," Kristen said.

"Well, there's nothing wrong with living for the Lord. As a matter of fact, I'm saved now. Actually, I have been saved since I was 7-years-old, but I re-dedicated my life to the Lord and I go to church now."

"Hold up! Were you saved when you and Dee were trying to push my buttons?" Kristen asked and then waited for an answer but continued without one. "Yeah, she told me."

"Look, we were just having a little fun," Chris said.

"It wasn't fun to me," Kristen replied.

"You did place a second order earlier, sir?" A waitress said as she stared at Chris.

"Want to share this pizza?" Chris asked Kristen as the waitress placed the pizza on the table. "Anything else?" The waitress asked as she turned to Chris.

"Kristen, do you want anything sweetheart?" Chris asked. He had noticed how the woman was simply ignoring Kristen.

"Give me a minute. I got some making up to do," Kristen said. "That tiny piece of grilled chicken was a snack."

They both laughed. Chris thought about trying to reunite with Kristen, but he felt things would be just like it was before. At one time, he loved her and even wanted to marry her.

"Let me ask you something." Chris was just about to ask a question when his phone rang. He glanced at the screen and decided not to answer it. He knew that Kristen hated when he ignored calls. *'It must be another woman,* she would yell. *You scared to talk around me?* She would ask. When the phone rang the second time, he didn't bother looking it.

"I'll go wash my hands so that you can have some privacy," Kristen said, grabbing her purse and quickly heading to the bathroom.

Chris was surprised that she didn't respond as usual, but he could tell it bothered her that he didn't answer the phone. "I guess she's over that stage of showing her jealous rage in public, even though she is jealous. Chris watched her walk to the bathroom, but he still didn't answer the call. He knew it was someone calling about the Vet, which he had already sold. When Kristen returned, she grabbed a slice of pizza and placed it on Chris' plate and then placed a slice on her plate.

"You know, when you decided to go back to school, it felt as you were saying that I wasn't good enough for you," Kristen confessed.

"Baby," Chris said, looking into Kristen's eyes.

"Baby," she repeated back. "Be careful now, don't start something that you cannot or do not intend to finish."

"After all these years, you still don't know do you," Chris replied.

"Know what?" Kristen asked.

"Never mind," Chris said, grabbing his pizza and stuffing his mouth.

"Can't you even look at me? Can't you at least tell me how you feel right now?" She asked.

"Look Kristen," Chris began and then paused for a long time. He didn't know if how he felt, would even made a difference. "I can't say that I don't love you anymore, but you don't make it easy for me to want to be with you either."

"I know, I guess I was trying to make it easy for you to go," Kristen said. "And when you did, I assumed that you weren't really mine anyway. I didn't want you hanging around just because you had gotten me pregnant. I want a man to want me and not settle for me or just simply tolerate me. It took me a long time to realize it, but I know it now, you are a good man. I guess I was so quick to judge because it seemed that you ran from woman to woman."

"Really," Chris said without even trying to defend his reputation.

"Sometimes women think that men are sorry, but maybe some men are just as confused as us women are. Looking in all the wrong places for love. We do it as women, and we make excuses, but when men do it, we cast judgment," Kristen said and then paused to give Chris the chance to respond, but when he didn't, she continued. "My mom told me that you were a good man. Even after some of the things you did, she still thought you were a good man. I guess you were right, you just had to grow up. I guess we both did," Kristen said.

"True! We both had to grow up, and now you have someone and maybe one day I will too," Chris said. He didn't see the point of Kristen's heartfelt speech.

"Really, who are talking about?" Kristen asked, grabbing her pocket book and searching for something. "Are you referring to him?" She asked, showing Chris a picture.

"I guess," Chris said. "I don't remember seeing your friend before, I just remember you talking about someone and seeing a picture when you opened your wallet the last time I was here. You know, when I asked for a wallet sized picture of Naija'."

"Oh him," Kristen said and put a picture on the table. Chris immediately noticed that the picture was not on photo paper.

"He came with the wallet," Kristen said.

Chris looked at the picture again and then balled it up and threw it at Kristen. They both shook their head and laughed.

"I had a few failed relationships. After the last one, I simply decided to just concentrate on my daughter. I didn't want a parade of men in and out of her life or a new man for her to call uncle every week. Oh no! Not me. After dropping out of college when I got pregnant with my daughter, I promised myself that if I ever got the chance to go back, I would."

"Well," Chris replied.

"Well, and that's what I did. One more semester and I will have my college degree. I almost decided to drop out again, but well, with you sending me good money, I had the money to pay somebody to keep Naija', at night. I couldn't live the life I wanted, but I had enough to do what I needed to do. I really didn't have to worry about working. I wanted to, but I knew that if I worked and tried to go to school, it would be hard, and I would pay for it later. I just decided to wait it out. Yeah, I know a lot of people think that all we do is sit back and collect child support checks, spend it on ourselves. Well, not me. I saved up, found me a cash car that was in good shape, kept my bills paid, went back to school, and now look. I will have my bachelor's degree in less than three months. Not all of us are the save."

"Wow, Kristen, that's wonderful. I am really proud of you."

"I know I didn't always make it easy on you and fussed every time a check was late, but I hated paying those extra fees for paying the car insurance late or not getting the tags renewed on time. I know it wasn't your fault," Kristen said.

"If only you had told me, I would have kept helping you. I imagined the worse, I guess. Anytime you do better, it means better for our daughter. I would have done anything to help," Chris said as he looked at her instead of his ringing cell phone. "All you had to do was ask."

"I guess I was too hurt," Kristen said, fighting back tears.

"I guess we both were hurt," Chris said.

They both sat silently for a few minutes.

"I'm not sure what we're supposed to do now," Kristen muttered.

"I guess we just continue on being Naija's parents," Chris replied.

"You live in North Carolina and I'm here, don't know how that's going to work other than how it has always worked. I guess like the orders requires, I guess," Kristen said as if there should be another option.

"Well, at least for the next three months," Chris replied as if there was another option. "You need to stay here, to finish school. What are you going to do after you graduate?" Chris asked. "Are you planning on staying here and finding a job? Is relocating totally out of the picture?"

"It depends," Kristen said. She wasn't sure what it depended on at the moment, but she didn't want to feel as if Atlanta was the only place she could be.

"Depends on what," Chris asked.

"The reason I would have to relocate. I might be willing to relocate if I find a really great job. Maybe one day a man will ask me to marry him; I'll move where he is. You never know, that just might happen?" Kristen replied.

"I have a question," Chris said, sliding his plate aside. He was not interested in hot pizza anymore.

"Sure," Kristen replied, then continued eating.

"If I didn't have a girlfriend and you didn't have a boyfriend, do you think we might could give us another try?"

Kristen finished chewing the pizza then swallowed, making a big gulping sound. "Long distance relationships almost never work out. And you made it clear that you are not moving back here, and my job is here.

"Thought you didn't have a job?" Chris asked.

"You aren't the only one who realized that it was time to grow up. I never finished telling you my story. Right before the child support check was lower, I started a paid internship, which I was required to do. I was looking even before you cut the check and I found out I had to do an internship. My pastor said, no self-respecting woman should rely on a sugar daddy."

"Wait, hold up, rewind," Chris said. "You said pastor. Did I hear that right?"

"Sometimes life can get so hard you know, that without God, you just can't make it. I told him, the guy I was seeing, that the only man that gets to live with me is my husband. He wasn't trying to put a ring on it, so he had to go. It was hard at first, his check was gone, then you cut the child support, but you know I found out just who I was trusting, everybody but God. I repented and asked God for help. I knew that He would help me through it. So, there it is, I'm standing on my word to God and myself. I've got a little way to go, but things are on the right track for me."

"Wow, I'm so proud of you," Chris said.

"Yeah, I'm proud of me too. Guess we both found peace after all."

"No, I think we both let go and let God. As for that peace stuff, I wouldn't say that I have it," Chris said, thinking about how he often felt when he looked at happy couples. "On second thought, you're right, I have found an inner peace. I stop looking for what I already had, and it wasn't until this very moment that I actually knew that I had found that peace. Let me ask you another question," Chris said.

"Ok, make this one multiple choice," Kristen jokingly requested.

"Okay give me a minute," Chris said. He thought for a few seconds then continued. "Okay I got it. Which of the following things keeps you from leaving Georgia? (A.) You love it here and want to stay. (B.) You don't want to leave because of your job. (C.) You have not been given a reason to leave. (D.) You don't have means to support yourself if you leave," Chris asked and then stared at Kristen, waiting for her answer.

"Wow! That's a hard question. Can I pick more than one?" She asked.

"Sure, why not," Chris replied

"C & D," Kristen answered.

"Question number two," Chris said.

"You said a question, 'a' means one, not more than one," Kristen said and bit into her pizza.

"Question number two," he continued, ignoring Kristen's objection. "Yes or no? Will you leave Georgia?" Chris asked, looking very serious. He paused for a few seconds, contemplating if he was doing the right thing or if he was rushing. He said a quick silent prayer and then continued. "And become my wife, if I promise that I will always love and support you, no matter what?"

"Oh my God, stop playing Christopher," Kristen said. She stared at Chris, waiting to see what he would do or say. "Chris please tell me you are playing: Wait! No! Tell me you are not playing. Say you are not playing."

"If I knew I was going to feel this way, I would have bought you a ring," Chris said without taking his eyes off her. "That's how serious I am. Come back with me, if you can. Just for a few days until you have to return for school. I want you with me, now. I want to put a ring on it, today, before we leave this mall."

"You for real?" Kristen questioned.

"You can keep your place here, until we get married. I will pay the rent for you. I know that you pushed me away because of your insecurities and I didn't do enough to show that I love you."

Kristen placed her hands over her face and just kept saying 'oh my God.'

"Sweetheart, it's a multiple-choice quiz, yes or no?" Chris asked as he pulled her hands from over her eyes.

Kristen quickly got up from the table. "I'll be right back," she said, walking as quickly as she could, without running to the bathroom.

Chris was shocked and wasn't sure what to think. He turned and looked towards the bathroom. After a few minutes, Chris could hear her screaming. He thought she had left to call her mom or one of her friends to get their opinion, but she returned to the table in less than two minutes. She set down as if nothing had happened.

"Come here," she said, motioning with her finger for him to come to closer to her. Chris leaned across the table as if he was about to hear some big secret. "Closer," she said motioning with her fingers for him to come even closer. When Chris was as close as he could get, she whispered something in his ear and then gave him a big kiss. Chris looked at her and smiled.

"So, it's all mine?" He asked with a big smile on his face. "So, your final answer Kristen is..." Chris said and then paused and waited. He wanted her to say the words.

"Yes," she said and kissed him again.

"Yes," Chris yelled as if his favorite football team had just scored the game-winning touchdown. "So, I guess we better finish eating so that I can get back and begin packing," Chris said and then began eating his food as if it was the best pizza in the world. They looked around for DeAnna and Naija'.

"Wait! This won't work," Kristen said.

"What won't work?" Chris asked with a heart-felt sinking feeling. He was afraid to hear the answer.

"Now that we are both trying to do things right, we can't live together before we get married."

"Oh," Chris said and let out a big sigh. "Yeah, you're right, but I got a plan B. You stay at my house and I can stay with Myles or Jeremy."

"Are you sure?" Kristen asked.

"Yup, it won't be for long. We have waited long enough. If not, your mom will let you stay with her, won't she?

"I don't know, she's pretty full with my sister and her kids already there," Kristen explained.

"That's right. I went by there last week just to say hello to her," Chris said.

"Are you serious? She didn't tell me about that."

"I visit her once or twice a month. For some reason, I always felt like she was a mother figure to me. I guess now she will be," Chris smiled and winked at Kristen. "Well, everything is going to work out. If I have to, I can move back in with my grandma, she is not that far from me. If I tell her that we are getting married and her grand princess will be less than an hour away, instead of seven and a half hours. She'll probably tell me to stay as long as I like."

"I don't know about that," Kristen said. "You know she didn't like me that good."

"My mom died when I was young, so she's just kind of protective. I'm already out of the house now, so there's nothing she can do. I think she'll be happy for us, especially since we are both living for God. She would want us to be married. We have a child together and we love each other. Well, at least I love you. There is only one love that will ever go in front of you, I promise."

"Who's that Naija'?" Kristen asked.

"Nope," Chris responded.

"Wait!" Kristen protested. "Wait one minute now. Your grandma cannot be the number one girl."

"Nope she ain't," Chris said with a hint of pride in his voice. "My first love will always be God."

"Ok," Kristen said relaxing a little. "You were about to get a beat down already, but I can deal with that."

"A beat down," Chris said and chuckled. "Ha-ha, for real?"

"I ain't all that saved yet," Kristen said and smiled.

They both laughed, enjoying their re-kindled love for each other. They both realized that lust and sex was the most important factor in their previous relationship, but not this time. They discussed wedding plans, moving plans, and living arrangement. Chris told her about the plan he had made for decorating Naija' room at his house.

When DeAnna returned to her hotel room, she quickly freshened up and changed her clothes. It was almost 6:45 pm and she knew that Bobby would be downstairs shortly to pick her up. She glanced at her phone, hoping that she had not missed a call from him. "Good," she said. "No missed calls." As soon as she tossed the phone on the bed and headed to the mirror to re-apply her lipstick, the phone buzzed. She immediately began to feel a little strange about going out with Bobby. DeAnna felt as if what she was doing was wrong. "Maybe this is what it feels like when God has already chosen your mate. You feel like you are cheating on him even before you see him or know who he is," DeAnna said, sounding as if she was talking to someone.

"Hello," DeAnna said, answering her phone.

"Hello beautiful," Bobby said. "Are you ready to hit the town?"

"I'm not sure, but let's do it anyway," DeAnna replied. "I'm headed down right now."

DeAnna hung up the phone and quickly finished putting on her lip-gloss. She grabbed a lightweight jacket and headed to the hotel lobby where Bobby was waiting for her. When she spotted Bobby, she smiled and waved as they walked towards each other. When they reached each other, they hugged and headed out the hotel.

"I got tickets for a show at the Fox Theater," Bobby said as they walked outside and headed to the car. "Then I thought maybe we'll get something to eat. You know, sort of a late-night dinner." He opened the car door and DeAnna got in the car. He waited for her response.

"Sounds good to me," DeAnna said.

Bobby smiled and then closed her car door and quickly walked to the driver's side. Once he was in, DeAnna added to her response. "A late dinner will give the food I ate earlier, time to digest."

Bobby drove off as if he were in a hurry to get somewhere.

"I tried to get permission for you to ride back on the company's plane, but well, my boss said no," Bobby told DeAnna.

"It's okay, we saved a lot by not having to pay for round trip tickets. We really do appreciate that. We are already booked on a flight for 10 a.m. I wanted to stay longer, but Chris has to get back to work." DeAnna didn't want to tell Bobby the truth, which was that she was ready to get back to see what Jeremy had to say to her.

"Guess you already knew, huh?" Bobby said.

"Well, it is always good to have a back-up plan," DeAnna replied.

"Right, always good to have a back-up plan," Bobby said as if he had something up his sleeve.

"So, what do you have a plan B for?" DeAnna asked.

"What are you talking about?" Bobby quickly said. "I'm just agreeing with you,"

"Oh, okay!" DeAnna said, but she was not fully convinced that Bobby didn't have something up his sleeves.

DeAnna tried to enjoy her time with Bobby, but she couldn't keep her mind off Jeremy. When they arrived at the Fox Theatre, the show had been cancelled, but Bobby didn't seem to be surprise. They decided to visit the Reflecting Pool outside of The King Center. DeAnna wanted to go in, but the museum closed at 6 p.m. Bobby drove DeAnna pass the house in which MLK, Jr. was born. He backtracked and pointed out Ebenezer Baptist Church. Bobby acted as a tour guide. He told DeAnna about the symbolism of The Eternal Flame, which represented the continuing effort to realize Dr. Martin Luther Kings' dream. He told DeAnna about Freedom Hall and the International World Peace Garden. DeAnna decided that someday she would return when she could actually go inside. She thought about getting up early and visiting it before their flight.

DeAnna really didn't want to get anything to eat or sit in a restaurant and make small talk. She was still satisfied from the earlier meals, so she asked Bobby to take her to places in which some of the movies were shot. Bobby agreed but wanted to get himself something to eat first. He stopped at a fast food restaurant and placed a takeout order. When he received his meal, he drove to Centennial Olympic Park. There was a free live concert going on. The place was packed with people, but they were able to find a place to sit down so that Bobby could eat his food. DeAnna seemed to enjoy the concert and the atmosphere so much that Bobby suggested that they stay. DeAnna was in total agreement. She enjoyed it so much, she didn't think about Jeremy until a young girl got on stage and began to sing. DeAnna sang along with the group.

"*In my mind, I'll always be his lady,*" DeAnna sang. When DeAnna got to the part about *seeing his mother the other day*, she stopped singing. "That's how it all began for us," she said. She wasn't even aware that she was talking aloud.

"That's how what began?" Bobby asked.

"Nothing, just thinking out loud," DeAnna said as she continued to sing "I'll always be your girl."

After Bobby finished eating, he and DeAnna decided to sit on the grass and enjoy the rest of the concert. They enjoyed jDenea' singing her famous song, Divvy That. They sang along with her.

The things you think I did, it blows my crane. I was your main, friend. I guess when time evolve it has to change. Ain't no time for the silly games, you playing. Boy go rest in peace, the mess you do is tied. I was down to ride, but you showed me another side. Time to split up, divide. Divvy that divvy, divvy, divvy that. Let's divide the facts and let it rain on your lies. See what time comprise surprise, over time, it reveals what's inside."

They laughed though the words that they didn't know and enjoyed the concert. The weather was prefect and the music was awesome most of the evening. It suddenly began to rain. Bobby jumped up and quickly offered to help DeAnna up. As he tried to pull her up, she pulled him down. They both laughed and then quickly pulled themselves to their feet.

"Frist one to the car is a rotten egg," DeAnna said and then watched Bobby take off like a schoolboy. "Gets them ever time," DeAnna said as she trailed behind him. "Wow," she said once she reached the car and they both quickly climbed in. "I got in my exercise for today. A few more days like this and the pounds will fall off," she said and laughed

"I hear ya, rotten egg," Bobby said.

"If you heard me, then you would know that you are the rotten egg. I said, 'first one to the car is a rotten egg,' not last one," DeAnna said then laughed and pointed at him. "Got'cha," she said.

"Okay, now that I think about, you did say that. Okay you got me," Bobby admitted. They both took a few more deep breaths. "You are so fun to be with DeAnna. When I jumped up to help you get up, I just knew you were going to start yelling about your hair getting wet and messing up your new do."

"Well, my do' ain't all that new and my hair just gets curly when it gets wet, so no big deal," DeAnna said. "I guess that's a wrap for tonight, but I had fun. I am so glad we had to stop for your gut, otherwise we would have missed the excitement."

"Me too!" Bobby said as he started the car. He was hoping to beat the crowd out of the parking lot. "You seemed to have been deep in thought for a minute back there," Bobby said as he flipped though the radio station, looking for some R&B.

"I was, but I really don't want to talk about it now. I will face the music that I have to face when it's time for me to do so. Right now, I just want to enjoy this music," DeAnna said then chimed in with the song that was on the radio, doing the best she could to remember the words.

"Finding' love ain't easy as it seems. People think it's easy as one, two, three. Sittin' here waiting for my date. He running late. Contemplating I should make him pay. Took me all day to get myself together. Did my own hair, nails, and the makeup on my face. Can't deny it, still excited. I can't hide it. Although my prides tellin' me that I should fight him. Getting' restless pacing back and forth. Thinkin' bout what will I say when he hit the door. Got me waitin.' Anticipation, getting' the best of me. He betta hurry, bout to catch this fee, He's bout to see the attitude in me. I'm tryin' to be as pleasant as can be. He pushing my patience. Gotta sista waitin. Make me wonder why I'm dating. Findin' love ain't easy as it seems. People think it's easy as one, two, three. It takes more than what you see on TV. Patience is one of the things you'll need.

"Sound nice," Bobby said looking at DeAnna wondering if they were on a date or just hanging out as old friends. "jDenea' is all over the music industry, I see. Her songs have really deep messages. I would love hearing her live.

"Me too," DeAnna said. "I love her music.

The ride back to the hotel room was filled with bad attempts from both DeAnna and Bobby to sing whatever came on the radio. They laughed at each other and sang with each other. When they arrived at the hotel, Bobby parked in the parking deck so that they would not have to battle the rain that turned from a sprinkle to a down pour. They entered the hotel from the garage entry. They stopped by the hotel's restaurant and got some dessert. They talked about old times and what classmates were doing great things and who wasn't. They talked about those who had died or who were sick. DeAnna thoughts began to drift back to Jeremy. After they finished their ice cream, Bobby walked DeAnna to her room door.

"Can I come in for a minute?" Bobby asked.

"I don't think that is such a good idea," DeAnna said, rambling through her purse for her room key.

"Why, you're single. I'm single. I am NOT going to try anything, and you know that," Bobby replied.

"I know that," DeAnna said. "You have always been a gentleman, but it's just doesn't look right."

"To who, Dee? Nobody here knows us. Just because a male and a female come to a hotel together, doesn't mean something is going on."

"The Bible does say we should avoid even the appearance of sin," DeAnna said and then swiped her room key.

"Nobody's looking," Bobby said, pausing to look around to see if anyone was looking. "Therefore, it doesn't look like sin to me if nobody's looking," Bobby said, turning back to face DeAnna. "Who is it looking like sin to? God knows and see all. So, why does it matter what others might think?"

"Look Bobby, I just don't want to put myself in a position to be tempted," DeAnna said. She thought about the few test she previously failed when she opened herself up to temptation. She had managed to escape temptation for the last 6-years and she wasn't about to back slide now.

"You're a strong woman and you aren't going to do anything that you don't want to do," Bobby said. "I'm just not ready to say goodbye to you.

"Tell you what, we can talk," DeAnna said as she thought about how lonely she was going to feel once she said goodnight. She thought it was much later than it actually was.

"Good because..." Bobby said as he motioned forward.

"Downstairs," DeAnna said. "Meet you in the lobby in ten minutes."

"Wow, you don't play, do you?"

"Not anymore, too many heartaches, heartbreaks, and feeling of shame to get over. After a while, a sho'nough saved person gets tired of repenting over the same old sin. If you can keep committing the same sin and not feel convicted, I would wonder if you are really saved or if you truly repented. I know saved people sin, but they should feel some conviction at some point once they know that what they are doing is sin," DeAnna replied.

"Good point. I guess we have to stop making provisions for the flesh and doing what causes us to get caught up in sin, huh?" Bobby said as he stepped back from the door. "Well, I'll see you in ten minutes."

As soon as DeAnna entered her hotel room, her phone rang and as soon as she pushed TALK on the phone, Bobby knocked on the door. She quickly opened the door.

"You forgot this," Bobby said, handing DeAnna her scarf when she opened the door wider. "See you in ten minutes," he said and winked at her as he turned and walked back towards the elevators.

"Hello," DeAnna heard a voice coming though the phone.

"Oh! I'm sorry. Hello," DeAnna said, watching Bobby turn the corner and disappear.

"Please, I need to talk to you."

"Can it wait? I promise, I'll be back soon," DeAnna said. She was careful not to sound mad, mean, moody, bitter, or angry. She intended to sound happy, busy, and pleasant.

"No, it can't. I waited long enough. Dee, I wasn't sure why you stop calling me or returning my calls. I guess I thought I was just a charity case with you," Jeremy stated.

"Jeremy no, that's not true," DeAnna said. She was shocked that he felt that way. She felt bad for not talking to him earlier. She would have explained that he was not a charity case.

"I know that now," Jeremy quickly interjected. "But that day I came to the hospital to tell you that I got my sight back, as I stood there asking the lady at the desk what time you get off, she insisted on calling you. I told her I just wanted to surprise you. She pointed to you. She said. "There she is." Then all of a sudden, I couldn't see. I turn and walk in what I thought was the right direction. I stumbled over a trashcan or something. The lady asked me if I was okay," Jeremy said and then paused as if his story was building up to something more. "I was so embarrassed; I just kept walking. I think she thought I was drunk and sent someone to help me."

DeAnna was in tears as she listened. "Oh Jeremy."

"DeAnna, I got so discouraged. I thought I was going to be blind forever. I began to cry. I didn't want anybody to see me or even know what happened that day. When you called me later that day, you said that you thought you had a date, or something like that. I thought I had loss the one thing I had found because of my blindness. The one thing my blindness allows me to see."

"Thing! What thing was that?" DeAnna asked. She knew he was talking about her, but she wasn't sure if it was more about her or the help she provided that he was concerned about losing or her love for him.

"That thing was true happiness," Jeremy said. "I mean, who would have ever thought that through blind eyes, I'd find happiness. Me, the one who is so judgmental and stuck on looks and appearances. God allowed my sight to be taken. Well at first, I blamed Him, until you explain that God doesn't do devilish things like that. He doesn't make people blind, but he doesn't stop everything from happening either. I guess in some respect, I was glad that he allowed it to happen, because…" Jeremy paused before finishing. "It allowed me to see what real beauty was… I mean is."

"So, if not for that, you would not have found me attractive?" DeAnna asked without thinking.

"I think you are very attractive, one of the prettiest ladies that I have ever dated, if what we were doing was dating. You know there are different categories of beauty, there is pretty, and then there is gorgeous. DeAnna you are gorgeous. But, to be honest, I couldn't see past the weight at first. I found it so ironic, Chris had a plus size woman that he loved in spite of and here I was about to lose the only woman, I've ever love because of…"

"Love?" Dee questioned.

"Yes! I know my timing is bad and maybe you've already moved on, but I know that you do or at least you did love me too."

"How do you know that?" DeAnna asked. She laid back on the bed and smiled.

"After all the superficial women I've dated, who only wanted me because I was a BMW."

"What?" DeAnna questioned and laughed.

"Black Man Working. I know when somebody loves me verses just love the idea of me or how we look together. I know it all too well. My question to you is, do you believe that I love you?" He asked.

"Yes! Do you think that I love you?" DeAnna asked.

"Honestly, I think you are the only woman who ever has," Jeremy said and then paused for a long time. He was waiting, hoping for her to confirm his words. "So, am I wrong?" He asked after two minutes of silence.

"Let me ask you a question?" DeAnna said. "When did you discover that you loved me? Was it when you heard I was with an old boyfriend or when you heard we were flying to Georgia on a private plane?" DeAnna paused, but not long enough for him to answer. "No, let me guess, when you realize that all the other girls were just using you," DeAnna said.

"It was the day I shared my dreams about having children, a wife to come home to and mess over when she gets sick. I told you about the boy's room with trucks and my daughter's room decorated in purple. You fell asleep on me that day and I almost pee-peed on myself, because I wanted you on me for as long as possible. I had Kimberly buy you a sofa blanket, just so your perfume would stay in my house. I refuse to let anyone else use it. I smelt you in my home. Your presence belonged there."

DeAnna was totally and completely shocked as she thought about that day. She remembered him suddenly gazing off like he was looking out the window. She remembered falling asleep on his lap. She remembered him putting the blanket over her feet.

"So why did you wait so long to tell me?" DeAnna questioned.

"Dee, I promised myself that I would be honest with you no matter what and I am. At first, I kept thinking about you saying something about a date. I sort of thought, I was the date you were talking about, but then I thought about my childhood. Growing up with plus-sized ladies in the family was challenging," Jeremy said and then hesitated. He didn't want to hurt her feeling, but he had promised to be honest.

"Challenging for who? Them or you?" DeAnna asked.

"Both. Watching TV, sitting between my mom and my aunties, I was pinned in and down until they wanted to move. I felt crushed sitting on the church pew between my mama and my sister. I felt like I couldn't move or breathe. I got smooshed riding in the car on the way to church, on the church bus, riding on rides at carnivals, the list goes on. A simple hug and my face was smashed between two humongous boobs," Jeremy said then let out a sigh. "It didn't change much when I became a teenager either. When I got my driver's license and had to drive everybody here and there, I practically drove with my left shoulder out the window," Jeremy said.

He doesn't sound like he is picking or making fun of the situation as some people might have thought. He sounded as if he was traumatized as a child, DeAnna thought. She had heard all the jokes and comments most of her life.

"I see, so that's how you got a phobia about big girls. You are afraid you're going to roll over one night and she's going to crush you?" DeAnna asked. She wanted to lighten the mood a little. She wanted to laugh, but she realized he was serious. She thought about how people treated her because she was big, but she never considered how people felt around her. She remembered one day at church, a lady kept trying to slide over to the left as if she was trying to get away from her. DeAnna was a little upset at first. Then she remembered thinking, *maybe she just needs a little bit more room.* DeAnna once told an usher to stop seating all the big people side-by-side, *all we going to do the whole service is arm wrestle.*

"When I was 17-years old," Jeremy continued. "My favorite cousin Tammy, she died. She was considered morbidly obese, had high blood pressure at 19. Diabetes too. My mom kept saying, *'she better loose that weight. She is too young to be carrying all that fat around her heart.'* I used to go walking with her, then we would stop by the store and she would buy candy and chips," Jeremy said and then paused. He took a deep breath. "When she died, I was so angry at her. I just don't see how you could love food more than life," Jeremy said, remembering how hard he cried at the funeral.

"Jeremy, not all big girls are big because they love food or don't exercise. Some people have thyroid problems. Now some say that it's a hereditary issue. That's what they want to keep claiming as their excuse, but not me. Sometimes when people keep saying 'it runs in the family,' folks just give up and accept it. I always say, 'if the family would just run, maybe diabetes wouldn't have to be the only one running the family.'

"I know Dee, but since her death, I thought about all the complaints I used to hear from my mom, sister, and aunties. 'My knees hurt, my back hurt, my hips hurt, and this is giving out.' Seems like all they did was complain. Got to 'get the weight off' was stated so much, it should be a workout song. It was like the national anthem at our family reunions. But none of them ever did or even tried, so I was determined; I wasn't going to be big like my family members."

"So, is it now like a taboo for you to be with big women?" DeAnna asked.

"You know," Jeremy said. "I knew you were plus-size long before I regain some of my sight. And yes, at first, I thought about all the complaints that I had heard in the past.

"You didn't think about your image; I mean being seen with a big girl?" DeAnna asked.

"Well at first, I did, but then I thought about how I felt with you. You didn't do all that complaining like I expected. But then again, how could a blind man judge anyone else?" Jeremy said as he thought about all the irony that exist in his little love triangle. He had more to complain about then anybody. "Then I looked at how you cared me to health. Well, in my spirit. I just thought, couldn't I do the same thing with someone."

"Wow! So then, why did it take you so long to make your mind up?" DeAnna asked.

"Well I must admit, I would let myself think about having children and going on family vacations," Jeremy smiled as he talked. "But then I thought about what if she gets sick. I began to hear all those complaints that I had heard every since I was old enough to remember. What if she dies and I have to raise the children by myself? I want my kids to have a mom."

"Wow, you do have some imagination. Jeremy not all big girls are unhealthy. That's a common misconception, see some of us are healthier than the salad eating sisters," DeAnna said and then laughed. She had never talked to a man like this before. She had gained a whole new level of respect for his honesty. She even respected his logic.

"I know that now," Jeremy laughed.

"Besides, have you ever thought that maybe, just maybe, that a healthy living and long life can be accomplished at a greater level when a person feel loved and appreciated?" DeAnna asked him. "Love, peace, and joy produces good health too."

"So they say," Jeremy said.

"Well, it's true, for most of us anyway. Did you ever think about just going for a walk with me or working out with me?"

"I noticed that I didn't hear all those complaints that I normally hear from the big women, so I didn't think about it," Jeremy explained.

They both were silent for a few minutes. DeAnna wanted to finish their conversation, but she suddenly remembered Bobby was waiting downstairs.

"DeAnna," Jeremy said and took another deep breath. "I know that this might not persuade you to consider dating me seriously, but when Chris talked about how lucky I was that I met you first, I got a little jealous."

"He told you that?" DeAnna asked. "I'm shocked."

"Yep! Then I heard that y'all left together," Jeremy said, sounding upset. "I was fuming mad. I thought he was trying to steal you from me."

"Steal me," Dee chuckled. "Now we are not in high school, besides Chris loves you like a brother. He would never do that."

"You know what they say, all is fair in love and war," Jeremy said.

"That's in love and basketball," DeAnna said and laughed.

"I just know that I had to step up," Jeremy said. "Then when I heard that guy's voice in the background when you answered the phone, I realize that I was jealous. I know enough to know that he was probably walking you to the door and that you wouldn't dare share a room with him," Jeremy said, sounding as if he was asking for confirmation.

"How can you be so sure?" DeAnna asked.

"Baby, I know so many 'so-called Christian women too and I know that not all of them are truly living as if God is really watching, so I know fake when I see it. Some are trying; I know that too. You are not perfect DeAnna, but you're not fake. Most of the time, men can handle a woman who has let go of being with another man. Meaning she no longer want anyone but us, but if he still wants her and if we think sex is involved, it would break us apart. I know you, and I know I don't have to worry about that," Jeremy said and then paused. "If I thought that something more would happen, I probably would not be able to talk to you right now. I would have Chris banging at your door every two minutes," Jeremy said and then paused again before finishing. "So now, back to my original question."

"Which was?" DeAnna asked.

"Was I wrong? I need to know, because I got a wedding to go to in a few months and I don't want to go alone," Jeremy said. "I want you by my side."

"A wedding? So does this mean, if I go with you, I'll be meeting the family?" DeAnna asked.

"Well, you already know my mom and my sis. You'll probably meet a few more, but since it is not one of my family members getting married, you'll have to meet my family another time."

"So, who's getting married?" DeAnna asked.

"Chris and Kristen," Jeremy said.

"Are you serious?" DeAnna questioned, bursting with joy and excitement. She was a little disappointed that it wasn't a secret proposal.

"Chris called earlier with the good news," Jeremy said.

"That's so wonderful. Surprising news and a quick decision, but wonderful," DeAnna said.

"When you love someone, as long as they have, all the separation did was allowed them to grow up while apart, so they wouldn't end up hating each other. When God sends your mate to you or back to you, you don't need to date forever," Jeremy said. "Oh, Chris also told me what you and he did. You were about to get a Georgia Carolina beat down."

"I must admit, she kept her cool pretty good," DeAnna said.

"Looks like change and growth is in the air," Jeremy replied.

"Yes and no," DeAnna responded.

"No, what?" Jeremy asked.

"Well," DeAnna said and then paused. She suddenly heard a loud crash in the background. "Hello, Jeremy what's going on? Is everything okay?" She asked, but he didn't answer, so she yelled again. "Jay are you there?" Jeremy still didn't answer. DeAnna could hear a lot of background noise. She could hear people talking and yelling.

"Call 911," she heard someone yell.

"Don't panic," DeAnna told herself. "Pray," she said. "God, I am not sure what's going, but please keep everyone safe. Lord, I just thank you right now that you put a hedge of protective around Jeremy and everyone that is around him. You are a merciful God. Lord, you allowed this man to see me even though he couldn't see with his eye. You allowed him to see and feel with his spirit, so Lord don't allow the devil to take him away from me."

Chapter 28

DeAnna continued to pray. She prayed so hard and loud that she became weak. She fell to her knees and rebuked the devil for trying to steal Jeremy's sight and his joy. "What you meant for evil devil, God will turn it into something good. Jay will glorify God with his testimony. Now, I demand you to go, in the name of Jesus. You have no authority in this man's life." *We don't always know what to pray*, she thought. "Just pray in the Holy Spirit," she said to herself. "The Holy Spirit knows what to pray for." DeAnna told herself. She quickly gathered her things and ran out of her room, speaking in tongues and praying as she entered the elevator. She didn't care who was looking or listening. She prayed as she entered the lobby. She immediately began looking for Bobby. He was sitting in the lounge area.

"Something happened," DeAnna said as soon as she reached Bobby. She was out of breath, but she began forcing words out of her mouth. "I'm not sure what, but I was talking to my friend, I heard a crash, the phone line is still open, but I can't hear him. I heard yelling..."

"Wait, slow down. What are you talking about?" Bobby asked.

"I have to call Chris," DeAnna frantically said, flipping through her phone contacts, but was careful not to touch the END button on her phone. Jeremy's line was still open, and she did not want to hang up. She got a little frustrated when she saw several contacts, all with the name Chris. "Why didn't I put last names beside them?" She asked herself. "Wait his number should be on the screen. Think Dee," she said and looked at the number that was at the top of the screen. "NO, NO, NO, DeAnna you are not looking for Jeremy's number, you are looking for Chris' number. I'm confusing myself," she said and then looked at the numbers again to see which ones looked familiar. "This is it, but I just don't want to use my phone. Bobby can you call this number," DeAnna read the number to him.

"DeAnna, you're scaring me, what's wrong?" Bobby asked as he dialed the number.

"I'm not really sure," DeAnna told him.

When Bobby heard the phone ringing, he gave DeAnna his phone.

"Chris this is DeAnna, I was talking to Jeremy and I heard a loud crash or something. He didn't hang up the phone and I haven't hung up either. I don't know if he's involved or what, I keep calling his name and no one says anything. I don't know if he just dropped his phone and maybe cannot find it, but I heard people in the background. Someone yelled, call 911," DeAnna said. "Have you heard from anyone?"

"Dee slow down sweetheart. Let me call Myles, they were together earlier when I talked to him," Chris said.

"Call me right back please," DeAnna pleaded. "Okay, call me at the number on your screen; I'm going to keep my line open." DeAnna explained.

"I will. Why don't you check on an earlier flight?" Chris suggested.

"I checked earlier, before I talked to Jeremy and the next flight out is tomorrow at 3:00 p.m.," DeAnna said.

"Okay, I'll call you right back okay," Chris promised.

DeAnna ended the call and gave Bobby his phone. She checked her phone to see if the line was still open.

"Okay Dee," Bobby said. "So, from what I gather, you were talking with Jeremy and then you heard a crash. Jeremy must have dropped his phone or something, but he didn't hang up and so you are still connected with his phone, is that right?" Bobby asked.

"Yes, I hear background noises. People yelling, but I can't tell what anybody is saying; they seen too far away."

"Can you hear sirens or fire trucks or anything?" Bobby asked.

"No," DeAnna replied.

"Maybe it was a car accident or something," Bobby said as he pulled DeAnna down on the sofa.

"Oh, I hope not. You see Jeremy was shot over six to eight months ago. He was temporarily blinded," DeAnna said. "I just hope he wasn't driving."

"Think positive," Bobby said, not knowing what else to say.

"I hope Myles or one of his friends is with him," DeAnna said. "Oh my God. He just has to be alright. I have to see him God, please Lord. Let him be okay."

"Dee," Bobby said, suddenly realizing something. "Who is Jeremy to you? Is he your ex-boyfriend?"

"No, I am, well he's, hum... Well, to make a long story short, I was his personal nurse after the accident. We both began to feel for each other, if you know what I mean, but never really admitted it. Well, at least not to each other, until tonight."

"So why did you come here with me?" Bobby asked.

"Well, like I told you, we didn't admit it to each other. I didn't think he liked me the way I liked him. Bobby, we, you and I, have not made any commitments to each other. There was no understanding that we were going in order to build a relationship. It's just a friendly thing, I thought. We never made any promises of a relationship."

"So, you really like him?" Bobby asked.

"Yes! Actually, I love him," DeAnna replied.

"Well, I guess I lose out again," Bobby said. He grabbed her hand and kissed it as if to give her a kiss goodbye.

"Bobby, I am sorry," DeAnna said.

"We'll always be friends, right?" Bobby asked.

"I guess that's all we were meant to be," DeAnna said as she placed the phone back to my ear. "Hello," she said, listening for background noises, but she couldn't hear anything.

"Why don't you rent a car and drive back?" Bobby asked. "It's only a seven or eight-hour drive."

"That's better than waiting around here," DeAnna said. She glanced at Bobby and suddenly realized how insensitive her statement must have sounded. "No offense," she said to Bobby.

"None taken; I understand," Bobby replied.

DeAnna asked to borrow Bobby's phone again to call Chris. She wanted to see if he was up for a long drive. Chris was already one step ahead of her. He informed DeAnna that he would be by to pick her up soon. They were headed to drop Naija' off at her grandmother's house. He was going to drive Kristen's truck back to North Carolina.

DeAnna and Bobby headed up to DeAnna's room. She wanted to be packed and waiting downstairs when Chris got there. She was packed and back downstairs in fifteen minutes. She talked to Bobby about her relationship with Jeremy while she waited. When Chris arrived, Bobby helped Chris load DeAnna's luggage into the car. "This is the last one," DeAnna said, handing Chris her duffle bag.

Chris arranged the bags in the trunk. DeAnna said goodbye to Bobby and got settled in for the long ride home.

Chapter 29

DeAnna was surprised to see Naija' with them. She thought Naija' was going to stay with her grandmother, but she was happy for back-seat company.

"Times to hit the road," Chris said, trying to sound as if there was no sense of urgency. Chris asked Kristen to pull up the direction on her phone. There is an accident on 85," Kristen said.

"So, you one of those people," Chris jokingly said, as he fasted his seat belt.

"Yup, don't like surprises," she replied.

"Well, today is one of those days that I don't either. I am just ready to get there," DeAnna said.

"Everybody buckled in," Chris said as if he was a flight attendant.

"Check," DeAnna said as she winked at Naija', trying to forget about what could be going on in North Carolina.

"Check," Naija' said.

"Check," Chris said.

Everybody waited for Kristen to say check. She was still searching for directions. Chris wasn't concerned. He knew the way; he just liked hearing the directions. He didn't want to miss something because he was not paying attention. He thought she might be looking at or for something else.

"Mommy, you got to say check," Naija' said.

"Oh, Sorry," Kristen replied. "Check."

"So, let's go," Naija and Chris yelled.

Chris turned the radio up they all began to sing as they pulled off.

Ain't no body trippin,' living' life God has given. Happy to be spending time up-out with my girls, umm! Don't have to struggle on your own, I'm here for you, you know I got your back Girl, don't give up, umm! If you got ya girls, you don't have to worry, nah! Let your hair down girl. Free yourself from problems, yeah! If you got ya girls. You don't have to worry, nah! Let your hair down girl. Free yourself from problems, yeah (ohhhh). Pack your baggage, ship them off. Let the devil have it. Relax your mind. Free your spirit; Sista let's get lifted. I see you stall. Ain't gonna let you fall. Let's get, get it! Take back what you lost, don't let the devil get it.

The all laughed and began singing the next song on the radio.

"Our God is an awesome God," Chris sang with pride.

"Wait!" Kristen said as she held her hand up, "You?"

"Yes me," Chris replied. "And I am not ashamed to admit it either."

"So, you were not joking about going to church and living for God," Kristen asked, staring at Chris. "You, Mr. I-GOT-A-LOT-MORE-LIVING-TO-DO-IN-THE-WORLD. This is a game, right?"

"So, you thought I was joking back at the food court?" Chris asked.

"No, I just didn't know you were at this level already," Kristen said.

"No," DeAnna chimed in on Chris behalf. "It is not a game."

"So, I guess, I really do have to stay at your grandma's house after all, it is a sin …" Kristen began, but didn't finish.

"Or the appearance of sin," Chris said.

"DeAnna, he is joking?" Kristen asked, knowing Chris wasn't joking.

"I'm afraid not," DeAnna answered.

"So, you and I can't," Kristen said, and then winked at Chris, "ride the marry-go-round?"

"Nope, we can't," Chris said and then started laughing.

"Like that's really going to happen," Kristen said.

Chris quickly turned and looked at Kristen in disbelief.

"So, you think this is all some kind of joke? You think that I was just saying something to impress you for the moment. Did you think I was just going to take you back with me for three days on a mini-vacation to good old North Carolina and fornicate with you for three days and then send you back to Augusta, as if all you are to me is my baby mama?" Chris asked.

"Well, I guess I saw it more of us having a romantic fling with each other like we used to," Kristen said.

"She," Chris said, pointing in the rearview mirror at Naija. "She deserves a better example."

"So, you really are serious," Kristen asked.

"Yes, I'm really serious," Chris replied.

329

"Wow! All this time," Kristen said and then stopped.

"I'm not saying I'm perfect, I still have a lot of issues to work out, but I just don't want to waste any more time. I've wasted enough in loveless relationships, being a daddy to everybody else's child and not my own. No more playing house. You know DeAnna's pastor." Chris paused. "Wait! I mean my pastor, he did a message about being a real man."

"And?" Kristen questioned.

"And according to him and the contents in the message, which were the qualifications, I wasn't a real man. I wasn't submitted to God, I was saved, but not serving. I did not have a relationship with God. A relationship is more than just praying and going to church. How could I be the spiritual head of my house, when I did not know God and wasn't obedient to His word. I had no covering. Couldn't even get a prayer though to God at that point. How can I teach Naija' what to do if I didn't know? The Bible says train up a child and when they are older they will not depart. Or something like that. Well, either the Bible wasn't true, or it was just a matter of time before I was going to return, because we were all bought up in the church, under the Word. The Bible doesn't lie, so I returned about two months ago." Chris looked at Kristen who had set quietly and listened to him without interrupting. "It gives me great comfort in knowing that Naija' will be trained up right and if she ever strays, she will come back. The Bible does not lie, but we have to make sure we train her up." Chris paused and looked at Kristen. "Why are you crying?"

"Two months ago, that's when I gave my life back to Christ. And as I told you earlier, I broke up with him because of it. I didn't want to do things my way anymore. I asked God to send me a God-fearing man to be a husband to me and a father to Naija'. Then I saw you and DeAnna together, I could tell something had changed about you. When I saw you and Dee, I instantly and secretly hated her, no offense Dee," she said to DeAnna who sat quietly listening. "I thought she had gotten the man I prayed for," Kristen paused. "You know, it was hard to even hate her too, she seemed so nice. Boy, did I feel convicted. The Bible says love your neighbor."

DeAnna laid her head back and silently cried. She was happy that Chris and Kristen have reconciled, but she longed for her own mate. When will it be my turn? She instantly thought about Jeremy and questioned if he was serious about dating her. *It is always everybody else*, she thought to herself. *When God, when will it be my turn?* She closed her eyes, but she couldn't sleep. She listened to Kristen and Chris talk.

"Look at God. He is so good," Chris said. "I didn't see this coming at all. Hit me from the blind side. I'll talk to Jeremy about me staying at his house."

"Dee are you okay back there?" Kristen asked.

"I'm okay," DeAnna replied. "Thanks for asking."

"Good," Chris said. "Don't worry about anything. Like you always tell us, worry about nothing and pray about everything. Jeremy probably just dropped his phone and can't find it. He has not regained his full sight yet," Chris said.

DeAnna tried to get some sleep, but only manage to close her eyes for fifteen minutes at a time.

"So, I hear you are a nurse slashed interior decorator," Kristen said to DeAnna.

"Nurse slash a wanna-be interior decorator," DeAnna replied with a lack of enthusiasm in her voice.

Chris could tell that Dee was not in the mood to talk.

"Dee ain't no telling what we are about to find when we get home. A welcome back party, a girl gone wild party, little Kimberly or Jason walking around, and you know if the word is out that Jeremy's off the market, then the whole town is turned upside down. Get some sleep sweetheart, you gonna need the energy. You know can't nobody handle Jeremy, but you."

"Oh, he's off the market?" DeAnna asked. "Interesting."

"Well, he told me that he was," Chris replied.

"So, he finally gonna let someone in his heart?" Kristen asked.

"According to him, he already has, a few months ago," Chris said.

"She must be a lucky or a mighty crazy woman," Kristen replied.

"You right about that. She's going to have a mess to deal with," Chris said.

"What kind of mess?" DeAnna asked.

"Well," Chris began. "There's a lot of women out there who thought that they were going to be the one."

"I don't think that's gonna be a problem," DeAnna said.

"Oh yeah," Chris replied.

"Me either," Kristen said. "Not too many girls gonna want to be burdened with a blind man. Now a grown woman, that's a different story."

"He's not blind anymore," DeAnna said. "Well, sort of not blind."

"Bet the women don't know that; otherwise, they would have been flopping their little behind wherever he was," Kristen said. "I remember how women would flock to him; baby in their arms and one hanging around the hips. They didn't care how they looked when they saw him, they seized the chance to try get him."

"Now that's true," Chris said.

Kristen and Chris talked almost the entire way back to NC.

"Dee, your phone is ringing," Chris said as Kristen turned around and gently shook DeAnna. Kristen was careful not to wake up Naija'.

DeAnna jumped when she heard the phone. She wasn't sure when the phone had hung up. "Hello," she said. DeAnna perked up when she heard Ma Phillips' voice. "Ms., I mean Ma Phillips."

"Where's you at honey?" Ma Phillips said. "Jeremy has been acting strange since you left."

"I just took a mini-vacation, but I, I mean we are on the way back now. I'm in...." DeAnna looked around for road signs, but she didn't see any. "I'm on my way back from Georgia. Is everything all right? I heard a crash."

"Okay, honey how long foe' you's back?" Ma Phillips asked.

"I'm not sure. We been riding now for about four or five hours, I guess. Ma Phillips, what's wrong? You don't sound like yourself. Is everything okay?" DeAnna asked. She could tell Ma Phillips was avoiding some of her questions by pretending to be hard of hearing and hard of understand.

"Yeah, all is well in the Lord," Ma Phillips said. "Do me a favor and call me once you get back, okay."

"Yes ma'am," DeAnna said. "Hum..." as she looked at the time.

She noticed that she had a few missed calls from Ma Phillips and Myles. "Something is not right. I got that feeling something is wrong with him."

"What's wrong DeAnna?" Chris asked

"Well, I'm not sure, but something is wrong. I feel it."

"Wait!" Chris said as he grabbed his ringing phone. He looked at the phone and handed it to DeAnna. "This is Myles. He and Kristen are oil and water, so please answer it, please."

"Hello Myles. This is Dee, what is wrong?" DeAnna asked with no hesitation.

"Why you assume that something's wrong. Where's Chris?" Myles asked.

"He's driving," DeAnna said.

"Well, how long before you back in North Carolina?" Myles asked.

"The way Chris is driving, in about 2 hours. What's wrong with Jeremy?" DeAnna asked with an, *I demand to know tone*.

"You love that man don't you sugar?" Myles asked. "Look when you get here, give me a call."

"Myles, what is wrong?" DeAnna asked again. "First Ma Phillips, now you."

"You talk to Ma Phillips?" Myles questioned.

"Yes," DeAnna said. She felt like yelling, but she knew that it wouldn't help. "Where is Jeremy?" DeAnna pleaded. She heard static on the phone. She could tell it was about to cut off. The battery was almost dead. She could hear Myles saying something, but she could only make out a few words. "Hit, dead," she repeated. "Hello, Myles, No!" DeAnna cried. "No! The phone can't be dead."

"DeAnna calm down. What's going on?" Kristen asked.

"The phone is died, but it sounded like Myles was saying Jeremy was hit and I heard the word..." DeAnna couldn't say the word dead. She handed Kristen, Chris' phone back. "I don't think you had this charging," DeAnna said. She didn't try to stop the flow of tears that ran down her face. She just began to pray. She prayed so loud she woke Naija'"

"What's wrong Aunt Dee?" Naija' asked as she sat up.

"Oh, baby, nothing. I am sorry I woke you," DeAnna said. "I hope I didn't scare you."

"You didn't scare me, because I heard you talk to God. So, I know everything is fine. Those must be victory tears, since they're tears. You told me that people cry sometimes when they're happy. You said God sees and hears victory tears. You said he counts them. So, you crying victory tears? I wish I could make myself cry victory tears with you."

"That's right baby," DeAnna said. "You are one very smart little princess," DeAnna said and managed to smile at Naija.

"I can't seem to find my phone," Kristen said. "Do you see a phone anywhere back there, Naija'? Have you had my phone playing games?"

"No, mommy. I have not had your phone. Daddy bought me one to play games on."

"I wish I had a good signal," DeAnna said, glancing out the window. The phone was almost dead, and she figured by the time she had a better signal, it would be completely dead.

DeAnna was pre-occupied, she didn't even hear the conversation between Naija' and Kristen. Everyone seemed to be in his or her own private world. Chris was trying to remain calm, so he would not upset Naija'. DeAnna was trying to call someone to find out what was going on, but all the calls kept dropping. She suddenly realized that the devil seemed to be testing her faith.

"Not today," DeAnna suddenly said. "Not today, devil."

DeAnna flipped through the contact list in her phone and quickly jotted down a few numbers.

"Chris, do you have your phone charger? I think this one has a shortage. I put your phone on my car charger, so I thought it was charging the entire time," Kristen said. "I almost forget where I put yours and now I don't even know where my phone is."

Kristen's phone is fully charged; none of the numbers we need are stored in her phone. But if she knew where it was, I could call the numbers that I was able to jot down from my contact list, DeAnna thought.

Chris' phone was dead, Kristen's phone was lost, and DeAnna's phone was fading in and out. Chris didn't want to stop, but he had to. He pulled over and both he and DeAnna rambled through their bags, but they only found Chris' charger. They were back on the road in less than five minutes. They charged Chris' phone first, since he had most of the numbers they needed.

As soon as DeAnna was able, she tried to call Ma Phillips back, but she got no answer. DeAnna looked at her phone and noticed she had a few text messages. She thought she had check them. She saw a text from Jeremy. She quickly read it. More tears flowed as she scanned the long text for keywords.

'**I love you with all my spirit, heart, and soul…. You are my favor, my good thing**…. Come back to me.' I can't believe this," DeAnna whispered to herself. "God, my God thank you for him. Lord, I know you won't let this end like this. If I am his good thing, if he has favor; it can't end." DeAnna looked at the last text from Jeremy; she read the first word before the phone completely died. "Will," she read. "Will what?" DeAnna asked. She kept saying the word 'will,' and asking herself, "Will what?" She wanted to snatch Chris' phone off the charger and plug her phone back up, but she resisted. They had been alternating their phone with each other's, on the only charger they found, every fifteen minutes, but now it was Chris' turn. "Lord, please let this be what I've waited to hear. I just trust you Lord to protect him. For over two and a half hours, DeAnna repeatedly called Ma Phillips and Myles.

Chris' phone was almost fully charged. He tried to reach one of the guys and even their wives. DeAnna's phone was now on the charger. Kristen had found her phone and DeAnna used Kristen's phone a few times, so her phone could charge without her being on it while it charged.

"Nobody's picking up. I just know something is wrong," Chris said without thinking. "They're avoiding the calls to avoid the answer."

"Don't say that," DeAnna quickly demanded.

"Poochie!" DeAnna said. "Call her.

"Yup! She can't hold water in a cup," Chris said. "But I don't have her number, she changes it every few months."

"It's seems like we had this conversation before," DeAnna said. "Just try the last one you have."

Chris gave his phone to Kristen. He didn't want to keep making calls while driving, especially if he had to search for a number.

335

"The passcode is 1228, find Drama queen. That's her last number."

Kristen was shocked that Chris willing gave her his passcode, which seemed to be her birthday. She strolled through a long list of women's names, until she found Drama Queen14. Kristen hit the number and handed the phone to Chris. He refused to take it.

"Don't want no ticket," Chris said. "Just tell her that you are my girlfriend and I told you to call to see if everything is okay with Jeremy; if she answers."

Poochie answered the phone on the first ring.

"What you want boy?" Poochie yelled into the phone.
"Hello, this is… Kristen, Chris's girlfriend."
"Stop lying trick," Poochie said. "Chris ain't got no girlfriend. Nobody good enough for his 'think he's so fine self.'"
"This is Kristen, Naija's mother. Is this drama," Kristen paused when she saw Chris shaking his head no, indicating not to call her drama queen "Is this Jeremy's sister?"
"Yes, it is Ms. Chris' baby mama," she said as if she didn't believe that she was talking to Kristen.
"What can I help you with? I don't know where Chris is."
"Oh, he's here with me, I mean I'm with him, wait, well actually, I'm calling for him. We are trying to find out what's going on with Jeremy."

DeAnna set up so she could hear the conversation.

"Put her on speaker," DeAnna whispered.
"I'm going to put you on speaker phone, so Chris can hear you," Kristen said.
"I hate speaker phones; my mouth big enough, as a matter of facts so is his ears," Poochie said and then burst out laughing. "I've always thought Chris had some big old ears."
"Poochie!" Chris yelled "What's going on?"
"Don't be yelling at me like that. You know I don't play that. I won't tell ya' stuck-up behind nothing."
"Poochie!" Chris yelled again.

"I's just playing Chris. You know I's always liked you, but you just act like you didn't like women. All you do is work, play ball, and sleep."

"Poochie!" Chris said again in a very calm voice.

"Okay-okay, all I know is there with a car accident and everybody is at the hospital, just like last time. Maybe this time it knocked his sight back in socket. I'm waiting on Ma to call me now. I'll call you back as soon as I hear something. Oh, and let your girlfriend answer, you can't take a joke." Poochie laughed and hung up the phone without saying goodbye.

"God," DeAnna said. "I'm trusting in you. Keep that man safe. Let him be okay. We'll be there in less than an hour."

"You just keep sending the prayers up, DeAnna," Chris said. "You know there is power in agreement. Why don't we all pray?"

"I'm not good with prayer just yet," Kristen said.

"Me either, but practice makes perfect. It's like talking to your father. We don't need fancy words. I have to be the man of the house, so I will pray, but I ain't closing my eyes," Chris said.

Chris' prayer was so comforting that DeAnna dose off to sleep for the last hour of the ride.

Chapter 30

When DeAnna woke up, Chris was pulling into the hospital parking lot. He found a park close to the emergence entrance. Kristen got out and told Chris and DeAnna to run on as she walked with Naija'. DeAnna jumped out of the truck and ran into the hospital.

"Where is he?" DeAnna asked, approaching Myles and Malcolm, but she saw Jeremy walking to them. "Jeremy, what happened? Are you okay?" DeAnna asked, briskly walking towards him. She wanted to run to him, but she suddenly noticed a strange woman following closely behind him. DeAnna stopped walking as if she had become paralyzed. Jeremy continued approaching her. When he was close enough to smell DeAnna's perfume, he reached for her and pulled her into his arms. When DeAnna noticed the strange woman staring at her, DeAnna tried to ease her body from Jeremy's hug, but he didn't seem to want to let her go. DeAnna assumed that the woman was not a threat to her relationship with Jeremy, if that's what they had.

"What happened?" DeAnna asked.

The woman stood impatiently waiting for DeAnna and Jeremy to release from their hug, but she didn't give Jeremy time to respond to DeAnna's question. She extended her hand toward DeAnna as if to shake hands, but the lady quickly turned to Jeremy and grabbed his hand and then she turned to face DeAnna.

"Your husband tried to save my son," the woman said.
"Save your son?" DeAnna asked. The word *tried*, bounced around in DeAnna's head.
"Yes, my son was riding his bike on the sidewalk and a drunk driver began to swerve out of control. Your husband tried to get my son, but by the time he reached him, my son had been hit," the woman fell in Jeremy's arms.

DeAnna was familiar with women like this. She could tell by the woman's flirtatious display of body movements and lack of tears, that the boy was probably not dead and okay. DeAnna could also tell by the way

338

the woman said '*husband*' that the woman was trying to figure out if Jeremy was indeed DeAnna's husband. *This woman has probably already noticed that neither of us is wearing a ring and I don't have on an engagement ring. She has probably also noticed that neither of our fingers even had signs that rings had ever been there. She keeps using the word husband, hoping for clarification, but she ain't getting it, at least not from me. I am sure she has decided that we don't look like we could be sister and brother and we hugged too long to be just friends, so she is unsure of the relationship,'* DeAnna skillfully summarized. *If she is more into getting Jeremy's attention then she is concerned about her son, then there is nothing for her to be in real distress about, or at least that what she might think. The boy is probably hurt, maybe a few broken bones, but no real major damage. Flesh wound perhaps,* DeAnna thought to herself. *I have waited too long to get a good man, hurt child or not, I'm not going to allow an under-emotional, non-teardrop having, over-dramatic, opportunist man-hunting pretender, who is trying to use her son's unfortunate accident as a means of hoarding in on my man,* Dee thought to herself.

"Ma'am, why don't you sit down?" DeAnna softly said. "We wouldn't want you to go into shock, now would we? Over here." DeAnna grabbed the woman and led her by the hand to a nearby seat.

The lady tried to pull Jeremy along with her, pretending to stumble with weakness.

"I got you," Dee said. "I'm a nurse here who just happened to be off duty today. I'm used to these types of situations. I'm here for you. Have you heard anything from the doctor?" DeAnna asked, guiding the woman down.

"Yea," Jeremy said. "I think he has a broken leg. The bone actually penetrated the skin."

"Yeah," the lady said, rising to her feet as Jeremy move closer to DeAnna. "It would have been worse if," the woman said looking at Jeremy as if she was begging for attention with her eyes.

"Let's not think about the worst," DeAnna said, interrupting the lady and coaching her back down to her seat.

"Your husband," the lady said again and paused.

"Speaking of husband," Jeremy said as he turned to face DeAnna, but before he even had the chance to say anything else, two police officers entered and ask to speak with Jeremy and the lady. DeAnna walked off and joined the group. As she sat and waited for Jeremy to finish up with the officers, she suddenly remembered the text message that she didn't finish reading. She rambled through her purse and grabbed her cell phone as if it was life or death. She found the last text that Jeremy had sent, and she read it. Her eyes flooded with tears as she read the entire text this time.

Dee,

I want a second chance to make a first impression. Now, that I see just how beautiful you are inside and out, will you give me the chance to win your heart as you have won my mines. I love you with all my spirit, heart, and soul. I know God didn't cause me to be blind, but what the devil meant for evil, God turned it into something good, really good. You are my favor, my good thing. If I had- had my sight, I would not have seen you. If that makes any sense. DeAnna, once again, I ask you to please Come back to me. Please! Will you have me as your first date when you return to NC, DeAnna Wright?

J'

DeAnna stared at Jeremy and even though she wasn't sure if his sight had been fully restored, she felt as if he was staring at her. When he finished with the questioning, DeAnna slowly rose from her seat as Jeremy slowly and carefully walked towards her. He played no attention to the woman following closely behind him. He acted as if she wasn't even there.

"Jeremy, I just don't know what I would have done without you," the woman said and threw her arms around him.

"And I just don't know what I would have done without him either," DeAnna said, then took what she was sure was her position beside him.

"Oh, I am so sorry," the woman said, sounding slightly offended. "Is he your husband?" The woman asked, sounding shocked with DeAnna's statement and position beside Jeremy, although she had been calling him DeAnna's husband the entire time.

"No," Jeremy said.

The woman's face suddenly seemed to look less tense. Jeremy continued as he grabbed DeAnna and turned her to face him. For the first time since they met, DeAnna allowed her body to be totally comfortable and relaxed pressed up again his. She felt as if she belonged in his arms. She looked at him and smiled. She knew that his answer 'No' to the smirking woman was a conditional one, but DeAnna's smile was what he was waiting on to continue his response.

"Not yet," Jeremy said as he turned to the woman. Then he kissed DeAnna on the cheek.

"Oh, anyway thanks for your help," the woman said as if 'no' was the answer she was looking for and she didn't even hear the 'not yet' comment. "If you had not seen that car coming and pushed my son out of the way, he might have more than just the broken bones. So, thanks. I could have killed that driver."

"Oh Jeremy," DeAnna said. "You saved his life."

"Actually!" Jeremy began. "I didn't even see the car and I bumped into the kid because I stumbled over something," Jeremy told DeAnna. "My sight has not fully been restored. It was, I guess you can say, coming in and out, but it had not completely returned. I see images with more form now."

The woman stared at Jeremy. DeAnna explained to the woman about the accident that left Jeremy blind.

"Oh my God, blind fate saved my son's life," the woman said.

"Blind fate showed me just how blind I have been all my life," Jeremy said as he looked at DeAnna. He looked at her as if she was the only one in the room that he could see. His friends had allowed him to have his time with DeAnna,

"So, Jeremy can you see now?" DeAnna asked.

"Not really?" Jeremy said as if it didn't matter. "What's that scripture in the Bible, I see men walking as trees; something like that," he said and smiled at DeAnna.

"So, when I came though the double doors, it appeared that you were looking straight at me, "DeAnna said.

"When I came out, I could see an image. I felt your spirit and I could smell your perfume," Jeremy responded. "I looked in your direction and I heard God, at least I think it was God. He said, 'that's her.' I had asked him to show me my wife weeks ago. So, when I heard that, I knew it was you. On the phone earlier, I asked you about giving me another chance to date; I realized I want to be more than just a date. We have been dating all along."

"You do?" DeAnna asked, hoping he would feel the same when his sight was fully restored.

"DeAnna, I see you clearer than I've ever seen any woman. I see your heart, your spirit, and your soul. You helped me to see with the most powerful eyes we have been given, my spiritual eyes. You showed me so much about real love, self-love, and I learned to truly love me ...and I love you. Dee, I would have wanted a more appropriate setting, but I refuse to wait another week, another day, another hour, or another minute. It's for this moment that I waited for," Jeremy said then paused. "It's so ironic, this is where we meet, this very same hospital. So, it feels like fate that brings us back here again." Jeremy said then kneeled down on one knee.

Chris looked up at Jeremy. "Look," he quickly said to get the groups' attention. "Look!" Chris said again and pointed at Jeremy.

Everyone turned around and watched Jeremy.

"DeAnna, I never want to lose sight of what real love is. If I had not lost my sight, I would have never seen you or seen what real love is. This is *blind fate* for sure." As Jeremy talked, he noticed that DeAnna face became clearer. He could see her long black hair. He wanted to look her in her eyes. So, he slowly pulled himself up.

DeAnna wasn't sure if he had changed his mind. He let go of her hand and gently wiped a tear from her cheek.

"I only have my sight on you, my love, I only have eyes for you." He grabbed her hands and placed both of them around his neck. He slowly rocked her back and forth. "This is where my blind fate began," he said as he looked around the hospital. "The worst tragedy of my life ironically led me to the best thing that has happen to me, DeAnna," Jeremy said as he pulled her hand gently back down as he kneeled back down in the traditional proposal position, on one knee. "Will you do me the honor of being my queen, my best friend, my baby mama? DeAnna Wright, will you continue to be my good thing, and please be my wife."

DeAnna didn't answer. She pulled him back up gently until they were eye-to-eye. She softly wiped a tear from his eyes. He blinked as her hand moved toward his face. He smiled. She knew that he could see her clearly, but she asked anyway. "Do you really see me?" She asked.

"Yes," he replied, smiling.

"Do you really want me?" She asked.

"Yes, I really do," he replied with no hesitation.

"You only have eyes for me?" She asked. "When I was a little girl," DeAnna began. "Somehow, I felt as if I always would know my husband when I kissed him, really kiss me."

Jeremy kissed her, really kissed her for the first time.

When Jeremy released DeAnna, she whispered in his ear, "Yes! My King."

He kissed her again.

"Yes," she said again. The second time she spoke loud enough for everybody to hear. "Yes, yes, yes," she excitedly repeated.

"Looks like we are going to have a double wedding," Kristen said as she flashed her ring. She looked at Dee and whispered, "Thanks."

DeAnna knew that Kristen was thanking her for encouraging Chris to reach out to her again. DeAnna also wanted to flash an engagement ring too, but she knew it was a spare of the moment thing. "Besides," she said to herself, "I don't want to take the ring glow away from Kristen." DeAnna smiled as she looked at Naija' hanging onto both of her parents. After all the congratulations finished circulating for both couples, Jeremy grabbed DeAnna and whispered in her ear.

"I have your ring, but I didn't want your ring to upstage Kristen's ring, so I decided to wait to put it on your finger later. I know you would have preferred it that way."

"You think you know me, don't you?" DeAnna said and kissed her fiancé."

"Yup," Jeremy replied with no hesitation. "I study everything that is important to me. Actually, I master it." He stared DeAnna eye-to-eye. "So, am I wrong?"

"Nah," DeAnna said, knowing that she would not have wanted to upstage Kristen's moment. At that very moment, DeAnna looked in Jeremy's eyes again and she loved him even more. She realized that he truly did see her. DeAnna suddenly remembered, as she thought about the ring, that he answered a question that she never even asked him directly. *I love him so much,* she thought to herself, "Thank you God," she whispered.

"I love you too," Jeremy said as if he had heard her thoughts and words to God.

"How ironic," Poochie said, as she approached her brother. She had been watching him for a while. "He had to go blind, to see that beauty comes in all shapes and sizes and only when he accepted her as she is, it's then that he gained his sight back, in the very place that he lost it. The very place that he met his wife is the place that he accepted his wife. The man who finds a wife, finds a good thing and obtained favor from the Lord," Poochie said. "You brother, you didn't 'just' get your favor, you got it the day she walked into your room. God sent her. She has been your helpmate the entire time. She has been eyes when you couldn't see. Now, that's just what I believe. Think a lot of men are too blind to see their good thang. Blinded by the lust of the flesh. Some men are married, but their wives don't act or seem like their good thang, well not at first. Even though some women are the true world's definition of a wife, they are not the spiritual definition. Maybe when the women start acting like wives, maybe that's when the men get their favor. I'm just saying."

Jeremy kissed his sister on her cheek and then turned and hugged his future wife again and said, "To God be the Glory."

Ma Phillips, who had been quiet the entire time, smiled at the loving exchange of affection between her grown children and her future daughter-in-law. "Amen," she said. "Amen."

DeAnna smiled. Tears of joy freely flowed.

"Thank you, my Heavenly Father for answering my prayers," she said, looking towards Heaven. "Pastor always says, 'every delay works in my favor. He was definitely worth the wait."

"And she was definitely worth the delay," Jeremy said and kissed his future wife.

"To God be the Glory," they both said.

Robin M. Manley

About the Author

Robin Manley was born in Halifax, North Carolina, but raised in Rocky Mount, N.C. with her mother and three siblings. She is a graduate of South West Edgecombe High School in Pinetop, N.C (1988). She earned an AAS-Paralegal Technology from Wilson Technical Community (2002), BA Degrees in Criminal Justice and Psychology, from North Carolina Wesleyan College (2012), MA-Human Services: Marriage and Family Counseling from Liberty University (2014) and is currently pursuing a PhD in Social and Community Services (EDG, 2022).

Ms. Manley is the single parent of Jasmyne and Jerika Williams. Jasmyne (a.k.a jDenea') a third-generation graduate of NCWC, is an actress, model, singer and the songwriter of all the songs mentioned in this novel (all songs copyrighted, 2015). Jerika (a.k.a Dani) has many talents. She would one day like to open her own bakery, as she is well-known for her delicious Honeybun cakes and many others. She also has one step-son from a previous marriage, Denzel Davis, whom she loves with all her heart

Ms. Manley and her daughters are members of Showers of Blessing Christian Center. Robin is a motivational speaker and travel to different cities speaking at public group events, women's conferences, and church groups on topics which such as date rape, domestic violence, anti-bullying, divorce, self-esteem building, educational empowerment, customer service skills, and many others. She was the radio host of the 'Relationship and You' radio show on the BFTM Christian Radio Network.

Ms. Manley writes, produces, and directs plays and often uses her creative talent as a means of delivering visual and powerful messages on the topics that she speaks about. It is Ms. Manley's dream to write, produce, and direct movies and films that will minister to those in need of solace, to encourage individuals to believe in themselves, to inspire people to discover and reach their full potential and purpose in life, and return to and live for God.

Ms. Manley published two books, which were inspired after the end of her 15-year marriage. *To Hungry Souls Every Bitter Thang Tastes Sweet* is Ms. Manley's first novel. After starting her own publishing company, she self-published her second novel, *Entangled Again in the Yoke of Bondage*, released in June 2014. It's her dreams to turn her books into a movie. *Blind Fate is her first* romance novel, written totally from her imagination. This book teaches many life lessons though the lives of the characters. She also desires to turn this book into a movie.

Book Clubs interested in booking Robin M. Manley, can contacted her via Facebook, or e-mail (redbrd007@hotmail.com). She is also available for speaking engagements. Ms. Manley manages of the singer/actress mentioned in this book, jDenea'. Bookings for singer, songwriter, and actress can be arranged via Ms. Robin Manley.

Robin M. Manley
From the Author's Desk

Thank you for selecting this romance novel for your reading enjoyment. In an effort to help improve relationships, I have provided two questions for book clubs members, singles, married couples, and even Marriage Counselors to think about and discuss.

Singles
1. What are some of your standards that others may see as superficial or cosmetic that you would /will not compromise on that may have or could cause you to lose the love of your life? (ex. Women: You refuse to date short men. Men: You refuse to date women who are taller than you).

Married
2. What are some standards others may see as superficial, that you are glad you compromised on in order to be with the love of your life? (ex. At one time you refused to short men, but you end up falling in love and or now happier than ever).

www.ingramcontent.com/pod-product-compliance
Lightning Source LLC
Chambersburg PA
CBHW072315020726
47501CB00002B/520